WORLD
WAR
MOO

ALSO BY
MICHAEL LOGAN

APOCALYPSE COW

AN APOCALYPSE COW NOVEL

WORLD WAR MOO

MICHAEL LOGAN

ST. MARTIN'S GRIFFIN
NEW YORK

WORLD WAR MOO. Copyright © 2015 by Michael Logan. All rights reserved. Printed in the United States of America. For information, address St. Martin's Press, 175 Fifth Avenue, New York, N.Y. 10010.

www.stmartins.com

Designed by Jonathan Bennett

The Library of Congress Cataloging-in-Publication Data is available upon request.

ISBN 978-1-250-06165-2 (trade paperback)
ISBN 978-1-4668-6769-7 (e-book)

St. Martin's Griffin books may be purchased for educational, business, or promotional use. For information on bulk purchases, please contact the Macmillan Corporate and Premium Sales Department at 1-800-221-7945, extension 5442, or write to specialmarkets@macmillan.com.

First Edition: June 2015

10 9 8 7 6 5 4 3 2 1

FOR NATS,
even though she told me
to dedicate this book to
somebody else

Acknowledgments

As ever, I have a bazillion people to thank, but I'll restrict myself to those with the most direct impact. First up is my wife, Nats, who reads my books at least ten times during development, poor thing. She still manages to come up with excellent feedback every time, and as of yet hasn't thumped me over the head with a rolled-up manuscript.

I am also indebted to Rebecca Dempster, Kat Urbaniak, Scott McDonald, Mick Sailor, Tom Dixon, Peter Abraham, Dani Solomon, and Andy Dunlop for their services as beta readers. If any other author needs a bunch of eagle-eyed readers who are not afraid to stick the boot in, they're available for hire as a job lot. John Berlyne also helped with his early comments on the tone of the book, and I am grateful for this.

Finally, thanks to the readers of *Apocalypse Cow* who entered my competition to have their names, and in some cases appearances and quirks, used in *World War Moo*. They are, in no particular order: Ruan Peat, Jack Alford, Glen Forbes, James Anthony Hilton, Andy Scholz, Tim Roast, Eva Gilliam, Hannah Campbell, Scott McDonald, Peter Abraham, Tom Dixon, and Andy Dunlop. Andy Dunlop really is a competitive egg thrower and Scott is genuinely a giant with an addiction to tie-dye, which goes to show real life really is often stranger than fiction.

WWM

1

General Carter was standing on the seventeenth tee of the Augustine Golf Club, using his wood as a leaning post and stifling a laugh as his Russian counterpart shanked a ball into the rough, when the call came in. General Kuzkin broke off from his incomprehensible cursing, and General Zhang turned from where he was sifting through his clubs. They looked at the American expectantly as he listened. He nodded once, said, "Understood," and hung up. A broad grin sprang up so quickly that it set his pockmarked jowls wobbling.

"Good news, gentlemen," he said, adjusting his red golf cap to a jaunty angle. "Our glorious leaders have finished their little powwow, and they've finally had enough of waiting on this multilateral UN crap. This time next year, I'll be teeing off at Gleneagles again."

"Lovely course," said Zhang, miming a swing with his delicate hands.

"Yes indeed. I laid out five thousand bucks for my membership last year and only got to play once before those goddamn zombies shut down the country. Didn't even get a refund. Eight months without a round at the best course in the world. That, my friends, is a tragedy."

"How soon do we move?" Kuzkin asked.

"They want us ready to go in twenty days. No warning. Catch them with their pants down and their pasty British asses dangling in the breeze."

Kuzkin threw his club back to the caddy. "We should go to the clubhouse to start planning."

"Hold your horses," Carter said. "We've still got two holes to play. I do my best thinking on the course."

"In Russia, we do our best thinking in the *dacha* with a warm fire and a bottle of vodka. This is a stupid Western game."

"Hey, it's team building. This is our first joint mission: Russia, China, and the U.S. working together in the interests of humanity. It's a brave new world, my friend. We need to understand each other's cultures."

Kuzkin's pale blue eyes peered out from beneath a canopy of shaggy eyebrows. "Culture is literature, classical music, and art, not hitting a stupid little ball at a stupid little hole you can't even see with binoculars."

Zhang slid a wood from his bag and pointed it at the Russian. "You only want to stop because you are losing."

"I don't care if I lose. You can have my money now. Or we can go double or quits and play Tiger Has Come in the clubhouse."

"What is that?" Zhang said.

"Russian drinking game. I am the army champion."

"You are the top general. They let you win."

"*Nyet.* I have the stomach of a bear. Every day I drink bleach and disinfect the urinals in headquarters with my piss."

"A bit of focus here, gentlemen," Carter said. "Before we do anything else, we've got to take care of the most important part. We need to name the mission."

The Chinese general whacked his ball hard and true down the fairway, prompting a disgusted snort from Kuzkin. The three men climbed into their golf cart and trundled off, the caddies following in their own vehicle.

"How about Operation E-limey-nate?" Carter said, letting out a chuckle as he steered. The others offered up blank expressions. "It's a joke. We used to call the Brits 'limeys,' and we'd be . . . oh, forget it."

"We need a strong Russian name. Operation The Great Terror would make them quake in their boots."

"You can't make it sound like there's killing going on," Carter said. "You may as well call it Operation Mass Murder. It has to be evocative. Woolly enough so folks can pretend what we're doing in their names isn't all that bad. Like Operation Desert Storm, that was a great name. Geographically appropriate, dynamic, and suggestive of a force of nature."

"But we will be killing a lot of people. There should be honesty, no?"

"Hell no. The first rule of any military campaign is that you lie your ass off to the folks back home. And, you can't refer to them as people. Always call them zombies, especially in public."

"They are not zombies."

"They're near as dammit. Look, we can't have the public thinking of them as people, or they might start feeling sorry for them. As it is, we're damn lucky we've had all those zombie films and TV shows swimming in blood and guts for the last few years. Actually, we're even luckier the Brits didn't turn into vampires. If my daughters are anything to go by, we'd have every pubescent girl that's ever read *Twilight* trying to get over there and find some sparkly five-hundred-year-old teenager to tongue wrestle."

Zhang, who clearly hadn't been listening as he stared off into the distance, held up his closed fist and opened his fingers. "Operation Unfurling Petal," he said.

"That's too far the other way. We're not dropping flowers on them. It doesn't even make any sense."

"We call it after my president," Kuzkin said.

"No."

"Why not?"

"Hurricanes get people's names, not military campaigns. And we're doing this jointly, not under the command of a man who can't seem to keep his top on."

"He has a manly body, not like your scrawny president. Why should he not show it?"

"No man I know gets his bitch tits out when he's fishing or horse riding. It's borderline homoerotic. But if you insist, we can call it Operation Topov."

"His name is not Topov," the Russian said, frowning.

Carter sniffed. "Damn language barrier's killing my puns. Let's just move on. Any other suggestions?"

"Operation Flaming Wind," said Zhang.

"Sounds too much like the gas you pass after a hot chili."

"Operation Deliverance," offered Kuzkin.

The American shook his head. "We've had that one already. Canada in Somalia, 1993. Made everybody think of banjos, buggery, and Burt Reynolds."

They fell silent, faces scrunched up in concentration as the buggy shuddered to a halt in the general area where the Russian's ball had skittered into the long grass.

"How about Operation Excision?" Zhang said as Kuzkin clambered out and gestured to the caddy to find his ball.

"What's that mean?" Carter asked.

"It is the surgical procedure of cutting out a diseased organ or tissue. Very appropriate, since we will be stopping this disease from spreading."

"You know, I think that might just work," Carter said. "It sounds clean. Precise. Tidy. Agreed?" The other two men nodded. "Excellent. Now we just need to draw up a plan. Twenty days, gentlemen, and the fireworks commence."

Kuzkin stood over his ball, which the caddy had located, and slashed at it. It curved into the trees a few dozen feet ahead.

"If we are off this course by then," Zhang said.

Carter gave up trying to hold in his spiteful mirth at Kuzkin's golfing ineptitude and released a guffaw that startled a swan dozing on a nearby water hazard. The bird spread its great wings and took to the air. It flew overhead, casting a dark shadow like a bomber, and unleashed a stream of white shit to splat on top of the buggy.

"I just hope our boys are as accurate," Carter said, and laughed again.

EIGHTEEN DAYS TO EXCISION

2

The waters of Loch Long lapped at Ruan Peat's ankles like a slobbery and cold-tongued dog as she crouched in the shadows, entranced by the siren song of soft light spilling from the bar. A glowering mountain stabbed its peak into the pale moon slung low over the village, and the wind blew strong and cold into her chafed face, setting her body shivering. She imagined walking into the low white building, where the awesome power of her breasts would warp the barman's pitiably fragile male mind and stop him noticing she was far too young for a vodka and coke. She would then defrost before a crackling fire, sipping her drink and listening to the local yokels' boring small talk as the crackle and spit of frying fish and chips drifted through from the kitchen.

She blinked rapidly to dispel the dangerous fantasy. The welcoming façade of the bar was as genuine as the bogus *Facebook* profiles her teachers used to warn her about—behind which fourteen-year-old Jenny, who "hearted" chatting about boys with her online mates, was really a dough-faced pedo who typed with one clammy hand. Within that bar lay monsters—probably wearing comfortable shoes and 1970s Noel Edmonds jumpers from the look of the place, but monsters all the same.

No sixteen-year-old girl, especially one once so painfully hip that she almost qualified for replacement surgery, should have been as intimately acquainted with the life of one of British TV's most persistent unflushables. However, Ruan's mum had nursed a crush on the hamster-faced presenter and kept a scrapbook spanning thirty years of the most egregious knitwear known to humankind. Ruan's dad, a facial-fuzz offender himself, hadn't seemed to mind. Ruan considered her regular subjection to the book far worse abuse than anything skulking beneath *Facebook*'s veneer of chumminess. At one point she'd threatened to call ChildLine. Now she longed to sit in their spacious apartment in Edinburgh's New Town and leaf through the album one more time, rolling her eyes as her mum advised her to "find a nice man like Noel when she grew up."

Ruan again blinked five times in quick succession, the physical cue she'd picked up from a sports psychology book to change unhealthy thought patterns. She then employed her other technique to ward off this miserable reality, which was to fill her mind with ridiculous images. She pictured the bar full of bearded and smirking Noels cavorting in Christmas pullovers so garish they should have carried an epilepsy risk warning, playing pranks on each other and grinning smugly. Not that she could mock anybody's clothing choices these days. The ankle boots, skinny jeans, and designer tops she wore before the virus had long been ditched. She sported hiking boots, cargo pants, and a thick fleece—all of them black, to help her dissolve into the night, and tattered from countless miles of hard traveling. She wore a WWI-era saber across her back under a stuffed rucksack. A Glock handgun was strapped to her right hip. All these items had been salvaged from abandoned homes, hundreds of thousands of which now gathered dust across Britain.

Even with the harmless images playing in her head, she knew she should return to where she'd left her mountain bike on the outskirts of the village, a few hundred meters down from a roadblock where an indistinct figure held what looked like a shotgun. Instead she edged closer, drawn in by the faint chance of pilfering some hot grub. Her boots emitted a worryingly loud crunch on the loose scree of pebbles as she crossed the beach. Coming through the trees would have provided better cover, especially since the moonlight glittering on the lake's surface framed her creeping shadow, but the dark woods held worse dangers. Water dulled her scent, and in the open she could at least spot incoming trouble at a distance and scarper. Seven months spent as a mobile buffet for every living creature on this forsaken island had developed her acceleration to the point where it would startle a cheetah.

She grabbed the edge of road, which was raised six feet above the beach, and pulled herself up. Streetlights shone sodium orange light onto the deserted road. She'd been to Arrochar, a small village huddled on the northern tip of the loch in the west of Scotland, once before on a school trip. Then it had been a dinky hamlet with a population of a few thousand. As in every village, town, and city across the U.K., the carnage would have slashed that number. She would never forget the bonfires of bodies, animal and human alike, which had cast a smoggy pall of organic matter across the land for months after the outbreak.

Don't go there, she thought, blinking so hard her eyes hurt.

She refocused on the seam of flavorsome odor that had attracted her in the first place. If she wasn't mistaken it came from a freshly cooked beef stew. Warm saliva slicked her lips. She hadn't eaten a proper hot meal in months, living on increasingly scarce tins retrieved from cupboards in empty houses and scraps raked from bins in the dead of night. Nor had she touched a morsel of fresh meat. What little meat remained was infected, but anything that passed her lips couldn't harm her. She had no idea why the virus slipped off her like an overly moistened spitball from a distracted teacher's back, didn't even know if it could be called good fortune considering the life it forced her to lead, but there was nothing she could do to change that.

She glanced along the road one more time and hauled herself over the guardrail. Her long legs swiftly carried her to the shelter of a thick tree trunk. Beyond lay an overgrown lawn strewn with tables that in summer months gone by would have been packed with hikers slapping at swarms of midges nibbling on the pale legs that protruded from khaki shorts. She scuttled to the wall of the building and chanced a peek through the closed window. Five men ranging from teenage to late sixties were gathered around a rectangular wooden table, staring at a flat screen fixed to the rustically bricked wall. Weirdly, they did all look rather like Noel Edmonds. Either Noel had gone on a sexual rampage in his wild years and impregnated every woman within a twenty-mile radius, or the village's gene pool wasn't deep enough to wet the shins of a toddler and had created a weird anomaly.

The window was thin enough for her to hear a former *Big Brother* contestant called Amy something-or-other tongue-trip her way through a news bulletin presenting the government propaganda line that "all was, and would be, well." Keep Calm and Carry On. God, she hated that phrase, which was plastered on banners and advertising hoardings in every town and city. In her experience, calm was in as short supply as razors seemed to be in this town.

"Another round," said one of the Noels, a stocky 1980s model with thick chunks of hair curling from behind his ears like warthog tusks.

"No bother," said the barman, who bucked the trend by being clean-shaven and wearing a plain white T-shirt. "That'll be 140 quid."

"The last round was only 120!"

The barman shrugged. "Hyperinflation. Blame market forces."

"Who do you think I am, Richard Branson?" the first man said, his fingers curling up into a fist.

"Aye, well. You're a dick with a beard so that's close enough."

"Just sell us the bloody beer."

A sneer crossed the barman's face. "Wait a minute. Prices have gone up again. A hundred and sixty quid or you can find another pub that's open. Oh wait, there isn't one."

The youth kicked back his chair, lunged at the counter, and slammed his fist into the barman's face. Every man in the room threw himself into the fight, teeth bared through bristling beards. A woman came running through from the kitchen and shouted at the combatants, although she stopped short of wading in to separate them. Given the empties strewn around the table and the all-male rural Scottish company, Ruan couldn't be sure if the fight was down to tempers inflamed by the virus or business as usual. It made no difference to her. She'd learned to take her chances when they presented themselves, so she quick-stepped to the kitchen and glanced around the doorframe.

Steam curled up from a casserole dish, seeming to form a hazy beckoning finger. She scampered in and slipped on the oven gloves next to it. Just as she was about to snatch up her bounty and disappear into the night, a growl rose beneath the bawling, clattering, and profuse swearing from the bar area. She froze as a creamy white Alsatian raised its head from a basket in the corner. Its hackles rose and the growl turned into a bark—and not a friendly "can I have some stew" one at that. Ruan was out the door, not even giving herself time to curse her stupidity, before the dog got to its feet. Even so, she heard the sounds of the fight die away. Every living being in the bar would be on her tail in seconds.

She ate up the ground with the intention of hurdling the guardrail. She'd been a serious modern pentathlete before her life fell apart, so she could ride, shoot, fence, and swim as well as she could run. She could lose her pursuers out in the loch, although that would mean ditching the rucksack. Unfortunately, the road was no longer deserted. Beneath the streetlamp were two men, again in beards and jumpers. The wind was at her back and blowing toward them. They looked at her and took simultaneous deep breaths through their noses. Lines of shadow slashed across their orange faces as muscles bunched, the viral rage seeming to open a vortex that sucked all their features toward one gnarled point between the eyebrows. Lips pulled tight across teeth clamped together by straining jaws. Their bodies snapped rigid as though their clenched hands were clutching high-voltage wires.

At the beginning of her ordeal she'd tried to conjure up silly images to soften the impact of this change, which she'd witnessed more times than she cared to remember. She'd imagined them as sufferers of extreme constipation straining on the toilet or woeful community theater actors overemoting in a desperate attempt to engage an audience of bored school kids. After a near miss, she'd realized this was one thing she shouldn't allow her imagination to gloss over: she needed the fear to put her body into fight-or-flight mode.

"This is our village," the one on the left screamed. "No strangers."

Ruan's hand dipped to the holster, but the floral oven gloves she still wore frustrated her attempt at a quick draw. She shook them off and kept running, resisting the impulse to shoot as the occupants of the bar poured out behind the two men. Freeing the weapon, clicking off the safety, and firing would slow her down and do little to increase her chances of escape: infected on the hunt were either fearless or thick as shit. Plus gunfire would attract the attention of any others in the area, if the shouts hadn't already done so. The houses she sprinted past seemed empty, but the infected had a habit of multiplying like fruit flies on a rotten banana once the chase was on. She glanced toward the water, wondering if she could still get over the rail. She dismissed the option. At the speed she was moving, there was every chance she would twist her ankle at the end of the drop. Equally, remaining on the road would give the dog a chance to catch up. One bite to the leg could fell her and it would all be over. Even if she kept ahead of the chasing rabble, the roadblock she'd avoided was only a few hundred meters ahead.

The row of houses gave way to woods, and, despite what might be lurking amidst the shadows, she cut left into the trees in the hope of losing the pack. The light died off beneath the canopy, and her shoulder cannoned off a trunk, sending her body spinning. She caught herself and began weaving through the dark columns. It didn't take long for the animals to find her. The squeak came first, followed instantly by a small furry blur that streaked through the air, paws akimbo. She ducked and the animal sailed over her head. Seconds later, another furry missile launched itself at her. This squirrel managed to snag its front paws on her shoulder and nip her ear with its buckteeth. She grabbed the bushy tail, swung the filthy rodent round once, and hurled it high into the trees. It squealed all the way, sounding like a cheap firework. Rustling came from all around now, but she didn't look to see what else was coming; she needed all her attention for the slalom through the trunks. The trees cleared and the moon once again lit her way as she vaulted a wooden fence into a field that tilted upward into the foothills of the mountain. She turned back to the right to avoid tiring herself too quickly. That was when she heard the shuddering chorus of moos.

"You're taking the piss!" she found the breath to shout.

The fence vibrated behind her as her pursuers leapt over. She chanced a look back, and what she saw brought hysterical laughter bubbling up. A handful of cows, several squirrels, a posse of rabbits, a young deer, what may have been a badger, the Alsatian, the barman, and seven variations on Noel Edmonds were strung out in pursuit. They all lent their baying, shouting, barking, cursing, and mooing voices to the air. It hadn't been that many years since she realized that the whole Disney princess thing she loved as a little girl was sexist drivel, and she couldn't help but be reminded of how the animals in the cursed forest had flocked to help Snow White. Only the birds were missing; even the Noels could have passed for dwarves if she squinted. She bit down on the hysteria and focused on running; these woodland animals weren't coming to sing a merry song and lead her to the safety of a cabin until a handsome prince slung her across the back of his horse and hauled her off for a life sentence of sewing dresses and looking pretty. They wanted to chew out her eyeballs. At least the small animals were already falling behind, and just before she turned her attention forward again the two front-running Noels collided and went down in a bearded, jumper-clad heap. Only the dog was gaining, now lolloping along a good five meters ahead of the others.

Ahead, she saw tiny globes of light floating in the far corner of the field. In happier times they could have been mistaken for fireflies or even sprites of the forest by those of a more imaginative bent. Ruan knew what they really were. As they rushed onward, the sheep, whose eyes were reflecting the moonlight to produce the glowing orbs, materialized at the gallop. Ruan bared her teeth at the sight of the animal she hated above all others. Her right hand pulled the sword from its scabbard in a smooth arc. She transferred it to her left without breaking stride. Still tracking the flock with her eyes, she unholstered the gun and flicked off the safety.

The sheep were close enough for her to see their eerie silvery-blue eyes and teeth jutting out from their waggling lower jaws. A few seconds later, she was amongst them. She slashed at the nearest one's snout. Snapping jaws brushed against the sleeve of her fleece and she shot the attacker in the mouth. She shimmied past the falling body, slammed another sheep between the eyes with the butt of the gun, and leapt. Her right foot landed square on the back of a particularly matted and shaggy specimen, prompting a winded bleat, and she jumped again. As she sailed upward, a savage joy seized her. She pointed the gun downward and squeezed the trigger once more. She felt rather than saw the bullet burrow into its target as her heels cleared the top of the fence by inches.

The impact of landing jarred her knees and spine, but she kept her feet and disappeared into the trees. She raised her head and let out a primal, adrenaline-fuelled howl. Too busy giving vent to her elation, she ran full tilt into a tree and toppled backward. Above the wheezing of her stuttering lungs, the din of the pursuers grew louder. The thrill of the chase knocked out of her, part of her welcomed the end. She was so tired: of the constant stress of flight, of the loneliness, of the tormenting memories that kept slipping through her mental defenses. But her survival instincts remained, so when she saw a figure slip through the shadows ahead she drew in a rasping breath and lifted her weapons. The silhouette raised its hands, pointing the left in front and drawing the right back.

A bowstring twanged and the air whispered as an arrow flew past. The dog yelped. The silhouette lowered the bow and stepped into a shaft of moonlight breaking through a gap in the foliage. At first, Ruan couldn't make sense of the shadows on the woman's angular face. Then she realized she was looking at deep scars running across jaw, cheek, and forehead. The woman shouldered the bow and held out her hand.

"Come with me if you want to live," she said.

Ruan took the hand. She hadn't touched another human being for what felt like an eternity—not counting violent encounters—and the contact sent delicious signals scampering along her nerve endings. The woman must have felt something similar, for she gasped and squeezed so tightly that Ruan's bones clacked together.

"I know you are here and it makes me happy," the scarred stranger said, emphasizing each word.

The report of splintering wood echoed through the forest, and the chorus of animal and human voices grew louder still. Ruan snapped back to herself. "That's very sweet, and I'm happy, too, but can we get the hell out of here?"

The woman opened her eyes and yanked Ruan to her feet. They ran through the woods together, leaving behind the sounds of pursuit.

3

Lesley McBrien waited at a tiny table in Nancy Whiskey Pub, where laughter and the click of pucks from the shuffleboard table added random and incongruously cheerful percussion to the somber music of Arcade Fire drifting out from the stereo—rather like an uninvited and enthusiastic busker playing the bongos at a funeral. The dissonance did nothing to ease her frazzled nerves. In front of her sat a Jameson's and lemonade, her second in the twenty minutes she'd been here. She fought to stop her regular sips from turning into gulps as she kept glancing toward the front door.

She'd arrived early to the bar on the corner of Lispenard, Sixth Avenue, and West Broadway to give it a quick once-over. Her contact had chosen well. A close-packed affair with a long wooden counter behind which twinkling fairy lights wove through row upon row of liquor bottles, the bar wasn't the kind of high-end place frequented by New York's contingent of highly paid UN twats. It was instead full of a mainly young, casually dressed crowd swigging on beer, chatting, and casting occasional glances at the muted television screens overhead.

It was refreshing to be away from the UN staff, diplomats, and hangers-on, most of whom were as useful as a fart in a spacesuit, a one-legged man at an arse-kicking contest, or any of the other overused similes the pathologically cynical journalist crowd working the UN beat bandied around. They did nothing but form working groups, a misnomer if ever she'd heard one; craft resolutions full of loopholes so large a grinning dictator could, and often did, merrily lead a convoy of tanks through them on his way to massacre his own people; and hold meetings, meetings about meetings, and meetings about meetings about meetings. It could take two years to decide whether to deploy lemon- or orange-scented urinal blocks in the delegates' lavatory, never mind whether to deploy an intervention force.

Lesley was too recognizable to take the chance of one of these numpties seeing her chatting with the man she awaited. She was the leading pundit on the infection: her face was plastered over the news, and her book about her flight from Britain as the virus turned animals into killing machines had sold a hundred thousand copies in the first week. The advance had swollen her bank account to bursting with money she couldn't bring herself to touch. Her dream of eclipsing her famous war correspondent father had come true, much to his chagrin: on the rare occasion they spoke he dropped snide comments about how her efforts didn't compare to his former exploits. He had no idea how right he was. As if to demonstrate her ubiquity, one of the screens flipped to a promo for the interview with Jay Leno she'd recorded the previous evening. Her fingers tightened round the glass, which she wanted to hurl at the screen. Instead, she put her head down and let her hair hide her face.

The book portrayed her as a sparky journalist who—with grit, determination, and a firmly starched upper lip—had uncovered a moronic secret government weapons program aimed at decimating enemy nations' food chains. In reality, she'd chanced on the story and made a big hairy dog's cock of the ensuing investigation. Only blind luck allowed her to escape with the world's biggest scoop. The sole thing she'd done right was to shoot dead the pursuing Alastair Brown, the government security operative who'd been the first recorded case of the virus crossing to humans and a glistening purple bell end to boot. In the first draft of her book, she'd stuck closer to the truth, only glossing over her more idiotic moments—such as allowing herself to be lured to an out-of-the-way location, on a flimsy pretext any decent journalist would have seen through, and kidnapped. Her editor, unimpressed by the fecklessness of the "lead character," had given the facts the kind of brutal massaging normally only dealt out by a heavyset, moustachioed woman in an East European bathhouse. Once the fiction of Woodward in high heels had been created, Lesley couldn't back out of it.

Worst of all, her success had been bought with death. For the hundredth time she ticked off the victims: Gregory Strong and Constance Jones, the scientists who gave her the information about the viral program—dead because she hadn't got the story out in time; Fanny Peters—dead because she had to go on a food run when Lesley turned up at her house with extra mouths to feed; James Peters, David Alexander, and his twin sons—killed by Brown because they were in her company; Bernard the helicopter pilot—dead in a crash because they'd hijacked his aircraft. She tried to pay homage to these people by talking about them in interviews, but the host always turned the subject back to her. They wanted to celebrate the heroic tale of a survivor, not dwell on the grim topic of the dead.

The kiss of death had even followed her to New York. She'd witnessed—probably caused—two fatal car crashes, a pedestrian squashed by falling scaffolding, and a woman struck dead by lightning. Animals were not immune either. She and fellow escapee Terry Borders had bought three rounds of goldfish as they tried to build a cozy domestic life. Each of them had quickly floated belly-up in the murky water for no discernible reason other than Lesley's malicious proximity. She was a jinx to every living thing in her vicinity, the rose that grew strong and bright as its roots burrowed into the fertile depths of a mass grave.

It had gotten so bad that she suffered a recurring nightmare in which she stood alone in the middle of a desolate landscape. Off in the distance, the crumbling buildings of a ruined city clawed at a sky blackened by storm clouds. As she stepped across the desiccated soil, her foot crunched on something. This was the only variable in the dream: sometimes the animal she'd stepped on was a cockroach, sometimes a mouse, once an unbearably cute chinchilla. Always, though, as the creature expired she was seized with the certainty she'd killed the last living being on Earth apart from her. She would wake with a scream dying in her throat. Terry assumed she was having nightmares about being back in Britain; she didn't disabuse him of this notion. He would try and convince her it was a delusion, like the smell of death he'd thought clung to his skin when he worked in the abattoir. Unlike Terry, she had proof of her curse: the corpses that trailed in her wake.

Her phone rang, interrupting her self-flagellation, and she looked at the caller ID. Her finger hovered for several seconds before she accepted the call.

"Hi, Terry," she said.

"Hello. Just wondering when you're coming home. I've made vegetable risotto."

"Sorry. I meant to tell you I was going to be out late."

There was a long silence. "Right. Working again. I can tell that from the music."

"I'm meeting someone about a tip," Lesley said, her voice tight.

"There's always something, right?"

"You know why I have to work so hard."

"I suppose I do. It would just have been nice to have some company."

Terry never said anything direct about how their escape had been presented. She wished he would, wished somebody would confront her about the damage she'd done so she could take her punishment now rather than store it up for the day of reckoning that must be coming. Instead he only referred to it obliquely, in snide little comments like, "I suppose I do." She knew he thought her selfish, pouring everything into her career to become a star. He didn't believe her when she told him she didn't want to be so lucky, that she only wanted to deserve whatever success came her way without having to clamber up a pile of bodies.

"It's not my fault you don't have enough to do," she said.

A heavy sigh flooded the speakers. "I just meant it would be good to see you, specifically."

He hung up without saying good-bye.

She thumped the phone down, her mouth dry, and tried to focus on the night's business. Ever since she'd been posted to New York, the Security Council had been meeting regularly behind closed doors to discuss the British crisis. She knew from sources that they'd talked about using nukes—a proposal vetoed by the Brits, who wouldn't have a country to go back to, and the French, who would have to deal with the fallout. Recently, though, there'd been a sense of growing momentum: whispers in the corridors of power and tougher language in off-the-record briefings that pointed toward the decisive military action many—including North Korea and Iran, who were delighted that a new pariah state had displaced them from the top of the international hate list—had been calling for. Tonight, she hoped to find out exactly what was afoot.

Jack Alford was a member of the delegation from the British government in exile, which had kept its role as one of the five permanent members of the Security Council despite being responsible for the virus in the first place and not having a country to govern—two pretty fucking compelling reasons for their being kicked off, in Lesley's view. She knew he was uncomfortable with the use of force, so when he'd slipped her a note asking to meet, she suspected he was going to tell her a lot of things he shouldn't.

The door swung open and in walked Jack—a tall and rangy man in his early forties, with short black hair verging on curly, a cute face, and an easy way that meant he was often buttonholed by female journalists looking to pump him for information, as well as just pump him. After a quick detour to the bar, he picked his way through the crowd and air-kissed Lesley. The soft rub of his cheek sent a shiver down her spine. She pulled away abruptly, picturing Terry sitting alone at home and staring resentfully at her untouched plate.

Every meeting began with a game in which they created farcical scenarios that the pallid UN chief would condemn, strongly condemn, or ignore. Lesley plowed right in. "I've got a good one for you tonight. Germany invades Poland again."

"The Germans are the only ones keeping the European economy afloat, so they can invade whomever they bloody well like," Jack said. "Ignore or encourage."

Lesley smiled, but Jack kept his face straight. Around his eyes were circles so dark it made him look like he was wearing mascara.

"My turn," he said. "Armed forces wipe out millions of people deemed subhuman and a threat to humanity."

That's a bit grim, Lesley thought, but still tried to answer in a jokey tone. "Are you talking about gingers? Ignore. Ginger hair is bogging. There was a story last year about a sperm bank refusing to take donations from gingers. If I ever want a kid, that's where I'll go."

Jack's lips stayed tight. "Actually, I'm talking about something closer to home."

Lesley raised a quizzical eyebrow, realizing he meant business.

"You can't use my name," he said.

"A senior official close to the negotiations okay?"

He nodded.

"Let's start with the cure," he said. "There isn't going to be one any time soon. They might be close to a treatment to control the symptoms, but it would be a series of shots. And how would they administer them? You can't get near the infected, and you can't trust them to take it themselves. Even if they did, the costs would be astronomical and the virus could still be passed on."

The shit journalist Lesley had been would have interrupted to say she knew all that. Her months in New York striving to deserve her ill-gotten reputation had taught her you never stopped somebody talking even if they were covering old ground; it gave the speaker the ego boost of feeling they were imparting crucial information, thus loosening the tongue, and some nugget you didn't know could crop up. Applying this rule, she'd already gleaned off-the-record information on the virus from the team working on a cure. They were calling it The Bloody Mary, as it had proven to be a cocktail of viruses rammed together willy-nilly. Some of the viral components—the sneezing and the sores—served the same purpose as a booster rocket putting a space shuttle into orbit, allowing the virus to spread more quickly in the early stages. After a while they sloughed off, dealt with by the immune system, to leave the core virus responsible for the urge to attack. That was the real bugger. Like most viruses, it hid itself inside cells. The sneaky part came when it stopped hijacked cells from sending out specialized molecules telling the immune system they'd been compromised. You couldn't fight what you couldn't see.

"This is why we are where we are," Jack said. "They can't keep Britain ring-fenced forever. The cost of the operation is crippling."

Lesley nodded in agreement. Estimates put the outlay close to one trillion dollars and rising, straining a global economy still battling the hangover of recession. It wasn't just the military: humanitarian aid was draining the coffers at an alarming rate. Never mind aid deliveries to

Britain, there were over fifteen million expats dependent on handouts—middle-class Britons who were either on holiday abroad during the peak August season when the virus broke out or had fled the country in the expectation of spending a few weeks drinking wine and visiting art galleries while the army sorted out the animals. When humans got infected and the U.K. banks collapsed along with the rest of the country, they became a dishevelled and hungry horde with no money and nowhere to go. The largest camp, known as Little Britain, had been set up outside Calais, sprawling across miles of formerly beautiful countryside. At least five million people lived there in makeshift shelters, littering the fields and polluting the rivers. There had already been several outbreaks of cholera. France, fearful that the foreign masses might also spread the more pernicious disease of the English language and culture, was desperate to send them back home—which meant the current occupants of Britain needed to be cleared out in a tidy fashion.

"Putting the money aside, at some point the virus is going to get out. Unless it no longer exists," Jack said. He took a long pull on the beer he'd ordered. "At the next Security Council meeting, military action is going to be vetoed again. But that's just for public consumption. They need the infected to be off guard for the plan to work."

Lesley leaned forward, her knees gripping the table leg. "And the plan is?"

"The U.S., China, and Russia are going to take action on the grounds that this is a clear and present threat to humanity's existence. At the next set of food drops after the meeting, they aren't going to deliver aid. They're going to drop nerve gas, which should take out a sizable chunk of the armed forces working on distribution."

"Is that why they've been doing food drops? To create a Trojan horse?"

"No. The food drops were to encourage the infected to stay put. If they'd all been starving, even more would have tried to pile over to France. Anyway, the gas is only part of phase one. You've heard of neutron bombs?"

"It's another type of nuke, right?"

"Yes, but they have lower blast power than a standard nuke, meaning less damage to infrastructure and so less reconstruction. Neutrons have a short half-life, so the radiation dissipates quickly. But anybody exposed to the blast radius that doesn't die from the explosion will die within weeks. This takes care of the British and French objections as far as possible, so they're happy to let it go ahead as long as they don't have to publicly back it." He slugged from the beer again and banged it down on the table. "They'll be dropped on every major population center, with an added focus on the command and military structure. In phase two, they'll start a more conventional bombing campaign: jets and helicopters, missiles and napalm. Once that's over, they'll send in ground troops to mop up." He shot her a grim smile. "It'll be over by Christmas."

Lesley pulled on her fingertips in lieu of the cigarette that New York's antismoking rules prevented her from having. She would never forget the sight of an infected bull trampling that poor scientist to death, the bodies that littered the streets, the cows rampaging through the refugee camp as army helicopters rained down fire. She didn't want to have to live through that again, and so had been all for a swift cleansing. However, now that she was hearing the stark details of what this would entail, she felt queasy.

"What about the British nukes? Won't they get a chance to fire them off?"

"They're hoping they'll be able to shoot the missiles down and take out the subs before they can pop off any more."

"Sounds like a slim hope."

"It's considered an acceptable risk. It's the chance of a few cities being flattened versus the world being infected. There's never been a threat like this to humanity. All bets are off."

"So you're for the attack?"

Jack frowned. "I wouldn't be talking to you if I was. If they were mindless, brain-eating beasts, it would be an easy decision. But they're not."

"So why now? They've had months to do something."

He picked at the label on his bottle. "Something happened a few days ago that made them very nervous. I'm not sure what."

Jack uncharacteristically refused to meet her gaze. He clearly knew what had happened but didn't want to tell. Lesley let it lie: he didn't seem in the mood to be pushed, and in a way it was irrelevant. All that mattered was that they'd decided to act.

"When's the vote?" she said.

"Seventeen days from now. Everything will be in place to get going the next day."

Lesley drained her drink, bringing back some of the color that had leached from her cheeks. "Why are you coming to me? You know where I stand on this."

"I'm coming to you precisely because of where you stand. If you come out with this story, if you oppose the attack, it might make a difference."

"Why would I oppose it? I've seen the infected up close. I know how dangerous they are."

"You've seen a few of them," Jack said. "Let me show you something."

He whipped out his smartphone and slid it across the table to Lesley. The screen showed a *Facebook* page. She scrolled through page after page of young children, from infants to gap-toothed older kids, smiling out from dozens of pictures.

"What's this?" Lesley said.

"Pictures people have posted of their family members still alive in Britain. All infected. Are you really telling me you want to see them killed? Don't you think they deserve an opportunity to be cured?"

Lesley focused on one chubby boy, no more than six months old. He was smiling behind fingers jammed into his mouth, giant blue eyes glittering with mirth. She remembered Tony Campbell—the leader of BRIT, or Brits for the Rights of the InfecTed—holding up the picture of his daughter when she'd interviewed him on CNN, something she'd dismissed as a tactic to throw her off. She slid the phone back across the table, her guts gnarling further.

"If I write this up, they'll know what's coming."

"Yes."

"And they might do something desperate."

"It's possible."

"And if the story does stop the attack, the virus might get out."

"Sure. But let's call this what it is: genocide. If you don't write the story, you'll be a party to it. If you write it, maybe you can create a public outcry and stop the bombing from taking place at all."

Lesley stared at Jack. Here she was again, at the center of a massive story—this time with the responsibility for millions of lives in her hands. Perhaps she was actually Death and nobody had bothered to tell her. Not for the first time, she asked herself what her father would do. Insufferable as he was, he'd earned his reputation. He would tell her that as a journalist her first responsibility was to the truth. On those grounds alone she should write the story. There were plenty of other reasons. The attack was a typical half-arsed strategy from the international community. Never mind the possible nuclear response: the staggered nature of the assault meant plenty of people would be left alive to flee after the initial bombing. The blockade had coped so far, but if everybody tried to cross the English Channel at once, some of them would get through and precipitate the very thing the attack was aimed at avoiding. And finally, if she refused, Jack would take the story to another newspaper and she would miss out on a scoop she really had worked for. There was only decision she could make.

"I'll do it," she said.

Jack touched her hand and headed to the toilet, leaving her sitting with her reeling head in her hands. She glanced at the bar. A stocky youth with tattoos running the length of both arms was staring at her. For a moment she thought about bolting, sure he was a spy. The youth tipped her a wink and held up a glass. He was trying to pick her up. She exhaled and shook her head. Seconds later, the young man was winking at somebody else.

Even though it had just been a burst of paranoia, she was glad of the pick-up attempt. This was an explosive story the powers that be would want to keep under wraps. She needed to be careful. She was going to stay right there in the very public bar and write her story on the laptop. Instead of e-mailing it and giving any cyber spies a chance to intercept the communication, she would take her computer physically to the *New York Times* office to upload the story. That way, there was no chance they would find out what she was up to.

It was almost midnight by the time she finished. Jack had left after one more drink, and she'd moved to a table in the corner to hide her screen. When she typed the final word, a sense of pride swept over her and she temporarily forgot her doubts and fears. While this piece was not as groundbreaking as the initial story about the virus, it wasn't far off. More pertinently, it came from the sweat of her brow. For the first time in her life, she felt like a real journalist.

She read it over again for typos. Jack had wanted her to come out strongly against the attack, and suggested opening with an analogy painting an alternative history in which sufferers of HIV/AIDS were rounded up into gas chambers. Even if she'd been going to editorialize, she wouldn't have taken that route. The gas chamber mention risked linking the Jewish people to flesh-eating zombies. Given she lived in New York, making a link that could be construed as anti-Semitic would have put her in more danger than if she'd been plopped down in middle of London wearing an "Eat Me" T-shirt. Instead, she wrote it as a straight news piece. She really should have called the appropriate officials for comment, but that would alert them to the story and possibly prompt them to kill it—or even her. The paper could add the denials once the story was published and they were safe.

She pulled on her jacket and headed out into the chilly night to flag a cab to the *New York Times* building. After being immersed in the story, it felt strange to watch so many New Yorkers going about their normal business: looking for late-night food, rushing to catch the subway home, and generally looking pale and interesting. She supposed the vast stretch of Atlantic between the U.S. and Britain gave them some comfort and got it that many Americans only vaguely understood the rest of the world existed; all the same, she found this capacity for getting on with life in the face of a potentially planet-altering event astonishing. This resilience was what so many people loved about New York. To her it seemed like willful ignorance. Why couldn't they fret, worry, and generally be miserable about the future like the Scottish? New Yorkers were probably as close to Brits as you could find in the States, and they certainly had a spikiness she liked, but she still found everybody more upbeat than she was used to.

Thinking about dour Scots, she realized she should let Terry know she wouldn't be home until the wee small hours. After all, it wasn't his fault their relationship was floundering. It wasn't anybody's. They'd been thrown together when escaping Britain and were still caught up in that whirlwind when she invited him to New York. Now that the initial shag-frenzy had waned and life settled down into a routine, they were two near-strangers rammed up against each other in a cramped apartment in the East Village. Terry was trying to keep busy. He'd joined a vegan cooking class and was volunteering at a food bank, but he still couldn't find any work. She could tell he struggled with being reliant on her. She struggled with it, too. The little things that had once been endearing were now irritating, such as the smell of Old Spice that permeated the apartment; Terry may have finally accepted he didn't smell of meat, but his habit of wearing too much aftershave remained. But he had nowhere else to go, so she couldn't kick him out. Then again, they couldn't keep going this way. Something had to change.

She resolved to be at least a little kinder to him, but the call didn't go through. She looked at the screen. There was no service. She gave the phone a shake, just in case the SIM card had dislodged, and stared at it suspiciously. It seemed a little too coincidental that her phone had stopped working not long after she got her hands on an incendiary story. It was possible she was just being paranoid again, but Lesley's breathing quickened as she hurried to the curb. A yellow cab turned the corner and she waggled her arms at it in a decidedly uncool, non-New York manner. The locals usually just held up a nonchalant arm and let it hang there at half-mast. Lesley, who thought she was missing some subtle signal only natives got, usually had to leap in front of a cab to make it stop.

Somebody else was trying to flag the vehicle, but on this occasion her semaphore won the day, and the cab drove past the closer fare. As she stepped forward, she accidentally kicked a cat that had been lurking unseen by a lamppost. It yowled and ran onto the road, where it disintegrated with a pop under the wheels of a passing truck. The jinx had struck again. Hanging her head, she ducked into the cab without sparing the driver a glance. "*New York Times* building, please."

When the cabbie didn't drive off straight away, she looked up. "Can we get going? I'm in a hurry."

"Everybody's in a hurry, lady."

Lesley started as the door flew open. A man with his jerkin zipped up to his chin and a woolly hat pulled down to his eyebrows stuck his head in. "Mind if we share?"

"You don't even know where I'm going."

He climbed in, forcing Lesley to scoot across, and pulled the door closed behind him. "I'm pretty sure we're going to the same place."

The doors locked and the driver pulled out into traffic. Even before she felt the gun poke into her ribs, Lesley knew what was happening.

"It's amazing what you can overhear when playing a little shuffleboard," the man wielding the gun said.

Lesley, her heart sinking down to bounce off the top of her bladder and bring on the urge to pee, raised her face to the scarred ceiling of the cab. "Not again," she shouted.

4

Cold water trickled through the first hesitant sprouts of ginger hair on Geldof Peters's chest, which still heaved from the exertion of his long swim, as he sloshed through the shallows of the Adriatic Sea. A gaggle of girls lolled on a blanket halfway up the pebbly beach, gazes trained on the water polo match taking place in a nearby inlet. Croatia was going through an unseasonably warm spell, and the girls wore tiny bikinis intended to draw more attention to the areas they were barely concealing. It was working. Geldof smoothed his hair out of his eyes, blinking away the saltwater that stung his contact lenses, and picked his way through the slippery rocks on the seabed; he didn't want the girls to notice him only when he tripped and went face first into the shallows.

He trudged up the beach to the spot he'd staked out beneath some trees and sat down, alone. A cheer went up and the polo players, each one six-foot plus and displaying an anatomical marvel of musculature, emerged from the water to join the girls. Perhaps if he'd been able to play the game Geldof would have found a niche in the village. He knew better than to try. While he could cover long distances when swimming solo, anything that involved serious hand-eye coordination left him looking like a string puppet controlled by a hyperactive toddler on a sugar rush. Still, after an initial chubbiness brought on by a binge on the meat and fish his mum had once denied him, the daily swimming had added a wiry layer of muscle to his once-scrawny frame. He would have made a reasonable physical specimen back in Scotland, where wrestling open a particularly tightly wrapped fish supper had been considered strenuous activity. In Croatia, however, every man under the age of twenty-five could claim direct descent from Adonis.

When his grandfather set him up in the villa overlooking a village just south of Dubrovnik, Geldof had hoped being British and red-headed would make him exotic and thus appealing to the opposite sex. All it made him was shorter than Zlatan, the man referred to as the village midget even though he was a perfectly reasonable height, and prone to scalding sunburn that sent his skin sloughing off in the same way his hemp allergy once had. He hadn't realized that Brits, before they got too busy killing each other to worry about the national obsession of a holiday in the sun, had been making their presence felt for years: soaking up the rays like hairy white lizards after a freezing desert night and demanding tea with milk, not a bloody slice of lemon, in voices that substituted volume for even the most rudimentary effort to learn a few phrases in the local language.

Geldof had tried to learn Croatian, but most people just laughed at his attempts before responding in flawless English. If they'd spoken binary, he would have been on much firmer ground. He'd plugged away, attempting to fake a convincing accent in lieu of learning the grammar, until one humiliating day in the baker's. While summoning up a vehement *h* in the back of his throat to pronounce the word for bread, he propelled a gob of phlegm onto the glass counter behind which they kept the cakes. He'd had to slink out through a gauntlet of tutting older women as the result of his final attempt to speak a foreign language slid to the floor. Further proof that he didn't fit in came when he posted an advert for the Croatian wing of Maths Club around the village. The poster started with a line saying, "If you think you have what it takes to join Maths Club, call the number below." Beneath he arranged a series of infinite sums, integrals, trigonometry, and imaginary numbers, which, when solved and added up, gave his phone number. Nobody ever called.

The one benefit of having no friends was that he had time to catch up on all the movies and TV series he'd missed over the years. His mum had been opposed to every strand of popular culture save for those once deemed kooky—such as yoga, meditation, and other assorted Eastern mysticism—that the mainstream had now embraced. As a result, she'd forbidden television in the house. He'd been forced to watch what he could on his computer late at night, when she was otherwise occupied with riding his dad senseless in one of their tantric love marathons. Now he spent each evening and weekend plopped in front of the flat-screen TV, working his way through every list of classic films he could find online.

Biting his lower lip in concentration, Geldof set about teasing off a long sliver of peeling skin from his shoulder. Even the weaker March sun proved strong enough to cook his delicate flesh once the water had washed off the sun lotion he so carefully applied. Lost in the simple pleasure, he didn't notice the girl until her red toenails were wiggling in front of him. He looked up—gaze tracking along her long legs, flat stomach, and sumptuous breasts to land on her supermodel face—just as the skin separated with an audible rip. It dangled from his fingers, swaying in the breeze.

"What is that?" she said, her voice barely accented.

Geldof was already so red from the sun that she didn't notice him blush. He tossed the scrap over his shoulder and rifled his mental files for some of the ridiculous lies he'd used to disguise his condition during the flaky rash years. "There were some baby snakes here. Just a minute ago," he blurted out. "They must have shed their skins. I lay down on them."

She half-closed one eye, looking at the shoulder where many other alleged snake skins were still attached to his body, before saying, "Yes, those baby snakes are a problem in Croatia. I am Jelena. You are Geldof, aren't you? The boy from the book about the zombie animals. You were very brave."

Geldof had forgotten that Lesley's book detailing their headlong and chaotic flight from the U.K. was due to be released around now. He couldn't recall doing anything brave; the way he remembered it, the whole bunch of them had fled screaming and flapping their arms at every confrontation. Still, he wasn't about to admit that.

"I just did what had to be done," he said with a nonchalant shrug.

She was smiling now, her hip cocked toward him in a suggestive manner. Like most Croatian girls he'd observed from a distance, she was sixteen coming on twenty-five. "We are having a beach party tonight, from ten. You should come and tell us all about it."

"I'll be there."

"Excellent," she said, and sashayed off.

He tried not to stare too obviously at her buttocks, as her friends were now looking in his direction. He'd never considered what his role in Lesley's memoir might mean for him. Given he'd received his first social invite in all the months he'd been here as a result, it seemed he might become something of a celebrity. With the first unstrained smile on his lips for weeks, he gathered up his towel. He had to resist the urge to skip back to the villa.

At first, the party went well. He'd been in Croatia long enough to know nothing started until at least an hour after the appointed time, so when he came down at 11:15, wearing a blue sweater and a pair of canvas trousers, the beautiful youths were trickling in. Off behind the portable stereo, stacked beer coolers, and plastic bottles of homemade *rakija*, a grizzled old man with gray hair that thrust out from between his shirt buttons was kindling the fire beneath a spit pig. Although life had long since fled its basted body, Geldof thought he saw its snout twitch and dead eyes roll toward him. He shuddered and looked away.

Jelena waved him over and thrust a beer into his hand. He took a long swig, trying not to screw up his face, and held the bottle down by his side where nobody could keep checking how much he'd consumed. He knew from sitting alone on his balcony, watching other parties and hoping somebody would wave him down, that Croatian mothers must have hard liquor instead of amniotic fluid sloshing around their wombs. It was the only way to explain how everyone seemed able to knock back endless amounts of beer and spirits and remain upright. To date, Geldof's experience of drinking had involved the odd glass of wine with dinner. Even a few mouthfuls made him lightheaded. He would have to be careful—particularly since his grandfather had called earlier to announce an unscheduled visit the next morning to discuss something important. He couldn't face the hardheaded businessman with a brain softened to mush by booze.

"So, what's it like to fight a zombie?" Jelena asked.

"Technically, they're not zombies," he said.

"Why not?"

Horror and fantasy geeks had already got their knickers in a twist about the use of the term in the media, arguing that the British hordes didn't meet the classical definition and should be referred to as "infected." However, since the preferred term of BRIT didn't convey the same sense of drama or peril as the emotive z-word, the geeks were ignored and left to froth at the mouth on their message boards. Geldof wholeheartedly agreed with the geeks.

"None of the animals or people rose from the dead," he said. "They don't shamble about, groan, and slowly decompose—although there is another school of thought that says zombies needn't be undead, that the state of being a zombie is about the loss of humanity and individual thought, about being driven by a simple desire to infect others. Both of these definitions disqualify beings with this virus, since they appear to be capable of relatively normal behavior when there aren't any victims around."

He sat back, confident he'd kick-started a long debate on the relative merits of the terms, thus sucking the others into his geeky world and improving his chances of having it off with Jelena.

"That which we call a shit, by any other name would stink as bad," said one of the older boys who'd been playing water polo earlier. "That's Shakespeare. Well, an approximation of Shakespeare. We're studying him in English lit. It's irrelevant what you call them. They still want to kill us all."

Everyone nodded in agreement. Geldof pretended to vigorously scratch either side of his nose with his index and middle finger. He was really giving the smartarse boy a two-fingered salute, which was not as well known internationally as the single-digit insult. The response, irritatingly delivered in perfect English, had derailed his plan.

"Never mind what to call them," Jelena said. "Tell us what happened."

And so Geldof began talking about what it was like to live through a zombie animal apocalypse. At first, it felt good to tell his story: the craziness of the early days, the evacuations, the encroaching animals, and the constant bickering between his mum, Fanny, and their meat-obsessed neighbor, David. Others, boys and girls alike, arranged

themselves nearby and leaned over to listen. They laughed out loud
when he described getting his hands stuck in the side of an infected
cow during the abortive cow-tipping episode. He'd never had so many
people intent on his every word. When somebody handed him another beer and *rakija*, he took them, fearful of breaking the spell cast
by the sparks floating up from the crackling fire, the yawning vastness
of the starry sky above, and the convivial company he'd so sorely lacked.
The liquor burned his gullet when it went down; his novice splutter-
ing was greeted with encouraging thumps on the back.

It all began to go sour when, inevitably, he got to where people began
to die. His head already swimming, he snagged a third beer as he laid
out how his mum met her end at the very snouts of the snuffling, raven-
ous pigs she'd refused to eat. He glanced at the pig as he spoke, convinced it had winked at him. By the time he narrated how Brown shot
his dad in the Channel Tunnel as they fled, he'd sloshed down another
two beers. His words were now slurred, his voice a flat monotone. There
was no more laughter; of his audience only Jelena remained and she was
casting glances around, looking for some way to escape this torrent of
pain. Geldof knew he was losing her, but he couldn't stop. He didn't
want to stop. For all those months, he'd had to internalize his grief.
David's wife, Mary, still living with Geldof after their escape, was coping
with the loss of her husband and twin sons by refusing to talk about it;
Lesley and Terry were on the other side of the Atlantic getting on with
their lives; even Nadeem, the only surviving member of Maths Club,
shied away from Geldof's attempts to express how he felt on their Skype
chats.

Finally, near spent, he tried to catch Jelena's eye: a task made impossible by his swaying, double vision and her fixed stare at the ground.

"You'd think the worst thing would be that I got my dad's brains on
my face," he said, slapping his cheek and running his fingers down to
illustrate. "Right in the face. But it wasn't. At least I had a chance to
talk to him, you know? To rebuild our relationship a bit. But my mum.
My infuriating, hectoring mum. I was such a little shit to her. I never
got a chance to tell her I loved her. I'd give anything to do that: to say
good-bye, to say sorry."

He fell silent, the full stop firmly placed on his tale of woe.

"I'm sorry," Jelena said. "I have to go."

She slipped away, leaving him marooned in an island of stillness as those who'd once surrounded him danced to Gogol Bordello, a crazed gypsy punk band the kids of the village seemed to adore. He watched her join in the dance, which seemed all the more frenetic as they exorcised the unhappiness with which he'd contaminated them.

"You wanted a cheery little adventure story, didn't you?" Geldof whispered.

He drained the rest of his beer and rose unsteadily, intent on making it to bed before he barfed. His gaze fell on the pig, now dripping crackling juices into the roaring flames. Again, it seemed to be staring at him as it revolved; grinning as it mocked his pain and taunted him for his loss.

"You killed my mum, you malodorous swine," he said.

Without any conscious decision to do so, he broke into a weaving run and launched himself through the air to catch the pig square with a thumping tackle. The supports of the spit gave way. He landed on top of the evening's dinner and began to dish out flailing punches. The pig's crisped skin split under his blows and scalding fluid spattered his forearms. He was faintly aware that the dancing had halted and every youth in the party was gaping at him as his fists pistoned in time to the beat. He only stopped when he became aware of heat around his ankles. He looked down to see his feet were still in the fire and his trouser legs were beginning to smoulder. He leapt up, leaving his vanquished foe on the ground, and grabbed a half-full glass. As he was about to throw it on his trousers, a strong hand grasped his wrist. The old man shook his head and pointed at the glass. Geldof had been about to toss hard liquor onto the fledgling fire. The old man poured a bottle of beer over Geldof's feet and put an arm around his waist.

"Time for you to go home," he said.

"I can't go home," Geldof said, his words barely audible, and let the man half carry, half drag him back up to the villa.

SEVENTEEN DAYS TO EXCISION

5

Despite his throbbing head and the burns clamoring for attention on his limbs, Geldof felt surprisingly untroubled as he sat on the steps of the villa the next morning, waiting for his grandfather to arrive. He wasn't upset that he hadn't copped off with Jelena. Deep down he'd known it would end that way, and he'd pretty much accepted he would remain a virgin for life. In many ways, it was a blessing. Virginity was only a burden if you entertained serious notions of the relief you would feel upon getting the three-hundred-pound gorilla off your back. Once you acknowledged you would be carrying it around for the rest of your life, you stopped noticing your spine was concertinaed under the weight. Yes, he still thought about sex, and released the pink pressure valve as and when required, but he could go weeks without feeling the urge to masturbate—which must have been some kind of Guinness Record for a boy of his years.

He should have felt worse about making such a fool of himself, but he couldn't bring himself to care. Perhaps it was down to finally being able to express how he felt, albeit to an unwilling audience, or the catharsis brought by punching twelve bells of shit out of a roasted pig. Or maybe it was the freedom brought by the understanding that now, with his reputation as a weirdo cemented, he would never be accepted by the local kids. After the way they'd reacted, he no longer wanted their approval. They were children housed in adult bodies, unable to relate to what he'd been through and far too quick to turn their faces away from his pain. He didn't want to build friendships that would rely on his pretending to be happy all of the time.

Whatever the reason, he was able to close his eyes and enjoy the simple warmth of the sun on his face, his mind momentarily stilled. He was on the verge of dozing off when the crunch of wheels on gravel and the purr of an engine announced the arrival of his sole surviving relative. Grandfather Carstairs, dapper as ever in a linen suit, white hat, and bushy silver moustache, eased his way out of the black Mercedes and shook Geldof's hand as the chauffeur carried his leather valise up into the villa.

"You're looking good, my boy."

"You, too, Granddad."

This was something of a white lie. His grandfather was approaching eighty, and even the few months since his last visit had been enough to deepen his stoop, which was now so pronounced he had to raise his eyes to look at Geldof. Beneath the gray pallor of his cheeks, blue veins fluttered as his blood tried to summon up the enthusiasm to make another weary circuit of his body.

"How's business?" Geldof said.

In contrast to his appearance, his grandfather's voice remained strong and even. "Recovering. The U.K. crisis hit profits hard, but at least I don't have to pay wages there any longer, and we're diversifying into new markets. Your legacy is secure, my boy."

That at least was good news. Geldof was living in the villa at his grandfather's expense, and if the company were to collapse he could well find himself not only an orphan, but a homeless orphan. From there, he may as well throw in glue-sniffing, drug use, and becoming a rent boy—which would at least lose him his virginity on a technicality. He supposed if there'd been any sign of collapse his grandfather would have divested himself of all the assets, uncaring about the jobs lost, to safeguard his personal fortune. Geldof still marveled at how far apart his mum and grandfather were, or had been, on the pragmatism/idealism scale. Then again, Geldof had spent most of his time in Scotland trying to be as dissimilar to his mum as he could, so he supposed it was natural that she'd done the same thing with the father she'd fled and whose continued existence she'd hidden for so long.

Geldof's grandfather took off his hat and dabbed at his brow with a handkerchief. "Let's have a nice cool drink on the balcony. I have some news for you."

Frowning, Geldof followed him up through the cool interior of the house and onto the large balcony overlooking the sea. Recently, his grandfather had been sending e-mails full of hints that it was time for Geldof to move on from his seclusion. He kept raising the prospect of business school so Geldof could take over the coffee empire one day—a day that would come soon enough. As much as Geldof liked the idea of being obscenely rich and knew he needed a goal to stop him drifting along like the flotsam and jetsam the sea washed up on the beach, he didn't fancy having to run a corporation. He wanted to study mathematics and get a research job probing the mysteries of the universe, not spend his days worrying about coffee prices and exploiting poor workers on plantations. Increasingly, he felt like he'd escaped one set of expectations for another: from being encouraged to bring down The Man to becoming The Man. Nobody seemed to think about what he wanted.

Anyway, discussions of his future were moot. Geldof had no doubt about the inevitability of the virus—which he thought of as a malicious, sentient entity—escaping the cordon around his former home. He'd tried to encourage his grandfather to cut loose enough cash to buy a small island and had identified several likely candidates in the South Pacific and Caribbean on *privateislandonline.com*, where he could live an idyllic life of fishing, swimming, and not being munched up by hordes of angry infected. The six million dollars or so required would be small change to his grandfather, but the old git refused to part with the cash. Buying such a refuge was the act of a quitter, according to the ruthless businessman, and he wouldn't have a quitter for a grandson.

They settled at a wrought-iron table amidst a jungle of potted plants. The housekeeper brought them two glasses of peach iced tea. He could see Mary walking up the beach off in the distance. His gigantic crush on his former neighbor and math teacher had backed off completely. She would never replace his mother, but she was trying to fill that gap; thus thinking about her in a sexual way, as he'd once done constantly, now seemed very creepy. Perhaps sensing his reluctance to allow her to take on a maternal role, she'd started stalking the twin boys who lived in a nearby villa, who, despite not being evil little toe-rags, clearly reminded her of the sons she'd lost.

Geldof's grandfather took a sip of his iced tea and placed his hat on the table. "I thought I should tell you this to your face to try and ease into it, but now that I'm here I don't know any good way to introduce it gently. So I'm just going to say it."

Here we go, thought Geldof. *He's probably booked me a place in some awful business school.*

"Your mother is still alive."

Geldof sprayed iced tea all over the immaculate white suit.

"I thought that's how you might react," his grandfather said, dabbing at the stains with his hanky.

6

If this is the best Britain has to offer, thought Tony Campbell as he looked at the predominantly slack faces of the cabinet members gathered in Cabinet Office Briefing Room A at 70 Whitehall, *then we are well and truly screwed.*

His advisors sat around an orange table so large they couldn't lean back in their plush leather chairs without butting against the wall, which was painted a grotty shade of shit brown. Only the bank of monitors displaying a drawing of a human brain proved they hadn't returned to the seventies, when the whole of Britain had been tarred with the same two-tone brush. The young Tony had even owned a brown corduroy suit, matched with a lurid orange kipper tie and a shirt with collars so wide that a gust of wind could have sent him soaring off like a hang glider—a sharp contrast to the sober blue outfit he wore today. His cabinet members were dressed just as conservatively, which would have given a casual observer the mistaken impression they actually knew what they were doing.

In the days before the virus brought the country not so much to its knees as left it lying face down in the gutter soaked in its own piss, crisis meetings such as this one were known as COBRA after the location in which they were held. Tony considered the acronym too thrusting for the gatherings held by Brits for the Rights of the InfecTed, the self-appointed rulers of a formerly proud nation. His unspoken term SLUG—short for Sluggish Laggards in Useless Government—was far more appropriate.

He leaned forward, the overhead strip light glaring off the smooth brown skin of the vertiginously high hairline he'd suffered since he was a boy. His young self had often buffed up the front half of his scalp in an attempt to redirect light and create a Dalek-style death ray. Had he that death ray now there would be piles of ash on the chairs where his advisors sat. Only a few members of the cabinet were remotely useful. To his right sat Glen Forbes, Secretary of State for Defense and Commander in Chief of Land Forces. A stocky man with tiny ears out of proportion to his bulbous, bald head and skin several shades darker than Tony's, Glen had been a lieutenant general before the outbreak. After, as the highest-ranking military official left alive or in-country, he took up the task of marshaling the remnants of the armed forces and attempting to restore order through the standard military fallbacks of curfews and brute force. It was Glen, an old acquaintance from Oxford, who'd sought out Tony to head up a largely civilian government in order to make the new rulers seem less of a jingoistic military regime to the world.

By virtue of his experience, Glen had a working knowledge of the process unfolding across the Atlantic, where the UN was drawing closer to passing a resolution authorizing military action. Sure, they were keeping the food drops going and sending reassuring messages about researching a cure, but every article Tony read portrayed the infected as bloodthirsty beasts who loved nothing more than snacking on a dollop of brains washed down with a nice chug of blood. He entertained no doubt the media was being encouraged to demonize and dehumanize the infected so there would be no public outcry when the hawks swooped in to eradicate the threat of a global apocalypse. Only the nuclear missiles BRIT still controlled were delaying that moment. That deterrent wouldn't hold forever.

While Glen possessed certain skills, he was himself a ferocious hawk with claws far sharper than his brain. He'd been a firm backer of the Iraq invasion and unrepentant when the WMDs proved to be as hard to find as a four-quid pint in London in the days before the virus. He adhered to the school of thought that there was little point in possessing weapons if you weren't going to use them. Or as he'd once put it, "Why buy a Ferrari if you aren't going to take it out for a spin?" Glen's attitude helped convince Tony that the clock was ticking down to the moment when the warships and warplanes maintaining a protective cordon around Britain would dump their deadly payloads on the mainland: if Glen was representative of most generals, they would be champing at the bit to play with their toys.

To Tony's left sat Amira Farouk, his spin doctor. A rotund woman with protruding teeth and thick, sweeping hair, she'd been Tony's trusted media advisor for years. She came up with the BRIT acronym, using the word "infected" to emphasize that they were sick and thus could be cured; the Keep Calm and Carry On campaign; and the tactic of whipping out a picture of Tony's daughter during his first televised interview—recorded in the fledgling weeks of his job as leader of the new infected Britain—to remind the world that the lives of millions of children were on the line.

It hadn't been Amira's fault that the CNN interview had gone as tits up as Pamela Anderson in zero gravity. The stress of his new job, the lingering sores and sniffles from the early stages of the virus, and the high stakes of the attempt to present a softer face to the world had put him on edge. So, when that sodding journalist Lesley McBrien goaded him, the virus had awoken and he came across as a slavering maniac with his threats—futile, of course, since she was in a studio in Paris—about unravelling entrails and gouging out eyeballs. After the interview, the world's media had focused on his pointy teeth, speculating that he sharpened them with a file to make it easier to tear human flesh. That was completely unfair. He'd always had sharp teeth and had worn a moustache for over twenty years to partially shield his dentally challenged mouth. That now was gone, thanks to Amira.

"You need to lose the moustache," she'd said in her post-interview debrief. "It makes you look like a mad dictator. You do know you pet it when you're nervous, don't you? You looked like a Bond villain stroking his cat."

"Oh, come on. It's just a bit of hair."

"No, it's a symbol of all that is dark, cruel, and twisted in mankind. Think about all the evil leaders with moustaches. Hitler being the obvious one."

"Mine isn't a toothbrush moustache though, is it?"

"You're right. It's more like a dental floss moustache. Still has to go."

"I'm not going to cave in just because you brought up Hitler. Who else you got?"

"Genghis Khan."

"That was more of a beard-moustache combo."

"How about Ming the Merciless then? You can't deny that was one evil mouthbrow."

"He was a bloody movie villain."

"Exactly. The all-consuming evil of moustaches is so well accepted that it's become a trope in Hollywood. Bad guys are either effeminate English toffs or they have facial hair. Sometimes both."

"Don't we have bigger things to focus on than the contents of my top lip?"

"I know it seems trivial, but after that psycho performance we can't afford to have any more negative associations. You don't want to give *cracked.com* the chance to put you in a Top Ten Evil Moustaches list. Just humour me and shave it off, okay?"

Tony, a regular on the satirical Web site, had complied.

Beyond Amira and Glen, the cabinet swiftly ran out of talent. Tony's gaze tracked along the other dozen individuals who, through blunders or lack of ambition, had butted up against low glass ceilings in their careers before everything went to shit. It didn't help that many of them were doped up on the diazepam and nitrazepam the UN included in its aid drops. While the drugs were useful for dampening tempers, they turned the users into the sluggish laggards of Tony's acronym. Tony avoided the drugs, preferring to deal with the bursts of anger in his own way. The advisors were the best he could scrape up given that the greatest minds in the U.K. had buggered off before the quarantine. It had all been a question of money: those who could afford to go abroad did so, leaving behind those who couldn't afford the rocketing ticket prices as the virus bit. Of course, not every Brit with the skills he needed was able to make it out in the panic, but of those who remained, many had either been killed or were lying low.

When Tony's gaze fell on the sorry excuse for a chief scientist, one of the chief pill poppers, he ground his teeth. Before the outbreak, Tim Roast had been a biology lecturer at a provincial university—one of those pokey affairs that somehow attained university status and ran around trumpeting its credentials like a lottery winner flaunting his newfound wealth. This position was a step down from a government research post, from which he was sacked when he contaminated crucial samples with his own saliva. He looked exactly the way Tony felt a lecturer should: V-neck pullover, badly knotted tie, and a pair of glasses so enormous they made his eyes look like snooker balls. This, unfortunately, was the man who was leading their hunt for a cure. The problem, apart from Tim's utter crapness, was that the government facility where the virus was developed had been blown up in an overzealous cover-up. That journalist had smuggled out the data, but the world wouldn't share it; presumably they were concerned BRIT would use it to synthesize more of the virus.

Enough moping, Tony thought, and slapped his hand on the table. "Right, let's get on with it. Tim, please tell me you've made some progress."

Tim stood up and tugged on his tie. "Actually, we think we've tracked down the part of the brain the virus targets."

Tim nodded at his assistant, who handed out briefing papers. This was the first time Tim had done anything other than look vacant when asked about the virus, so Tony eagerly snatched his up. His face reddened as he looked at the top page. In the death ray scenario this would have been the point when he incinerated the muppet. He pulled out his wallet and opened it: Mr. Spock's impassive face regarded him from alongside pictures of his wife, Margot, and daughter, Vanessa.

This is your reflection, he thought. *You are calm. You are in control. You are Vulcan.*

Tony had been relying on Spock to calm him for over forty years. When he was a boy, his parents had done nothing but argue; his mother had been fond of telling Tony he was the product of a burst condom and the reason they were so miserable. He was always on edge, waiting for the shouting to start. He was seven years old when the first episodes of *Star Trek* aired on the BBC. He became entranced by Spock, whose calm angular face radiated magical tranquillity amid the bright, fuzzy colors and exotic aliens. No matter how chaotic the situation, Spock remained untouched by fear and despair. He would never cower in the corner as crockery flew. Tony's curly hair frustrated his plans to give himself a bowl cut, so he started plucking on his ears and eyebrows in the hope they would develop into Spock-like points. When the physical transformation didn't occur, he practiced steepling his fingers and raising his eyebrows until, after months of repetition and fierce concentration, these gestures started to calm him in moments of stress. After his father left for good, his mother still blamed Tony for ruining the marriage, so he had plenty of reason to carry his emulation of Spock through his teens and on into his adult life.

Now it felt like he was catching up on a lifetime of unspent ire. The virus slumbered inside him, fingers curled loosely around his brain and ready to squeeze. Already he could feel the pressure, although it was nothing compared with the iron grip exerted in the presence of the un-infected. It was worse when the hold of his conscious mind loosened and the virus was given free rein in his dreams. They couldn't be called nightmares, for he was the monster that bit and tore—although the savage joy he felt in the dream turned to gut-wrenching sickness when he awoke and wrestled for control of his mutinous mind. His need for Spock had never been greater.

Tim adopted a lecturing drone as Tony summoned up Spock to fight off his rising temper. "We suspect the virus targets the amygdala, which is part of the primal limbic system. Animal studies have shown that stimulating the amygdala, or more properly amygdalae, since we have one on each side of the brain, increases sexual and aggressive behavior. It also seems to control fear."

Tim paused, waiting for acknowledgment. Tony, fingers now stee-pled and right eyebrow straining upwards, didn't respond. The delay seemed to send Tim into a trance, and his assistant had to nudge him.

"Where was I?" The assistant pointed to a line on the sheet of paper Tim was clutching. "Super. So, the olfactory bulb, in fact all our sensory apparatus, is directly wired to the limbic system. We believe that when the scent of the uninfected is fed into the amygdalae, the virus activates, prompting increased aggression, heightened sex drive, and lack of fear."

Tony, whose invocation of Spock had calmed him down enough to speak, said, "And how does this explain that people are still angrier when the uninfected aren't around?"

"The virus rearranged the furniture when it moved in, so there are bound to be residual effects."

"Do you have any evidence of this?"

"It's still a theory. But it all fits. Birds don't have amygdalae, which could explain why the virus didn't affect them. Mammals do. Plus women have smaller amygdalae and larger prefrontal cortexes."

"This is getting too brainy for me," said Glen. "Can someone explain it in layman's terms?"

"Think of your amygdala as a dog and your prefrontal cortex as its owner," Amira said. "Women have a French poodle . . ."

"Hang on," Glen said. "Don't be fooled by the fluff. Poodles are vicious little bastards. Nippy. Treacherous. Yelpy. Just like a woman in fact."

Amira kept her cool. "Fine. Then women have a well-trained golden retriever on a strong leash. In men, it's a slavering pit bull on a tattered piece of string held by a pissed-up skinhead."

"Good analogy," Tim said. "Like Amira said, in most cases the members of the fairer sex do seem better able to keep a lid on their tempers."

"I thought that was because they didn't have any balls," Glen said.

"Why don't we just snip off your shriveled scrotum in the name of science, then?" Amira said sweetly. "You could definitely use a bit less testosterone."

Glen's ears wiggled, driven by his grinding jaw—a sure sign he was heading toward an explosion. Fortunately, Tim got back on topic before it could escalate into Glen lobbing furniture around.

"Testosterone may be a factor," Tim said. "But I want to point you to teenagers as another example. Puberty brings about rapid development of the limbic system, but the prefrontal cortex takes years to catch up. This is what causes all that erratic emotional behavior: the anger, the mood swings, the desire in boys to hump anything that moves."

"So the virus has turned people into teenagers," Tony said. "What's your solution? Ground everybody until they learn not to be snotty brats?"

"We're thinking we could remove the amygdalae in a few test subjects to see if it makes a difference."

"Do we have any neurosurgeons capable of doing this?"

Tim scratched his nose with the electronic pointer he'd forgotten to use and recoiled as the laser shone into his eye. "Not exactly," he said, blinking. "But we could figure it out."

"So what does this amygdala look like?"

Tim squinted at the screen. "Kind of like a peanut?"

"Better not do it on yourself, then. You'd remove your whole brain." Tony tossed the report down. "If you're going to cut and paste from *Wikipedia*, make sure you delete the bloody logo. You just googled a few key phrases and came up with this, didn't you?"

Tim fidgeted with his glasses. "Well, yes, but it does make sense. And *Wikipedia* is a valid source."

"For lazy cretins. Anyway, if by some miracle you were right, could you treat it with drugs, or are you proposing we crack open the head of every man, woman, and beast in this country?"

With a longing look toward his chair, Tim said nothing. Tony massaged his temples. While Tim was clearly a grade-A buffoon, there did seem to be some logic to the theory. Plus the clock was ticking louder and faster every day. They needed to find a solution or face obliteration. Better to pursue a possible dead end than stand looking down the alley, not sure if it led somewhere.

"Fine, give it a try," Tony said, now feeling more fatigued than angry. "What else do we have?"

"There is this," said Frank Maybury, a former chief inspector now serving as secretary of state for the Home Department and the only other member of the cabinet who'd shown he could do his job.

He slid a piece of paper up the table. It was a pamphlet calling on people to resist the virus and giving some techniques to maintain calm. Some of the strategies appeared to be based on the tenets of Buddhism, although Tony didn't recall Buddha encouraging people to get thoroughly stoned and have frequent sex to release calming endorphins—or in the case where no partner was available, masturbate regularly to achieve the same effect. If Buddhism had advocated that, it probably would have supplanted all other religions centuries ago.

Amira grabbed the leaflet. "Resist: You Are More Than Your Urges," she read out loud. "Don't think much of their tagline. I'd have gone with, 'Meditate. Vegetate. Copulate.'"

"Why are they telling everyone to have sex?" Frank said, with a significant look at Amira. "Most of us don't need any encouragement."

Amira blushed and hid behind the leaflet. Tony's mood lightened. There was indeed no need to promote hanky-panky. The frequency and intensity of sex with Margot had exploded since the virus came along, and when he walked through his offices at Number Ten Downing Street he would often hear broom cupboards and meeting rooms vibrating with the moans and thumps of quick knee tremblers. From the way the men's loos never seemed to have any toilet paper, it was pretty clear there was a significant amount of solitary activity to boot. He never flagged it up. People needed a release, and as long as it was consensual or the soloist managed not to splash on the toilet seat, he didn't have an issue with it.

"Where'd you get it?" Tony said.

"A patrol caught a bloke with a bag of them."

"I don't recall handing out flyers being illegal."

"They saw him in a garden in the middle of the night and thought he was a burglar. We only found out what'd he been up to after we nicked him."

Tony turned the leaflet over. He knew from his own experience it was possible to slow, if not entirely stem, the tide of anger. Yet could an entire nation be trained to resist? The majority, once lucidity returned, were filled with shame at the acts they'd carried out but were still unable to resist when another uninfected person came within range. Now the uninfected were all gone, some—like this insane Blood of Christ group that was causing so much trouble—still allowed their tempers to turn to violence or simply used the virus as an excuse for preexisting psychotic tendencies. The average punter was struggling to keep calm. Others seemed barely affected. Amira was a perfect example of this last group: always cool and collected. Tony had never seen her take a pill.

Glen, who also didn't take any sedatives because "the anger gave him an edge," showed exactly what he thought of the leaflet. "Great idea. Let's all sit cross-legged and wish the whole thing away. In fact, let's start distributing candles and incense. Maybe chuck in a few *Best of Enya* CDs and free passes to a spa. I'm sure that'll do the trick." He looked around the table. "You know how strong this virus is. You know the things we've done. If one of the uninfected came in that door right now, you know what would happen."

Tony knew, all right. No matter how hard he tried, he would never forget what the virus had turned him into. He'd never asked the other members of his cabinet what they'd done in those awful early days, as he was sure they wanted to forget just as much as he did. From the stricken looks on their faces—Amira aside—he knew it wasn't good.

"In the unlikely event everyone learns to control it, we'd still be an infection risk," Glen said. "Do you really think they'll let us live out our days in splendid isolation when we're all carriers?"

Even Amira, who often sparred with Glen just for the sake of it, didn't argue that point. Each and every person in Britain was a threat and would remain so until a cure was found, if it ever was. Glen stood up, holding his briefcase, and walked to the head of the table. The brightness of the monitors haloed his head, cloaking his face in shadow.

"I have a plan," he said. "One that will actually work."

Tony had a feeling that the plan would involve large explosions of some sort, but he couldn't shut Glen down after having given others a shot at presenting a solution. "Let's hear it."

"First, can we agree that sooner or later—most likely sooner—the UN is going to give the go-ahead for every living thing in Britain to be obliterated?"

Everybody nodded.

"And do we agree we'd much rather this didn't happen?"

The nods were more emphatic this time.

"Great. Next, what's their motivation for doing this?"

"They don't want the virus to get out," said Frank, stating the obvious.

"Bingo. So, we take away their motivation."

"We've been through that," Tony said. "The only way to take away their motivation is to cure it or assure them it's contained long term. That's what we're trying to do. Rather ineptly so far, I might add."

"There's another way to take away their motivation." Glen reached into his briefcase and threw his own set of briefing papers onto the table with a heavy thud. "We spread it."

The silence that filled the room could only have been more stunned had Glen announced he wanted to live out the rest of his life as a woman and whipped off his uniform to reveal a basque, miniskirt, and stockings. Nobody reached for the papers, so Glen pressed on. "Tony, I'd like to quote what you said during your CNN interview, 'Would everyone having the virus be such a bad thing? If we all had it, there would be no need for violence.'"

Tony, still struggling to get his brain to come up with some response to relay to his slack mouth, remembered the comment. It had been an off-the-cuff remark, not a policy recommendation, and he'd realized it was ill judged as soon as he said it. Now it was being tossed back in his face.

"In that spirit," Glen continued, "I propose we refit our Trident missiles with refrigerated warheads filled with blood collected from soldiers and fire them at Europe. We can have infected blood raining down on Paris, Berlin, and Rome within a few minutes, too quick for them to respond. They'll assume the lack of a mushroom cloud means the missiles were duds or simply a warning of our capabilities. It'll take them a while to figure out what really happened, and when they do there'll be no point in launching a response. The virus will be out, and they'll be too busy trying to contain it. Plus, they'll have more motivation to find a cure, or everyone will be infected." Glen paused, his teeth shining white in the dark shadow of his face as he grinned. "Now, any comments?"

Amira, who was shaking her head so vehemently that her dangly earrings almost slapped Tony in the face, spoke up. "I have one," she said. "You're off your bloody rocker."

Her voice broke the paralysis, and suddenly everybody was talking at once, hands waving and fingers stabbing the air. Amira was up on her feet, her composure gone for the first time since Tony had known her. Glen ignored the storm of voices and slid one of the briefing papers along the table to butt up against Tony's fingertips. Tony hesitated. Their gazes met, and Tony realized that the military man, normally so volatile, seemed utterly calm.

"It's the only way," Glen said, his strong voice cutting through the hubbub.

Tony picked up the document and began to read.

7

Ruan awoke at the stealthy click of an opening door. She opened her sleep-encrusted eyes to a boxy room, where the single mattress she'd slept on was the only furniture, and prepared to bolt. She always slept fully clothed, shoes and all, in preparation for just such a moment, but when she threw back the duvet she found she was wearing only a T-shirt and frayed white knickers. Even her rucksack and sword, normally packed and ready to snatch up, lay discarded in the corner instead of beside the window. She thrust a hand under the pillow and settled on the reassuring heft of the pistol. At least she hadn't been totally lax. Still disorientated, she had no idea where she was, how she'd gotten here, or why she'd been so careless, but she knew that she would have to sacrifice her belongings.

She was up on her feet, fumbling at the catch on the window with nerveless fingers, when the door swung open fully and a soft female voice said, "You don't have to run."

The gun rose as Ruan spun and tightened her finger on the trigger. She saw the woman and her arm dropped. It all came flooding back: her failed stew heist, the flight through the forest, the hand reaching out to her.

After they'd been sure the pursuers were shaken off, the woman had doubled back. Ruan had tried to talk, but her new companion held a finger to her lips. She led Ruan high around Arrochar at a jog and curved back toward the road, following it around the loch from just inside the tree line. There were no streetlights on this bank, so when the woman crossed the road and plunged into the bushes Ruan was surprised to find more tarmac beneath her feet. After a few more minutes they came out onto the side of the loch.

A hulk of a building sat on a pier that ran out into the water. At the end of the platform, Ruan spotted a small group sitting in lotus position around a roaring fire, encircled by flickering candles stuck into glass jars. Beyond, the reflection of the moon shimmered on the black water. It would have seemed almost idyllic were it not for the jumble of old machinery and rubble by the water's edge. Ruan moved toward the light, but the woman put a hand on her shoulder and shook her head. It had been seven months since Ruan had spoken to anybody—in fact, she'd barely said a word, since she considered talking to herself an early sign of going loopy—so she didn't know how to break the silence that had built up between them. Ruan allowed herself to be led into the house—one of around a half-a-dozen that sat shoulder to shoulder. She'd collapsed onto the mattress and, her guard lowered by the thought of so many clearly uninfected people around her, shucked off her clothes and slipped under the sheets to fall instantly asleep.

Now, in full daylight for the first time, she took in the woman's face properly. With no shadows to act as a soothing visual balm, the scars presented themselves in full pink and twisted glory. The worst was a bite mark on her left cheek, a crater so deep Ruan could have put her pinkie in up to the first knuckle. The same bite had removed a chunk from one side of a long, sharp nose. Other deep grooves and troughs pitted her face, running up into the gray hair she wore close to her scalp and plunging below the neckline of a long-sleeved black cotton top. Strangely, her face looked peaceful, like the ruins of an old castle. Her watery blue eyes betrayed no signs of bitterness at what had befallen her. When she smiled they seemed to lighten in the same way as a sun-dappled swimming pool.

"I see you've noticed my scars," the woman said.

Ruan's cheeks flushed and the instinctive urge to apologize nudged her vocal cords into life. Her voice sounded low and hoarse. "Sorry, I didn't mean to stare. It's been a while since I've had company. My social skills are a bit rusty."

"It's okay. If it was a problem, I would wear a mask. I want people to see them."

Something about the forthright way the woman spoke, about the way her gaze was challenging and encouraging at the same time, emboldened Ruan to ask a question that seemed rude the moment she said it. "Why? I mean, not that you should hide your face if you don't want to, or that I don't want to look at it . . ."

Ruan trailed off. She was sounding even more insulting with every word she added. The woman seemed unfazed. "It reminds me that I'm not the person I used to be."

Staring into the ravaged face, Ruan felt she'd seen this woman before. She closed her eyes and held the face in her mind. Ruan had always been highly visual, able to store near-photographic shots of any face or scene and conjure up images of startling clarity. She examined the mental picture of the face, turning it left and right like an animator playing with a 3-D model. There had been no scars, so she filled them in with healthy, if rather pallid, flesh. The woman's hair wasn't right. It had been longer; something scruffy and unwashed. Dreadlocks, that was it. She scribbled them in and then she had it.

"I've seen you before," she said. "At a demonstration in Edinburgh last year against Trident. You . . ."

Ruan thought it best not to continue. The protest had been one in a series of many against the U.K.'s nuclear weapons program, which was housed at Faslane naval base on Gare Loch, not too far from where they were now. The protests were normally rowdy but peaceful affairs attended by a mix of students, Campaign for Nuclear Disarmament activists, professional crusties, and genteel gray-haired old ladies. This particular protest involved a "die-in" outside Scottish Parliament, with everyone lying on the ground and feigning death during a visit by the defense secretary, who'd no doubt wished that they would stop pretending and get on with really being dead.

The woman had stripped off her green caftan, thick purple tights, and skimpy knickers, hurling each item at the line of police. The knickers landed right on a policeman's hat. When everybody else ignored her shrill cries for mass nudity, she kicked off the hand grasping her ankle, which belonged to the ponytailed man lying next to her, and skipped through the prone bodies. She hurdled the barricade and dashed toward the startled politician as he was about to climb into his car. The police intercepted her and dragged her off as she screamed abuse. All of this had been caught on camera and played repeatedly on the news, accompanied by smirking jokes from the presenters.

The woman looked at the ground. "As I said, I'm not that person any longer."

Ruan realized that she'd just repaid the woman who saved her life by reminding her of an incident she clearly wanted to forget. She hadn't even expressed her gratitude for the intervention. "Thank you for helping me last night."

"You're welcome."

"What were you doing out there anyway?"

"Hunting."

"Ah. That explains the bow and arrow. Which, by the way, you're very good with."

"Thank you. I used to do archery when I was younger, before I became a pacifist."

From the way she'd ended the dog, it was clear pacifism had only been a phase. "I don't even know your name. I'm Ruan Peat."

"Fanny Peters. Come on, let me show you around."

"Can I get dressed first?"

"Ah, of course. Old habits die hard, I'm afraid."

They smiled at each other, and Ruan felt the warmth that only human companionship brought bleed through her. She had to fight to stop it thawing the emotions she'd done her best to keep on ice to maintain her sanity. She pulled on her clothes. As she did so she noticed that the smartphone she'd lifted from an empty house was plugged in and charging. She grabbed the phone and her sword through force of habit and walked to the door. As she approached, Fanny's breathing slowed. The ruined nostril quivered as she drew in deep breaths.

"I know you are here and it makes me happy," Fanny said quietly, repeating the phrase she'd uttered upon their first meeting.

Ruan frowned. The lines on her forehead deepened when she passed through the door and noticed the key. It protruded from the outside of the door. Fanny had locked her in.

I'm sure she had a good reason, Ruan thought.

The state of the hallway didn't help her discomfort. Fungus bloomed around the skirting board, while only a few scraps of wallpaper remained on the blistered walls. It smelled and spoke of ruin.

Fanny seemed to sense her unease. "Sorry about the state of the place. Nobody was in this one, so we left it. We'll decorate it for you if you decide to stay."

Ruan stepped into the fresh air, reaching out to flake stones from the gray pebbledash covering the walls. As she did so her arm brushed the guttering, which creaked and swayed. The view outside was just as cheerless. Across the overgrown lawn sat the building she'd seen on her way in. It formed a large part of the pier that ran out over the water on a lattice of warped and worn wooden struts. Scudding layers of gray cloud and the houses and shops of Arrochar across the loch were visible through the charred skeleton of the building. Underfoot, weeds and clumps of moss sprouted from what appeared to be rails set into the concrete. The rails led from the ruined pier to semicircular stone structures with heavy steel doors. Hangars, perhaps.

"What is this place?" she said.

"It was a torpedo testing station, shut down in the eighties and left to rot."

"Why do you stay here? I don't mean to be rude, but it's a bit skanky."

"Lots of reasons. It's remote. It's easily defensible. And it has a rather appropriate symbolism considering what we do."

"And what do you do?"

"Let me show you."

Fanny followed the tracks to one of the hangars and rapped on the door. A steel plate slid open and a cloud of smoke puffed out. It held the same sweet, pungent fragrance that used to emanate from her brother Bryan's room when their parents were out. A pair of gold-rimmed spectacles appeared, from behind which lidded blue eyes peered out. The glasses darkened in reaction to the sun outside.

"Are you ready?" Fanny said.

The man took several deep breaths and said, "I know you are here and it makes me happy."

Bugger, Ruan thought. *Just my luck. This is some crazy cult.*

As Fanny and the man talked in whispers, Ruan pulled out her phone and opened her messenger app to send a quick note to her best friend,

Bridget. "Had a crazy night," she wrote. "Just got more mental. Walked into a den of FREAKS! More later."

She hit send and, as she always did, allowed herself a brief moment of hope that she would see the two little ticks that showed communications were working again and her friend was listening. When the clock icon indicated the message had gone nowhere—just as in the hundreds of other messages in her one-sided conversation—she squeezed the phone so hard the plastic case creaked.

She blinked rapidly, took a step backward, and considered running for it. For all she knew the hangar contained a sacrificial slab and dozens of robed acolytes with sharp knives, ready to sacrifice her to some freaky god. On the other hand, these were the only uninfected people she'd come across, and Fanny had saved her life last night. Metal scraped as a bolt was drawn back and Ruan stepped inside, fingers tightening around the hilt of her sword. The man who'd answered the door shuffled backward until his head butted up against the curved hangar wall. Instead of a robe, he wore a red and blue tie-dyed T-shirt and a pair of jeans. He was enormous, towering over Ruan by almost a foot, and had a bulky frame to match. The sparse covering on top of his scalp became a waterfall of blond hair that cascaded down his back in a long ponytail.

"This is Scott McDonald," Fanny said.

"Ruan," she said, holding out her hand.

He flinched, as though she were offering him a dead mouse lollipop instead of a handshake. Fanny stepped over and put a hand on his shoulder.

"It's okay," she said. "You can do it."

These people are seriously weird, Ruan thought.

Then again, it was little wonder after all they'd been through. She'd developed her own strange habits, such as enjoying the taste of Pedigree Chum with fish oil and chicken, a tin of which she'd discovered at the bottom of a skip around the back of a supermarket at a particularly desperate moment. Perhaps it was just that serendipitous combination of hunger and thirst, but the moist, meaty chunks had electrified her taste buds and, as a regular taker of cod-liver oil in her old sporty life, she'd been aware of the benefits of added omega-3s. Since then, she'd always kept an eye out for that particular brand and flavor and ate it even when human food was readily available.

Scott, after a long puff on the joint he was clutching, reached out to take her hand. The contact from the massive paw was limp and fleeting, but it seemed to prompt palpable relief in him. Ruan turned her attention to the rest of the interior. A metal grille with an inset, padlocked door separated her from a windowless room lit by three harsh fluorescent strips. It seemed Fanny had a thing for locking people in. Bog-standard office furniture was crammed into every space above a snaking mess of cables connecting battered computers, monitors, and printers. The room was a fug of dope smoke, emanating from fat joints clutched between the fingers of three men and two women who'd risen from their seats to stare at her. Ruan curled her fingers around the grille.

As one, they said, "I know you are here and it makes me happy."

A mass inhalation followed and the smoke jetted out added to the clouds swirling around them. Ruan coughed, beginning to feel light-headed.

Give them a chance, she thought, and parroted the phrase back at them. They looked surprised.

In the far corner of the room, half hidden by a stack of what looked like pamphlets, was a youth who hadn't joined in with the greeting. Although he couldn't have been more than seventeen and only had a light dusting of beard, he reminded Ruan of the Noels. He had to be local. His right fist was convulsing, mashing one of the pieces of paper into a crumpled ball.

"Where did you get all this stuff?" Ruan asked.

"My old friend Scott here has been putting this together for a few years," Fanny said. "It was going to be our command-and-control post when the revolution came."

"What revolution?"

"We were never clear on that," Fanny said with a rueful smile. "But I'm very glad he did it. Now we really are the resistance."

"The resistance to the government?"

"No. To the virus."

"I don't understand."

"Rory," Fanny called. "Hand me one of the leaflets."

Avoiding looking at Ruan, Rory scuttled out from his refuge like a furtive crab, handed a pamphlet to the woman with wavy brown hair who marked the end of the row of watchers, and scuttled back to his paper cave. Ruan rolled her eyes. Back before every human wanted to kill her, she'd often had this effect on teenage boys. Her Irish descent on her father's side had given her creamy skin and big green eyes, while her mother's Slavic genes provided jet-black hair, sheer cheekbones, generous lips, and a tall, lithe body—not to mention breasts that at one point she'd feared would keep growing until it looked like she'd been in a car crash and her chest had somehow fused with the inflated air-bags. Even though she knew many women would kill for her figure and she found them useful on occasion, such as when she wanted to get served in bars, she'd hated those breasts. She hated them still. They got in the way of her athletic pursuits—she kept a stack of sports bras in her rucksack—and their sheer heft seemed to exert an extreme grav-itational pull on any male eyes orbiting in her vicinity.

Men employed a variety of techniques when faced with her breasts. They stared at the ground and turned an alarming shade of red (most of the teenage boys at school); they stared at her face with the occa-sional downward flick of the eye (the male teachers); they pretended to be interested in the design or logo on her T-shirt (the sneakier older boys); and, in the case of older, more-experienced tit watchers, they waited until they thought she wasn't looking and drank their fill in long, greedy gulps or stood off to the side and feigned interest in some distant object that just happened to be in the same eye line as her breasts. Out of all the methods, she preferred the blatant staring, which had the virtue of honesty. At one point, after meeting a particu-larly discomfited fifteen-year-old whose eyeballs were vibrating with the effort of not looking, she'd snapped and said, "Why don't you just bloody stare at them for ten seconds to get it out of your system, and then we can try to talk to each other like real people?" Unsurprisingly, he'd skedaddled in a fugue of embarrassment.

Some of the girls at school weren't much better, basing their as-sumptions on her appearance and accusing her of trying flirt with their boyfriends. Early in Ruan's development, one girl had made the mistake of slapping Ruan when her boyfriend began writing unwanted soppy love notes to her. Nobody made the same mistake again. Her fondness for nice clothes had only made it worse. The girls assumed that choosing to adorn her body with well-fitting, gorgeous outfits was a deliberate ploy to steal their men, when in fact she just loved the way they looked and felt. There had been a point when she considered dressing in the frumpy rags that passed for clothes in her mum's cupboard, but she decided not to change her behavior for other people. It was their problem, not hers. Yet she couldn't escape the fact that people often made up their minds about her based on genes, over which she had no control. Sure, exposure to the elements and the scars and worry lines she'd picked up over the last seven months had no doubt dimmed her youthful glow, but it hadn't reduced the size of her chest. Rory's reaction came as no surprise.

The woman handed the leaflet to Fanny, who in turn passed it to Ruan.

"Resist: You Are More Than Your Urges," Ruan read aloud from the bold headline.

Underneath, an introductory paragraph exhorted people to remember that they were human and not to give in to the imperatives of the virus. She stopped after the first few lines and looked at Fanny. "Do you really think the infected can resist the urges?"

Fanny looked at her companions and put an arm around Ruan. "Come outside."

They strolled to the water's edge, where Ruan picked up a flat stone and skipped it across the loch. A sad smile kinked Fanny's lips. "My son used to love doing that."

Ruan took note of the past tense and chose not to pursue it, for it could lead to a conversation she didn't want to have. They fell silent, listening to the wind rustle through the trees. There was no birdsong. Virtually every bird that could be caught had long since been wolfed down by the hungry population, while the rest had presumably developed the sense to keep their beaks shut or migrated permanently. After a suitably sensitive time elapsed, Ruan held up the leaflet. "So, you really believe this?"

Fanny nodded. "The fundamental question is: Are we creatures of biology only, or are we something more? I've never believed in any one god, but I think we are creatures of spirit. A virus can't infect our spirit."

Ruan's experience had taught her the exact opposite. "Look at that village," she said, nodding across the water. "If they knew you were immune or uninfected, whichever it is, they would be over here in a shot to tear you to shreds. How can you believe anybody can resist?"

"I think a line has been drawn with this virus, between those who want to evolve and those who want to devolve," Fanny said. "We all have to choose which side of the line we stand on."

We? Ruan thought.

The strange behavior of Fanny and her band suddenly made sense. The residents of Arrochar must have known that people lived here. The fires would have been visible at night across the loch, which was only a few hundred meters wide at this point. Surely they would have come to investigate and discovered a whole community of uninfected. Unless . . .

"You don't understand," Fanny said, reaching out even as Ruan began to back away. "We're living proof that it does work. We're all infected."

Ruan turned the leaflet over. There, in an oversized purple font, she saw the mantra every member of the community repeated when they saw her. They'd only been saying it because they wanted to kill her. The leaflet fell from her fingers and she turned to run. Behind her, in a semicircle blocking her escape route, stood the occupants of the hangar.

"I know you are here and it makes me happy," they said in their freaky one-mind voice.

Ruan unsheathed her sword and blinked away her fear. She narrowed her focus down until it was just her, her gleaming weapon, and the targets standing between her and freedom. She set her sights on the apparent weakest point of the chain—a frail, wizened old man with soft brown skin and an Oriental hint to his features—and charged.

8

Geldof wheezed out the droplets he'd inhaled at the revelation his mum was still alive and stared at his grandfather with eyes so wide his contact lenses crinkled.

"Zounds!" he said once he'd recovered his breath.

His grandfather gave up trying to wipe off the pink stains. "Still playing with medieval expletives, I see. Zounds, indeed. I didn't want to tell you until now so you wouldn't get your hopes up, but when I sent in my team to sprinkle your father's ashes over the house, I had them go to the supermarket to look for your mother's body so we could do the same. They found a trail of blood leading from an aisle to a walk-in freezer. No body."

"But Terry said he saw the pigs kill her."

"I spoke to him. He was perched on top of a shelf and only had a few seconds to look before he fell and the pigs began chasing him. He didn't have time to take a pulse. He thought she was dead, but she must have just been badly wounded. Your mother is a tough woman, Geldof. You know that better than anyone."

"Why didn't she come back to the house? We were there for at least another day."

Geldof knew he was trying to pick holes in the theory; not because he didn't want her to be alive, but because he wasn't ready to believe it. While he hadn't come to terms with her death or his inability to say farewell, to have her resurrected so abruptly freaked the shit out of him. It seemed too much like a far-fetched plot from the cheap South American soap opera the housekeeper watched on her lunch break. Any minute now he would probably discover he had a moustachioed evil twin he didn't know about.

"Maybe her wounds were too severe to move immediately," his grandfather said. "Or maybe she had to wait for the pigs to leave. All I knew was that there was no body. So I started looking around."

"You mean you've found her?" Geldof said, aware his voice was rising so quickly in pitch it would soon only be audible to dogs.

"Your mother didn't know, but I knew exactly where she was after she ran off with you and that washed-up soldier husband of hers. I kept tabs on her movements and known associates, looking for some opportunity to either reconcile the family or, in the worst-case scenario, have her arrested so I could claim custody of you."

"You would have done that?"

"She named you after that awful Irishman. That alone almost made the case for her parental rights to be revoked."

Fair point, Geldof thought. Even though he'd ditched his long-standing plans to change his name after the death of his parents, the reaction of others when he told them what he was called still brought choking embarrassment.

"And then filling your head with all that woolly nonsense," his grandfather continued. "I loved your mother, and I love her still, but she was a principled fool. She was making you weak, my boy. There's no room in this world for the weak."

Geldof frowned. He'd had months to think about his relationship with his mum. She hadn't made him weak; that was entirely his own doing. She was one of the strongest people he'd ever met and had only being trying to transmit this strength and moral certitude to him. Yes, it had been a spectacular pain in the arse, but the clear-eyed distance the final absence of death brought allowed him to see past his teenage resistance and appreciate her actions.

"That's not fair," he said. "Mum was a good woman."

The old man rolled his eyes. "Oh, please. You're far too intelligent to make the mistake of idealizing the dead."

"I'm not."

"You are. Everybody does it. When somebody gets knocked over or has a heart attack, the obituary piece is all sweetness and light. Nobody ever writes, 'John was a shiftless, odious toad who was too fond of cheap lager, slapped his wife around, and smelled like ripe feces. We're glad he's dead.' Even if it's true."

"Well, she's not dead, is she?"

"Not for the last five minutes, as far as you're concerned. Anyway, back to the point. She was aligned with all kinds of crazy people: mystics, peace campaigners, would-be eco-terrorists. 'Beardy-weirdies,' I believe they are referred to in the common parlance. These people had hideouts across the country, so I had them investigated."

"But the country is full of infected, not to mention the fact that anybody who tries to leave gets filled full of lead. You can't just wander in and poke about."

"Correct. But, with enough resources at one's disposal, you can get your hands on any satellite image."

Geldof, already irritated with the questioning of his new image of his mum, was growing frustrated at his grandfather's long-winded approach. It was so typical of him: he always had to give a lead-up that showed how rich, powerful, and resourceful he was. The better Geldof got to know him, the more he understood why Fanny had spirited the family away. "Just tell me where she is."

"I'm getting to that. At one of the locations on my list, a remote camp up in Scotland, the satellite images showed people living there. Quite a few people actually. One of them—a very large man with a propensity for tie-dye who is a known associate of my daughter—was recognizable from the shots. The resolution wasn't high enough, so I had some friends in the military send a drone over to take some better pictures." He reached into his valise and placed an envelope on the table. "I warn you, it's not pretty."

Geldof slid out the first picture and quickly put it down, tears brimming in his eyes. He'd only caught a glimpse of the hollow, scarred face and cropped hair, but he knew it was his mum. The pigs may not have killed her, but they'd destroyed her poor face. He took a minute to compose himself, unsure whether the tears were a result of how damaged she looked or having proof that she was still alive. "What's she doing up there?"

"That I'm not sure of, but I assume doing what she does best.

Surviving. Resisting. It appears to be a commune of some sort: one can only presume immune or uninfected from the way they're hiding out."

Uninfected. That's when it hit him: he might get to see her again, might get to say what he should have said instead of being so immature and contrary, might get to erase the distance that had grown between them down the years until it became what he'd believed was the impassable chasm of death.

"If she doesn't have the virus, we can get her out," he said, his irritation forgotten in a sudden burst of hope. "We have to get her out."

His grandfather raised an eyebrow in what may have been a gesture of approval. "I concur."

"You can send the people you hired to look for Mum's body, right?"

"Alas, no. They got killed before they could get out again. It was all very messy. That's why I stuck to air-based surveillance afterward until I could be sure your mum was alive. However, I happen to know some other gentlemen who may be prepared to undertake such a mission for the right kind of money."

"What sort of gentlemen?"

"They're a mixed bunch, led by a very capable South African chap. I used them when I was having a slight problem with a West African president who wouldn't cooperate with my plans for expanding my coffee plantations."

"You mean lawyers? How's that going to help? Are they going to parachute in with their black umbrellas and smuggle Mum out in a giant briefcase?"

His grandfather twiddled his moustache. Geldof was still getting used to his signals, so he wasn't sure whether it was an evil genius twiddle or an awkward confession twiddle. It was only when his grandfather gave the chops a final twang and bared his white and even false teeth that Geldof figured it was the former. "You have a lot to learn, my boy. I mean mercenaries."

Geldof's mouth dropped open. "You organized a coup?"

"I wouldn't say 'organized.' 'Funded' would be more apposite."

"Isn't that illegal?"

"Not if you don't get caught. Some would call it immoral. I console myself with the fact that he was a very bad man that nobody missed when he was deposed. I must hasten to add he wasn't killed. It was all relatively bloodless."

"Relative to what?"

Grandfather Carstairs looked at Geldof, his eyes devoid of any remorse. "Relative to other coups in which more people died."

This man, whose blood flowed through Geldof's veins, had killed in the name of profit. Now Geldof understood why his mum had been such a relentless campaigner: her father was a heartless blackguard. Geldof hid his disgust behind a large swig of iced tea, pretending to grimace at the tartness. Now was not the time to reveal how he felt. It was clear that he needed his grandfather and the men he could command to see his mum again. He couldn't let emotion get in the way—although his automatic moral outrage revealed just how much of his mum's teachings had seeped through his defenses. He felt a burst of closeness to the maddening woman that only increased his desire to see her again.

"Can you call them?" he said.

"They prefer to do business face-to-face," his grandfather said, apparently unaware of Geldof's reaction. "It's a trust and don't-get-caught-talking-over-the-phone thing."

"So you'll have to go see them?"

"No," his grandfather said, his eyes crinkling. "You will."

Geldof almost laughed. "Me? What do I know about negotiating with mercenaries?"

His grandfather leaned forward and slapped the table. His voice became low and hard. "When I was your age, I was well on my way to earning my first million. You, on the other hand, mooch around this villa on my dollar feeling sorry for yourself. It's time to earn your keep."

"But . . ."

"No buts. You are my sole male heir, and I want you to take over my business one day. I need to know you're up to the job. Are you?"

And there, finally, was the expectation. Admittedly, being asked to prove himself by hiring a team of mercenaries wasn't the same as attending business school, but it amounted to much the same thing. Geldof swallowed his desire to tell this horrendous old man where to stick it. His mum—unexpectedly, amazingly, and wonderfully alive—was still in peril. Regardless of his resistance to becoming a business tycoon and his growing disdain for his grandfather, he needed to play along until she was free. "I think so."

"Don't think. Know. To succeed, you're going to have to deal with some bad men, and these men are just about as bad as they come. I need to know that you will do whatever it takes to get the job done. The job in this case is saving your mother's life."

Geldof forced himself to meet his grandfather's unwavering gaze, imagining the moment when he would unflinchingly kiss his mum's wounds and make it all better. "Where do I need to go?"

The old man leaned back, reverting to what Geldof now understood was a studied, and very misleading, image of a fragile old man. "Nairobi."

After a moment's silence, Geldof said, "Sorry, where's that exactly?"

His grandfather sighed. "Given your name, I would have thought you would know. Africa. Kenya, to be precise. I'll see if I can set the meeting up for a few days from now. We need to move fast. It's looking increasingly like they're going to finally get around to bombing Britain, and I'd hate for something to happen to her now that we've found her."

As his grandfather called his assistant over and instructed him to set up a meeting and book tickets, Geldof walked to the edge of the balcony, keeping his back to the table so his face would not betray him. Once he'd hired the men to get his mum out, he was done here. His grandfather was right that he'd been floating and feeling sorry for himself. This turn of events had broken his paralysis. There was no way he was going to follow in the footsteps of such a man, and staying on in the villa would give the impression that was what he wanted to do. Plus, he was pretty sure his mum would refuse to come here and see her father again. Once Fanny was out of Britain, another disappearing act would definitely be in order.

9

Tony stared pensively out of the window as the black Mercedes purred along Oxford Street. Many of the store fronts were still boarded up from the broken-window shopping—Amira's euphemistic phrase for looting—that went on during the initial orgy of violence, while those that had reopened were closed for the night. There was no point in staying open late when you had nothing much to sell and not much of a market to sell to. The depressingly quiet street represented another policy failure. Tony had lifted the curfew after coming into power, knowing that to have any hope of restoring normalcy he needed to create space for people to get on with a semblance of everyday life. Forcing everyone to hole up after dark, particularly when night fell early during the recently ended winter, only created a greater atmosphere of claustrophobic hopelessness and reinforced the belief that the country was knackered. However, few felt comfortable enough to venture out in the darkness, which provided cover for the criminal element. Only a smattering of people wandered past, stopping to linger at storefronts that displayed goods rendered unaffordable by hyperinflation: even the cheap stores were charging thirty quid for a pair of wafer-thin socks now they didn't have access to their foreign sweatshops.

Amira, whom he was dropping off along with Frank, screeched and pulled him out of his thoughts. He clutched the armrest and looked out the window for the source of her alarm. They'd been attacked before—usually by criminals so seduced by the thought of the riches within the sleek vehicle that they didn't notice the armed escort until it was too late. Something else had prompted Amira's response, however.

She tapped the driver's shoulder to get his attention. "Pull over." Crooked teeth burst from between her smiling lips. "Kebabs."

The car pulled up alongside a large metal drum set up on the junction with Regent Street. Flames flickered through ragged holes punched in the metal, and smoke rose from a barbeque grill placed over the top. Amira rolled down the window. The smell of charring meat wafted in.

"Hello, Ruth," Amira said. "Long time, no see."

"Not been much to sell," the vendor, a thin-faced woman bundled up against the cold, said.

"Well, you're here now, praise the gods. What's tonight's mystery meat?"

"Guess."

Amira took a deep sniff. "Pigeon?"

"Nah. Pigeon ran out ages ago. The dopey little sods are too easy to catch. Just chuck a few bread crumbs and bag 'em with a big net."

"Cat, then."

"With the Cats Protection League Militant Wing on the prowl? Anybody who so much as looks at a moggy the wrong way is likely to get thumped with a brolly."

"Dog."

"Either too trusting, and so already eaten, or too aggressive. A few of my mates have lost fingers."

"Squirrel?"

"All done, too, I'm afraid. They were a pain in the arse to sell anyway. All that bushy hair kept getting stuck in the meat. Customers thought they were pubes. Anyway, you're getting warmer. Definitely rodenty."

"Rat?"

"Bingo!"

Tony grimaced as Amira pulled out her purse and ordered two kebabs. "What?" she said. "If you've ever eaten a fast-food burger or a chicken nugget you've probably had a lot worse."

"Beaks and arseholes," said Frank, who'd nodded off after taking one of his pills but now seemed to have perked up. "I'll have one as well."

"Exactly," Amira said. "Anyway, beggars can't be choosers."

She had a point. The madness reached its peak during harvest season, which meant crops had rotted in the fields. Nor was there any
way to import food: the days of sun-dried tomatoes, olives, and cous-
cous were long gone. They couldn't even fish the seas, as boats were
shredded before they got to the fishing grounds. Pretty much everybody was dependent on food aid, which the helicopters couldn't deliver fast enough to fill every hungry belly. To bridge the gap, traders
such as this woman had sprung up to sell the meat of those pets and
urban animals too slow to realize humans were no longer so reticent to
eat creatures once considered either too cute or too covered in lice. But
the supply of animals was growing thin, and the lice themselves—as
well as beetles, cockroaches, and any other creepy crawlies that could
be scooped up—would probably be considered a good source of pro-
tein before long. Farmers could soon begin planting what seeds they
had salted away, but Tony wasn't sure people could hold out for the
months it would take the crops to grow. Yes, the initial attempted exodus that saw boats and planes full of infected blown apart had died off
in the face of the impenetrable cordon and a public appeal from Tony
asking people to stay put in order not to goad the world further. That
would change as hunger grew. It wouldn't matter that their motivation
was only survival; they would flee, they would be shredded on their
makeshift rafts, and the new migration would undoubtedly prompt Britain's cleansing—if it hadn't already happened by then.

Amira handed over a freshly minted thousand-pound note and got
her change. They sat in silence as the car rolled off again, the only sound
that of teeth mashing up stringy rat meat. After a few minutes of chewing, Amira nudged Tony in the ribs and brought up the subject he'd
been hoping to avoid. "You aren't really considering Glen's plan, are
you? The man's a loony."

Tony had thought of little else since he adjourned the meeting amid
chaotic scenes, with his advisors split down the middle on whether to
support or oppose the bloody missile. It was barbaric and insane, Tony
knew, but he also couldn't deny it held a certain twisted logic. He had
a duty to his people to at least consider it. However, he didn't want
Amira to know what he was thinking. She'd probably try to choke him
to death with the remains of her kebab. Calling on the ancient political

skill of artful dodging, and hoping Amira wouldn't do a Paxman on him, Tony put the onus back on her. "If you can think of something else, I'm all ears."

"It's the same thing as the *Facebook* page with the kids. As Stalin said, 'A single death is a tragedy; a million deaths is a statistic.' We need to keep trying to humanize this. Let them know we're still people. Restore Internet access and mobile communications. Let everybody get their stories out."

"I can't do that," Tony said. "It's bad enough now with all these sneaky sods using satellite connections to talk to journalists. We'd have even less control. It would just make things worse."

"How can it be worse? *YouTube* is full of the videos people shot on their mobile phones when everybody was killing each other. That's what the world is watching: Brits as bloodthirsty monsters. We managed to make Hannibal Lecter seem like Mary Poppins. We can't persuade anybody we can be trusted if that's all they see."

"Fine, but look at the news stories now. They're all about how angry we still are and what a shambles the country is. Then it's crazy homemade shit from Blood of Christ promising to murder everyone. We open it up and we'll get more of that."

"And we'll also get videos of people doing everyday boring stuff. Killer zombies don't post videos of themselves doing crap cover versions of Bruno Mars songs or twerking in the fruit and veg aisle at Tesco."

"They can see us doing normal stuff on the BBC."

"Come on, that looks like obvious propaganda."

"Aren't you supposed to be a spin doctor? You know we need to manage the story. Anyway, it isn't just them looking in. It's us looking out. If we give everyone Internet access, they'll see for themselves that the world wants us dead. They'll panic. Which means they'll start trying to get out again. Which will just make it more likely we'll be attacked."

"Fine. If it's more propaganda you want, let's do something with this," Amira said, pulling out the leaflet about the resistance movement. "I know it's thin, but we can use it. If we find them, I could make a film showing there are people who can control the virus and are helping others to fight it. It'll buy us some time to explore other options."

Tony was at the point where he wasn't so much clutching at straws as trying to catch drifting filaments of spiderweb with chopsticks, as evidenced by allowing Tim to carry out his mad scientist operations and giving serious thought to Glen's suggestion. He turned to Frank. "What do you think?"

Frank shrugged. "It's worth a shot, I suppose."

"You still have the guy who delivered the leaflets in custody?" Frank nodded. "Ask him who's behind this. Find out where they are."

"I'll take care of it," Frank said.

Amira put her greasy hand on Tony's. "I'll make this work, I promise. Just don't do anything rash in the meantime, okay?"

"You've just eaten a rat kebab, and you're telling me not to do anything rash?" When Amira didn't smile in response, he placed his free hand over hers. "I promise I'll think it through."

The conversation lapsed, and the movement of the car lulled Tony into a daze, which he only snapped out of when his phone shrilled.

"Shit," he said when he looked at the caller ID.

In the madness of the day, and his whirlwind of thoughts about Glen's plan, he'd forgotten about his scheduled call with Piers fucking Stokington, who'd been appointed to serve as the international community's liaison with BRIT. They'd no doubt done so because he and Tony had a personal relationship. Piers obviously didn't mention to his superiors that Tony considered him an egregious cunt. Piers had been an active member of the Tory student association when Tony was studying law at Oxford, and despite the political differences they'd been friends until Tony began to rise fast—he'd been lined up for a ministerial post in the next Labour government—while Piers went nowhere. Jealousy cracked their friendship, which was shattered when Piers made an advance on Margot at a party, telling her he'd long loved her from afar. It had been the one time in his adult life that Tony resorted to using his fists.

Tony raised an eyebrow, took a deep breath, and answered the call.

"Hello, Tony. How's life on our once fair isle?" Piers said.

"Getting better every day, which you would know if you'd stayed instead of scurrying off like a hamster on speed."

Piers ignored the jibe. "You're being economical with the truth. Our intelligence reports suggest you're struggling to keep things under control."

"We're getting there. We just need more time. In fact, one of our scientists has come up with an interesting theory about the virus."

"You mean Tim Roast? I hear he set his assistant's hair on fire with a Bunsen burner a few weeks ago."

"Tim's a good scientist," Tony said, almost choking on the words. "He thinks the virus directly targets the amygdalae and believes there may be a surgical or chemical option to control the symptoms. Can you confirm we're looking in the right area?"

"You know I'm not allowed to reveal any of those details."

"At least tell me if you're getting closer to a cure."

"We're putting all of our resources into it."

"Spoken like a true politician. Why don't you just say no?"

"When we have something, you'll be the first to hear. In the meantime, I want to talk about something else. There's been a rather worrying incident. A few days ago, a French outpost on the coast intercepted an inflatable assault boat full of your infected chums as they beached."

"Intercepted. That's a nice way of putting it. You mean you killed them. Just like you killed thousands of other innocent people on planes, boats, and in the Chunnel. They weren't coming to get you. They were trying to escape."

"It doesn't matter why they were coming. We couldn't let them get in."

"You could've turned them back."

"Not this lot. When a containment team picked up the bodies for burning, they found all five people on that boat had a chalice tattooed on their forearms. Sound familiar?"

Tony's heart sank. The chalice was the symbol of Blood of Christ, the extremist group led by Michael Moran, a former pastor who now referred to himself as Archangel. He claimed the virus was sent by Heaven as a tool to allow the righteous to wipe out the ungodly. As far as anybody could tell, most of Archangel's followers were former members of the radical right English Defense League, which probably had something to do with the fact that under Archangel's interpretation the ungodly were Muslims, Hindus, Sikhs, gays, atheists, agnostics, and anybody who looked like they may have read *The Guardian* at least once. Archangel was overlooking the fact that the virus didn't discriminate according to race or religion, but fanatics were expert at selectively picking which logic to apply to justify their doctrine. Tony needed to put an end to the den of nutters to have any hope of proving Britain wasn't full of slavering maniacs. Unfortunately, the security services still hadn't been able to track the group to its base.

Tony somehow managed to keep his voice steady. "It was probably just a wine-tasting club trying to get to Bordeaux."

"Don't be facetious, Tony, it doesn't suit you. They almost managed to get out this time. You told me you were on top of the situation."

"We're going to take them out this week," Tony said, aware that, as ever in these calls, he was telling a lot of lies.

"I don't know if I can trust you on that."

"You're talking about trust when you're planning to kill us all?"

"Let me assure you that any military plans are only contingencies to be used in the event you fail to keep your people under control or try anything silly."

Lying bastard, Tony thought. He could always spot when Piers was telling big fibs: he slowed down, speaking in measured tones to ensure he didn't slip up. And he'd also "assured" Tony that he harboured no designs on Margot, right after he hit on her and just before Tony hit him in response. Tony, feeling his anger levels nudge up towards the red, played his trump card. "And let me assure you that the intercontinental nuclear missiles we have at our disposal will only be used should you fail to keep your people under control or try anything silly."

Piers fell silent, as Tony had known he would. Piers didn't know how precarious the nuclear deterrent was. When the virus came down, two of the four Trident submarines that carried the nuclear missiles were at sea. They didn't return. The third had smacked against the seabed under the control of enraged submariners—a fact Tony needed to hide at all costs. As long as the world believed that there were two submarines and that one was prowling unseen beneath the seas while the other was in dock at Faslane, they would think twice about coming in all guns blazing. If they found out there was only one sub, it would be a simple matter of blowing it up when it came in to resupply.

"We're not going to do anything," Piers said finally. "You have my word on that."

"And you have mine," Tony said.

He hung up. "And so we're both liars," he said softly.

10

Even as she sprinted at the old man, Ruan noted that he remained utterly still, his brown eyes calm. With the virus clawing at his brain, he should have erupted into a frenzy by now. Still, she hadn't survived this long by indulging in analysis when it was time to kick arse, so she put the incongruity aside. Blood coursed through her veins, feeding her muscles for the swift sword stroke that would clear her path. At school, her fencing lunges had been so rapid that almost nobody could parry a perfectly timed attack—particularly one aimed at the balls of the many sexist boys who assumed a woman would be easy meat. Fast as she was, though, the old man was faster: before she could bring the blade arcing forward he swiveled, went down on all fours with his bum in the air and shot his back leg straight up. His heel smacked her funny bone, and the sword slipped from her numb fingers. As she crashed into him he wrapped his legs around her trunk and used the momentum to flip backward. Ruan somersaulted through the air to land flat on her back with a jarring thud.

She'd been lucky enough to fetch up on a patch of grass still soft from recent rain, so she suffered no serious damage. That was as far as her good fortune went: before she could scramble to her feet, the occupants of the camp had surrounded her. She looked straight up into a dozen hairy nostrils. As the last thing she would see on this earth, the view lacked a certain poignancy. She felt no fear, just anger at being so stupid as to walk blithely into a den of infected.

Instead of setting to frenzied work with teeth and nails, they backed away to make room for Fanny, who held the dropped sword. "We aren't going to hurt you. Think about it. We could have killed you a dozen times over already."

"But you've got the virus," Ruan said, getting her feet under her.

"We control it, not it us." Fanny held out the sword, hilt first. "Take it."

Ruan snatched her weapon. The point waggled as she swung it around the circle. "Just let me go."

Fanny leaned forward and placed her throat against the point. Ruan grew still. "Nobody here will harm you. If you have to kill me to prove that, do it."

Ruan had killed three times, not counting animals. Each time it was done in the heat of the moment, when she needed to fight with every ounce of her being or die herself. This was different. She'd spoken to this woman, who seemed relaxed despite the sharp blade tickling her jugular vein. The camp followers were still retreating, leaving Ruan with a clear route to the exit. She looked at them all in turn, trying to process what she saw. Smoldering joints were being transferred to lips at regular intervals. The average carrier of the virus couldn't last a few milliseconds in her presence without transforming into a rabid beast, yet these people were keeping themselves in check. All the fight went out of her. She still knew fleeing was the sensible option, but she was so tired. And what did she have to run to?

Life on the road had taught her there was fat chance of making it out of the country. Any time she trudged along the coast, helicopters buzzed back and forth beneath a crisscrossed pattern of jet contrails. If the day was clear, she could sometimes see the outlines of the war-ships the helicopters had taken off from. The beaches were studded with the splintered remains of boats, and occasionally a fragment of aircraft fuselage would wash up. She was trapped on this island, where it was only a matter of time before her luck ran out. Nor could she re-turn home. That life was gone. It was a life she'd thought she hated: stuck at home with her well-meaning dad, who cringingly tried to relate to her by learning what he thought was cool teenage speak; fighting with Bryan over her desire to play One Direction, which he called Wanked Erection to annoy her, at ear-splitting volume; suffer-ing the indignity of her mum's insistence on picking her up after train-

ing even though all her friends got the bus home on their own. She'd
wanted nothing more than independence, to go to university to study
something easy like social studies while she worked at becoming a
professional athlete, and assumed the adulthood that was being denied her. Now she had that independence and all it had brought her
was a life as a fugitive, running in every direction but home, holding
on to a useless smartphone and writing stillborn messages to a friend
who was probably dead. These people might represent the closest
thing to a normal life she would ever have. She lowered the sword.

"What in God's name was that?" Ruan said, looking at the old
man who'd proven to be as far from the weakest link in the chain as
possible.

"Combat yoga," Fanny said.

"There's no such thing."

"Sometimes when the mind does not want to hear, only the body
truly listens," the old man said in a soft voice rich with Eastern tones.
When Ruan looked at him blankly, he switched to a Scottish accent.
"Tell that to your bruised arse."

Stoned giggles rippled around the audience. Ruan scowled, forcing
herself not to rub her injured bum. She wasn't used to being bested so
easily and wouldn't give her conqueror the satisfaction of seeing she
was hurt.

"Let me introduce everyone," Fanny said. "This is Nayapal: origi-
nally from Nepal, longtime resident of Cumbernauld, and now our spiritual advisor and martial arts coach."

Ruan gave Nayapal a cool nod. She'd made the same mistake that
countless men had made when facing her on the fencing piste: she un-
derestimated an opponent. If they ever went into combat again she
wouldn't be taken so easily.

"This," Fanny said, indicating a man with deep angled lines that
branched from his nose to form a shallow triangle filled with a bushy
grey moustache, "is Andy Dunlop. In his previous life, he was the president of the World Egg-Throwing Federation. Now he's responsible for
our crop cultivation."

Andy raised a bushy eyebrow in greeting, sending his wrinkled forehead bunching up. The woman with wavy brown hair who'd handed

Ruan the pamphlet was introduced as Eva Gilliam, a former public re-
lations officer for Oxfam who now drew up the copy for the commune's
leaflets. Tom Dixon, an Englishman in his early thirties with a chirpy
demeanour, was next up. He was in charge of leaflet delivery. Hannah
Campbell, a tiny woman who peeked out from behind a thick fringe
of blond hair, introduced herself as a general dogsbody. Scott she already knew. Finally they reached the youth who'd hidden behind the
stack of pamphlets.

"This is Rory, one of our newest recruits from across the water,"
Fanny said.

Rory lifted his hand slightly in greeting but refused to look at Ruan.
She noticed that only Fanny appeared comfortable enough to come
close. The rest hung back, whether to set her at ease or because they
didn't fully trust themselves, Ruan didn't know. They hadn't attacked
her so far, but that didn't mean they wouldn't lose their cool at some
point. She resolved to keep her wits about her. The door would be
locked at night, from the inside this time, and her weapons would always be at hand. If there were any signs of twitchiness, she would take
off.

"Now that we all know each other, let's get back to work, shall we?"
Fanny said. As everyone turned to go, Fanny plucked Andy's sleeve.
"Can you finish the tour for Ruan? I've got some stuff to do."

Once everybody had wandered off, Andy's moustache twitched up
into a smile. "That was the most excitement we've had in months. Now,
I expect you have a few questions."

Ruan had plenty of questions, but the first one that cropped up was
rather random. "Were you really the president of the egg-throwing
thingy?"

"Yes, indeed. I was also the 2011 Russian Egg Roulette Champion."

"Do I really want to ask?"

He narrowed his eyes and deepened his voice until it sounded like
a movie voice-over. "Six eggs. One raw. A battle of wills. A game of
chance to the death. Well, until you get egg on your face."

"So how good are you at throwing eggs?"

"I can knock a lit cigarette out of a builder's arse cleavage from one
hundred yards."

Ruan picked up a rock and held it out. "Show me."

"We don't have any builders around."

"Just hit something small at a distance, then."

"I can't throw a rock. The heft and aerodynamics are all wrong."

"Don't you have any eggs?"

"Yes, from the chickens we keep out back, but they're too precious to waste. I only throw them in emergencies. You'll have to take my word for it." He crooked his finger in a come-hither gesture. "Anyway, let's get on with the big tour, shall we?"

As they walked around the back of the hangar, where a satellite dish poked up from the roof, Ruan said, "Am I the first uninfected person to come here?"

"Yes."

"So how did you know you were ready?"

"Fanny said we were. We believed her."

That seemed a risk that Fanny had no right to take. These people had been nonviolent in theory only. Ruan wondered if her savior had one eye on a human guinea pig when she saved her. While not best pleased at this thought, she tried to shrug it off. If she planned to stay for any length of time, she couldn't afford to be resentful of the leader of this odd little band. Anyway, Fanny's motivation paled in insignificance compared with the fact that Ruan would have been dead without her intervention.

"She seems to get a lot of respect," Ruan said.

"She's a leader. That's what people need in times of crisis."

"Have you known her for a long time?"

"Twenty years. We were young activists together, me, Fanny, Scott, and Eva. There were a lot more of us, people who were supposed to come here if anything ever went wrong." Andy paused and his voice grew soft. "Nobody else made it."

"Who are the others then?"

"People who drifted in or we picked up and convinced to give our methods a go."

"And your methods work? I mean, I can see you're not like the others, but you don't feel any urges?"

"I'm a man. I've spent my whole life trying to ignore my urges. Look,

I'm not going to lie to you. When I smelled you, I felt a ... twinge. I still do. But we really do have it under control."

Andy's words confirmed something Ruan had long suspected but never been in a position to ask any of the infected since they were usually too busy trying to bite her face off. "So it's smell then?"

"Mainly, although virtually any sense can trigger it. Even the imagination. Look, if it'll make you feel better, I can ask everyone to collect their sweat in jars. We can rub it on you to mask your scent."

"I'll take my chances," Ruan shot back, before realizing Andy was chuckling.

"Only kidding. Seriously, you don't have to worry. Once you know the triggers and the signals, you can condition yourself to ignore them. Although I'm not sure it would work in a mob."

"What do you mean?"

"You've never been swept along in a crowd? Felt that mass hysteria? That's why it was worse in the camps and the cities. Anywhere there was a concentration of people, individuals had no chance of staying in control. Look, this is Fanny's theory, which I happen to agree with. The human brain hasn't evolved at all. We're just as savage as we were thousands of years ago. However, society has evolved. Humans are like individual cells in this structure, and generally they don't indulge their violent impulses because society developed in such a way that it was frowned upon. We became cooperative to succeed. In the microsociety of the mob, on the other hand, violence is completely acceptable. Everybody is anonymous and just as culpable. It's too easy to give in. Even without the virus, perfectly ordinary people do awful things in a mob."

That made sense. While she'd never taken part in real mob violence, Ruan had seen the principle operate on a smaller scale. At school, she'd known a girl called Samantha with a gammy leg, bad breath, and no social skills whatsoever. Ruan had nothing against Samantha and usually left the girl to her own strange devices, which included jamming a finger in her ear and writing her name on the wall in a seemingly endless supply of sticky orange earwax. However, when gathered with her friends in a tight little knot, it was all too easy to join in with the catty remarks and cackling. Desperate to hang out with the cool kids, Samantha kept coming back for more, the strained smile she wore allowing her to pretend they were laughing with her, not at her. One day they took it too far. They rounded on her and shoved her until her bad leg gave way and she crumpled to the concrete playground, still trying to pretend it was a game among friends even as her eyes moistened. It had been the most shameful moment of Ruan's life. She spent the rest of the school term trying to make it up to Samantha, oohing and aahing at her waxy skills and teaching her how to be less of a weirdo. Nobody had dared to give Ruan a hard time for the association, for they knew they would be the recipient of a slap around the lughole.

"What does it feel like when, you know . . . "

"When the virus takes over? Everybody has their own analogy, their own way of visualizing it so they can control it. I used to fly planes recreationally, so for me it was like being in a plane on autopilot. I did things my rational mind, sitting in that pilot's chair, didn't want to do, and no matter how hard I pulled on the joystick I couldn't stop." He paused, his moustache drooping and his eyes distant. Ruan didn't want to know what he'd done, and didn't ask. "That's how I control it now. I breathe, I recite the mantra, and I imagine myself switching back over to manual. Tom, on the other hand used to dabble in ventriloquism, so he imagines the virus as a puppeteer sticking its fist up his . . ."

"Got it," Ruan said.

Andy smiled and didn't continue with the example.

"And this," he said, stopping in front of a large greenhouse, "helps a lot."

Ruan peered in the window. Row upon row of the distinctive green, spiky fingers of the marijuana leaf grew under bright lights. It was the first time she'd seen the plant anywhere other than on a T-shirt.

"Ever smoked weed?" Andy said.

"A little," she lied, prompted by a desire not to seem unworldly. "At parties."

She'd been presented with plenty of opportunities to smoke dope but always refused, not wanting to reduce her lung capacity even a fraction and lose her competitive edge.

"Resin or grass?"

"Resin," she said, picking one at random.

"Then believe me, you haven't tried anything like this. On this stuff, anybody who is infected might be angry but just couldn't be bothered to kill anyone. I smoked five joints one evening and ended up wetting myself where I sat because I couldn't summon up the enthusiasm to go to the toilet. And it felt amazing."

"Eeeewww. TMI," said Ruan.

"TMI?"

"Too much information."

Andy laughed. "Fanny wants to get everybody smoking, as it's better than the drugs that come in the aid supplies. Unfortunately there isn't enough to go around. They'd need to import it, but the blockade means nothing can come in. Anyway, we do what we can. We print up the leaflets laying out the method, and we have a network of people who deliver them by bicycle."

Ruan waved in the direction of an old, high-backed truck that was parked almost out of sight in an area where the vegetation began to thicken. "Why don't you use that?"

"Like the eggs, for emergencies only. It's got a full tank and we have spare diesel for the generator in case the lights go out, but once that's done there's no other fuel to be had. The army's stockpiled what's left and all the cars have been siphoned, which is a good thing if you ask me. Road rage was bad enough before. Could you imagine what it would be like now? If you cut somebody off, they'd pull you out of the car and beat you to death with their emergency triangle."

Ruan indicated the satellite dish. "Couldn't you set up a Web site?"

A look of irritation flashed across Andy's face. Ruan backed off a step. He seemed to sense her flash of wariness and raised his hands. "I'm not going to bite your head off just because you're asking some admittedly very annoying questions. Look, we do know what we're doing here. If we set up a Web site, who would look at it? Almost nobody can get online. We've got to go old school. Besides, we try to keep the satellite connection use to a minimum in case they track us."

"They?"

"The government. They might not approve of what we're doing."

Ruan thought the government likely had bigger concerns than a bunch of hippies, and, considering BRIT was also encouraging people to keep calm, she didn't see the problem. Then again, Fanny's gang did smoke a lot of dope and were bound to be a bit paranoid. After a few seconds, her gaze lit on a shed penned in by a fence. This time she phrased her question so it didn't seem like criticism. "What's over there?"

"The chickens. Behind that we've got another greenhouse for fruit and veg. And we all take it in turns to hunt, although Fanny's the best. There are plenty of rabbits left out there, too, since they breed like, well, rabbits." Andy rested his hand on the greenhouse door. "If you don't mind I'll leave you to make your own way back to your room. I've got to check on the plants. See you at lunch on the pier in a few hours."

With a cheery wave, he disappeared into the greenhouse. Ruan looked up at the satellite dish. She had a message she would love to send, one she couldn't deliver in person, but it was pointless since the Internet was off elsewhere. Then an idea hit her, something that should have occurred to her as soon as she understood that these people proved the virus could be controlled. She ran back and burst into the hangar where they were producing the leaflets. Tom, the man she was looking for, was stuffing bales of leaflets into panniers.

Too excited to bother with niceties, she blurted out her question: "Do you distribute in Edinburgh?"

"Yes."

"If I give you an address, could you deliver one of the leaflets there?"

"I could get one of our people to do it."

Ruan snatched up a leaflet and, tightly gripping a borrowed pen, wrote along the top, "Please try this, then we can talk. Love, Ruan."

She folded it over and wrote the address on the other side.

"Do you mind if I ask who you're writing to?" Tom said.

Ruan handed the leaflet over. "My parents."

11

After he dropped off Frank and Amira, Tony told the driver to take it slow on the way home. He wanted to clear his mind so that he would be able to spend an hour of quality time with Margot and Vanessa before getting back into it, yet no matter how hard he tried he couldn't block out the babbling mental newsfeed of things to worry about. In particular, Blood of Christ's latest attempt to set off on some continental capers had been the last thing he needed. This near miss would nudge the world closer to action, if not tip them over the edge. He needed to do something fast to stop that from happening, and for the moment the only option that seemed to offer any hope was to do what Archangel's men had failed to do: get the virus out into the world quickly and efficiently.

When he finally got back home thirty minutes later, feeling utterly exhausted and useless as he tried to ignite the spark of inspiration that would provide a way out of this mess without killing half of the world, he paused before the front door. He pulled out all the stops with his Spock mannerisms to ensure that, when he walked into his house, he wouldn't be shunted from the thoughts of the barbaric act Glen wanted him to carry out back into the memories of the barbaric act he'd almost carried out. With a final logical eyebrow raise, which he hoped would be enough to keep him anchored in the present, he inserted his key in the lock. When he pushed open the door and saw Vanessa's innocent little face light up with the simple pleasure of seeing her daddy, the memories engulfed him all the same.

He'd been at a meeting of the Labour Party just as the virus jumped to humans. Even though the threat appeared on the verge of containment, the Tories were holed up in a nuclear bunker in Northwood. Labour leader John Spencer, never one to miss a PR opportunity, even one as ridiculous as taking advantage of a zombie animal infestation, had instructed those party faithful who hadn't already done a bunk to show solidarity with the people through a public meeting. He had one eye on the next election and saw this as a chance to flag up the Tories as snivelling toffs cringing in hiding while the average voter suffered. Solidarity only went so far, though: half a dozen armed police were stationed outside the room for protection, and a squad of helicopters sat on standby a short car ride away from the Hilton Brighton Metropole to whisk off the Labour elite should the situation worsen again.

Tony was in the middle of the packed room, safe in the knowledge he and his family had a spot on one of the helicopters, when former leader Tony Blair took the podium. Sitting in the presence of his namesake, Tony was reminded of how he himself had been touted as the next Blair. They'd both gone to Fettes College in Edinburgh and then to Oxford to study law, although ten years apart, before joining the Labour Party. They shared the same first name and May 6 as a birthday. That, as far as the younger Tony was concerned, was where the similarities ended.

While Blair had been a fee-paying student, Tony reached both prestigious establishments through scholarships awarded for academic brilliance. While the public school education had influenced the centrist policies with which Blair infected the party, it made Tony more of a leftie. He didn't encounter any racial discrimination, but there was plenty of snootiness directed his way from the Tory students for being a working-class lad from a poor background.

At first, in a party still dominated by the old left, Tony could give full rein to his politics. As it drifted to the right, though, and those who couldn't adapt dropped out, Tony kept quiet about his discomfort. He knew that to be too obviously leftist would lead to his being frozen out. To change the system, you needed to be in it. He'd played along, all the while thinking that once he was in a position of real power he would subtly fight to drag the party back where it belonged. So, all in all, he wasn't too impressed with Blair's presence.

Ostensibly there to support the party in this moment of national crisis, it took Blair thirty seconds to get his first subtle dig in at Spencer, saying that Labour now had a golden opportunity to get back to the glory days of the late 1900s and early 2000s. Spencer clenched his jaw so hard you could almost hear his fillings squeak, and, despite himself, Tony stifled a laugh. Blair was just warming to his theme when the emergency exit crashed open. A chambermaid, her uniform clinging to a heaving chest streaked with red, swayed in the doorway. Tony's first thought was that she'd been chugging red wine from the minibars and was horrendously drunk. He wasn't alone in that assumption.

"She's pissed as a newt," somebody said. "Get her out of here."

Before the security guards could move, the woman streaked toward the stage. Blair crumpled sideways under the impact of a flying tackle and landed hard with the chambermaid on top of him. She writhed and wiggled until she slipped past Blair's defending arms and sank her teeth into the easy target of one of his jug ears. The former prime minister screamed like a little girl. Suddenly everybody was on their feet. Three delegates joined Blair's burly bodyguard, and together they managed to disengage the kicking, screaming, and snapping chambermaid.

"I'm okay," Blair said loudly, getting to his feet. "It's only a flesh wound."

"I think she bit part of your ear off," Spencer said, peering at the side of Blair's head.

"She's done him a favor then," somebody near Tony whispered, prompting a few giggles.

Blair shook his head, as though trying to clear it. "I suppose you think this is funny," he said.

"Of course I don't," Spencer said.

Yells continued to come from the posse trying to restrain the chambermaid, who'd somehow managed to free her damaged hand and was slamming it into the face of the bodyguard. Blair ignored the commotion. "Yes, you do. In fact, you probably set it up."

"Steady on, Tony," Spencer said, his large brown eyes goggling. "You're obviously in shock."

"You ruined my party, you smug little Tory-lite fucker, and now you're trying to make me look stupid."

Spencer lost his patience and stepped closer to Blair. "You're calling me a Tory? You had us goose-stepping all the way to the right when you were in charge."

Blair yanked Spencer nose-to-nose by his blue silk tie. "At least I was a strong leader. You should resign and let me take over. I am the Labour Party. I am Britain!"

"Just go back to your lecture circuit, you washed-up old loon," Spencer said.

With no warning, Blair delivered Spencer a crunching head butt and followed the falling man to the ground. The crowd surged forward, voices raised in protest. Tony found himself carried with the masses even though he longed to go in the opposite direction. Something was very wrong here, and he had an awful feeling he knew what it was. The crowd tried to change direction as a wail rose from ahead. With the opposing masses pressing up against each other, the middle collapsed like a rugby scrum. Blair had abandoned Spencer, who sprung to his feet with a guttural yell and leapt into the heaving crowd like a stage diver. Blair was momentarily still, his glittering eyes roving the room. Tony had always thought Blair looked evil: particularly the grin that seemed to stretch beyond the confines of his face, as though the skin was about to peel back and reveal a grinning imp skull, ears working as demonic wings to take the head flapping off the body. Now, with blood staining those huge teeth beneath glittering pinprick eyes, Tony expected exactly that to happen. Unreality washed over him.

As more people began to struggle with each other and the din grew, Tony scrambled toward the emergency exit. This was no hallucination. The only thought in his sputtering mind was to reach the room where his wife and daughter were waiting. He was almost at the exit when somebody grabbed his ankle. He looked down to see Melissa Braithwaite, the shadow home secretary, half trapped beneath a pile of writhing bodies. She reached up with her free hand.

"Help me," she shouted.

Tony reached down and grabbed the hand. Braithwaite promptly sank her teeth into the gap between his thumb and forefinger. Yelling at the jolt of pain, Tony pulled away and looked at his hand. Tiny beads of blood welled up from around a perfect circle of teeth marks. Braithwaite looked up at him, blue eyes swimming with confusion.

"I don't know why I did that," she said, and lunged at his ankle.

He skipped backward to avoid her snapping teeth and dived for the exit. He skidded as he landed, cracking his head against the far wall. Braithwaite was clawing at the bodies around her, crying as she did so, while chairs, microphones, and even plastic water bottles were put to use as blunt objects elsewhere in the chaos. Tony, vaguely aware of a thrumming sensation racing up his arm, got up and staggered to the lift. As the door slid shut, gunfire crackled from the conference area.

When he emerged into the corridor on the third floor, somebody was screaming. He ignored it and ran to his room, thinking only of protecting Margot and Vanessa. He inserted the key card with shaky hands and clicked open the door. Vanessa looked up at him from where she was working on a jigsaw puzzle, smiling from behind a mass of curls.

"Daddy!" she shouted.

Tony staggered backward as a shockwave of rage battered him. His heart rate soared and his body flushed with a roaring heat. Margot came out of the toilet, a white towel wrapped around her body, wet strands of black hair clinging to her bare freckled shoulders. Her eyes widened. "Tony, are you okay?"

"You're dripping water on the floor!" he yelled, the anger finding a focus.

He could smell them both, the scent of clean skin and warm blood pulsing through their veins as enticing as freshly baked bread. His mouth dropped open to bare his sharp little teeth. He took a step forward. It felt like his rational mind was trapped in a tiny cell, watching in horror through the bars as somebody else, this savage beast that had been locked away in the recesses of his mind, ran amok with his body.

What would Spock do? he asked himself, the voice so quiet amidst the tumult of his rage that he could barely hear it. Yet somehow it was enough to stall his forward advance. He roared at the ceiling and turned his despairing eyes on his wife.

"Lock yourselves in the toilet," he said, voice straining with the effort of speaking.

Margot didn't move, so Tony began punching his balls as hard as he could in the hope of incapacitating himself. He hardly registered the pain, but it felt so right to be hitting something that he kept going until he sank to his knees. It was the sight of her husband pummelling himself in the groin that sent Margot sprinting across the room to snatch up Vanessa. They disappeared into the toilet and the lock clicked. Still he could smell them and it drove him crazy. He fought every inch of the way as his arms hauled his body toward the door. He could hear his daughter sobbing. This only made him angrier, reminding him of all the sleepless nights he'd passed when she was a baby, fighting the urge to slap her. Now he would slap her, all right. This strange voice, so alien and harsh, gave him enough of a jolt to attempt to reclaim his mind one last time.

"This is highly illogical, Captain," he screamed, trying to force his trembling fingers into the steeple position and falling on his face as the support left his arms. It was just enough to allow him to divert his course. He knew he couldn't hold on much longer and, focusing his mind on the one thing that could save his family, beat his head against the heavy metal legs of the bed until he passed out.

Tony fingered the scars the bed legs had left, the memory of what he almost did to his beloved family setting his cheeks burning. Vanessa, who'd either forgiven or forgotten that awful moment, flew over and grabbed his legs. "Daddy! Let's dance!"

God knows dancing was the last thing he felt like doing, but he let Vanessa drag him to the stereo and put on Katy Perry's "Firework." He shuffled around while Vanessa skipped, rolled, and threw some disturbingly adult poses. Margot smiled softly, and the heat of shame bled out from him as he twirled the little bundle of energy and threw her up in the air. He'd hated this song, had even been embarrassed to download it in case any of his friends noticed it on his iPad, but ever since Vanessa saw *Madagascar 3* she'd been obsessed with it. So he'd made the sacrifice, as parents always did for their children, and didn't force her to listen to Desmond Dekker instead. He'd even developed some affection for the song, which brought him these little moments of happiness that were so sorely lacking in his life. For a while he forgot he was anything other than a father lost in the simple pleasure of bringing happiness to those he loved.

He spent the next half hour calming Vanessa down with a relaxing bath and bedtime story. After she was asleep he ate a quick dinner and sat on the sofa, Margot's head resting on his chest as the *Eastenders* theme played. He'd intended to take a last half hour of downtime before getting back to work, but as ever his mind wouldn't let him find peace, analyzing all of the decisions he'd taken and wondering if they were the right ones. One of his first priorities when he took up the reins of power had been to get the BBC back on the air. The British public could stand just about any privation, but take away their flat-screen televisions and it really would be anarchy. Fortunately they had enough uranium stockpiled to keep the nuclear power plants servicing the reduced electricity demand for decades, and Tony was looking into reopening as many coal mines as possible just in case a plant went down and they couldn't fix it.

As part of his plans to give people something to do apart from roam around and kill each other, he'd considered reviving the English Premier League, and so set up a friendly between Chelsea and Spurs to test the waters. It hadn't been his greatest idea. Ten thousand spectators showed up to watch two teams full of cloggers, promoted in the absence of the skillful foreigners, lump the ball up and down the pitch. Eight minutes in, a heavy tackle prompted a brawl, which then transmitted to the stands. It made the football violence of the 1980s look like a slap fight in a nursery. When a performance of *Hamlet* he authorized at the National Theater ended just as badly—the audience took offense at the lead actor's bad performance and decorated the stage lights with his intestines—Tony realized that the passivity on the part of the viewer and the distance separating the performers from the audience made TV the safest form of entertainment. Reruns, with a heavy focus on *Doctor Who*, dominated the programming. The only shows they produced were *Eastenders* and the heavily censored and positively slanted news broadcasts—both filled with people whose only experience was fucking each other under bedcovers on reality TV or acting in infomercials on crap cable channels.

The *Eastenders* episode began with the usual plots of infidelity, business skulduggery, and family squabbles. Then the camera focused in on Dot Branning—the only character portrayed by the same actress as before the outbreak, who appeared to have been alive since the dawn of time and was probably immortal—standing outside the Queen Vic with cigarette smoke wreathing her cadaverous face. A rustle came from the center of the square, and the camera panned in on a shadowy figure raking through the bins. Dot's nostrils flared and the cigarette dropped from her fingers. She opened her mouth to unleash an ululating scream and, displaying surprising agility for a woman who was at least one hundred, burst through the gate in the park and caught hold of a teenage boy, who'd tripped over a fallen branch. As Dot set her gnashers to work on his face, the regulars came pouring out of the Queen Vic to lend their hands to the bloody task. Tony got to his feet, drawn toward the screen as though he could cross over and join the fray. The scene ended with everybody standing silently over the ruined body as Dot lit another cigarette, staining the end with blood rather than lipstick.

As Spock fought the virus in his mind, Tony turned to Margot. "I can't believe they did that. Everybody's going to be going mental."

Margot, still seated, took a deep breath. "It's social commentary, love. That's what the soaps do."

"But I told them to keep the themes light."

Margot put her hands on his shoulders. "You can't control everything."

"I can't control anything," Tony said, rubbing his forehead. "My government is the very definition of an omnishambles. I must be the worst prime minister this country's had."

"That's hardly fair. Nobody else has faced the problems you have. And, anyway, there are plenty of positives."

"Name just one."

"Well, the Tory cuts to the welfare state have been reversed. We're all dependent on handouts now."

"I'm sure Red Ken Livingstone and Arthur Scargill would consider that a glorious triumph for socialism if they were still alive. Considering the country had to be turned into a big pile of shit to bring back the social safety net, it's a bit too Pyrrhic a victory for my tastes."

"Okay, then. No more traffic jams."

"That's because we've got no bloody fuel, and I can't persuade anyone to give us any."

"At least the air's clean. You must be the only leader in the Western world who's managed to meet his emission reduction targets. Britain's an environmentalist's wet dream."

"I think you've hit on something there. Al Gore probably created this virus to fight climate change. We should call the media."

Margot pinched him on the arm. "Stop being a misery guts and get into it."

"Fine. The tube's empty, so you don't have to be a contortionist to fit into a carriage at rush hour and then spend the journey with your ear pressed into somebody's sweaty oxter."

"That's the spirit. Keep them coming."

"No more annoying tourists stopping in the middle of the pavement to rustle their big maps, smacking you in the face with their enormous backpacks, or asking when the Piccadilly Circus starts and if they have clowns."

Margot snorted and looked at Tony expectantly. However, try as he might he could find no more positives. All he could think about now was the lost income from the tourists that no longer came, money that Britain's economy desperately needed. Margot read the worry in his face and hugged him. After a few moments he broke away, gave her a peck on the cheek, and went to Vanessa's room to escape the rest of the show in case they did something else to wind him up. The room was bathed in the soft pink glow of Vanessa's night-light, and he plucked away a curl that was tickling her nostril. She shifted beneath her Barbie duvet and reached for his hand in her sleep. His insides dissolved into warm goo.

He'd come late to marriage and to fatherhood. He'd always focused on his career, first as a barrister and then as an MP, and had never thought he would meet somebody he could commit to. Then, at a party, a woman with black hair down to her waist and eyes you could lose yourself in came up to him. By way of introduction, she rubbed the top of his scalp and said she loved a man with a high forehead. They married within the year and she was pregnant instantly. Vanessa was born when he was forty-four and Margot was forty-two. It was a difficult birth—twenty-four hours in hospital that culminated in an emergency C-section—and at one point he thought they would both die. He'd almost lost them then; five years later he would have lost them again had it not been for the intervention of Spock. He had no intention of letting it be third time unlucky.

He imagined Vanessa waking in her cot as jets roared overhead and the ground shook. He saw fire billow in the window, roaring up to the ceiling and engulfing the bed as his daughter screamed for him to save her. He clenched his fists, but this time he did not search for Spock. This wasn't unfocused viral rage looking for an excuse. It was the justi-fied anger of a parent whose child was threatened. Amira believed the world could be convinced of their humanity. He doubted that. The soldiers who killed the refugees in boats were close enough to see they were still people. It didn't stop them. As for the civilian population, any shrinking violet could watch a thousand people killed in *Batman* or *Die Hard* so long as the deaths weren't graphically portrayed. If they didn't put close-ups of the burning bodies on television, everybody could accept the death of millions of infected as the price that had to be paid for their safety. They would all just be statistics, even his innocent little daughter.

Last year, during a drunken conversation in the MPs' bar, somebody had asked him a question about his opposition to the drone strikes on terrorists that often caused civilian casualties. The question was, "If somebody held a knife to your daughter's throat and said they would cut it unless you pressed a button that would kill one hundred strang-ers, people whose pain you will never see or feel, would you do it?" He'd prevaricated at the time, saying it was an impossible choice. Now he realized that if it really came down to choosing between the lives of faceless strangers and the lives of Vanessa and Margot, he wouldn't hesitate.

Putting off the call to Glen he knew he must make, Tony went back through to the other room and wrapped his arms around Margot. He squeezed her so tightly she let out a little gasp.

"Are you okay?" she said.

"I'm fine," he said, laying his head on her lap so she couldn't see his face. He couldn't tell her what he was thinking about doing. She would try to talk him out of it. Glen had said it would take around two weeks to get everything ready, and then it would be down to Tony to give him the nod. If he said yes to Glen, he would still have time to find another way. If the others failed to deliver on the slim hopes they offered, the missile would be ready should they have to use it.

He was still holding Margot tightly and felt her breathing quicken. Her hand reached under his shirt and stroked his back.

"There is one other positive you didn't mention," she said.

"And what's that?"

"More shagging," she said, and bit his neck.

Even though his head was not remotely in a place to have sex, his body responded—as it always had since the virus took over. Soon they were naked and on the floor. Tony entered his wife; they both gasped. His balls contracted and he felt that telling preorgasm tingle. He withdrew slightly and held his breath until the feeling passed. Unbidden, the image of another phallic object rose in his mind, and he grasped the obvious fact that had been staring him in the face all day as he agonized over whether to give Glen the go-ahead.

"Just because you have a payload, it doesn't mean you have to fire it," he said.

"Seriously, are you okay?" Margot said. "You're acting really weird tonight."

"Oh, I'm totally fine," Tony said.

Viral missiles would be the ultimate deterrent. The world's armies might risk a nuke or two for the sake of eradicating the virus, but there would be no point in dropping bombs if the consequence was the definite release of the virus the attack was aimed at neutralizing. Those missiles would guarantee their safety. He would call Glen and tell him to start preparing, although initially he wouldn't reveal he had no intention of firing the missile. That would only piss him off. Nor could he tell Piers the good news, for Britain at least, until the submarine was out at sea—it was likely their satellites would spot activity at Faslane and figure out the submarines were being refitted, which would risk the missiles being targeted. He would have to keep pursuing the other avenues offered by Tim and Amira to mollify the international community until the missile was ready. For the first time, he began to believe he really could save this country.

He began to move again, gently this time. Margot responded in kind.

FIFTEEN DAYS TO EXCISION

12

Half asleep in the heat blasting through the rolled-down window of the Land Rover, Geldof didn't notice the cows until they were upon him. When the first large head loomed by the side of the car—long tongue lasciviously exploring a nostril, one stubby horn tapping off the bodywork—he scrambled across his seat and knocked the hand of his driver, Mwangi, as he shifted gear. The engine stalled just as the long line of cars ahead lurched forward, prompting an instantaneous blaring chorus of horns.

Heart thudding, Geldof scrabbled for the button to raise the window. The cow regarded him with watery, incurious eyes as the window snicked shut. A tall man with stretched lobes looped over the tops of his ears flicked at its behind with a thin stick. The cow walked off at the head of a ragged line of scrawny compatriots and bent down to munch on wild grass growing from a roadside ditch. Now awake enough to remember that the virus had not spread to this part of the world, Geldof let out a shaky breath.

"Sorry," he said to Mwangi, who'd got the engine going and was fending off the cars trying to squeeze into the gap his momentary panic had created.

"You are afraid of cows?"

"Just the horny ones," Geldof said.

Mwangi laughed, his round face splitting to display yellow teeth. "They all have horns."

Too jittery to correct the misunderstanding, Geldof kept silent. He'd caught an overnight Kenya Airways flight from Amsterdam to Nairobi, and his reaction was largely down to sitting up all night reading the copy of Lesley's book he'd purchased in Schiphol Airport. The threat of the cows was fresh in his mind once more. At least now he knew why Jelena had thought him brave. Lesley's tale, while built around true events, portrayed all of them in an unrealistically positive light. There was much stoic gritting of teeth and heroic taking of tough decisions as they fought their way through the country to bring the truth to the world. He supposed it made for a better story; all the same he felt a little icky at the manipulation of facts.

He put the book out of his mind and concentrated on the exotic city they were travelling through. Mwangi, a fixer hired by his grandfather, had picked him up in the shiny new Land Rover and driven them down a long highway past the wide-open plains of Nairobi National Park. The park, Mwangi had informed him, was full of lions, hippos, crocodiles, giraffes, wildebeest, and other hulking animals. It was just as well the virus hadn't come to Kenya: there were far too many dangerous beasts on the loose already.

They gathered speed once Mwangi cleared a four-car prang, around which the drivers huddled, chatting into their phones and making no attempt to sort out the blockage. The campaigning of his namesake, Bob Geldof, had prepared him for a montage of poverty: ruined shacks, snotty-nosed kids in rags, fly-blown faces, and swollen bellies. Contrary to his expectations, they were cutting through factories, shiny hotels, shopping malls, and the tower blocks of the city center. Sure, the traffic was chaotic, old buses pooted out large plumes of black smoke, massive hunch-backed birds brooded on acacia trees by the roadside, and people streamed everywhere on foot. But he got no sense of a city defined by desperation. Nor, despite all of the media stories about the terrorism threat in the East African nation, did anybody try to lob a grenade into his car.

Once they reached the hotel, his media- and Bob Geldof–driven expectations were confounded further. The Sankara was an ultramodern, ultraposh slice of glass and steel stuffed with spas, bars, and restaurants that overlooked a shopping mall. He checked in and handed Mwangi a thick packet containing background documents on the mission he was in Nairobi to set in motion. Mwangi, promising to return for him at ten that evening, set off to deliver the package to the mercenary to allow him time to gather his thoughts. In an era of instantaneous global communication, it felt strange to be using such an old-fashioned method of passing on information, but this was the way the mercenary preferred to do business.

Up in his sleek, minimalist room, Geldof lay down on his bed and tried to catch up on the sleep he'd missed. He couldn't quiet his whirring mind. Provided the mercenaries were insane enough to agree to enter a country in which every man, woman, child, and animal would want to kill them, Geldof would soon be with his mum again.

The dance floor in Black Diamond, a bar on a busy strip jammed with neon lights and nightclubs, was a gyrating tangle of young women with sweat-slicked black skin and achingly beautiful faces. Geldof was having some difficulty figuring out why so many of them had chosen as their dance partners old white men with beer guts, bright-red faces, and saggy necks like turkey wattles. Some of the men even danced like turkeys, unsure on their skinny little legs and pecking their chins forward with their hands on their hips. The old turkeys and young chicks were moving to a live band flying through some rock number Geldof faintly recognized. Those not dancing were knocking back drinks in the dimly lit bar, talking and laughing or tapping away on their smartphones without a care in the world. Again, this was not the Africa of Bob Geldof: sure, no rain or rivers were flowing here, but the booze certainly was.

He nodded at the dance floor. "Why are those girls dancing with those men? They're a bit old."

"They're working."

"You mean they're barmaids?"

Mwangi let out a hoot of laughter, which he did often and with little provocation. "Prostitutes. Or girls looking to find a sugar daddy."

Geldof gaped at the revelry anew. The only time he'd seen a prostitute was in Glasgow, when a snaggletoothed old crone had pounced out of a doorway to bray "Business!" at him as he walked through the city center one early evening. This was about as far from such seediness, both in terms of furtiveness and physical attractiveness, as it was possible to be.

"But it's so open," he said.

"*Karibu* Kenya," Mwangi said, grasping Geldof's wrist. "Come, let's get a drink."

Geldof settled at a table on the balcony. He peered down at the cars jostling for parking spaces amid groups of baton-wielding security guards as Mwangi waved over a waitress. Geldof got busy digging out the fake ID he'd had made in Dubrovnik. She didn't even look twice at him and returned a few minutes later with two Tuskers. Geldof took a tiny sip of the sweet beer. Mwangi nudged him and pointed at the door leading between balcony and dance floor. The man who stood there was so broad his shoulders almost brushed either side of the doorway. A black, short-sleeved shirt revealed forearms corded with muscle, although his jeans were cinched beneath a protruding belly. He looked like he could crumple up Geldof and toss him aside like a piece of paper. Strong body aside, his face betrayed no sign of his profession. He had a weak chin, feminine lips, and eyes crinkled with laughter lines. It was as if he'd undergone a head transplant; somewhere out there would be a thin, weak-bodied man—a clerk or traffic warden—with a grizzled, battle-scarred face. Adding to the incongruity was the girly drink, pink in hue and slopping around in an ornate glass, clutched in his right hand.

Geldof knew the face was misleading. His grandfather had told him all about the man he would be hiring. His name was Andy Scholz, a South African who'd served in 32 Battalion—a group of soldiers who earned the nickname "The Terrible Ones" during South Africa's border wars with Namibian and Angolan forces. Scholz had excelled, gaining medals and promotion to captain for his planning skills and cool under fire. Once the force was disbanded in 1993, many of the soldiers went on to form mercenary groups. Scholz set up on his own, fighting in dozens of conflicts and carrying out one shady gig for the coffee magnate. In 1998, when South Africa banned mercenaries from operating from its soil, Scholz shifted to Nairobi: according to Grandfather Carstairs, officials were easier to bribe there, and Kenya was closer to the action now that southern Africa was quieter. He was not a man to be trifled with.

As Geldof battled to slow his quickened pulse, Mwangi got up and met the mercenary halfway to the table. After a quick conversation Geldof couldn't hear above the blaring racket of the band, Mwangi wandered off to start chatting to one of the prostitutes. Scholz sat down across from Geldof.

"So you're the progeny, heh?" he said.

"I'm sorry?"

"You're that old bastard's grandson. You don't look like him."

Unsure how to respond to such an opening, Geldof held out his hand. "I'm Geldof."

"Like the wizard?"

"No, Geldof. Like the scraggly old Irishman."

"Jesus Christ. That's worse," the mercenary said, taking the offered palm and giving it a firm squeeze that indicated there was a lot more power lurking in those fingers. "I'm Andy Scholz. You can call me Scholzy. Tell me, how are you enjoying the delights of Nairobi?"

Geldof shot another glance at the girls and tried to paint a worldly look upon his face. "I've not been here long enough to enjoy them properly."

"Well, let's get business out of the way first and maybe you'll get the chance."

Geldof took a deep breath. Even though no other mercenaries were in the frame, his grandfather had been very clear that he shouldn't seem too keen. He'd been instructed to ask some probing questions, so he stuck to the only script he knew: that taken from his unsuccessful interview for a part-time job in a small newsagents' booth in Partick train station.

"Thanks for agreeing to meet me," he said. "We've got a few people to talk to about this. Perhaps you can start by telling me why you want this job."

Scholzy crossed his arms. "I didn't say I wanted it. You came to me."

Geldof shifted in his seat. "Okay. What's your greatest strength?"

"Doing bad things for money."

Already this wasn't going terribly well, which wasn't surprising considering he was looking to employ a man to stage a raid in the world's most dangerous country, not stock shelves with Mars Bars. In the absence of another plan, he ploughed on with his questions. "Perhaps you could outline your relevant experience?"

"Your grandfather knows what we can do."

"I'm not my grandfather," Geldof said, narrowing his eyes into what he hoped was a mean squint.

"I can see that," Scholzy said. "Let me put it this way: Simon Mann and Nick du Toit are babes in the woods compared to us."

Geldof's research on mercenaries had largely involved downloading Frederick Forsyth's *The Dogs of War* and watching a DVD of *The Wild Geese*, both of which Google alerted him to when he was searching for appropriate literature. However, he'd also read some old articles about real-life cases and recognized the names as the men caught planning the botched Equatorial Guinea coup Mark Thatcher was involved in. "I've heard of them. How come I've never heard of you?"

Scholzy leaned across the table. Geldof flinched as the hard gaze met his. "We've overthrown dictators and democratically elected presidents; we've put down rebel uprisings; we've rescued hostages from Somali pirates; we've done just about every dirty and downright dangerous operation you can think of. Nobody knows who we are because we never get caught. If you want something done, we're your men."

As it often did when he was nervous, Geldof's mouth merrily skipped out of reach of his brain, shot him the finger, and blurted out something utterly stupid in an attempt to introduce some levity it idiotically thought was needed. "I suppose you're better than the A-Team as well."

Amazingly, instead of plucking out Geldof's Adam's apple to use as a grisly cocktail cherry in his drink, Scholzy let out a snort of laughter. "You're damn right. The *A* stands for amateurs."

Encouraged by the response, Geldof pushed a little further in an attempt to build up some rapport. "So you can make an armored car in half an hour with just a blowtorch, a beat-up old truck, some scrap iron, and a couple of bolts?"

"No. But we do manage to kill people every now and then," Scholzy said, no longer smiling. "You've had your little joke. Time to stop dick-ing around. I've looked at your briefing. I'll need a team of four. One week to prepare. We'll be in and out in three days."

"Really?" Geldof said, unable to hide how impressed he was with the deadpan response. "You're not concerned about the whole infection thing?"

"We'll have guns. Anybody tries to bite me, I'll shoot his bloody teeth out through the back of his head."

"And it'll really just take one week to prepare? I thought it would be a few months. Don't you need to buy weapons, forge certificates, move money through Swiss bank accounts, all that kind of thing?"

"You've been reading *The Dogs of War*, heh?"

When Geldof nodded his assent, Scholzy sighed. "If I had a dollar for every person who read that book and thought they could tell me my business, I wouldn't have to do this for a living. That book was written over thirty years ago. The world's moved on. It'll cost you one million dollars, including equipment and running costs."

Geldof's grandfather had given him a budget of one and a half million dollars, but he'd been told to talk down the initial quote. However, coming from a culture where you automatically paid the price that was on the sticker in the shops, bartering was as natural to Geldof as putting the toilet seat down after a pee. The steady look in the mercenary's eyes told him he would be wasting his time trying. Plus, he wasn't finished yet. There was something he'd resolved to do, something he hadn't told his grandfather. "There's one more thing. I'm coming with you."

"No way. We don't take passengers."

Now it was Geldof's turn not to react. He didn't want the mercenary to see how terrified he was at the prospect of returning to Scotland. In the days since meeting his grandfather, he'd spent his time deep in thought. There was no guarantee these men, good as they were supposed to be, could extract his mum. The mercenaries and Fanny could be killed, and he would never see her again. He didn't even know if she would agree to leave. If she'd decided to play some messianic role in Britain, the only way to get her to depart would be to drag her. That wouldn't exactly lead to a pleasant reunion. If he went with the mercenaries he would have a better chance of seeing her one more time, and, if she really did love him, he could persuade her to leave with them. There was, of course, a strong chance he could get killed, but that was something he chose not to dwell on.

"You take me, or I find somebody who will," he said.

Scholzy held his gaze for what felt like hours. Geldof had to fight hard not to look away.

"You've got guts," Scholzy said finally. "I'll give you that. We'll take you for an extra five hundred thousand."

"Done," Geldof said.

His grandfather wouldn't be happy that he'd spent the whole budget and would freak out if he found out about Geldof's plan to tag along. Considering Geldof didn't intend to go back to the villa, he didn't really care as long as his grandfather didn't discover his intentions until it was too late. "What happens now?"

"You give us half the fee up front. Then we get planning."

"That won't be a problem," Geldof said. "Can you send us your bank details and we'll do a transfer?"

"No banks. You send the money through Hawala." Scholzy grunted at the look of incomprehension on Geldof's face. "You don't know a damn thing, do you? It's a trust-based transfer system run by the Somalis, beloved of many a jihadi. Your grandfather hands a wad of cash to somebody, tells him where and who for, and then we pick it up. Totally untraceable. The old man knows the drill."

"So, we have a deal, then?"

"We have a deal."

Fighting the conflicting emotions of sheer terror at going back to the U.K. and elation at the prospect of seeing his mum, Geldof held out a trembling hand to shake on it.

Scholzy lit a cigarette and blew a long stream of smoke toward the ceiling. "So, tell me. Are you still a virgin?"

Geldof blushed. "That's a very personal question, and I don't feel comfortable answering it."

"Ah, so you are a virgin. How about I buy you one of these ladies to get you going, heh? A little gift to seal the deal."

Before Geldof could respond, Scholzy waved over a woman in a tight, glittery dress that struggled to make it over her curvaceous hips. "Tell the boy your name."

"Lucy Pussy."

Scholzy slapped the woman on the behind. "Don't worry, it's just a name. Her pussy isn't as loose as it should be considering the number of cocks that have been up there."

Lucy rubbed her firm breasts against Geldof's arm and put her hand on his thigh. His body thrummed in response. It would be so easy to say yes and lay his lack of sexual experience to rest. The fact that he was about to put himself in mortal danger and may never get another opportunity made it more enticing. Yet as much as his body urged him to respond in the affirmative, he brushed her hand away.

"The boy's nervous, Lucy," Scholzy said. "He's a virgin. You have to be gentle."

Lucy nibbled on his ear, sending fresh waves of electricity coursing down his neck. "I like virgins. It's over fast fast. I'll do you for a special price."

Even though every hormone-soaked muscle in his body resisted, Geldof pushed back his seat. In all his fantasizing about his first sexual experience, he'd never imagined an impersonal transaction. With Mary and other focal points for his nocturnal fiddling, there had always been one commonality: the object of his affection finally realized what a handsome, smart, and beautiful human being he was and fell into his arms in a fugue of passion. Most likely this would never happen, but better to wait decades for that special moment than toss his cherry away on a seedy encounter that would make him feel as grubby as the wanked-in socks he used to stuff down the bottom of the washing basket in more horny times. None of these romantic sentiments made the mutinous erection he tried to hide by tugging down on his shirt any less throbbing.

"I'd better go back to the hotel now," he said, signaling Mwangi with a tilt of his head.

Lucy, seemingly unoffended, moved off and draped herself over a short, fat white man who looked as though his seventieth birthday was a distant memory.

"I've got one last question," Geldof said, keeping his hand firmly on his shirt. "How do you plan to get us in?"

"When you want to get something insanely suicidal done," Scholzy said with a broad smile, "you call the Russians."

SEVEN DAYS TO EXCISION

13

In this, Lesley's second incarceration while chasing a story, nobody had interrogated her. Considering the last time it happened she'd been reduced to a quivering wreck, this could be chalked up as a positive. Unlike Brown, who needed to find out if she'd backed up any of the information and seemed to delight in tormenting her, these men didn't have to grill her. They saw her meet Jack and heard everything he told her. They would have checked she hadn't contacted anyone and they had her laptop. They most likely also kidnapped Jack. The worse thing was that they'd been there all along as she bashed away on the keyboard, so sure she wasn't repeating the mistakes of the past. She hadn't even noticed the watcher. The ghost of the old, incompetent Lesley hadn't been as thoroughly exorcised as she'd believed.

At least Terry would have reported her disappearance. However, he didn't know she was working on such an incendiary piece, and there were all manner of ways to go missing in New York. He would most likely think she'd been murdered or fallen down a manhole cover. Given her heavy drinking lately, the latter would probably be his chief suspicion. The police would be looking for her, but if they probed too closely she was sure they would get the message from above to back off. She didn't know if Homeland Security, the FBI, the CIA, or the Secret Service were holding her. Not that it mattered. A turkey ended up just as firmly trussed whether it was the farmer or his wife who tied the knots. All she could do was hope a Thanksgiving Dinner wasn't in the offing for this particular bird.

On that front, she wasn't too concerned. The cab had headed up

Sixth Avenue before her captor jammed a black canvas bag over her head. That relieved rather than terrified her. The fact they were obscuring her vision meant they didn't want her to know where they were going, which in turn suggested they would release her once the attack was under way and couldn't be stopped. She tried to keep track of their movements through Manhattan, but quickly lost her bearings. Her best guess, once they hit a straight stretch of road, was that they were heading upstate. They drove for what felt like hours. The only break in the monotony came when the car juddered and the driver cursed.

"I think I just hit a coyote," he said in a New Jersey accent.

Lesley sunk down in the seat. Even while being held captive in a moving vehicle, her malign aura was so powerful it could suck creatures in to their deaths.

Finally they pulled off the main road and rattled along at a slower speed before coming to a halt. Once the engine died, the only noises were the night whisperings of nature. Her captor pulled off the bag and helped her out of the car. A small log cabin sat in a forest clearing, hemmed in by soaring pine trees. The only way in or out was the narrow dirt track they'd driven down. Although her minder was barely pointing the gun at her any longer, Lesley didn't try anything. She smoked far less now thanks to the restrictions in New York, but that didn't mean she'd partaken in anything as vulgar as physical exercise— although she did purchase trainers and a gym membership, which in her book should have conferred some honorary fitness upon her. Her guard looked as though he could overpower her using his pinkie, and if she somehow did manage to knock the gun from his hand and make a break for the trees she would get only a few hundred meters before collapsing in a sweaty heap. And so she'd let him lead her inside as the cab crunched off through pebbles and strips of bark.

Now she'd been cooped up for over a week, stewing in her own juices. Her guards rotated every twelve hours, standing outside the door while she showered, sitting across from her as she stared at the television, and watching her as she slept—which at first ensured she lay awake for hours staring at the ceiling until she got used to it. They brought her clothes to change into: ill-fitting dresses, blouses, and jerseys snatched randomly from the racks of Walmart by the look of it. All the while they refused to talk to her, get a message to Terry that she was alive, or buy cigarettes and booze.

Despite the isolation and mindless wait, it was a relief to have the responsibility for all those lives taken out of her hands. Whatever consequences arose from the military onslaught, or lack thereof, she could console herself with the knowledge that none of it was her fault. Her jinx was as safely locked up as she was. All the same, she thought obsessively of the preparations that would be taking place—bombs being loaded into crates and planes, soldiers mobilizing, drones being fueled up—and the face of the blue-eyed boy haunted her uneasy sleep. Escape, however, was not an option.

That night, as she was about to climb into bed, her kidnapper returned and held out the bag.

"No questions," he said. "Just put it on."

She complied and allowed him to tie her hands. It was possible that the attack was in full swing and she was about to be freed. Although it was earlier than Jack had anticipated, they could have accelerated the timeline for fear of further leaks. While she was happy at the thought of getting the hell out of there, her freedom would mean the bombs were falling. She no longer knew how she felt about that.

This time the journey was much shorter. When she got out of the car, they left the bag on and led her stumbling through a series of gates and doors. From the exchanges between her companion and those manning the entry points, it seemed they were in an air base. She walked across a wide, open area, cold wind whipping around her, and up what felt like a metal gantry. Somebody shoved her into a seat and clicked a belt around her waist. She was definitely on a plane.

"Where are you taking me?" she asked.

"You're going on a little holiday. All expenses paid by the U.S. government."

"Can you at least take the hood off? If it gets bumpy I might puke in it."

"At least you won't have to reach for the sick bag. I'd sleep if I were you. You're going to need your strength."

Lesley was beginning to get the strong feeling that her assumption she would be released had been misplaced. The air-conditioning came on as the plane's engine fired up, and footsteps receded as her guard walked away. She began to fumble at the seatbelt with her bound hands, sucking the cloth into her mouth with each panicked breath. Somebody delivered a stinging slap to the backs of her hands.

A male voice, low and hard, sounded close to her ear. "The fasten seatbelt sign has now been lit, so I'll have to ask you to remain in your seat."

The following hours were nightmarish in both wakefulness and fitful sleep. Her dreams were full of images of buildings crumbling and bodies disintegrating in the heat of blasts. When she woke amidst a rattling bout of turbulence, she was convinced she was trapped beneath the rubble with bombs still raining above her. Only a helpful slap to the side of the head brought her back to reality, which was almost as bad. The bag came up once, just as high as her nose, to let her gulp from a bottle of water and be spoon-fed greasy spaghetti.

When the plane landed, she stumbled on numb legs, aided by prods to the back, onto what seemed like another airfield. There, after an interminable wait, she was tossed up like a sack of potatoes into another cabin, which she realized belonged to a helicopter when the blades began to whine. This was worse than being held by Brown, who'd at least got to the point quickly. What they were doing felt like mindless cruelty with no apparent end—unless it was an attempt to break her so she wouldn't talk about her capture upon her eventual release. She fervently hoped that was the case; the alternative was that she'd become a victim of rendition and was en route to a country where human rights treaties were used only to stabilize the wobbly leg of the table upon which they kept the pliers, scalpel, and blowtorch.

After another unquantifiable period in the air, her stomach registered that the helicopter was dropping. A door clunked and air whistled into the cabin. Somebody cut through her bonds and the bag was yanked off her head. Outside of the helicopter was blank darkness. Between two men in U.S. Air Force uniforms sat Jack, his hair dishevelled and skin pale beneath the cabin light.

One of the soldiers yanked her to her feet and jockeyed her to the brink of the helicopter. With no further ado, he gave her a hard shove in the back. She didn't even have time to scream before her hands and knees smacked onto wet grass. Almost immediately, Jack landed face-first beside her with a thud. The wind from the blades buffeted her, and she looked up to see the helicopter silhouetted against a sky full of fragmented clouds backlit by the moon. It banked off to the right, gaining altitude until it was lost in the darkness. She grabbed Jack by the shoulder and helped him to his feet. His face was caked in mud, and he seemed unsteady on his feet.

"Where are we?" he said.

Lesley looked around, trying to get her bearings. With the helicopter gone, she could hear the wash of waves on rocks nearby, although she could still see little other than a field fading off into the murk. She didn't need to see anything to have a good guess at where they were. "The bastards dropped us back in Britain."

Jack wiped mud from his lips and flicked it to the ground. "Jesus," he said shakily. "I'd like to say it's good to be home, but I'm afraid that would be a lie."

Lesley took in a whooping breath. The oxygen fed the spark of anger smoldering in the pit of her stomach, boosting it to a roaring conflagration. She turned to Jack and began beating her fists against his chest.

"This is your fault, you fucking arsehole," she shouted. "Why didn't you pick some other idiot for your stupid bloody story?" Jack didn't even try to fend her off; he just stood there and let her beat her rage out against his breastbone. When the coals of the fire had gone cold, Lesley sat down heavily, uncaring that the muddy grass chilled her buttocks. She dropped her head to her knees. "We're dead."

"Not yet, we're not."

"Yes, we are. You just don't know it yet. Were you here during the outbreak?"

"No," Jack admitted. "I was stationed in New York."

"I almost died, several times, and that was before people got infected. Now every living thing on this island is going to want to kill us, and there's no way off."

Jack sat down and put a tentative arm around her shoulder. She could tell from his heavy breathing that he was just as scared as her. However, he put a brave face on it. "Look, I know this isn't ideal."

"That's the fucking understatement of the century."

"At least we're free. And while we're alive, we've got a chance."

"Really? If the bloody zombies don't get us, they're going to bomb the shit out of this country any day now. You can choose which one of those ways to die suits your personality. I'm just going to sit here and starve quietly. In fact, I might suffocate myself."

Lesley plunged her head into the mud.

Jack pulled her up. "Stop fucking about. They've left us here to die, no doubt about it, but they've made a big mistake."

"You're right. They should've pushed us out from much higher up."

"We've still got time. Somewhere on this island there must be a way to get a phone call or an e-mail out. I mean to find it and let everybody know exactly what they've done and are going to do. They're not going to get away with it."

"That's very action hero of you. Shame we don't even know where we are."

"I'll have you know I used to be a scout. Troop leader, no less. And I have my orienteering badge."

"Okay then, Baden-Powell. Where exactly are we?"

"If you get up out of the mud, we can start walking and figure it out."

"Why bother?"

"Because getting this story out and maybe stopping the attack is the only chance you've got of surviving this. Nobody's going to stop and ask if you're a zombie before dropping a big bomb on your head or shooting you."

"Are you just going to keep nagging me if I don't get up?"

"Yes."

"Great. Do me a favor and nag me to death."

"For fuck's sake, Lesley," Jack said, "try to find some positives."

Lesley ran through a mental list: fresh air, the great outdoors, a chance to pee without a guard listening to her tinkle. None of them were particularly heartening. Her life seemed to have become a cycle of repetitive events. For the second time, she found herself kidnapped and trapped in a zombie-infested nation as she tried to disseminate a story that would have wide-ranging repercussions. Once had been quite enough, thank you very much. The only thing missing to make the awful sense of déjà vu complete was a very large bull. Once more wrapped in the comfortable blanket of self-pity she'd worn so many times down the years, she said nothing.

"If you want to sit here and be pathetic, that's fine," Jack said. "I'm off to do something about it."

He stomped off into the darkness. Lesley, stung by being called pathetic, got to her feet. Just as she'd fallen back into a similar situation, she'd fallen back into being the old Lesley: a useless woman who spent her life bemoaning her fate rather than doing something to change it. Well, she'd shown in New York that she wasn't that woman any longer, even if that was what had ultimately brought her back here. She wasn't about to give up those hard-won gains so easily. Yes, they were in a whole lot of trouble, but Jack was right: they still had a chance, no matter how slim.

"Hold on," she shouted. "I'm coming."

Jack reappeared, suggesting his plunge into the unknown had only been a performance to snap her out of her funk. "Fantastic. Let's try and find a bit of cover until the sun comes up so we don't freeze to death. Then we can make a plan."

As she opened her mouth to acquiesce, provided the plan involved getting food into their stomachs as soon as possible, a deep bellow sounded from the darkness. Lesley, completely unsurprised, almost smiled at the ridiculousness of the last element of her Groundhog Day falling into place.

"I don't suppose you used to be a matador as well," she said.

Jack shook his head, peering into the field to figure out which direction the sound had come from.

"Then I suggest we leg it," Lesley said, and demonstrated what she meant.

14

Geldof, his gaze darting left and right, tried not to run as he approached the Paris tower block where he was due to meet Scholzy and his team. It was just after midnight, and all around him shuffled loose packs of youths in hoodies, who turned the shadows where their faces should be toward him. He put on a fake pimp walk as he mounted the narrow stairs, hoping he looked mean rather than just lame in every sense of the word. He still hadn't told his grandfather he was going in and had booked the ticket to Paris under the pretext of carrying out a last-minute check that everything was in order. With luck, he would be out with his mum and starting a new life before his grandfather realized what was really going on. Provided, of course, he even made it out of the tower block alive.

Scholzy didn't waste any time when he answered the door, ushering Geldof inside to stand in front of three men lounging on a beat-up old sofa.

"Introductions," Scholzy said.

First he pointed to a short man who appeared to be entirely hairless, although it was hard to be sure since he was wearing a chunky, hard-plastic mask that covered the lower half of his face. Geldof could only presume it was an air filter, which was odd since his grandfather's comprehensive briefing packet said the risk of air-borne infections had passed. They just needed to make sure they didn't have sex with anybody, get bitten, or both. Considering Geldof's record to date, he wasn't too worried about the first one. Plus they weren't even in the country yet. Even so, the mercenary was also already wearing what looked like body armor. Although they were clearly in a dodgy area of the French capital, such precautions seemed a touch excessive.

"This is Peter Abraham, our logistics and techy guy," Scholzy said. "Bostonian, with tours in Iraq and Afghanistan before he saw the light and decided to make real money."

Peter raised an eyebrow and said something unintelligible behind the mask.

"Next, we have James Anthony Hilton," Scholzy said. "Don't let the posh British name his father bequeathed him fool you. He's as Belgian as they come, with the exception of pedophilic tendencies. He's heavy weaponry and explosives, plus the keeper of the first aid kit. He can blow legs off and then sew them back on. And don't tell him he looks like Harry Potter, or he'll cut your nipples off and wear them as earrings."

Geldof stared at the lightning bolt scar running across James's forehead. Even without the glasses, he did look rather like Potter—albeit a version of the boy wizard who grew up in a Glasgow housing scheme, where anyone bringing a magic wand to a fight would get a broken glass in the face, and spent his adult life hanging around dimly lit basement gyms with an assortment of thugs. James didn't even bother returning Geldof's nod.

Scholzy pointed to the last mercenary, whose blond hair was parted in the middle and swept past his ears. He had a goatee, which emphasized his chipmunk cheeks, and a wide nose that appeared to have been broken repeatedly.

"Last and definitely least is Mick Sailor. He was in the Irish army until he punched one too many officers. He's our official psychopath. Every good outfit needs one."

Mick scowled and pointed a finger at Geldof. "Sociopath."

"I'm sorry?"

"The discharge papers said 'sociopath.'"

"Is there a difference?" Geldof asked as politely as he could.

"Of course there's a fecking difference," Mick said, his face pained. "Psychopaths are psycho, sociopaths are more sociable. Charming, so. Like me."

Scholzy laughed. "Fortunately, Mick's far better with a sniper rifle than he is with the nuances of psychiatry."

Geldof stood in the middle of the room, unsure what was expected of him. They hadn't even got going, but he already felt more out of place than ever—which was really saying something. Although only Peter wore armor and a mask, everybody was dressed head-to-toe in black combat gear and wore sturdy boots. Geldof had been provided with neither dress code nor packing list and so was wearing red Converse, light-colored jeans, a fluorescent blue waterproof jacket, and a woolly hat. His rucksack contained two spare shirts, a toothbrush, and three changes of socks and pants.

"Err, should I change or something?" he said.

"Don't worry," Scholzy said. "We brought gear for you as well. It's in the bedroom. Throw it on and we'll get going."

An hour later, driving to Charles de Gaulle Airport, Geldof felt better. It was amazing how dressing all in black could make you feel harder and more capable. When they'd walked down the stairs together, the hoodies had melted away in the face of the tight posse of fierce-looking men. Geldof felt his swagger had possessed far more authority than on the way in. He sat up front alongside Scholzy while the others crouched in the back of the truck with the gear. They'd brought an astonishing amount of equipment with them: quad bikes; satphones; sleek, black automatic weapons; grenades; radios; RPGs; mines; assorted explosives; rucksacks full of food and spare ammunition; and lots of other little toys—such as a remote-controlled spy car.

Since the others were out of earshot, Geldof took the chance to ask the question he'd wanted to pose from the moment he walked into the apartment. "Why was Peter wearing a face mask? And body armor?"

Scholzy spoke without taking his eyes off the road or changing his slow, measured driving. "He's had more close shaves than a ladyboy's legs, so he's grown a little paranoid. He likes to prepare for every eventuality."

"But we're still in Paris. How's that going to help?"

"Better safe than sorry, he says, and his neurosis saved my ass a few times. You may have noticed we brought a lot of kit. That's down to him. You'd be surprised how often you need some of the weird shit he brings."

"What about the others? Do they have any odd habits?"

"As I said, Mick's a mad bastard, so everything about him is odd. Just don't make any sudden movements and you'll be fine. And it's best not to mention Rwanda around James."

"Why not?"

"What do you know about the genocide?"

"Some people killed lots of other people."

"Ah, the young generation. The Internet gives you so much access to information and you use it to look at videos of amusing cats."

"I don't," Geldof said.

"I forgot. You're a teenage boy. You just download free porn, heh?"

"I play a lot of math games, actually."

"Sure you do. Anyway, potted history: the Hutus slaughtered almost a million Tutsis. When it started, James was serving as a peacekeeper. He was assigned to protect the prime minister, but he and another nine Belgians were taken prisoner. A mob of soldiers set on them with machetes—hence the big scar—while a whole bunch of other peacekeepers stood by and did nothing. The official story is that all ten died, but James fought his way out and disappeared. After the war he came back and found the soldiers who killed his friends. It didn't go well for them. He didn't feel kindly disposed toward the Belgian military either, so he started working for me."

There was another question Geldof had wanted to ask, and, even though he wasn't sure he wanted to know the answer, he posed it anyway. "How many men have you all killed?"

"I don't count," Scholzy said. "It's about getting the job done. Killing is secondary."

A chill ran through Geldof as the reality of their mission, and the strong possibility he would see more death, began to sink in. Still, at least he appeared to be in the right company, meaning any death would hopefully be restricted to the other side. "Can you give me details of the plan to get in?"

"My old pal Sergei and his Ukrainian sidekick Andrej are heading over as part of an aerial convoy to drop supplies at Ibrox Stadium in Glasgow, one of the agreed collection points. For a hefty bribe they've agreed to smuggle us in a container under their helicopter and make a slight detour to drop us off outside the city. We ride the rest of the way on the bikes, pick up the target, and a few days later head to a rendezvous point, where Sergei will detour from his next delivery and winch the lot of us up onto his helicopter."

"Sounds pretty simple."

Scholzy shot Geldof a sideways look, his face serious. "It always does."

The first thing Geldof noticed about Sergei, apart from the fact that he appeared to be little more than four feet tall, was that he was shit-faced. The Russian swayed like a flagpole in a strong wind as they disembarked from a truck round the back of the World Food Programme warehouse, which had been set up at the airport for the purpose of marshaling the food aid to be dropped into Britain and delivered to the camp down in Calais. Scholzy greeted Sergei warmly as the others revved up the heavily laden quad bikes and drove toward an open metal container. Once Sergei had staggered off, Geldof tapped Scholzy on the shoulder. "Is he drunk?"

"Of course he's drunk. He flies better that way. I've only flown with him sober once, and it was the most terrifying experience of my life."

"Where'd you find him?"

"Russians and Ukrainians are the best pilots in Africa. We've flown with Sergei in shitty old Antonovs across the continent. Now these guys are the only ones crazy enough to fly these aid missions over the U.K. We can count ourselves lucky that Sergei is doing this run. It means we're in and out with no fuss. Otherwise we would've had to try to sneak through the cordon on dinghies."

Geldof looked at the retreating Sergei who, silhouetted against the bright glare of lights overlooking the airfield, was slugging from a flask. "I hope you're right."

"I plan on coming back alive to spend my money. I wouldn't be doing this if it wasn't the safest way. Now, come on, we need to get all our shit loaded so Sergei can seal it up."

You'd better be pleased to see me, Mum, Geldof thought as he followed Scholzy into the yawning mouth of the crate.

A few hours later, Geldof was busy emptying the contents of his stomach over the bare metal floor of the container as it slipped and slid through the air. They'd had Chinese takeout before they left the apartment and the interior, lit by portable lamps in each corner, stank of acrid soy sauce. Scholzy told him the motion was so bad because their crate was suspended by hooks below the helicopter for ease of release, although Geldof kept imagining Sergei nodding off only to snort awake and jerk the controls. The lighter supplies were in the actual cargo hold, where they could be pushed out to fall to the ground. The pilots were under strict instructions not to touch down, even though the protocol was for the army units picking up the supplies to remain outside the stadium until the drop was complete. At any sign of the infected violating this rule, the pilots were to abort.

Mick, his pinched face harshened by the shadow of the lights, turned away in disgust as Geldof retched. "Remind me why we agreed to babysit this fecking eejit?"

"Because he's paying us a shitload of money," Scholzy said.

"I can't stand puke," Mick said.

"I've smelled a lot worse come chuffing out of your Irish arse," said James, prompting a snort of muffled laughter from Peter.

"So, Geldof," Mick said. "How you going to make yourself useful? What's your special skill, apart from chucking up your guts?"

Geldof wiped saliva from his chin. "I'm good at maths."

"Jesus. I hope you've at least sharpened your compass so you can stab somebody in the fecking eye with it." Mick rummaged around in his bag and threw something. Geldof caught it reflexively and found himself holding a heavy handgun. "Take that. If you're coming along, you may as well learn how to kill."

"I don't want to kill anyone," Geldof said, holding the butt of the gun by his fingertips.

"Happy to pay us to do it though, aren't you? Look, it's easy. Click off the safety, point, and pull the trigger."

Scholzy plucked the gun from Geldof and slapped it back into Mick's hands. "Enough mucking around. He's more likely to shoot one of us by mistake."

Mick looked like he was about to argue the toss when Geldof's stomach lurched up into his throat. The radio crackled into life and Sergei's voice, vowels equally thick with booze and his Russian accent, came through. "We are descending to the drop site. Twenty minutes to unload, and we are on our way."

Above the whining clatter of the rotors, something clunked. The rotor sound grew louder.

"That's the cargo doors opening," Scholzy said.

They hovered for five minutes as crates hit on the ground. After a particularly loud thump, Scholzy patted Geldof on the back. "Chin up. That's the other big crate under the helicopter gone. We'll be on our way in a minute."

"Why couldn't he drop us off first?"

"The other pilots would've noticed. He's going to claim the release mechanism for this crate is stuck. When we're out of the city again, he'll say it finally released itself."

Geldof had enough time to give him a wan smile before the floor of the crate dropped away. Scholzy, his eyes widening, appeared to float in the air beside him for a second before their heads thumped off the roof of the crate. With a chorus of swearing, they plummeted to the floor. One of the quad bikes slid toward Geldof and stopped with its tire just a few inches from his nose.

"What just happened?" Geldof said, his voice panicky.

"He dropped us," Scholzy hissed. He got on the radio. "What the fuck are you playing at Sergei?"

"Yes, I am here. I pressed the wrong button. Sorry, my friend."

"Never mind sorry. Get that fucking winch down and pick us up again."

"Too late," Sergei said. "We are the last helicopter. The army is coming now."

"I'll kill you for this, you drunken fuckwit," Mick shouted, raising his gun up to the roof.

For one horrible second Geldof thought he was going to pull the trigger, either sending bullets ricocheting through the interior or ripping into the helicopter and bringing it down on top of them. Scholzy, who'd let go of the call button, put a hand on Mick's forearm. "Zip it. We still need him to pick us up. He won't come back if he thinks we're going to kill him."

"He's right," said James. "Let's not tell him we're going to put a bullet in his brain. Until right before we do it."

"Sergei, how many soldiers can you see?" Scholzy asked once Mick had fallen silent and the airwaves were open again.

"Two trucks, about a dozen soldiers. But that is not your biggest problem."

"Christ, what else?"

"When the helicopters come, people know there is food. They always come. Sometimes the crowd can get ugly."

"And how big is this particular crowd?"

"Maybe five hundred people, all outside the stadium. There are more soldiers holding them back."

"And do they look ugly?"

"British people are always ugly. These ones look hungry. They are the worst kind."

"Fucking perfect," Scholzy said. "Sergei, you'd better be back to get us."

"We will have a drink and laugh about this little mistake when it is all over."

"Just be at the pickup point."

"Have I ever let you down?"

"Yes. Two fucking minutes ago. Literally and figuratively."

Sergei laughed. "This is why I like you, Scholzy. You always keep your sense of humor. I will see you in a few days."

The whine of rotors grew in pitch and then faded. Geldof heard raised voices and the chug of a diesel engine.

"We've probably got a few minutes before they open up the crate and find out it's not full of food," Scholzy said. "Everybody on the bikes."

Geldof's heart hammered in his chest as he stood there frozen amidst a sudden burst of controlled activity. Scholzy grabbed his wrist and yanked him to the back of his quad bike. Geldof wrapped his arms as far around the broad trunk of the mercenary as he could.

"As soon as the door opens, fire up the engines and gun it," Scholzy said. "Me first, then Mick, Peter, and James. Anybody gets in your way, kill them."

The crate was filled with the snap of excitement, the crackle of anticipation, and the pop of Geldof's nervous bowels. Somehow he found a little reservoir of Chinese he'd yet to evacuate and delivered it down Scholzy's back. Scholzy, utterly focused on the doors, didn't move a muscle. Vomit clogging his nostrils, Geldof closed his eyes and waited to die.

15

Lesley and Jack ran in the direction they judged to be the exact opposite from where the bellow had come, but in all honesty Lesley had no idea if they were blundering toward the enraged beast or away from it. The near-absolute darkness made their headlong dash even more petrifying. Any second she expected to see a pair of red eyes appear out of nowhere as a precursor to receiving a sharp horn up the jacksie. She could hear the thud of hooves and the occasional snort and bellow. It sounded as if they were growing closer. She could tell Jack wasn't running at his full speed, instead remaining by her side. She found his moral support simultaneously incredibly endearing and completely fucking stupid.

"Run faster!" she shouted. "One of us has to get out."

The effort further knackered her lungs, which were already protesting that she should have joined the joggers in Central Park instead of expending energy locating the elusive spots where she would be the requisite distance from public buildings and aggressive nonsmokers to spark up. Jack ignored her plea, grabbed her hand, and half dragged her along. The waves seemed louder now, which meant they were probably running toward the sea. If they could get into the water, they might be safe. Even if bulls could swim, she was pretty sure her doggy paddle would outpace a cow paddle. She chanced a quick glance backward and saw the thundering outline of the bull for the first time. It couldn't have been much more than ten meters behind them. Praying that the water's edge was just up ahead, she willed her aching legs onward.

In answer to her prayers, the grass disappeared into a darker area up ahead. They were going to make it. She lowered her head, sure her ankles would be splashing through the surf any second. Instead Jack yanked her off to one side, screaming "Shit!" at the top of his lungs. What she'd assumed was the sea was in fact the edge of a cliff. Lesley's legs swung out over the void and her upper body began to follow suit. In the shock of having the ground yaw away, she couldn't even will her heavy limbs to scrabble for purchase to defy the insistent pull of gravity. Fortunately Jack had somehow managed to find a handhold and held her up. She dangled there, staring back at the hooves coming straight toward them.

She closed her eyes, expecting any second to feel the weight of the bull crash into them and carry them all over. What she heard was a surprised moo. She snapped her eyelids open in time to see the rear end of the massive beast plummet past. The moo continued all the way down, getting quieter and more plaintive, until a meaty thud silenced it. Jack hauled her forward until her legs were on solid ground. They lay there together panting. Eventually, they crept forward and peered over the drop. She could just make out white foamy waves dashing against the rocks and what may have been a bull-shaped splodge.

"That's one way to tenderize a steak," Jack said.

He started laughing, and Lesley joined in, although her gasped hiccups sounded suspiciously like sobs. Once they'd calmed down, they sat together and stared out at the horizon. Lesley thought she could detect a slight lightening where sea met sky.

"Think there are any more bulls in this field?" Jack said.

"Doubt it. They always keep them on their own."

"Then let's wait here until the sun comes up. I don't want any more nasty surprises."

They watched the clouds dissipate and the sun, weak and yellow, lethargically spill its first rays over the rolling surface of the sea. As the adrenaline faded and their bodies cooled down from the exertion, Lesley's teeth began to chatter. She was still wearing a flowery knee-length woolen dress and a yellow cardigan, both embossed with splotches of mud and grass stains, but neither garment was enough to keep out the cold. Jack, also shivering, edged closer. "Mind if I steal some of your body heat?"

A young couple sitting on a cliff top watching the sun come up was so stereotypically romantic that Lesley couldn't help but make that association. Her first instinct was to refuse. Terry was back in their apartment, no doubt frantic with worry. Cuddling up to the handsome man who'd just saved her life felt like a betrayal, no matter how small and no matter how fragile her relationship with Terry. Then again, she was bloody freezing. She leaned into Jack. The sense of betrayal grew stronger when his nose brushed against her ear and sent a delicious shiver down her neck.

"Actually, I think it's time to get moving," she said, pulling away and getting to her feet. "Time for you to display your boy scout credentials."

Jack squinted at the sun. "We're obviously on the east coast somewhere, since the sun's coming up over the sea."

"Well, that narrows it down to about six hundred miles or so."

"No need to be snarky."

"It's my default setting," Lesley said. "Look, can I make a suggestion?"

"Sure."

She pointed back across the field, to where a little hamlet had appeared in the growing light. "Why don't we head toward that village over there and see if we can spot a sign?"

"Won't it be full of infected?" Jack said.

"Probably. But what choice do we have? We need to find a phone or a computer if we're going to get this story out. Anyway, don't they teach stealth tactics in the scouts?"

"Sorry, I didn't get my ninja badge."

They squelched back across the field, getting lower and slower. It was a sleepy little village that could have been anywhere along the coast of Britain, all winding strips of tarmac and one-story buildings built from large gray stone blocks. There appeared to be no sign of life. They crouched behind a bush and looked through the fence.

"Should we go in?" Jack said.

"It looks quiet enough, I suppose."

No sooner had Lesley spoken than an elderly man with a thick mop of gray hair and a bent back came out of the door of a house about fifty meters away. Propped up with a cane, he shuffled onto the road to stand looking up at the sky.

"He doesn't look like much of a killer," said Jack.

"Just wait until he gets a whiff of you. He'll probably try to intrude anally with his walking stick."

"I'm all up for new sexual experiences, but I think I'll pass on that one. What do we do?"

Lesley looked around, wondering if they might be better striking off farther into the mainland, although she had no idea what they might find there. Her gaze fell on a large mound of bullshit. A rather disgusting thought occurred to her. "Have you ever seen *The Walking Dead*?"

"No."

"How can you not have? It's been all over the TV the last few months."

"Yeah, and did you wonder why they've been showing that and lots of other reruns of zombie films on every channel?" Jack said. "Dehumanization. Makes it easier to swallow when they're all killed."

Lesley, all too aware she'd played a part in this dehumanization, moved the conversation on. "Anyway, there's a scene where they smear themselves in zombie intestines to hide their smell so they can walk amongst the dead. It might work for us."

"Are you suggesting we kill him and stick our heads in his guts?"

Lesley shook her head and pointed at the dung. Jack groaned. "You've got to be shitting me."

"Very funny. Look, I know it's nasty, but if we're going to survive we need to find a way to get around without being set upon every couple of minutes. This is a perfect test environment. I think even I could outrun him if it doesn't work."

"Fine," Jack said. "In that case, you go first."

Lesley crawled to the brown heap and, her face twisted, dug her hands in deep. She started on her bare legs, smearing it all the way up to her thighs, and stuck her hands up her dress to rub it on her stomach and breasts. Next, fighting the gorge rising in her throat, she slapped it onto her armpits and neck. "Think we need to do the face, too?"

"Definitely," Jack said.

She got busy, trying to pretend she was putting on a mud pack in an expensive spa.

"How do I look?" she said when she was finished.

"Like crap."

"You can stop with the shit jokes now. It's your turn."

"Actually, I think one person is enough for the purposes of our experiment. Off you go and talk to him."

Lesley scooped up a generous handful and lobbed it at Jack, who ducked. "Hey, it was your idea. I promise I'll do it if it works."

"Arsehole," she said and got to her feet.

She clambered over the fence and approached the old man, who was still seemingly lost in thought. Eventually he noticed her approach and turned to face her. As she came to a stop at a healthy distance, his nostrils twitched. She braced herself for the cane to come swinging up. He remained still.

"Fit like?" he said.

The crapouflage is working, she thought, and considered what he'd said. The only time she'd ever heard that phrase was on a hen weekend to Aberdeen, when she'd mistakenly thought the ruddy-cheeked oil worker who said it was being too forward in expressing his appreciation for her figure and told him to fuck right off. She'd had to apologize when a friend explained it meant, "How are you?" She made it up to the oil worker by getting horrendously drunk and sucking his face off.

"Fine, thanks." She expected him to say something further, perhaps comment on her unusual appearance and smell. He just stared at her with eyes that were the same color as the sky behind him, making it feel as if she was staring right through his head. "This is going to sound strange, but can you tell me the name of this village?"

"Aye. Portlethen."

"Are we near Aberdeen by any chance?"

"Aye. It's just up there a bit," he said, pointing north.

Again, he chose not to ask any questions, such as where she'd come from, why she didn't know where she was, and why she was covered in excrement. Lesley was beginning to wonder if he was senile. "I don't suppose you have a phone we can use?"

"No."

"Would anybody else have a phone?"

"The phones aren't working. There's no power. There's nobody else here. All dead or gone to Aberdeen. Just me and my pet bull, Jamie."

Lesley figured it best not to mention that, thanks to her and Jack, Jamie had taken a nosedive off a cliff. She'd killed somebody's pet and only companion, zombie or not. Yet another success for the Lesley Mc-Brien Death Curse. After issuing hasty thanks for the information, she went back to report to Jack. She felt the old man's gaze on her back as she climbed the fence, but still he didn't move.

"We're near Aberdeen," she said when Jack poked his head out from behind the bush.

"Why'd they dump us here?"

"Dunno. Maybe the helicopter took off from Denmark and this was the closest drop point. It doesn't matter. Anyway, the shit works, so you'd better get decorating yourself. There's nothing for us here. We need to get up to Aberdeen to see if it's any better."

Jack sighed and helped himself to the remnants of the dung. "Well, looks like you've saved the world. All we need to do is get everybody to cake themselves in cow plop and there'll be no more trouble."

"I'll be sure to put that in the story."

"So how are we going to get to Aberdeen? Walk?"

"There must be some transport in the village. The old boy said he was the only one there, so it'll be safe to look around."

They walked back into the village, nodding at the immobile local—who didn't bat an eyelid at the appearance of a second swamp monster. There were plenty of cars, but none of them contained keys and all of the fuel caps had been pried open. After a while, they began breaking and entering. They slaked their thirst with tap water, but no food—or cigarettes, which Lesley still craved despite ten days of cold turkey—was to be found anywhere. Eventually they lucked out and found two Raleigh racers, circa 1970 by the looks of the rusty chains, in the garage of a bungalow. They were just the right height for Lesley, but Jack's longer legs rose almost to his chin as they mounted up and set out along the main road toward the unknown dangers of Aberdeen.

16

The doors of the container creaked open and the engines of the quad bikes burst into life. Geldof opened his eyes to see three soldiers dive out of the way as Scholzy opened the throttle and sent the bike lurching into motion. They shot out onto the center circle of the stadium, right into a maelstrom of typical Glasgow stinging diagonal rain. The gray early morning light revealed soldiers humping sacks of food out of the dozens of crates, large and small, that the choppers had unloaded onto the rutted grass. Geldof expected them to reach for their weapons, but they just gaped at the four bikes tearing up the grass. The bikes sped toward the tall iron gates sitting open in one corner of the pitch, surrounded by old bricks and tangled metal from the seats and walls that had been gouged away to create a larger opening.

The four soldiers there had their backs to them and were busy trying to pacify a clamoring mob. Tears streamed down Geldof's cheeks, partly from the icy wind that eddied around Scholzy's body and partly from the icy certainty that he was about to die. For a fleeting moment, he regretted not having taken advantage of the working girl in Nairobi. Given his grandfather's opposition to eulogizing the dead, his newspaper obituary would probably bear the headline, "Geldof Peters. He Died a Virgin." The thought fled his mind as they drew closer to the bodies packed thick around the exit, arms undulating in the air and shouting for supplies. He saw no way they could get through the press even as they picked up speed, further churning up the once perfect football surface. Scholzy solved the problem by raising his automatic weapon and letting loose a burst of fire in the air. The crowd parted, falling over each other in their eagerness to flee. Scholzy led the wedge of bikes toward the thinnest part of the wriggling mass, but even as he did so the soldiers turned, hunkered down, and locked weapons to shoulders in one fluid motion. Geldof found himself wishing for a quick death. Better a clean shot to the skull than to be winged and sent sliding into the middle of the infected masses. Traditional zombies or not, he'd watched enough horror movies to know such situations invariably ended with intestines being tossed about like spaghetti. Those deliciously gruesome scenes had been his favorite moment of any zombie film; it was a very different matter when he would be the one providing the stringy pasta. The soldiers didn't get the chance to fire. With short staccato bursts, the mercenaries sent their targets spinning to the ground, adding further impetus to the scrambled efforts of the crowd to get out of the way.

They thrust right into the middle of the chaos. Scholzy's front right tire ran over the leg of a wide-eyed woman who'd fallen to the ground. The bike lurched to the left. Geldof started to slip, only managing to catch himself with a desperately flung hand on the side of the bike. Tilted out from the safety of his seat, he zipped inches by a forest of faces, close enough to see the whites of their eyes. Nostrils twitched, and suddenly the crowd was no longer fleeing. Hands reached for them, and the high-pitched screams of panic dropped several octaves into a rumble of anger.

Geldof brushed past a pinched-face youth in a white tracksuit, bottoms tucked into his socks, and a baseball cap with the rim pointing upward perched on his head.

"They're nicking our fucking drugs," the youth yelled. "Get the bastards."

The bikes had too much momentum to be snarled up and pulled clear to bump down onto the road. Geldof chanced a look back. The mob—young and old, male and female, short and tall, and all ordinary looking save for the identical gnarled looks of focused hatred and longing on their faces—was now sprinting after them. Even with the growl of the engine thrumming in his ears, he could hear the throaty roar emanating from their twisted mouths. One of the army trucks came barrelling out of the gate. The throng of people pelting through the rain, now spread out across the whole road, slowed its progress, but a soldier leaned out of the cabin and aimed a weapon.

They were driving up the hill toward the M8 when bullets whined around them. Scholzy began zigzagging, the tires designed for biting into soft grass squealing for purchase on the slick tarmac. Geldof clung on like a baby koala to its mother. The truck had nosed its way through the mob by knocking many of them over and was now roaring up the hill, gaining far too quickly. The intersection with Paisley Road West, and beyond that the on-ramp to the M8, lay ahead on their left, but Scholzy bumped onto the pavement and took a gap between leafless trees throwing their twisted branches up in protest against the relentless rain. They raced across an empty patch of ground and rattled over another curb onto the dual carriageway.

At this hour of day, back in normal times, the street would have been full of buses and cars trundling to work. Now it was empty save for a few sodden cyclists, who veered off at the sight of the four quad bikes. Geldof heard the sound of tearing metal and looked back to see the truck, which must have mounted the verge at speed, sideswipe a parked car. The door of the truck swung shut, mashing the soldier who was leaning out to fire again. The truck tore free and kept coming. On an empty main road they had no chance of outpacing it, particularly since so much shit was strapped over the bikes.

Scholzy pointed left and swung the handlebars to travel in that direction. The quad bike power-slid onto a street flanked by identical tenement buildings. Up ahead was a T-junction. Standing in the middle of it was an old Glasgow wifey. Her blue-tinted hair was done up in curlers wrapped beneath a clear plastic rain mac. She was wearing a shapeless gray overcoat that came down to her knees. Underneath her tan tights, thick varicose veins were visible even at a distance. One arthritic hand was wrapped around a tartan shopping trolley, a two-wheeled contraption with a little black handle that grannies across Scotland used to run over people's toes and jab the backs of the knees of anybody foolish enough to loiter in their way. It was a fearsome weapon in the right hands.

This particular wifey had clearly already sensed they were uninfected from the roar of the mob because she faced them, legs apart, and picked up the trolley. She hurled it with a strength Geldof did not think possible, forcing Scholzy to swerve to avoid its twisting arc. Mick's bike crunched it under its thick tires as Scholzy slowed to take the corner. Instead of leaping out of the way, the old woman dived at the quad bike and somehow managed to curl her fingers around the side bar. She held on as the bike accelerated and fixed Geldof with tiny eyes that brimmed with hate behind thick National Health specs.

"Joyriders!" she screamed. "You can't even let an old lady cross the road. I'll show you."

The drag of the road had already claimed her zip-up fleece shoes and was now grating the skin from her shins, but she somehow managed to pull herself closer to Geldof with one hand and reach out with the other to swipe at his eyes. She fell a few inches short.

"Get her off!" Scholzy shouted.

"How?"

"Tell her cat food is half price down in Tesco."

"I don't think that's going to work," Geldof said as the pensioner tried to pull herself closer for a more accurate swipe.

"I was being facetious," Scholzy shouted, his voice barely audible above the wind and engine noise. "Punch her in the fucking face."

"I can't punch her," Geldof shouted. "She's an old lady."

"She's also a flesh-eating maniac who'll kill you or give you the virus."

In the wild intensity of the moment, Geldof had forgotten about the risk of infection. Now he was even less keen to touch her. "Can't you shoot her?"

"I'm driving. If she gets her gnashers into you, I'll bloody well shoot you, though."

Geldof gritted his teeth and punched the woman as hard as he could, knocking off her glasses. It was only the second time in his life he'd resorted to violence. At least the last time he'd hit Mary's twin sons, who were both bigger and stronger than him and fully deserved it. Mind you, this woman was trying to kill him and so also deserved it, but in saner times he would be helping her cross the road instead of dragging her along it.

"Hooligan," she shouted and reached for him.

He punched her again, putting all of his weight behind it. The blow only enraged her further. She opened her mouth wide, like a cobra about to swallow its prey, and let loose a howl. Her false teeth shot out and hit Geldof on the forehead. He swiped at his skin, terrified that her saliva would drip into his eyes and turn him. He needed to get rid of her fast. He let go of Scholzy's jacket and allowed himself to fall backward, trusting his thighs to hold him onto the bike. The woman slashed at him as his head dropped. Her yellow fingernails brushed through his hair. Now that he was within reach, she bit down on his forearm. With no teeth, she only succeeded in giving his sleeve a moist gumming. Geldof grabbed hold of the swollen thumb on the hand securing her to the bike and, swallowing hard, yanked it backward. The thumb snapped, her grip released, and she rolled along behind them like human tumbleweed, the other bikes dodging past her, before coming to a halt. Unbelievably, she got to her feet and began tottering after them, shaking her fist.

The pursuing truck flew round the corner, too fast. It went up onto two wheels and, still tilting, overtook the pensioner. The undercarriage snagged her plastic rain mac and pulled it off her head. She didn't even notice, just kept coming after them in an angry little shuffle. The driver yanked the steering wheel back to the right, but the turning wheels slipped away underneath the vehicle and it toppled onto its left side. The metallic screech that followed sounded like nails on a blackboard amplified through a public address system. Geldof hauled himself into an upright position. He scrubbed again at his forehead, but he knew he wasn't infected, for he felt only fear.

She almost got me, he thought, and barfed onto Scholzy's back again.

"I'm adding the dry cleaning to your bill," Scholzy shouted.

Geldof looked over his shoulder again. The old woman kept after them, overtaking the wreck of the lorry that hissed steam from its bonnet like a vanquished dragon. She receded into the distance, but Geldof could see her still in his mind's eye, stalking them relentlessly across the country on her bandy little legs.

The next thirty minutes of driving through Glasgow—sticking to the back streets as they hurried toward the Erskine Bridge, where they would cross and begin making their way up to Arrochar—were utterly surreal. Geldof's mind went into partial shutdown as it tried to recover from the frantic first few minutes of his return home. By contrast, the mercenaries seemed elated by what anybody else would have counted as a bloody setback. They rode two abreast down the traffic-free roads, Scholzy and Mick shouting across to each other as the other two fell in behind.

"That was mental," Scholzy said.

"Crazier than the Congo," Mick said. "Did you see the looks on their faces? They wanted to murder us, bring us back to life, and murder us some more. This whole fecking country's hostile."

The cheerful inflection he put on the word "hostile" did not indicate that he considered this a bad thing.

"And what about Geldof here?" Scholzy said. "He engaged his first enemy."

"Right," Mick said. "He shoved an old lady off of a bike and still managed not to kill her. I'm not shitting myself at his ruthless fecking killer credentials just yet."

Geldof tuned out their banter and tried to focus on his surroundings as they doubled back through Govan, the River Clyde on the right-hand side. Although there were no cars, there was plenty of life. Mothers pushed their children in prams, kids listlessly kicked a ball against a wall, and a huge queue of people stood outside a branch of a store that appeared to be called Tennerland, where they were being allowed in a few at a time as others emerged with plastic bags hanging limp with meager shopping. As they passed, somebody tried to cut in line. The queue broke up as everybody started shoving and bawling at the transgressor. Geldof gaped. In the past, such an act would have been extremely rare and only resulted in lots of passive-aggressive tutting and eye rolling from the offended parties. The country really had gone to the dogs if Brits had lost their ability to queue in a civilized manner.

Another thing he noticed was that there was not one fat person in sight, which in Glasgow was astonishing. Everybody was hollow-cheeked, and when the bikes went past their gazes followed them. Nobody reacted, however. Geldof guessed they were too far and moving too quickly for the infected to pick up their scent, although two scrawny dogs did try to tail them, barking furiously, before they fell behind. No army vehicles pursued them, nor did any police helicopters take to the sky to track their progress from above. This came as no real surprise. Part of the reason Scholzy had been so confident was the parlous state of the security apparatus, which had been reduced to a threadbare force struggling to keep order in the cities and not even bothering to try outside.

Geldof assumed that this last fact was why, by the time they'd nipped onto the motorway and passed through the raised tollgates of the Erskine Bridge, the mercenaries had fallen silent. The intelligence report talked of gangs of brigands, essentially highway robbers, roaming *Mad Max*–style through the countryside. It would only be a few hours to Arrochar, but to get there they would have to travel through this bandit-infested countryside. Not that the mercenaries seemed concerned, just alert. Scholzy had said they would easily deal with any of the ill-disciplined rabble they encountered. From the way they'd dropped the soldiers and driven to safety, Geldof had no cause to doubt him.

The bikes sat idling by the side of the road as James peered through binoculars toward the village of Arrochar. Fanny's camp was on the other side, up and back around the top of the loch. Geldof climbed down to ease the pins and needles in his buttocks and hopped from foot to foot as he waited to get going again.

The few hours it had taken them to get to this point after the chase in the city were uneventful. They'd continued to take as many back roads as possible, just in case the army was looking for them. There were few people in sight in the small towns and villages they passed through, and those who were out in the street withdrew to their homes well in advance of their approach. Geldof didn't blame them. They must have looked like a fearsome bandit gang as they roared along the road in their squat little vehicles, all dressed in black and, Geldof aside, weapons at the ready. Of the real bandits that were supposedly out in force, they saw no sign. Maybe they were there, lurking off the road and waiting for travelers to ambush, but their little company was far from an easy target. Any watching eyes may have judged it wiser to wait for lower-hanging fruit.

He had to admit that ripping through the countryside was all rather exciting, now that the fear of the chase had passed and the rain sputtered out. If he'd been entrusted with a gun, he would have been tempted to fire it in the air as he'd seen so many excitable gunmen do during various televised uprisings across the world. It had seemed very much like the worst was over, and he'd grown increasingly nervous as the miles ticked by, knowing that in a very short time he would be with his mum again. He didn't know how she would react or even how he would react, for that matter. For so many months he'd thought her dead. Now it would be like meeting a ghost.

James laid the binoculars on the seat of his bike and scrunched up his face in thought. "One guy, with a shotgun. We could take him out, but we'd have to slow down to weave through all the crap they've blocked the road with. And then we'd probably have to fight our way through the village. I don't think we need that kind of attention. I suggest we go around."

Scholzy grunted and looked at his GPS. "This is the only road, so we'll need to go up through the hills. Ready for a bit of off-roading?"

They mounted up and set off through light shrubbery. Thorns snagged at Geldof's clothes as they bounced and jostled. Before long every muscle in his body ached. They climbed ever higher, bumping over grassy tufts and small rocks, until the village lay far below. Off in the distance, just above the settlement, Geldof saw a few paddocks in which white and brown dots indicated the presence of livestock. Even though they were way out of range, Geldof still shuddered. He had no desire to get any closer to one of those evil animals.

The view across the valley was spectacular. The rippling loch reflected the sun that had chosen to make an appearance, while off in the far distance heavy clouds unloaded slanting sheets of rain on the rolling hills and peaks. It was typical Scotland: brooding yet beautiful, sparse yet inspiring. Momentarily entranced, he forgot the tragedy that had befallen the nation until the wind carried a shout of alarm up the slope. He looked back at the paddock and saw a figure running down toward the village. He tugged Scholzy's shoulder.

"I think they've spotted us," he said.

"Then we'd better get a move on," Scholzy said.

He pulled the throttle back further and Geldof's pelvic bone suffered a severe pummeling as the heaving, lurching bike threw him up and down. After half an hour of having his internal organs jarred, they rounded the top of the loch and began to nose toward the road, traveling down a narrow track hemmed in on both sides by tall trees. He kept expecting some large animal to come bursting out. The only thing they encountered was a weasel chewing at something on the ground. It lifted its head at their approach and bounded straight toward them. Geldof could swear it bore a predatory look. As they came together, it tensed its back legs to leap. It didn't get the chance, disappearing under the heavy tread of the front right tire as James swerved to squash it.

"Another kill!" James shouted.

"Doesn't count unless it's armed," Mick shouted back.

"It had sharp teeth. That's a weapon."

They emerged from the track and swung onto the road, where they came to a halt. Geldof looked across the water. Halfway up the hill where they'd been, a small group of men was trekking upward.

"Do you think they're going to come after us?" he said.

"Doubt it," Scholzy said. "They probably thought we were bandits. When they see we've moved on they'll go back home."

Geldof wasn't so sure. They were perilously close to the village, separated just by the water. While he was pretty sure that the residents of Arrochar wouldn't be able to tell that the riders were uninfected from sniffing their tracks, he couldn't rule it out. He'd seen just how tenacious an infected animal or human could be. All he wanted to do was get in, sweep his mum off her feet, and get out again. They could find somewhere farther away from inhuman society to hole up until Sergei came back for them. Before he could express his concerns and make his suggestion, Scholzy pointed up the road. "GPS says the camp is just over there."

Geldof put his fears aside. His reunion with his mum was only minutes away. They inched along the road, searching for a gap in the trees. Peter whistled and pointed toward where undergrowth partially obscured a track running off the main road.

"Weapons up, nice and slow," Scholzy said. "They're going to be jumpy."

They pushed through the undergrowth and trundled along, waiting for the moment they would be challenged. It didn't take long.

"That's far enough," a female voice shouted from somewhere in the trees. "This place is taken."

All four bikes halted and Scholzy held up his hands. "We're not looking for any trouble. We're just here to talk to Fanny Peters."

A long, tense silence followed, before the invisible watcher spoke again. "Why do you want to talk to Fanny?"

"I think this is your cue," Scholzy said in a low voice.

Geldof swung his legs off the back of the bike and, with his hands spread wide in a gesture of peace, peered into the trees. "Her son's here to see her."

"Geldof? Good Lord, is that really you?"

A tree branch almost directly overhead rustled and something dropped to the ground. A woman, her face smeared with camouflage paint and curly hair tied back, emerged from the greenery. It took Geldof a moment to realize it was one of his mum's friends, a woman called Eva who came over to stay whenever there was a protest rally on in Glasgow. They were definitely in the right place.

Eva was normally one of those people who felt you weren't connecting unless her palm was resting on your forearm or her hip was pressed against yours on the sofa. He expected her to come charging forward and give him an inappropriately lingering hug, but she stayed back and muttered something under her breath. After an appraising look at the mercenaries, she gave Geldof a sad smile. "Your mum is going to freak out."

17

In the predawn gloom, lights burned on the top floor of Fraser House, the twenty-three-story tower block on Brentford Estate that Blood of Christ had made its home. Tony stood beside the mobile command center and peered at the six identical gray blocks through the night-vision goggles Glen had handed him. Soldiers and police were fanning out across the football field butting on to the back of the estate, keeping low as they scuttled toward the building. Similar movements were taking place all around the estate, creating an impenetrable circle.

They'd finally caught a break in their hunt for Archangel the previous day when a policeman witnessed three members of the group corner a frail old imam out for a stroll along the side of the Thames in Brentford. As the blows began to rain down, the officer followed his instructions to shoot on sight when confronted with members of the extremist group. He killed two of the attackers and the surviving member took off running. In his blind panic he sprinted back to Fraser House. Fortunately, the copper had been smart enough to follow at a distance rather than go rushing in and had noted the armed men guarding the entrance to the building. He then lurked behind a bush for half an hour until Archangel himself emerged, surrounded by bodyguards.

Tony had wasted no time getting Glen and Frank to pull together an assault force. Sections of the city had been unprotected for the night as a result, but whatever chaos took place was a price worth paying to be rid of these maniacs. Tony shouldn't really have been there since he did have a country to run, but he needed to see Archangel brought low, and he would be back in the office by 8:00 a.m. if all went well.

As he watched the soldiers take up their positions, he felt confident they were about to bring the extremist rabble to heel. As fervent as the madmen were, they would be no match for a well-drilled fighting force. And stopping their cross-channel jaunts would surely buy him enough time to get the missile ready.

"They could've picked somewhere a bit nicer to hole up," said Frank, who'd stuck his head out of the command center.

It was a good point. Decades of rocketing house prices had seen people scrimp and save to get their feet on the property ladder only to find the gap between the first and higher rungs impossible to bridge. Even a pokey flat in one of the tower blocks they were looking at had been going for around 150,000, a sum that would have purchased a mansion, with enough change to buy a sports car and maintain a few floozies to drape over it, when Tony was a young man. The virus turned the property ladder into a trampoline. When the initial wave of violence faded and survivors emerged from the camps, they at first returned to their own homes. The mass upgrading started when looters realized the deserted homes they were ransacking could be taken over wholesale. With so many empty properties, those who jumped earliest and hardest got whatever they wanted. A mass exodus to the largely empty posh districts took place. Knightsbridge, Belgravia, Chelsea, Kensington, Mayfair, and all the other areas once reserved for those with bulging wallets were now thoroughly degentrified—stuffed with the kind of plebs the previous residents would have called the police on if they so much as stopped to tie a shoelace outside their houses. A group of particularly ambitious travelers had even taken up residence in Buckingham Palace, replacing the corgis with Alsatians. Tony had taken the decision to let everyone get on with it. If they ever extricated themselves from the mess they were in and people started returning home, they could sort it all out then.

"It's more defensible. Archangel is probably at the top, so our boys are going to have to fight their way up floor by floor," said Glen, who'd been in a splendid mood since being given the okay to prepare the missile.

Tony hadn't revealed his true intentions to anyone, not even Amira, who kept bending his ear. He was worried that if he told her what he was really planning she would let it slip to Glen just to get one over on him. It was better to let Glen focus on getting this ultimate deterrent ready. Once the sub was at sea and the international community was suitably cowed, he would inform Glen that the missile wouldn't be fired and deal with the fallout.

"Well, it has to be done," Tony said. "If these nutters get caught trying to get over to France again this country is toast."

The radio crackled into life with the mission commander's voice. "All units in place."

"Operation is go," Glen said.

Tony looked through his binoculars again. Soldiers sprang up from their crouched positions and ran toward the entrance of the tower block. They kicked in the doors and poured inside, guns at the ready.

"Come on, Tony," Frank said. "You're going to miss the show."

He clambered into the cramped interior of the vehicle and peered at the monitors relaying the view from the helmet-cam of each unit leader. One of the screens showed a boot splintering a doorframe. The others displayed jiggling views of a dimly lit staircase.

"Units two through five, secure each floor before moving on. Unit six, guard the exit. Unit one, go straight to the top and secure the principal target," Glen said.

Tony felt slightly nauseated as one of the cameras continued its crazy wiggle upward. "Why can't they take the lift?"

"They always smell of piss," Frank said.

"Come on, that's such a cliché."

"Clichés come from somewhere, don't they? Every time we had to nick somebody in a tower block, we held our noses on the way up."

"So they don't have flushing toilets in their expensive flats and have to take a slash in the lift?"

"No, but little boys like to pee through the crack in the door to hear the noise it makes on the way down. It's worse in the bigger blocks, because there are more of the little toerags and they have more time in the lift to let it rip."

"It isn't because it smells of piss," Glen said. "It's too dangerous. When the door opens at the top, it would only take one grenade tossed in, and they'd all be dead."

As the lead team continued upward, the labored breathing of the soldiers apparent, Tony glanced at the other monitors. Door after door was kicked in to reveal uninhabited homes.

"Where is everybody?" Tony said.

"Maybe there weren't as many of them as we thought," Glen said. "As long as Archangel's up there, we're all good."

"They had guards yesterday," Tony said, beginning to get a bad feeling.

Unit one finally reached the top floor. The camera showed a view of a long, silent corridor. The soldiers edged along the wall, applying boot to wood at each apartment. Again, they were all empty. When they got to the last flat—the one with the lights on—the unit leader panned his camera around.

"Nobody here, sir," he said.

"Are we sure this is the right tower block?" Tony said.

In answer, the squad leader picked up a piece of paper from the coffee table and held it up to his camera. The Blood of Christ logo was visible at the top, although the resolution of the camera made it difficult to read the handwritten text.

"What's it say?" Frank asked.

"I will punish the world for its evil, and the wicked for their iniquity. I will halt the arrogance of the proud. Isaiah 13:11. You cannot stop us, Mr. Campbell. We are tools of the Lord's will. Archangel."

"They knew we were coming," Tony said, resisting the urge to punch the screen. "How did they know we were coming?"

"Somebody must have told them," Glen said.

"You mean we've got a leak?"

"They've got sympathizers everywhere."

This time Tony did wallop the screen, regretting the decision when it turned out to be hard glass. He communed with Spock briefly and, sucking his knuckles, turned to Frank. "Why didn't we post some lookouts after we found out where they were hiding?"

"We didn't want to take the chance of alerting them," Frank said.

Tony stood beneath the light and dropped his chin so it shone on the front of his head. An imaginary laser bored a hole between Frank's eyes. Frank, unaware his brain had just been turned into Swiss cheese, pulled at his ear. Tony sighed. Chewing Frank out would accomplish nothing now, so he kept his voice level and said, "Well, they were alerted. Find out who did it. We're going to get these sods. Next time I want them to know nothing until we hit them."

Frank nodded. "I'll get on it."

"We should head up there," Glen said. "Maybe they left something behind that'll help us figure out where they went."

They went up in the lift, which did indeed smell of piss. The strong stench of urine acted as smelling salts and helped clear Tony's head. This was nothing more than a setback. He only needed to keep Blood of Christ quiet for another week; with luck the disruption of having to move headquarters at such short notice would keep them occupied for that period.

When he entered Archangel's lair, there was nothing to suggest it had been the epicenter of a terrifying movement. Apart from the sheet of paper, everything had been cleared out save the bland Ikea furniture. They would get no leads here. Still, there must have been witnesses to the pullout. They would find these people, locate the new headquarters, and finish it once and for all. Feeling a lot better, he turned to leave. His satphone rang. He wrestled it out from the clip attached to his belt. God, he missed his mobile phone. This beast made him feel like a 1980s stock market trader.

"Hey, love," he said, expecting to hear Margot's voice. When he left before Vanessa woke, she always called so he could say good morning.

"Hello, Mr. Campbell. How do you like my apartment?"

Tony clamped his hand over the mouthpiece. "It's him. Get a trace on it!"

"We can't even trace a kid's drawing right now, never mind a satphone," Frank said. "Most of our tech got trashed when everybody went bonkers."

"Shit. Look, he knows we're here. That means somebody must be watching us. Get some men out and find them."

As soldiers ran from the room, Tony got back on the line. "How did you get this number?"

"Same place I got the information that you were coming after us. I just thought I'd say hello before I set off the explosives we've seeded through the building. So, hello. I'm pressing the button now."

Tony's bowels loosened. He couldn't even open his mouth to get out a warning. It would be too late anyway. They would never get down twenty-three floors before the bombs went off. As he waited for the boom that would herald his end, all he could think about was that there would be nobody left to protect Margot and Vanessa.

In lieu of a gigantic explosion, a tinny chuckle came from the phone. "Did I scare you? I just wanted you to know I could have killed you. But you're not my enemy, Mr. Campbell. I want to give you a chance to come over."

Tony, simultaneously weak with relief and throbbing with the desire to reach down the phone and pull out Archangel's larynx, took a few seconds to compose himself before replying. "Come over to what?"

"Our crusade. You can't deny this world has got out of control. Single mothers spitting out mewling brats, who will grow up to spit out more mewling brats ad infinitum. Muslims with five wives and thirty children, all of them determined to destroy Christianity. Godless, directionless hordes of atheists turning to tai chi and meditation to fill the gaping holes in their tawdry little souls. All of them destroying this beautiful world God gave us to watch over. Humanity is a plague, Mr. Campbell. It's time for a cull."

Even though his words were pure madness, Archangel's voice remained utterly reasonable, as though he were laying out the merits of building a new bypass.

"I'm asking you to stop this," Tony said. "If you keep trying to get the virus out, you'll get us all killed. Give us a chance."

"No, Mr. Campbell. You're going to get us killed by doing nothing. Do you think you can appease these people with your press releases and statements? If we die, God's purifying weapon dies with us. I cannot allow that."

"Killing isn't God's work."

"Have you read the Old Testament? God was partial to unleashing plagues upon those who displeased him. We have displeased him greatly this time. He created a world of balance and harmony. We have disturbed that harmony. Think of all the wars we have fought,

Mr. Campbell, of all the new diseases that nature produces, of all the famines and natural disasters. God has been trying to keep us in line for many years, trying to pare back our numbers. We kept pushing back with science and medicine and diplomacy, ignoring his message. Now he is taking drastic action, using the weapon of science against us. I am the instrument that will spread this, his greatest plague, and save our world."

"But you're talking about turning the whole world into murderers. They'll tear each other apart. Billions will die."

Glen frowned, and Tony realized that he wasn't sounding like a man who'd given the order to do exactly what Blood of Christ aimed to achieve. He put his hand over the mouthpiece. "I'm just trying to talk him down," he told Glen.

"Is it wrong?" Archangel said. "Consider the Last Supper. Jesus said, 'Anyone who eats my flesh and drinks my blood will have eternal life.' There is a precedent."

Tony decided to toss diplomacy out the window. "That was a metaphor, you bloody nutbag, not an invitation to cannibalism. Even if you're insane enough to take it literally, which you clearly are, he was asking his disciples to eat him. He wasn't inviting everybody to gnaw each other's faces."

"It was a message for the faithful," Archangel said, unperturbed by Tony's insult. "Make no mistake. We will cleanse the world, with you or without you. When we are finished, only a handful of true believers will stand to carry on God's work. It seems you won't be one of them. Good-bye, Mr. Campbell."

The line went dead, leaving Tony gaping at the phone.

"What'd he say?" Frank asked.

"To paraphrase: blah blah blah, I'm completely off my fucking trolley, blah blah blah," Tony said, shaking his head in wonder. "Keep looking for the mole and find out where Archangel's gone to. I'm going back to the office."

When Tony got downstairs, he waved away the driver. It had been months since he took public transport, and he felt the need to be amongst the people. Archangel's insanity had got him thinking. As far as he could tell, Moran had been a normal pastor before the virus. His mind must have cracked when he killed, and Tony wanted to gauge how widespread this mental instability was. He could only imagine what it must have been like to emerge from the viral daze with blood on your hands, for he'd never taken a life.

The self-inflicted blows to his head had kept him out for a day; when he finally came to, Margot and Vanessa were both infected—from the vaporized snot Margot said started exploding from his nose shortly after she emerged from the toilet. The first thing he did was hold them close, wetting their heads with his tears, and ask them to forgive him. Margot told him there was nothing to forgive, as he'd fought the virus, while Vanessa brushed it off as though he'd come home grumpy from the office. They holed up, living on chocolates and nuts raided from the minibars of other rooms, until the awful sound track of screams and gunfire receded. While the bloodshed was still going on, Tony had stayed far from the window, terrified that if he saw the carnage he would be seized with an urge to join in. When they finally emerged to trek home, the streets were empty save for twisted, ruined bodies thick with buzzing flies. He'd spent most of the days on the road with one hand supporting Vanessa's behind, the other over her eyes, wishing there was somebody to carry him and close his eyes. No, he hadn't killed—he'd never seen another uninfected person since—but that awful journey and the memory of what he'd almost done to his wife and child had been enough to push him close to the edge.

He walked to South Ealing tube station. It was still early, but when he boarded the train there were a few dozen early-morning commuters. He couldn't see any overt signs of mental torment. He didn't even know how many people had taken a life. The animals took care of a big chunk to start with, over ten million fled the country, and the army shot dead many more—most of the dead he saw seemed to have died from bullet wounds. Despite what zombie films would have people believe, he suspected it was damn hard to bite somebody to death. Then there were the famously bad British teeth. Overbites and teeth sprouting off in different directions would surely have hampered efforts to rip out a jugular. Plus you had to consider the speed with which the virus took over its host; many attacks would have been curtailed as victim and victimizer joined forces to look for fresh prey. Plenty of blunt force would have been applied, he supposed, which could account for a lot of deaths, and the mob factor definitely made it worse. Still, since he hadn't killed anyone it stood to reason there were many more in the same position. It was difficult to know, as nobody talked about that period: it was as though a collective amnesia had descended over the nation.

As the train filled up, he noticed something else. In his carriage at least four women were pregnant, and, up in the far corner, a couple was indulging in heavy petting. Everybody stared at them. Their soft moans and the vibration of the tube prompted movement down below. He crossed his legs. A slim young woman with red hair and full lips caught his eye and gave him a saucy smile. He smiled back and held up his ring finger. She pouted and turned her attention elsewhere.

He was struck then by the strange dichotomy of the virus: how people were so ashamed of their anger but embraced the sexual aspect. The animals had mindlessly humped whatever came within range, but they were prone to a spot of random humping anyway. And they never actually raped anybody: they couldn't exactly take off clothes with hooves or paws and wouldn't have known where to put it. As far as he could tell the urge to do violence had overwhelmed the sexual element in humans. Perhaps it was a matter of expediency: it was quicker to bite somebody and pass on the virus than struggle with clothing. Now there were no uninfected around to fully unleash the beast, the virus seemed to have turned Britain into a nation of full-time slappers, instead of only shaking off their straitlaced attitudes when under the influence of drugs and booze. *The Sun*, the only newspaper still publishing, predictably loved it and ran stories with headlines like, "Brits Go BONKers!"

Perhaps people were happier to give in because sex was fundamentally a consensual act, and both parties usually enjoyed it—unless the man had a hair trigger or thought foreplay consisted of shouting, "Brace yourself!" Violence, on the other hand, was rarely consensual. Perhaps it was a choice: when handed two opposing urges, one more benign than the other, the easiest course was to take the more pleasurable.

Rapists still raped of course, and Tony came down hard on any of-fenders, but rape was an act of violence. It was about power and con-trol, not about sex.

If only they could create a selective cure for the virus, one that lost violent impulses and kept the sexual ones. That way the country would be transformed from a dystopia to a utopia overnight, and they wouldn't have any problem getting the population back up quickly.

As he looked along the carriage, plastered with Keep Calm and Carry On ads, he understood most people were trying to have a normal life. Tony had spent far too long cloistered away in his offices and in the car and was beginning to wonder if he hadn't overestimated the sever-ity of the situation. Extreme cases aside, the virus seemed to have trans-lated into more arguments, a lot more sex, and an inability to queue. They'd become Italian. Of course, all of this only applied when the uninfected weren't around. The acid test would come if they ever got the chance to reintegrate with the world. For that to happen, they needed to learn to control themselves come the crunch. He was beginning to wonder if he should make an effort to engage with the people handing out the leaflets.

He looked again at his fellow passengers: his people, his responsi-bility. He focused on one woman, her hand supporting her protruding stomach, and imagined the baby growing within. If the attack took place, that unborn child and many like it, the epitome of innocence, would never have a chance to grow up. He wouldn't let that happen.

First, though, he had other matters to deal with. His erection was refusing to deflate by itself, and he caught himself checking out the redhead. He got off the train early, taking off his jacket and draping it over his arm so it hid his groin, with the intention of paying Margot a conjugal visit. There would be no point trying to work with such an insistent stiffy.

18

It took Lesley and Jack just half an hour to reach the outskirts of Aberdeen. Emboldened by the success of their disguise, they followed the main road, although they encountered no other people to further test the worth of the layer of dung. Lesley was perspiring from the effort of keeping up with Jack and the shit had begun to dry out and crack, save for the areas on her face, armpits, and small of her back, where sweat kept leaking out. They stopped at a roundabout beside a Royal Mail depot and looked down the dual carriageway leading into town. Crumpled cars ringed the side of the road, piled up like kids' toys.

"What d'you think?" Lesley said. "Should we risk going in?"

"I'm not sure. With the smell, they might mistake us for livestock. I understand they're partial to a bit of bestiality in this part of the world."

"If you make any sheep shagger jokes, you'll definitely be killed."

"We need to take the chance. It's our best chance of finding some kind of link with the outside world."

"It's also our best chance of being torn up into fleshy confetti."

"We're as good as dead anyway if we do nothing. Let's give it a go. If anybody seems even a tiny bit aggressive, we get the hell out of there."

Lesley trusted neither her legs nor the squeaky old bike to shake off any pursuit but followed when Jack headed down the road. They passed an old church in which the gravestones were half hidden by long grass, squat metal-roofed industrial units, and rows of silent houses, many of them with front doors ajar and windows broken. Lesley felt that eyes were watching them from within those homes where washing hung on the line or smoke trickled out of chimneys. Nobody came out to challenge them.

They passed several public phones, which neither of them had any money or credit cards to operate—although they did stop to pick one up and found no dial tone, which did not bode well. Still, there were plenty of shopping malls and Internet cafés in the town center. With luck one of them would be operating. She knew from *Twitter* and *Facebook* that some people in Britain were still getting online somehow. Not that they would go into the shops when people were there. They'd agreed they would keep moving and stay in the middle of the road, out of nostril range, until they identified a likely target. They would return in the dead of night to break in. With luck they would be able to pinch some food and cigarettes as well. Specifically, she was thinking about the Trinity Center. If memory served her correctly the streets around there were wide enough to give them breathing space, and it would let them figure out if it was open or not. She was hopeful it would be. People said cockroaches were most likely to survive an apocalypse. She'd always put her money on consumerism.

She took them over the road bridge. On the other side, a teenage boy had his girlfriend mashed up against a wall.

"Does he have his hand up her skirt?" Lesley said.

"Looks like it."

"Bit public for that, isn't it?"

As the bikes squeaked past, the teenagers broke off from their lusty wrestling and stared.

"Just act normal," Jack said.

Lesley gave them a cheery wave.

"I said act normal, not like an overfriendly nut job," Jack said.

"How can we act normal? We look like we've just been shat out of a giant's ring piece."

"At least can the waving."

As they cycled deeper into the city, more people appeared on the streets, all of them seemingly wandering with no apparent goal. Even though Lesley knew the stares they attracted were the result of ingrained Scottish nosiness and their bedraggled, grotty appearance, she began to sweat more heavily. In a way, it would have been easier to cope if everybody had looked like movie zombies: all rotting flesh, teeth gleaming from jawbones, and atrophied muscles, which would also have the added benefit of making them easier to run away from. They all just looked so damn normal, which meant it could be easy to fall into a potentially deadly state of relaxation.

"This was a very bad idea," Lesley said, as the crowds grew thicker.

"We'll be fine. Just keep going."

As if to back up Jack's message, she looked up and saw a huge banner draped across the road. White letters on a red background, beneath a picture of a crown, read, "Keep Calm and Carry On." Underneath, however, some wag had spray painted "Eating Brains."

"The mall's just ahead," she said. "Let's have a quick look and get the hell out of here."

At the junction with Union Street, Lesley took them right. People wandered in and out of the mall doors, which stood open beneath the vaulted window and spires of the old building that modernity had converted to a collection of chain stores. The obvious differences from her last visit were the reduced numbers, fewer and less bulging shopping bags, and the guards in makeshift uniforms flanking the entrance. Another thing she noticed was the absence of phones. Normally every second person would have a smartphone jammed in their face to the exclusion of the outside world, texting, surfing the Web, or posting banal *Facebook* updates. Now people appeared to be talking to each other or taking in their surroundings. As refreshing as that was, it reminded her of the communications blackout. Still, the mall was open. The problem was that if it was guarded during the day, it would definitely be guarded at night. No doubt there were all kinds of desperate characters around, such as themselves, who wouldn't be averse to a spot of breaking and entering.

Jack, seemingly reading her mind, said, "We should go in now."

"Do you think they'd let us into a mall looking like this?"

"We could pretend we're an experimental dance troupe."

Lesley didn't dignify that with an answer.

They were both looking at the entrance, so neither of them saw the little girl step onto the road until the last minute. Lesley jammed on her brakes and stopped with her front tire inches from the girl's legs.

Jack juddered to a halt beside her. The girl was dressed in a ratty-looking jumper and jeans smeared with dirt. Her face was so thin that her sad green eyes looked huge, almost alien in size.

"Do you have any food, missus?" the girl said, revealing a gap where her front teeth had dropped out.

She reached out a wavering hand and Lesley's heart almost broke. The little girl was probably an orphan, roaming the streets and relying on charity. For the first time, she believed absolutely in the rightness of their quest to stop the bombing. This hungry child was no monster. At that moment, a droplet of sweat ran from Lesley's nose and landed on the girl's palm. She snapped her hand back as though it had been burned by acid. The hand drew up to her mouth and she licked the sweat. Her lips pulled back and her eyes seemed to darken. She let out a high-pitched growl as her hands curled up into clawed fists.

"Food!" she screamed. "Give me some food, you big poo-poo head."

Lesley backed off, the sweat now burning hot on her chilled skin. Around her, all motion stopped, as though God had pressed pause on the remote control to nip out for a cup of tea. Jack broke the paralysis by planting his foot in the girl's scrawny chest and shunting her out of the way.

"Move!" he shouted.

Lesley shoved off and set to pedaling furiously, the adrenaline turning her into a drug-enhanced Lance Armstrong. Jack swerved to the left down a narrow cobbled street, and as Lesley turned she looked back. Weirdly, not everybody was coming after them. Some started running, and then stopped to clutch their heads. Others stood by the side of the road, just staring. Still others were walking swiftly in the other direction, most of them women. These were in the minority, however: the little girl was lost in the throng of people pelting up the road. The contents of shopping bags became missiles: shoes, books, tinned goods, and other objects soared through the air like a hail of arrows and clattered onto the cobbles behind them.

"I told you this was a very fucking bad idea," Lesley shouted.

Jack didn't respond, concentrating on dodging a cluster of pedestrians ahead. Guttural yells and pounding footsteps echoed off the high walls of the gray granite buildings that penned them in. She felt the way Fanny must have when she went down under the weight of the pigs. She was trying to save these things—after her flash of sympathy she wasn't feeling kindly enough disposed to think of them as people—and they just wanted to bite her face off.

They wound through the streets and zipped past other Aberdonians. The only thing that kept them alive was the fact that the people ahead of them didn't quite realize what was going on until they'd passed, at which point they were sucked into the ever-expanding crowd. The mob stretched behind them in a ragged vortex of hundreds of screaming maniacs, among them a young mother pushing a pram and somebody in a motorized wheelchair. As the mob swelled, so did the chorus of voices. Those ahead of them began to react quicker, forcing them to bob and weave. By this point, Lesley had lost any sense of where she was. In any case Jack was out in front, changing direction at random intervals. He was starting to pull away as her exhausted body, deprived of food for well over a day, began to falter. The sounds of pursuit were louder now.

They found themselves on a long road with a large red brick building topped by a turret on their right-hand side. A roundabout ahead linked to a main thoroughfare. With luck it would give them a straight run out of town on which they could outpace the mob—provided her legs held out. She was just beginning to feel faint stirrings of hope when she heard the grinding of a locked chain. Jack flew over the handlebars and hit the ground face-first. Her heart thudding, she braked and leaned over to grab his hand. He looked up at her, blood leaking from grazed skin. From his dazed eyes she could tell he couldn't run, which he would have to do: his own bike was ruined, and two of them on her old banger would spell certain death.

"Get up," she shouted all the same.

"Go," Jack said. "Go, or else they've won."

She looked back and saw the tidal wave of infected course down the street. Still she couldn't bring herself to go and leave somebody else to die thanks to her bad mojo. Jack settled it for her, somehow pulling himself up, brushing off her hand, and staggering toward the infected. She got the bike moving as well as she could, willing herself not to look. When a savage roar went up from the mob, she couldn't help herself. Where Jack had been, dozens of bodies lay heaped on the ground, squirming and roiling and scratching and punching each other to reach down to the center of the maelstrom. Many of those following on either dived in or tripped over the growing pile. Soon the whole roundabout was filled with writhing bodies.

Through a blurry haze of tears, which made it seem as though she were driving a car through a downpour, she saw a small street on the left and took it. She turned and turned and turned through a maze of houses. Ahead, a door opened in one of the many gray homes that lined the streets. A man popped his head out and beckoned. "In here, quickly."

If this man was infected and she went inside, she would be dead for sure. But he didn't seem to be reacting to her presence, and there had to be some immune people in the country. If she kept going she would be caught and Jack would have died for nothing. She cycled toward the door, which opened directly onto the pavement, and the occupant moved back to let her bump up into the hallway. He locked and bolted the door and pointed up the stairs.

"Get to the back of the house," he said. "Don't look out the window."

She crawled up the stairs and curled up in a corner, putting a hand over her mouth to stifle her sobs. The sound of those pursuers who hadn't joined in the gruesome pile-on grew until they were beneath the window. For one horrible moment she thought they'd stopped, but the footsteps pounded on. It took almost five minutes for them all to pass. When they'd finally gone, she was shaking so hard her head kept bouncing off the floor.

Her rescuer came up the stairs, breathing deeply and muttering something to himself. He stopped near the top, so his eyes were level with Lesley's, and held something out. "Here, take this. It'll help."

She saw the smoldering tip and grabbed for the cigarette. Her lungs rebelled as the sweet smoke funneled in. Once the coughing fit passed, she took another draw. A soothing limpness bathed her muscles. She looked at the cigarette and saw that it was a very fat joint, which she proceeded to smoke in its entirety. After, the edge taken off her shock by the dope fugue, she lay in the corner. Her host sat quietly on the stairs.

Jack wasn't a good friend, that was true, but they'd spent many hours together over the last few months. She'd liked him. And he'd undoubtedly saved her life by turning back and forcing her to leave him. She knew he hadn't done it for her specifically: the story needed to get out. The powers that be had almost got exactly what they wanted: both of them dead and no need to explain it away. Well, they were going to be disappointed. She just wished her big scoops didn't always have to be tinged with the blood of those who'd died trying to get them out. It was just another part of the awful loop she appeared to have been thrown into. The anger she felt at her predicament and yet another death gave her strength to sit up. She looked at the man who'd given her refuge. He had brown hair, neatly parted, tiny dots for eyes that may have been a result of earlier indulgence in the industrial-grade weed, and a chin cleft she could have parked her bicycle in if he lay down.

"How did you know they were after me?" she asked, her voice hoarse from a combination of fleeing, crying, and smoking.

"They make a very distinctive noise when they're on the hunt," he said. "You can hear them a mile off. When I saw you bombing up the road looking petrified, it wasn't difficult to figure out who you were running from."

"Does that happen a lot?"

"Not anymore. It's a bit like making popcorn. Loads and loads of pops at the start and then just a few until it dies away. There can't be many uninfected people left. You're only the second I've seen in the last six months. I'm curious to hear where you came from."

Lesley told him, and his eyes widened until they were just about normal size. "Fuck. How long have we got until they start bombing?"

"What's today's date?"

"April the eighth."

"Seven days. If I get this story out, there's a chance they'll be forced to stop. A very slim chance, but it's worth a shot. Is there anywhere I can get online or make a call?"

"I think I can help you. This might be a good point to introduce myself. My name's Tom Dixon."

"Lesley McBrien."

She held out her hand, but Tom shied away.

"Ah, sorry," Lesley said. "I forgot about the shit."

"I did wonder about that."

"To block out our smell. It was working, too, until I turned into sweaty Betty."

And got Jack killed, she thought.

"Before we go on, there's something you should know. I've got the virus."

Lesley stared at him. "No, you don't. You're not like them."

"Because I choose not to be."

"You're serious," she said, trying to figure out if she could hurdle the banister and get past him.

He backed down the stairs. "I'm going to go into the living room. If you want to leave, you can. First, have a look in the room behind you and read what's there. Then, if you want, we can talk."

Once he was gone, Lesley looked long and hard at the front door. Then, with a sigh, she pushed open the door to the spare room. Inside were boxes and boxes of leaflets. She picked one up and began to read, squinting to get her revolving pupils in focus. Excitement mounted as she understood the significance of the pamphlet, and for a moment she put aside her guilt over Jack. She hurried downstairs, barely giving the door a glance, and went into the living room.

"This really works?"

"We're having a conversation, aren't we?"

"How many of you are there?"

"In total, across the country, a few hundred. But the numbers are growing."

"This is amazing. It's proof that Britain isn't a lost cause."

"My thoughts exactly."

"Are you the leader? I can interview you and make it part of the story. They'll have to call off the attack."

"I'm not the person you should speak to."

"Can you introduce me?"

"Yes, but we'll need to go to the base. This is just a staging point for distributing leaflets: my old bachelor pad. If we go, you can get your story out from there. We have a satellite."

"Then let's go."

"It's about one hundred fifty miles away by bicycle, with a lot of hills."

"Ah," Lesley said.

"Exactly. Let's wait until the morning and leave before dawn. You need to get your strength back to make it, and we need to make sure the streets are empty. We don't want a repeat of today."

The new lease of life ebbed away at the thought of a long trek across the country. She flopped down on the sofa. "Is it going to be dangerous? Should I keep my poo cloak on?"

"We should be safe enough once we're out of the city. Most of the villages emptied out because of the bandits."

"Bandits? I have to warn you, people die around me."

"Don't worry, they tend to raid the cities now. There's nothing for them out there. So, I'd appreciate it if you had a shower. You're a bit whiffy."

"Do you have any food?"

"Beans and custard."

"Not together, I hope."

Tom smiled. "We're not that uncivilized. Shower's upstairs. You can take your pick of my clothes, although they may be a bit baggy on you."

He lit another joint and pottered off to the kitchen while Lesley went up and stood under a hot shower, clogging up the drain with clumps of dung. Fatigue took hold, and her thoughts turned dark again. She wondered if Jack's body, what little remained of it, was still lying in the middle of the roundabout or if there was a cleanup crew who would come and take him away. There would be no decent burial for him, and she couldn't go back out there to collect his corpse—it was too dangerous, and she wouldn't be able to face the ruined body of the latest casualty in the relentless rise of the Lesley McBrien brand.

No matter what she did—whether she worked hard or skived, whether she was good or bad at her job—elements of the story she needed always seemed to land in her lap against all laws of probability.

She survived. Others died. It seemed she was little more than a black hole that sucked up the luck of those foolish enough to get involved with her. She didn't want this luck anymore. But she couldn't change what had happened. All she could do for Jack now was make sure his death was not in vain by getting this story out. This time she would make sure the dead would get their due. He would be the hero, not her.

19

The rabbit and parsnip stew, made possible by Fanny's return the previous night with a cluster of the small animals, scalded Ruan's gullet as she chowed down. She didn't care. She was still recovering from her hand-to-mouth existence and shoveled everything down her throat as if she were a competitor at a speed-eating contest. Her longing for a juicy tin of Pedigree Chum seemed a distant and disgusting memory and she could already feel the extra weight piling onto her thighs, a process aided and abetted by no longer spending half her time cycling over hill and glen.

For the first few days in the commune, she'd remained wary. However, as she worked safely in the printing press or under the bright lights of the vegetable greenhouse, and even took a combat yoga lesson from Nayapal, she began leaving her door unlocked at night. More than anything, she reveled in having human company again. She said nothing of any import. Nobody seemed keen to talk about the past; she was with them on that score. Still, it felt so good just to be able to open her mouth and get a response that, on the second day, she turned off her useless mobile phone and left it in her rucksack. She couldn't quite bring herself to delete all of the messages to Bridget, though: they served as a chronicle of her time on the run, and she still nurtured a faint hope that one day the Internet would come back on and the device would light up with messages from her friend.

Fanny's troupe was committed, hardworking, and organized, printing thousands of leaflets each day from their stockpile of paper. Bicycle couriers came and went, panniers laden with their message of hope, dope, and regular sex or masturbation—the latter, Scott told her, inspired by the fact that Fanny's son, who it turned out was still alive and had left the country, had been an unstoppable wanking machine. Tom disappeared to take care of distribution on the east coast, carrying Ruan's message with him, but the rest of them never left the compound except to hunt. At the center of the activity, like a benign spider who praised and cajoled the flies in her web rather than sucking them dry, sat Fanny. She possessed a natural authority that permeated the camp and brought harmony where discord could easily flourish. Ruan suspected that without her it would all fall apart.

It was this calmness and normality—the proof that resistance was possible after all—that led her mind down paths it didn't want to travel but, in the end, couldn't avoid.

The Rest and Reception camp had been a novelty on the first night— more like a camping holiday without the grief of fumbling with tent poles while being eaten alive by midges than a frightened huddle against nature's unleashed savagery. It struck Ruan as odd that the army had scooped up as many people as it could from within the city's urban armor and plonked them in the countryside—which did seem a more likely place for zombie animals to congregate. She suspected that this was the emergency plan the government had put in place for major threats, which it probably expected would revolve around dirty bombs rather than mad cows, and that it was sticking to it for want of any better ideas. Ruan would much rather have holed up in her bedroom, several floors up and therefore a safe haven from any barmy bovines, and glued her nose to her laptop. Still, the camp seemed safe enough: the previous occupants had been despatched in a speedy cull, the waters of the Firth of Forth provided a natural barrier to intrusion on one side, and the perimeter fence took care of the rest.

The novelty soon faded. Unlike Butlins, the camp didn't have sports facilities or a bar she could sneak drinks from, there was no Wi-Fi or even power sockets for her computer and phone, and they had to share with another family. As a result, the tent swiftly began to smell as ripe as her unwashed sports kit after a week stuffed under her bed. She was just grateful that Bryan had gone down to visit a friend in Leeds before the virus broke out. The musk of teenage boy would have pushed the pong levels beyond her tolerance. Still, she made the best of it: getting out of the tent to run as often as possible and spending the rest of her time down by the water, reading the sports psychology books she'd borrowed from the library the day before the evacuation.

She was doing just that after dinner, about a week into her stay, when she heard shouting from the direction of the main entrance. That wasn't unusual: tempers were fraying as people used to coming home to a comfy sofa and giant television rubbed up against each other. She'd witnessed three scuffles, all of them involving people who looked like the only thing they'd ever battered was a fish for tea. While the latest kerfuffle was probably just another uncoordinated slap fest, she set off in search of some voyeuristic entertainment. The last real excitement had come two days before, when an enterprising soldier used a combine harvester to take out a seething carpet of zombie rabbits bearing down on the camp, spraying fluffy bunny gore into the bucket, while his mates crisped those bouncy enough to avoid the grinding blades with flamethrowers. They hadn't even bothered cleaning up, which meant the acrid smell of hundreds of decomposing bunnies drifted through the camp when the wind blew in their direction.

As she drew closer, somebody let out a piercing scream. The only time she'd ever heard a noise like it was when a teammate tumbled from her bike and snapped her arm clean in two. Another shriek rent the air above the babble of voices. She heard a succession of little pops, followed by more screams. The hairs on her neck wafted upward and she did a U-turn. When she got back to the tent, it was empty. She'd forgotten her mum and dad were "going for a walk"—which, from their happy smiles after they came back from such excursions, she took to mean, "We're going to the toilets to get frisky because that's the only place we can get any privacy." She had no idea where the other family was. While Ruan didn't know exactly what was going on, her body's primal response told her it was bad. She struck off in the direction of the closest set of portaloos and knocked on every door, hoping to find her mum and dad. All she got was a succession of people telling her to fuck off. The next closest block was back in the direction of the awful

many-throated voice, which grew louder and hoarser with every passing minute, so she squeezed between two portaloos and, using one as
leverage, got on top of the other to get a better view. The loo she'd
kicked off toppled sideways and hit the next. The domino effect went
as far as three toilets, prompting sloshing and more swearing. She ignored it.

At first she saw nothing but thrashing tent tops. She could hear faint
and regular pops beneath the crowd noise, like the imperfections on
the old jazz albums her dad listened to, from the automatic weapons
soldiers in the perimeter towers were unloading into the area where
the tents shook. The closest tower, only about fifty feet away, began
to vibrate and the soldier pointed his weapon downward. A man in a
bright blue jumper scrambled into view above the tents, going hand
over hand up the struts of the tower. A red spray materialized around
his head and he fell, but others took his place. Ruan's legs turned to
jelly and she almost slipped from the roof. The virus had crossed to
humans.

Not more than ten feet away, a woman appeared in one of the smaller
lanes that snaked off from the camp's main thoroughfare. Clumps had
been torn from her voluminous head of blond hair, and blood ran down
her forehead. Her eyes, blue and unblinking, completed the impression of a raggedy child's doll tossed aside to rot in the corner. Without
a moment's hesitation she sprinted toward the portaloo, shrieking as
she came. From that moment on everything became a blur of unthink-
ing, adrenaline-filled fear. Ruan jumped from her vantage point, but
before she could rise from her landing crouch, the blond woman
pounced. Ruan had enough time to raise an arm, which the woman
seemed to take as an invitation to dinner. The pain that flashed up
Ruan's nerve endings from the bite prompted a wave of anger, which
transmitted itself back down her right arm. She balled a fist and hammered the woman repeatedly in the temple. The attacker rolled backward under the force of the assault, buying Ruan the time she needed
to find her feet and run to the main avenue.

Just before she turned toward the sea, Ruan glimpsed a pack running toward her. She didn't wait to find out if they were pursuers or
pursued. Now she was on the avenue, rutted from the tramp of thou-

sands of feet or not, nobody would catch her. As she sprinted, she realized that even though the bite had broken skin, she felt no desire to attack the campers who were poking their heads fearfully out of their tents.

"Run!" she shouted, not waiting to find out if they took her advice. Within thirty seconds, her feet were crunching on pebbles. She kicked off her shoes and plunged into the sea, settling into a powerful crawl before the freezing water could shock her muscles into immobility. Locked into the easy, simple motion, her whirring mind shut down for a few minutes. She snapped back to herself in a moment of reeling vertigo and remembered her parents. She spun and saw the tents were a few hundred meters away, although they were partially obscured by a mass of people on the shoreline. On the fringes of the struggling crowd, figures were spilling into the water or spreading off in both directions on the land. It was too late to return. She allowed herself one roar of anguish before shutting down the panic with several swift blinks and completing a slow circle. Nowhere on the mainland would be safe. The genie was out of the bottle, and it would quickly flit across the country. Her only option lay out where the firth began to widen into the North Sea: Inchkeith, the abandoned island where a lighthouse spun its circle of light by night. She put her head down and swam.

When Ruan finally hauled herself onto the island, which was little more than a craggy slice of rock that rose vertiginously from the sea, her muscles were trembling with fatigue and her body was chilled to its core. On a slanting slope to her left lay a cluster of old stone buildings. She made her way across but found they were crumbling, doors and windows open to the elements. She trudged up the steep path to the lighthouse. When she got to the yellow building, which looked like a miniature castle with a large metal lamp plopped on top, she smashed a window and undid the latch. Once inside, she stripped off her light summer dress and underwear and mounted the stairs. In the lamp chamber, she draped her clothes across the light to dry when it turned on. Then she crouched shivering in the corner, listening to the wind howl and staring in the direction of the distant camp. She looked down at her bleeding arm, almost willing the rage to come. Anything would be better than this emptiness. When nothing happened, she began slamming her fist methodically against the toughened glass.

At some point she fell into an uneasy sleep, punctuated by flashes of light that illuminated dreams of running back through the camp, searching for her parents as unearthly screams whistled through rows of blank tents. When she woke, the sun was up and the lamp had fallen still. She slipped on her now dry clothes and went outside. She looked across to Edinburgh. It was too far to see any movement, but columns of smoke drifted over the rooftops. When the wind gusted toward her from the city, she heard a faint jumble of roars, shouts, and screams. She refused to think of her parents as dead or turned. In any zombie movie, there were always survivors. Her mum and dad were the kind of smart and resourceful people who fit that bill. She imagined them waiting in the plastic cocoon of their portaloo for the madness to recede, flitting through the bloody streets of Edinburgh and holing up in their apartment. She would swim across to the city once she'd regained her strength and the city sounded less insanely violent and find them there.

She spent the next two days trying to catch the skittish seagulls, until she finally admitted defeat and chewed grass. It left a bitter taste in her mouth and brought wrenching stomach cramps, lurid green diarrhea, and a fever. On the fourth day, she looked down upon the beach and saw a young seal sunning itself on the rocks. Her head, which had been part of campaigns to stop seals being clubbed to death by evil Scandinavians, said no. Her stomach shouted it down with a vehement yes. She grabbed the largest rock she could find and crept to the edge of the bluff overlooking the beach. The drop was only six feet, so she leapt down and landed close to the animal. She expected it to scoot toward the water and got ready to pursue. Instead, it lifted its sleek snout and looked at her with baleful eyes. With a noise like the bark of an effeminate dog, it flopped toward her.

"You, too?" she said, her voice cracked. "What are you going to do: slap me to death with your fins?"

The seal opened its mouth wide and displayed rows of incisors that wouldn't have looked out of place on a lion. Had she been less hungry,

she would have run. Instead, she dodged its clumsy lunge, planted her
behind on its back and beat it on the back of the skull until it lay still.
She searched until she found a sharp rock and, gritting her teeth, set
about butchering. A few hours later, her hands were raw and chunks
of seal meat and blubber were piled up on one side. She tried for hours
to start a cook fire, fruitlessly rubbing sticks and stones in increasingly
frantic combinations. It took her another few hours of staring at the
meat, knowing it was infected but also aware that she must be immune,
before she fell upon it. She bit into the salty, livery flesh and chewed
it down between labored breaths, pretending it was sushi.

One week in, the fever dreams intruded on her waking hours, making her jump at every flicker of movement, and she knew she had to
risk the swim before she grew too weak. In her fragile condition, the
crossing almost killed her: at one point, not far from the shore, she suc-
cumbed and slipped under the water. Luckily the rising slope of the
seabed was just beneath her toes, allowing her to bob back up and close
the remaining distance to the beach that ran along Leith Docks. She'd
timed it so she would arrive around dusk, but it was far too early to
consider venturing into the city proper. Just beyond where the beach
gave way to loose soil, a squat stone tower jutted from the earth. She
leaned against it and scanned the deserted docklands. Feeling reason-
ably secure for the moment, although keeping one eye on the water in
case any zombie seals came flopping after her—a fear that had caused
her great stress in the water, where she didn't have the advantage her
biped status afforded her on land—she settled down to wait in sopping
wet clothes that at least cooled her fever.

When the glowing digits of her waterproof watch told her it was
3:00 a.m., she set off. She encountered her first dead body just outside
the docks. The darkness spared her any visual details, although her
nostrils were given a full whiff of decay. As she moved deeper into the
city, ducking from doorway to doorway, broken glass from storefronts
glittered in the faint moonlight and everywhere dark stains blotched
the pavement. The streets were eerily empty. She made a quick pit
stop to grab a box of powdered antibiotics and a large tub of paracetamol
from the jumbled contents of a smashed-up pharmacy.

Only when she'd reached the apartment did she remember she had no key. She considered climbing up the side of the building, as the deep gaps between the blocks provided handholds, but rejected it. She was weak and couldn't take the risk of falling and spraining her ankle or worse. She jammed her finger on the buzzer. After what felt like an eternity of standing in the exposed street, her dad answered.

"I've got a gun, so you'd best be on your way," he said.

Ruan pressed her mouth against the wall to muffle her squeal of delight. She'd known they would be alive. Everything was going to be okay.

"It's me, Dad."

"Ruan?" he said. "You're alive. Thank God, you're alive!"

In the background, she heard her mum babble excitedly as the door buzzed open. She took the stairs two at a time. Security chains rattled and keys turned in locks, then she heard footsteps on the landing above. As she rounded the final bend she saw their familiar silhouettes standing side by side at the top of the stairs.

"Mum! Dad!" she shouted, not caring who heard.

As she continued upward, a growl echoed through the stairwell. Her first thought was that a dog must have been taking shelter in the building. Just as she was about to bound up the final set of steps, she realized it was coming from her dad. She froze. There was something wrong with their silhouettes: they seemed bunched, vibrating with tension. Her dad sneezed, before he spoke. "Where have you been? Your mother was worried sick."

Something had changed in the time it took her to climb the stairs. His voice was low, hard, and choppy—as though he was a mechanical replica of her dad, and somebody was turning a crank to get the sentence out. Her mum shook her head before her voice broke into a yell that held a timbre all too familiar to the screeching in the camp. "We bought you everything you ever wanted, let you do whatever you wanted, and now you do this to us. You need some discipline, you spoiled little brat!"

Then they were coming down the stairs.

This can't be happening, Ruan thought numbly. *It's just the fever.*

Her mum got there first and grabbed her hair. Moments later, her dad punched her on the side of the head. Within seconds, she became a bone between two snarling, snapping dogs. When her mum sank her teeth into Ruan's shoulder and bit down hard, her mind shrank away from this awful reality. She mentally switched her mum with the blond woman in the camp and her dad with a savage stranger. Her elbow snapped up and hammered into the woman's face, forcing her to release her grip. She put both hands into the man's chest and pushed with all her strength. His hands came free and she fell backward, twisting to face back down the stairwell. She landed heavily, but immediately got back to her feet and ran.

At the bottom of the stairs, she yanked on the handle before remembering she had to release the lock. She pressed the button and opened the door just wide enough to slip out. She pulled it shut. A second later the man slammed up against the glass. So distorted was his face—neck muscles corded, eyes popping from his head, teeth clamped together in frustrated rage—that it made it easy to believe the fiction he wasn't her dad. He hauled on the door, too far gone to remember the button, as the woman thumped up alongside him and scrabbled at the glass. Ruan didn't even look at her. She just turned and ran.

During the subsequent months on the road, Ruan had never blamed her parents for what they did; after all, she'd never seen evidence that somebody with the virus could behave any other way in her presence. When she realized Fanny and her troupe were fighting their urges, her first thought had been to pass this technique on to her parents in the hope they could be together again. With every day that passed in which nobody attacked her, she began to reevaluate. Not one of these people knew her or felt anything for her, yet they controlled themselves. Her parents, with a lifetime of supposedly loving her behind them, had shown no such restraint. Then there were the hurtful things her mother said, which had to have come from somewhere. What kind of parents, no matter how sick, tried to kill their child?

On the fourth day, a new recruit came in with one of the couriers—a middle-aged man who appeared to give physical form to the phrase "mild mannered." Ruan was confined to quarters to head off any potential incidents but watched from her window as Fanny sat him down cross-legged on the pier and took him through a series of breathing exercises. After a while, Fanny brought out a chicken and sat it in front of him. He lunged forward, grabbed the bird and bit its head off. Fanny let him pull off the wings and beat the body on the ground until he was spent and blood speckled his glasses. Nayapal led the newcomer, now weeping and spitting out feathers, to one of the hangars. Fanny saw Ruan watching and came over.

"We'll keep him there until he can be trusted," she said. "You won't be in any danger."

"Was that a test?"

"Yes, to judge his levels of anger."

"You mean it varies?"

"Absolutely. Some people are better at reining themselves in; women more so than men."

"You have more men here, though."

"Andy, Scott, and Tom were pacifists. And they're pretty metrosexual. We have more women in the network across the country."

"So that guy was one of the angry ones? He looked so harmless."

"It's always the meek ones you have to watch out for. They've usually got a lifetime of rage to come out."

Ruan thought again of her parents. Perhaps she'd been deluding herself that they loved her. Sure, they'd backed her in whatever she wanted to do and never showed any overt signs of resentment at the sacrifices they must have made for her and her brother, but that's what all parents did for their children. It was an automatic response, built into the genes just as much as the urges that the virus amplified. There was nothing special about a parent caring for the fruit of their loins, no matter how intense and wonderful that relationship seemed to the child. Her whole life may have been a lie.

"Why use a bird?" Ruan asked, trying to distract herself from this painful train of thought. "Couldn't you just annoy him? Call him speccy or something and see how angry he gets?"

"The point of this is ultimately to reintegrate with the world, and that means being able to control ourselves around uninfected beings. We don't get angry enough with each other to really test it."

"So was I a guinea pig?"

Fanny looked uncomfortable. "Not purposely. I mean, I didn't help you for that reason. But it did cross my mind when you came back."

"Human testing always follows on from animal, right?"

"I know it sounds bad, but I wasn't taking any risks. I controlled myself, and I trusted everybody else to do the same. They all graduated by not killing the bird."

"But they all killed it the first time?"

"More or less. Some did it straight away, some held out for a few minutes. This one will take a bit of conditioning. If it's even possible. Some people just can't help themselves. We've had to let a few go."

That almost everybody killed the bird could serve in mitigation for her mother and father, and for a moment Ruan seized on it. Then again, she wasn't a bird. She was their child. Fanny had said that people needed to choose which side of the line they stood on. Her parents had made their choice, and that knowledge cut Ruan far deeper than any of the physical wounds she'd suffered. Even when the newcomer was locked away and Ruan was free to roam the camp once more, she lay on the bed, blinking until her eyes ached as she rewrote history. Time and again she replayed the scene of returning home, gradually replacing the reality with an alternative scene in which she pressed the buzzer to no avail. When she emerged from the room, she'd just about convinced herself that her parents were dead. This was her home now.

She encountered one other wrinkle in her attempt to build this new life—something she'd been expecting ever since she met Rory. He began following her around, not quite brave enough to talk to her, and she began to find little origami flowers on her bed in the evening. One day the flowers were accompanied by an unsigned note that said, "I fancy you." She tried to ignore it, as she'd ignored so many such clumsy advances in the past, but she could tell from the way Rory was beginning to look at her more openly, a hurt look on his face, that pretending it wasn't happening wouldn't cut it. Then, the day before, the approach she'd been dreading occurred. She was down by the water's edge, washing the dishes after lunch, when she heard tentative footsteps on the pebbles behind her. Turning, she saw Rory standing there, swishing the stones with his trainers.

"Have you been getting my flowers?" he said, looking at the tops of his shoes.

"Oh, they're from you," she said. "Thank you. They're lovely."

He looked up briefly and gave her a shy smile. He was kind of cute, she supposed, but God was he young. His cheeks were ruddy with the bloom of adolescence behind soft fuzz that heralded the beard that would one day, many years from now, take root in the Noel Edmonds–manner of his relatives. She couldn't stand such coyness. What she looked for in boyfriends was a confident maturity that only began to take shape once the early hormone storm settled down, usually in the early twenties. Her problem had been that most of those men wouldn't come near her despite their obvious desire—the French geography teacher who'd taken her virginity during a blissful weeklong exchange trip aside—as she was the very definition of jail bait: underage, fully developed physically, and looking for somebody way out of her age bracket. Now it didn't matter, as she'd celebrated her sixteenth birthday alone in an abandoned house with a bowl of Pedigree Chum topped with a single candle.

So, Rory just didn't fit her profile, even if you put aside the fact he had the virus. It didn't matter in terms of infection risk, but she suspected that once an infected person's dander was up violence could follow if they were getting it on with somebody uninfected. Her room was next to the one shared by Eva and Scott, and she'd heard them going at it. Their lovemaking involved lots of slapping and guttural, angry shouts, although she supposed they could always have been into S&M. Anyway, if she were to take the chance, it wouldn't be with a downy-faced boy who would probably spurt in his pants if she so much as cocked a hip in his general direction.

Rory stepped closer. He was wearing tight jeans, and with horror Ruan saw a lazy stirring of denim. She jumped up, clutching the bowl of dishes to her chest to hide the obvious spur for his growing arousal. "I'd better be going now. I need to stack these."

"Wait!" Rory said as she edged away. "I was wondering if you wanted to have dinner tonight. Just you and me."

His voice was tinged with desperation. She felt sorry for him, but it would be kinder to put a stop to it right now. "I'm sorry, Rory. I don't think that's a good idea."

If his face had fallen any farther it would have slipped off his skull and plopped to the ground. "You don't like me."

"It's not that. I'm just not ready to see anybody."

"So you might be in a while? Once you feel more comfortable?"

Shit, she thought. *Now I've given him hope.*

To illustrate the point, his trouser front twitched further. In an effort to ease her discomfort, she imagined it as a wobbly slug balancing on two new potatoes. This image made her giggle.

"You're laughing at me," Rory said, his fists clenching. Ruan edged sideways, looking to move around him, but he blocked her path. "You shouldn't laugh at me."

The bowl of dishes was just about to be tossed into his face when Scott, who'd been composting vegetable peels nearby, hurried over and placed his huge paw on Rory's shoulder. "I need you to help me with the vegetables."

Rory started. The petulant look of a little boy caught with his hand in his dad's wallet replaced the gnarled tension of his jawbone. "We were just talking, weren't we?"

Backing his lie with a dip of her chin, Ruan hurried off. For the rest of the day Rory avoided her as much as possible, eating his meals alone and no doubt nursing a sense of injustice. It was something he would have to get used to, for the world had become a very unjust place. That night, she'd locked her door again. Even now, as everybody else ate, she could see him crouched by the water, staring disconsolately into the lake—the wilderness equivalent of sitting on the stairs at a party and hoping a girl will take pity on you.

Ruan had just swallowed her last mouthful of stew when the throb of engines disturbed the calm. Suddenly everybody was on their feet and running to where they kept their weapons. Fanny picked up her bow, Scott grabbed a large wooden staff, and Andy returned with an egg in each hand. Ruan sprinted to her room to gather her gun and sword, and returned to join the line that faced the entrance. The engines cut off and a tense silence followed. When somebody came running down the road, Ruan flicked off the safety. The figure re-solved into a young boy with red hair and a flopping gait. She drew a bead on him, but Fanny slapped her arm down. She was too far away to stop Andy, who'd coiled back his arm. An egg arced through the air and exploded on the boy's forehead. Ruan almost applauded.

The intruder stopped to wipe off the sticky mess. "Who throws an egg?" he shouted. "It's in my contact lens."

Ruan relaxed. A raging infected human wouldn't have been stopped by something as paltry as a well-thrown chicken fetus. She felt an immediate kinship. This boy had to be immune, like her.

"Geldof?" Fanny said, half stepping forward.

What kind of idiot calls their kid Geldof? Ruan thought.

"Mum?" Geldof said, wiping egg out of his eyes. "Mum!"

He broke into a wobbly sprint again.

That answers that question, Ruan thought. *Lucky I didn't say it out loud.*

20

Geldof ran toward his mum, forgetting the egg slicking his forehead, the anguished months when he thought she was dead, the years when their relationship had been defined by strife. He became a young child again, with no complications to get in the way of the simple yearning to toddle toward his mum and be enfolded in arms that felt like an impenetrable shield against the world.

Fanny almost fell under the force of his charge. After a moment's hesitation, she curled one arm under his armpit and stroked his hair with the other. Even as Geldof wet her T-shirt, his heart swelled with a joy so fierce that it forced a torrent of words up through his throat like a burst water main. "I thought you were dead and I never got to say good-bye and I'm sorry I was so rotten to you and I never listened to you and I never appreciated you and I wanted to eat meat and I pretended to pray and never told you I loved you and masturbated all the time ..."

He stopped, realizing he'd gone too far with the confessions. Ignoring the titters from the others gathered around, he took a shuddering breath and pulled back to look his mum in the eyes. He'd never seen tears on her face before, but they were there now, glistening in the gullies of the awful scars. The pictures hadn't prepared him for how brutally she'd been savaged. Her face looked like the surface of the moon, ragged white craters rammed in by the force of passing asteroids. He wanted to kiss them away.

"I love you, too," Fanny said, mercifully glossing over his masturbation revelation—not that a sixteen-year-old boy admitting he was rather fond of tugging one off could be considered much of a revelation. "I should've told you every day."

He couldn't remember the last time he'd heard those words pass her lips. He hugged her tighter, as though the years of distance could be erased by this one moment of intense closeness. Fanny's thin body trembled as she took great sucking breaths through the ruin of her nose. A sudden heat flushed her body. In combination with the other physical ticks, it made her seem like an old boiler about to blow.

"You need to let go now, Geldof," she said.

As though he were holding a knitting needle jammed into the main socket, Geldof couldn't release his arms. Fanny's trembling became violent. With sudden force, she put her hands on his shoulders and pushed him away. She staggered backward, rapidly and repeatedly chanting a phrase that he couldn't quite catch.

"Are you okay?" he said.

"Just give me a minute," she said, squatting and holding up a hand. "Please."

When Geldof tried to go to her, somebody grasped his arm. He looked up to see a girl with astonishing green eyes.

"Seriously, you have to give her some space," she said.

He became fully aware of the other people, around half-a-dozen, who crowded around his mum. A bear-sized man Geldof recognized as another of Fanny's old cronies knelt down and began whispering in her ear. Eva, who'd followed on behind Geldof, stroked her cropped hair. Something wasn't right here. He still didn't know what happened after the pigs left her for dead. Perhaps she'd had a mental breakdown. All he could tell was that she was fighting some raging internal battle. A year ago, Geldof would have been hurt and resentful at being pushed away, but he'd changed. And so had she. He could see it in her eyes, hear it in the softer tones of her voice, understand it in the way she'd held him and told him she loved him. He stood at a respectful distance until Fanny's breathing began to return to normal and she got to her feet. Scott and Eva flanked her, holding her elbows in what looked suspiciously like a move to restrain her.

"I'm fine now," she said. "It was just the shock." With a look at each other, Scott and Eva dropped their hands. Fanny took one last whooshing breath and turned her eyes on Geldof. "I know you are here, and it makes me happy. But are you insane? You don't have the virus. You were out. Why did you come back? And how did you find me?"

Something about what she'd said niggled Geldof, but he focused instead on delivering the good news. "We've come to get you out."

"We?"

Geldof whistled. In response, engines started up, and down the track rode the mercenaries. They'd all agreed it would be wise for Geldof and Eva to go in together in order not to spook anybody—a plan he'd ruined by breaking into a run the moment he saw his mum. Fanny stared at them, her face darkening. "This is your grandfather's work, isn't it? He found you."

"Yes," Geldof said. "When he found out you were alive, he put up the money to get you out."

"And he sent you here with these men?"

"Not exactly. He didn't know I was going to come. But don't you see? None of that matters. A helicopter's coming back for us in a few days. It can sneak us out. We can be together again."

Sadness dulled Fanny's eyes. "I can't leave."

"I thought you might be stubborn enough to stay here for whatever crusade you're on now. I came to convince you to leave."

"You don't understand. I want to come with you, but I can't."

"Why not?"

Fanny looked at the mercenaries again. "Because I'm infected."

"No," Geldof said, backing away. "You can't be."

Even as he denied it, he knew she was telling the truth. Now her reaction to him made perfect sense. She'd been fighting her urges— hopefully just a desire to kill him rather than have sex with him first, which would have been a far more disturbing fate. He heard a chorus of clicks and looked at the mercenaries. Automatic weapons had materialized in their hands.

"This is turning into a right royal fuck-up," Scholzy said.

"We're all infected, apart from her," Fanny said, indicating the girl with the green eyes. Her voice was calm and authoritative, so unlike the shrill badgering Geldof remembered. "But we're not a threat to you."

"I prefer not to take any chances," Scholzy said as he locked the barrel of the gun to his shoulder. "Nothing personal."

Infected or not, she was still his mum. Geldof stepped in front of her. "You'll have to shoot me first."

"Considering I still have your puke on the back of my jacket, I'd rather like that."

"Go ahead. Then you won't get the rest of your money."

The gun remained pointed at his head for a few seconds before Scholzy laughed. "Now that, I wouldn't like." He lowered his weapon. "You've got one hour to say your good-byes. Then we're getting out of here. The mission's blown. And I warn you all: anybody who comes within spitting range of us gets a bullet in the skull."

Not taking his eyes off Fanny and her gang, he turned his head. "James, get Sergei on the satphone. Make sure the drunken moron remembers where and when he's supposed to pick us up. We'll hole up somewhere else until the rendezvous."

Geldof, still faint at the risk he'd taken, felt a light touch on his shoulder.

"We need to talk," Fanny said. She held out her hand, and Geldof looked at it nervously. "I won't bite, and you can't get it from just touching me."

"It's not that," Geldof said. "I just can't remember the last time we held hands."

"Does it matter now?"

In response, he curled his fingers through hers and they walked off toward the lake.

Once they were settled on a large rock, breath visible in the cold air, Geldof gave Fanny the news she needed to hear.

"Dad's dead," he said. "He got shot."

"I know."

In a flash, he realized what had niggled him earlier. She'd said that he'd got out with a certainty that meant it wasn't a guess. Now she knew that her husband was dead. "How do you know this stuff?"

"I read Lesley's stories."

"How?"

Fanny pointed toward a large satellite dish atop a hangar. "That's how."

"You have Internet access." For the first time since seeing her again, Geldof felt that familiar combination of frustration and anger she'd always engendered in him. "You have Internet access! Why didn't you send me an e-mail?"

"I sat in front of the computer so many times, but I could never bring myself to type anything. I thought you'd be better off without me. I wasn't a good mother. And I may as well have been dead. I was in a place I thought you could never visit and I can never leave."

"Don't you think that was my decision to make?" Geldof said, straining to keep his voice calm. She said nothing in response. Looking at the pain in her eyes, at the scars that ran not just over her face but down her neck and up her arms, Geldof forced himself to swallow his hurt. This was a new beginning. He didn't want to ruin it by falling into the same old pattern of arguments. "What happened? Terry said you were dead. He just ran away when they attacked, the villain."

"Don't blame him. He did try to save me. He did save me. If he hadn't come back, they'd have finished me off. They ran after him instead. While they were gone, I dragged myself into a freezer and closed the door. They came back and followed the trail of blood, but couldn't get in. After a while, they wandered off." She paused, her eyes distant with recollection. "Once they were gone, I got bandages and painkillers from the shelves and dressed my wounds as best I could. I was too weak to come after you, so I locked the doors of the supermarket and stayed there for two days. When I finally found the strength to make it back to the house, you were gone, and David and the twins were dead on the floor."

"What did you do then?"

"I buried them in the back garden and stayed. What else could I do? I had no idea where you'd gone and no way to contact you."

"Did you have the virus then?"

"No. It hadn't mutated yet." She rolled up her sleeve and showed another wound, a smaller bite mark than those from the pigs. "Courtesy of Mr. Brownlee in number 15 about a week later."

"The obsessive car washer."

"The very one."

"I don't understand why you're not like the others, though. Didn't you get it as badly?"

"I got it badly, alright. After he bit me, I smacked his head off the bonnet of his car until he passed out. Then I went roaming. When I saw my first uninfected person, I felt this unbelievable tide of anger rising up in me. All I wanted to do was kill."

"And did you?"

She shook her head. "When I was lying in that supermarket, sweating and feverish, I had an epiphany. I'd spent my whole life campaigning for animals, not eating meat, but it made no difference to those pigs. I'd always thought that all living beings were the same, but I realized then that we're different. Animals always act on their instincts. We don't."

"You mean we've evolved?"

"No. People always confuse evolution with civilization. The structure of our brains hasn't changed in thousands of years, but the way society developed forced us to cooperate, to learn to control these primal desires that still lurk inside us. This virus brings these desires to the fore again. But it doesn't have to be that way. When I felt those bestial urges, I chose to be human. It was the hardest thing I've ever done. Now, I mean to help people make that choice, too. That's what we're doing here. Even if I didn't have the virus, I would stay. It's the right thing to do."

She hasn't changed so much, Geldof thought. *Still fighting for a cause.*

"This is why I was so shitty to you," he said. "I never hated you. I just hated that you were so strong and I was so weak. I was never as committed or as driven as you and I took all kinds of crap from bullies at school because I wasn't strong enough. I should've tried to be more like you."

Fanny took his shoulders. "I wasn't strong. I was arrogant. I was a self-righteous, hectoring stereotype. Deep down, I even knew the hemp was causing your rash. And I still made you wear it, because I thought it was the ethical choice, that suffering would build character. I thought

I was opening up your horizons, when I was really narrowing your beliefs to match my own. I should've let you find your own way."

Looking at the aching regret in his mum's eyes, Geldof knew what he must do. It was funny that after all those years of her forcing her beliefs down his throat, it took the opposite approach to convince him. He was acutely aware of how immature he'd been. Everything he'd done was a reaction to outside pressures rather than a result of looking within.

"I'm staying," he said.

"No," she said. "You can't."

"I want to help. I want us to be a family again."

"And I want that, too. But I can't let you stay. It's too dangerous."

"Just thirty seconds ago you said you should have let me find my own way. Well, I've found my way. All I did in Croatia was watch television. And your dad was pressuring me to get into the business. He wants me to take over."

Fanny looked horrified, and for a moment he thought she was about to launch into a diatribe about fair trade, ethical treatment of workers, and the evils of international corporations. Instead, that old stubborn look, distorted by the scars but still recognizable, crossed her face. "It doesn't matter. You can't stay here. I forbid it."

His grandfather's words about idealizing the dead came back to him, as did the tight knot of anger in his stomach he'd nursed, like a stillborn evil child poisoning his blood, for most of his teenage years. "You forbid me? You're just the same as you ever were."

He got up to storm off, with no clear idea to where he would storm off.

"I'm sorry," Fanny said softly. "You're right, I shouldn't be forbidding you from doing anything. But try to understand: you're my son, all that's left of my family, and I love you. If you don't leave, you could die. I couldn't face that."

Geldof stopped as the pain in her voice disarmed his anger. He was behaving like a petulant teenager again. Well, this time he wouldn't let it happen. They would talk about this like adults. He would make her understand. "And you're my mum. I can't face losing you again. If I go, that's what would happen."

"We could Skype."

"I don't want to be your Skype buddy. Listen, you always wanted me to fight for something. Here I am, ready to fight. By your side. And don't forget that I'm the one paying those men. If I tell them to go without me, they'll go. So you don't really have any choice."

Fanny looked at him for a long time. Finally, a small smile turned up the corner of her scarred mouth. "You've grown up so much. I still want you to go, even though it would break my heart. But if you really want to stay, I won't stand in your way."

That was easy, he thought.

He hugged her again. This time she showed no signs of wanting to rip his head off. They had a whole new relationship to build from the ashes of their old one, and, although he knew there would be problems ahead, he felt the swell of optimism that only the hope of a new future could bring—which, he supposed, was a bit ironic considering he'd committed to living in a country in which he occupied the same position as plankton in the food chain.

They sat close together for a while, looking across the water to the hills shrouded in mist. "I wish Dad was here," Geldof said.

"He would've loved it, the dope at least. He probably wouldn't have been too happy about us eating all the squirrels."

"Hold on. You're eating meat?"

Fanny shrugged. "Somehow being a vegan just didn't have the same appeal any longer. Plus there's no tofu in the shops."

In Geldof's opinion, judging from the fleeting look of loathing that had crossed her face when she talked about the pigs, there was an element of revenge in his mum's new diet. He kept his opinion to himself, just happy that she wouldn't try to stop him from eating whatever dead animals were on the go. Nor did he confess to having given up the vegan lifestyle at the first opportunity. It would have seemed disloyal. He would just eat whatever they laid in front of him that evening.

Now that the important matters were out of the way, he turned his mind to something that he'd been itching to ask. "Who's that girl? The one that told me to give you some space."

"Now we get to the real reason you want to stay. She's only been here a week. She's immune."

"What's she like?"

"Tough as nails. Do you want me to put in a good word for you?"

Geldof blushed. "No. She's way out of my league."

Not to mention that her first impression was my admitting I'm a wanker, he thought.

"Don't be so sure," Fanny said. "From where I'm sitting, you look pretty handsome."

They talked for another hour, Fanny explaining about the camp, how they resisted the violent tug of the virus through meditation, visualization, dope smoking, and sexual release. She also promised to induct Geldof with daily lessons in combat yoga and hunting. Once they were done talking, they walked back to Scholzy to tell him about Geldof's decision to remain. Geldof intended to send his grandfather an e-mail informing him that he would have to find somebody suitably evil to run the company in his stead and instructing him to pay the rest of the mercenaries' fee. When he approached, the mercenaries were in deep discussion. They broke off as Geldof approached. Scholzy's cheeks were pinched and his lips set into a grim slash.

"I'm staying," Geldof said.

"You're not the only one," Scholzy said. "Fucking Sergei's got himself fired. He helped himself to the rest of his vodka flask on the way back and thought it would be funny to land his helicopter on a truck."

"You must have a backup plan, right?"

"Wrong. It was hard enough coming up with this one."

"So how are you going to get out?"

"That's a very good question," Scholzy said. He nodded at Fanny, who was standing nearby. "Can these people be trusted?"

"Yes," Geldof said without hesitation.

"What about the animals?" Scholzy asked, addressing Fanny. "Are we going to be attacked every five minutes?"

"Unlikely," Fanny said. "We've eaten everything in a radius of about a mile. We have to go farther out to hunt every day."

"Then we'll stay here for a few days while we figure out what the hell we're going to do."

After the sun set, the commune gathered to eat in the living room of one of the houses. Fanny served up a delicious-smelling casserole of potatoes, carrots, and wildcat. Geldof was banned from touching it. Salivating, he tried to protest that cooking the animal would surely have killed the virus, but nobody would listen. He reluctantly accepted they had a point. He felt a woozy sense of unreality as he sat, chewing on a meat-free version of the dish, and watched Fanny wolf down the flesh she'd once so vehemently rejected.

The mercenaries didn't join them. They'd set up their own separate camp on a rocky outcrop, chewing on their rations beneath a canvas sheet and warming their hands over a fire set in the middle of their ring of tents. The bikes were parked in a protective semicircle around them, and the lake guarded their backs, but looking at them through the window he could sense their watchfulness. He didn't blame them. Just about everything that could go wrong had, and then some, and they didn't know his mum as he did. If she said everything was fine, then it was.

Fanny, clearly with his inquiry about Ruan in mind, had sat him down next to the girl. It took him five minutes to speak to her. It wasn't that he was trying to formulate an opening gambit to impress her, for he'd meant it when he said she was out of his league and figured that there was no point trying. She didn't give the impression of wanting to talk, keeping her body angled away from him. Still, he found it a struggle not to keep looking at her and decided that not attempting to strike up a conversation would seem creepy. He waited until she shifted slightly in his direction and stuck out his hand. "I'm Geldof."

She gave what seemed like a tired sigh, before taking his hand. "Ruan."

The physical contact left him flustered, which had a lot to do with the idiotic pronouncement he made next. "So we both have daft names then."

"What's daft about my name?" she said, her eyes narrowing.

Wincing, Geldof tried to retrieve the situation. "Sorry, I didn't mean . . . I just meant to say we have unusual names."

"Ruan is the name of the village in Ireland my father came from. It's a perfectly reasonable name. I do agree that your name is bloody stupid, though."

Still a hit with the ladies, Geldof thought, but kept plugging away. "You can blame my mum for that one."

"Why'd she call you Geldof?"

"Big thing for Bob Geldof."

"Mine had a thing for Noel Edmonds."

"At least she didn't call you Noel."

"Well, names apart, your mum is an amazing woman."

"Yes, she is. I'm surprised, to be honest. She never used to be like this."

Ruan half-smiled. "I figured that. I saw her on television once, at that rally against Trident."

"God, the naked incident. That wasn't at all out of character."

"What do you mean?"

"She used to walk around the house in the buff and try to get me to do the same. Among other things, she believed getting air to your bits helped ward off infections."

"That must have been awful," Ruan said, turning her body toward him.

In the past, he'd refused to talk about Fanny, sometimes even telling people he was an orphan—something he bitterly regretted in the months he believed this had come to pass. However, Ruan was clearly interested in her and he saw it as a way to strike up some kind of rapport. "Oh, that's just the tip of a very large and ugly iceberg."

They talked all through dinner and remained at the table after the others had adjourned to the pier to pass joints around a roaring fire. Ruan's closed demeanor faded as she chortled at Fanny's many and varied embarrassing former peccadillos. At one point, he tried to steer the conversation around to Ruan by asking about her parents. She looked down at the table, not responding and blinking her eyes rapidly. He took the hint and went back to the subject of his mum.

Finally, Ruan began to yawn and Geldof's mouth ran away with him again. "Do you want to go to bed?"

Ruan's eyebrow shot up.

"I didn't mean with me," he said, hoping the dim light would hide the traitorous blood that rushed to his cheeks—an uncontrollable process he hoped would disappear as he got older. "I just meant I don't mind stopping if you're tired."

It was hard to read her expression, but he had a feeling that surprise flickered across her face as she responded, "That's okay. I'm enjoying myself."

"Then let me tell you about the time a lion almost ate us when she chained us to its cage at Glasgow Zoo," Geldof said, suppressing a smile.

"You've got to be joking," Ruan said.

As they talked on, Geldof glanced out toward the pier and felt a rush of love at the sight of Fanny holding court, the heads of her followers bobbing along to her words. Only one person wasn't paying attention: a young boy who sat outside the circle. It was too dark to make out his expression, but he appeared to be staring at Ruan and Geldof. From the way he was gripping his legs, it seemed something was bothering him.

He's jealous, Geldof thought happily.

He'd never had another boy envy his prowess with the ladies before. It was something he could get used to.

21

The Pillared Room at Ten Downing Street certainly lived up to its grand name. A glittering chandelier dangled from the ceiling, a decorative fireplace spoke of hushed late-night discussions before the hypnotic crackle of flames, ornate gold-legged chairs and sofas with plush upholstery dotted the shining floor, and the gold pillars after which the room was named stretched upward in the corners. So many great leaders had cloistered themselves away in here, making decisions that would affect the lives of millions. Tony knew he wouldn't go down in history as one of those men and women. Considering he would soon threaten to spunk off a missile filled with infected blood, he was more likely to fall into the Hitler, Khan, and Ming the Merciless camp after all. He may as well have kept the moustache.

After his trip through London and a spectacular hour spent with Margot while Vanessa was dumped in front of the television, he again asked himself how far he would be prepared to go to protect those he loved and those he led. God knows he didn't want to fire the missile, but what if it really was the only option? He dropped his head and drew in a deep breath. His nostrils filled with the scent of Margot, still clinging to his skin after their snatched lovemaking. He nodded softly. Nobody could ever be sure in a hypothetical situation, but he believed he could do it. He'd told Archangel it was wrong, but he was pretty sure he could justify it to himself. Archangel wanted the virus out there to kill people. If Tony fired the missile it would be to save lives. It wasn't as if it hadn't been done before. The bombs dropped on Hiroshima and Nagasaki were let loose in the name of ending the war early and thus preserving life. He shifted in his chair, trying not to dwell on the counterargument that the equation would be skewed the wrong way this time: more people would die than would be saved. It all came back to a more important equation: how many strangers' deaths was the life of a loved one worth? He thought of Amira quoting Stalin and got his answer. The death of his wife and daughter would be a tragedy; everybody else, no matter how many, was just a statistic.

He slapped his cheeks and got to his feet. It wouldn't come to that. He was about to set off to his working room, ready to start the day properly three hours later than scheduled, when Frank burst into the room. His face told Tony bad news was on the way. "Christ, what now?"

"Two things. While Archangel was making us look like country bumpkins this morning, heavily armed men on quad bikes came bursting out of a crate that was supposed to contain sacks of rice at an aid delivery site in Glasgow. They shot dead three soldiers and disappeared. We weren't able to track them."

Tony steepled his fingers, pressing them together so hard his fingernails whitened. "And the next thing?"

"A helicopter was spotted coming in over the east coast of Scotland around six a.m. We don't know what it was doing, and we didn't have any assets in the area to shoot it down. It could've been dropping somebody, or something, off."

"What do you think it means?"

"I think they've inserted some teams to carry out a mission."

"Do you think they know about the missile?"

"Glasgow is in the right geographical area, I suppose, but it's unlikely."

"Really? Somebody told Archangel we were coming. Why wouldn't somebody else grass us up about the missile?"

"Doesn't make sense. Whoever told them would be putting themselves in the shit as well considering what the response would be. They're more likely advance scouting missions to identify targets for a wider attack. We're trying to find out if there were other incidents. So far we haven't been able to identify any suspect activity, but that doesn't mean it hasn't happened."

Tony picked up his phone and got his secretary. "Get me Piers."

"It's the middle of the night there."

"I don't care. Wake him up."

While he waited for Piers to get on the line, Tony pulled out his picture of Spock and told himself repeatedly it was his reflection. It didn't work.

After five minutes, his secretary put him through to Piers, who said, "Hello, Tony. To what do I owe this unexpected pleasure at such an ungodly hour?"

"Worried that I disturbed your beauty sleep? Well, don't fret, petal. You'd still be an ugly sod even if you slept for the next five hundred years."

"You're hostile tonight."

"I'm hostile? What the hell are you playing at?"

"If you must know, I was playing strip poker with Margaret Thatcher and Helen Mirren. In my dreams, I might add. So you can perhaps understand why I'm feeling a little confused. Can you tell me exactly why you're calling?"

"At least two armed units were dropped onto our territory today, one of them carried in an official UN aid consignment. I want to know what they're up to."

Piers's voice, which had been fuzzy with sleep, snapped into focus. "Firstly, Tony, it's actually still our territory. We are the elected government."

"And look what you did with it."

"Labour would have been different? Politics only count during campaigning. Governments are governments, Tony."

"Stop trying to dodge my question. What fuckery are you cooking up?"

"I've no idea what you're talking about. We're continuing to respect the current détente and have no intention of changing our position."

"Then who are these guys? Extreme tourists?"

"Let me assure you that if what you say is true, it's nothing to do with us."

There was that word "assure" again, indicating that Piers was lying through his perfectly formed, attempted-wife-stealing teeth. "We're going to find these people. And we're going to interrogate them. If we find out this is part of preparations for a strike or invasion, you'll suffer the consequences."

Piers's voice took on a worried edge. "Hold on a minute, Tony. Are you suggesting you'll fire your nuclear weapons?"

Tony felt a near overwhelming desire to tell Piers about the viral weapon but kept himself in check. If they didn't already know, he couldn't afford to alert them to its existence before it was ready and give them a chance to destroy it. "I'm suggesting that any action, even the faintest whiff of an action, will be met with a commensurate response." Tony paused. The formal language of Ferrero Rocher–eating diplomats didn't quite convey how strongly he felt, so he rephrased his threat. "The moment I see a bomber, even a seagull that looks a bit like a bomber from a distance, some very large nuclear missiles will be fizzing your way. The first one has the coordinates of your hotel plugged into its computer."

"Think about what you're saying here. This is exactly the kind of talk that makes people nervous enough to consider the military option. Threatening us doesn't help."

"You're trying to blame us for this? You're the ones who've been talking about obliterating my country."

"If you weren't so aggressive and quick to wave your nuclear response around like a big stick there wouldn't be as much talk."

"We're being defensive, not aggressive."

"All I'm trying to say is that we should keep our heads."

"I am trying to keep my head. Attached to my bloody body. You and your generals should do the same."

Tony slammed the phone down and got up to pace the room. He picked up a lamp and dashed it into the fireplace, fragments of china pattering back out onto the floor. He stood for a long time, head resting on the mantelpiece and conjuring up Spock, before he was calm enough to turn back to Frank.

"They're really going to do it," he said.

"It's beginning to look that way."

Tony stirred the broken lamp with his foot. All of the morning's optimism faded in the face of the spurt of anger he'd been unable to contain. He was like one of those fragments, being swept along by far larger forces. Apart from the missile, all he had to hold on to was Tim Roast and his citizen brain surgery. He just hoped the deterrent would be ready in time, and that it would serve its purpose.

"There is one bit of good news," Frank said. "We've found out where this antivirus group is based."

There seemed little point in engaging the group at this stage in the game. If they got the missile ready and it served to hold off the attack on Britain, he could think about it. Then again, making the film Amira suggested would keep her out of his hair for a few days. Her constant attempts to talk him out of firing the missile were getting on his tits.

"I'll send Amira up to make the film," Tony said.

Frank's face fell. "Can't she just send up a camera crew?"

The anger Spock had just suppressed threatened to come back. Here they were in a race against time to save themselves, and all Frank could think about was the sex he wouldn't be having. Perhaps this epidemic of horniness wasn't such a good thing after all. "For God's sake, Frank, it'll only be a day or two. You've got hands. I'm sure you can manage by yourself until she gets back."

"That's like asking a forty-a-day smoker to chew Nicorette. The things that woman can do . . ."

"No details," Tony said. "She's going. And find these incursion teams. We need to know what they're up to."

As Frank huffed out of the room, other benefits of sending Amira occurred to Tony. Yes, these incidents were a bad sign, but a propaganda video could serve a purpose. With luck, Piers's paymasters would take the continuation of a PR offensive as a sign that BRIT had no other options. They'd find out how wrong they were soon enough.

SIX DAYS TO EXCISION

22

Geldof's combat training began at dawn when he was rudely awakened by his mum's voice. In his sleepy state, he believed he was in his bed at their Bearsden home being roused for school. Downstairs there would be a breakfast of chopped fruit in soy yogurt, which he would grumble about but eat nonetheless before heading round to Nadeem's to walk to class. His nostrils filled with the faint scent of dope smoke. He smiled. His dad was in the back garden, fiddling with his squirrel assault course and puffing on his first joint of the day.

"Just ten more minutes," he muttered.

When he opened his eyes in response to the shaking that predictably commenced and saw Fanny's ruined face, the fantasy fell away like the badly painted backdrop of a school play. His face must have mirrored the corresponding sinking in his stomach, for Fanny turned slightly to hide the more-ravaged side of her features. He reached out to touch her chin and turn her face back toward him. He brushed his fingers across the scars. She flinched, but didn't pull away. "Does it still hurt?"

"It's always going to hurt."

"I know," Geldof said, and pulled her in to squeeze her tight. Her grip around his back was tight, but he still sensed nothing sinister lurking behind the hug. It was simply the fierce embrace of a mother who'd missed her son. "Right," he said as emotion threatened to overwhelm him. "Enough soppiness. We are British, after all."

Fanny got to her feet. "Absolutely. Come on, it's time to start your training."

"Any chance of some breakfast first?"

"Shooting practice, then breakfast. A hunter aims better on an empty stomach. Meet me outside in ten minutes."

Geldof, now fully awake and rather excited at the thought of unleashing the fearsome warrior he'd always hoped lived inside him but had never been able to locate, gave his teeth a perfunctory brush, shrugged on his clothes, and hurried into the chilly morning. Fanny was standing in the middle of the clearing, a bow in each hand.

"We're going to start you off with a stationary target," she said, indicating a bull's-eye nailed to a tree.

Geldof eyed the target, which was a good twenty meters distant. "It's a bit far away."

"Nonsense," Fanny said. She dropped one of the bows, slipped an arrow from the quiver on her back, nocked, turned, and fired. The arrow thrummed through the air and hit the center of the target with a cartoon-style *thwock*.

Geldof whistled. "Where did you learn to shoot like that?"

"I did have a life before you were born. Your turn."

Geldof picked up the bow. The only time he'd held such a weapon it had been a plastic made-in-China effort that fired sucker darts. He'd never been able to hit anything then, and he wasn't feeling too hopeful now. "So, am I supposed to split your arrow or something? Or maybe you can stand over there with an apple on your head."

"Let's start with not shooting yourself in the foot."

She stood behind him, guided his hands to the correct position, and showed him how to nock an arrow with two fingers. "Now pull."

He hauled as hard as he could and managed to get the string back half as far as Fanny had. He pointed in the general direction of the target, his arms already wavering with the strain. When he let go, the string pinged his fingers and the arrow sagged through the air. It didn't even make it halfway to the tree.

"No problem," Fanny said. "Let's try again."

And so they did. Again. And again. And again. By the time they finished, Geldof's fingers were raw, Fanny's face flushed, and virtually every object around them—except the target—perforated. It seemed Geldof's inner warrior was still in hiding.

They broke for a quick breakfast, and then it was time for combat yoga. Nayapal was waiting for them down by the water's edge, doing a showboating handstand on a rock.

"Geldof," he said from his inverted position. "How is the rash?"

"Much better," Geldof said, refraining from adding, "No thanks to you." He still hadn't forgiven Nayapal for his consultation at the height of the hemp-induced itchiness, when he'd hovered his hands over Geldof's body for five minutes before diagnosing an extreme case of "spiritual malaise." He'd been correct about Geldof's struggling to find his place in the world, but that had no connection to the rash.

"Then let us begin," Nayapal said, lowering his legs to the earth in an impressive display of strength and balance.

The lesson began with ten minutes of sun salutations, which were intended as a limbering-up exercise but set Geldof's arms and hamstrings trembling with effort. Halfway through, Mick wandered over to sit on the grass and spectate. After the sun salutations, Nayapal had Geldof attempt to contort into a series of other poses—each agonizingly painful and as far from martial arts practice as Geldof could possibly imagine. He managed to fall on his arse during each one. Finally, when he almost broke his neck during an attempted handstand, he sat down.

"Come on, Geldof," Fanny said, frustration evident in the stiffness of her voice. "You never know when you're going to have to fight."

"I'm trying," he said.

"Either do, or don't do. There is no try."

"For feck's sake," Mick called across. "Are you quoting *Star Wars* at the poor lad?"

Fanny looked at him blankly. "I don't know what you mean."

"Yoda said that to Luke. What's next? Is this old bollix going to start spouting Mr. Miyagi at us?"

"It's pretty obvious I'm going to be crap at everything," Geldof said before his mum could shoot off a rejoinder, all too aware that this situation had the potential for escalation even given his mum's pig-induced personality makeover. "Can't we just stop?"

"You need to be strong of body and mind if you're going to join us."

"God's blood, I'm not John Connor. I'll be delivering leaflets, not fighting an army of killer robots."

"Who's John Connor?"

"The leader of the resistance in the *Terminator* films. You're acting just like his mum."

Fanny's eyes bulged out of her head, and Geldof began to worry the virus was taking over. "Can everybody just stop talking about films? Doesn't anybody have anything original to say anymore? I never owned a television, I never went to the cinema. I haven't seen any of them, and I don't care that I haven't."

"You're the one who just quoted a film," Mick said.

"I didn't do it on purpose!" Fanny shouted.

Geldof sighed. "Fine. I'll stop. But I just don't see how this can have any kind of combat application. Can't he teach me kung fu or something?"

"He's right," Mick said. "Yoga's for fat birds who can't be arsed with proper exercise and gay boys in ball-hugging pink leotards. I'll teach him some proper hand-to-hand combat."

"If it helps, I'm already an expert in face-to-hand combat," said Geldof. "My face. The other guy's hand."

"Do not listen to him," Nayapal said serenely. "There are many roads to the top of the mountain."

"You're going to make him run up a mountain?" Mick said. "That's not fair, now. Even Rocky only had to go up some stairs."

From the grin on Mick's face, Geldof could tell he'd thrown in another film reference just to wind Fanny up.

Nayapal folded his hands. "Allow me to translate," he said, before turning to Mick and saying in a thick Scottish accent that was pure Cumbernauld, "There are shitloads of ways to kick the fuck out of cunts like you."

Geldof burst out laughing, but Mick's face reddened. He stomped over to Nayapal, throwing off his jacket to reveal biceps that were larger than the Nepalese man's head. "How's about you prove it, then?"

"We do not practice in anger," Nayapal said, unflinching even as Mick lowered his face into his.

"I knew you were all talk and no fecking trousers," Mick said.

"I'll take you on," Fanny said. She wore the same scathing snarl that had always painted her lips when she argued with their neighbor

David about his environmentally unfriendly meat obsession. "Geldof needs a demonstration."

"I don't fight women."

"And I don't take kindly to sexists. Your swollen, misogynist balls should have done the world a favor and forgotten to drop. Whether you fight back or not, I'm going to right that wrong and kick them back up into your abdomen."

Geldof had seen his mum in action, jamming her armpit into David's face with steely strength when their game of Scrabble escalated into all-out warfare. With the virus inside her, she would be more likely to jam Mick's armpit into her own face and bite it. "I don't think this is a good idea," he said.

They both ignored him. Fanny advanced and Mick backed off to face her. "Fine," Mick said. "I can be modern."

As soon as Fanny came within range, the Irishman spun on the spot and whipped a booted foot toward her head. Geldof cringed, expecting to hear a crunch and see his mum's teeth fly through the air. The speeding foot whooshed through empty air as Fanny crouched low to balance on the balls of her feet. From there she came up onto one foot and slammed the other upward into Mick's exposed groin. He let out a keening grunt and collapsed to his knees. Fanny gave him no time to recover. She leapt forward, hitting him square in the face with her groin and sending him crashing backward. She squeezed her thighs round his neck. "You were saying?"

To Geldof's surprise, Mick began to laugh. He put his hands on Fanny's waist, in a way that was as far from combative as possible. Fanny, suddenly aware the timbre of Mick's arousal had shifted despite what must be a pair of firmly smarting testicles, loosened her thigh hold. Still holding her waist, Mick got his feet under him and hauled them both up. They stood face to face, both breathing heavily. Geldof remembered his mum's nymphomaniac tendencies. Two days without sex had been enough to send her running into the street to hump lampposts. He couldn't begin to imagine how seven months of abstinence had made her feel, particularly since the virus turned the bearer's sex drive up to eleven. Sure, the leaflet she'd given him called for regular sex, but as far as Geldof could tell she wasn't getting it on with anybody in the commune. With no suitable partner, she must have resorted to sorting herself out. That was something he really didn't want to think about.

Fanny's mouth was half open, and she made no attempt to pull away. For a moment, Geldof thought she was going to whip down Mick's trousers and give him a brisk seeing-to there and then. To Geldof's relief, she took a deep breath and an unsteady step backward.

"Lesson's over," she said, and virtually sprinted away.

Mick watched her go, a grin plastered across his face. "That's some woman, there. I'd like to have a proper wrestle with her."

"That's my mum you're talking about," Geldof said.

"Right you are. Not your wife or your daughter. So it's none of your business."

Mick was right, but Geldof couldn't help but feel protective: of both his mum and the memory of his dead father. The mercenary wasn't an ideal choice for a boyfriend—although admittedly neither of them appeared to be thinking of anything beyond the next couple of minutes. Still, he thought it wise to attempt to dissuade Mick from further pursuits. "Don't her injuries put you off?"

Mick scowled at him. "That's a terrible thing to say, so. Never judge a woman by her face. It's what's in here that counts." He thumped his chest. "Passion. Heart. And she's got them in spades."

Geldof, suitably reproached, felt awful about trying to use the scars as an impediment to Mick's lust. He wondered if he'd misjudged the mercenary: perhaps there was a tender soul under the crude, gruff exterior after all. What Mick said next ruined it all. "Anyway, I don't know about your cock, but mine doesn't have any eyes. Even if it did, it'd be too dark in there to see."

With that, Mick went striding off after Fanny. As he went, Geldof realized he had one card to play. "She's got the virus!"

"That's why God invented condoms," Mick said without looking back.

"God doesn't approve of condoms."

"Only the Catholic God. I'm a proddy."

"And you actually brought condoms with you?"

"You're such a virgin. Always have condoms in your wallet. You never know when you're going to get your end away."

"You thought you'd get lucky on an island full of bloodthirsty maniacs?"

"I'm a bloodthirsty maniac myself, so it was a fair bet."

"But she might attack you."

"I like it rough," Mick shouted.

Geldof turned to Nayapal. "Can't you restrain him or something?"

"Soul and body are two halves of the same whole," Nayapal said in his calm, mystical voice. "There can be no unity of purpose without completeness."

"Have you got a stash of fortune cookies somewhere? What does that even mean?"

Nayapal smiled and reverted to Scottish. "A good, hard shag never hurt anybody."

Even though he'd never been the recipient of a good, hard shag, Geldof couldn't argue with that sentiment. His mum had always known her own mind, and, virus or not, if she gave in to Mick's advances it would be because she wanted to. And after all she'd been through, and all of the problems that no doubt lay ahead, she surely deserved something for herself. If anything, he should probably be more worried about the mercenary. Should he succeed, he had no idea what kind of relentless pummeling his blind little friend would be in for.

23

Long before the sun had even begun to think about making another half-arsed attempt to illuminate the savage streets of Aberdeen, Lesley and Tom were heading out of the city. The blank windows of the silent homes stared at her like dead eyes, and their doors seemed like maws ready to vomit out a stream of infected. She did her best to hold her nerve and stuck close to Tom's back wheel. Only when they'd cleared the worst of the urban sprawl did she begin to relax a little, at least in terms of her fear of being disassembled atom by bloody atom. There was nothing at all relaxing about the bike ride. Her legs felt like planks of wood after the previous day's exertions, and the good night's sleep Tom recommended she enjoy hadn't materialized. She'd locked her bedroom door but still woke at every creak and rustle. At one point she'd plunged back into her dream of standing in the wasteland. This time, when she stepped on the last other living being, she looked down to see it was a tiny Jack.

"How many more people are going to die because of you?" he said with his last breath.

She jerked awake in breathless terror to find it had started raining. The patter on her windowpane sounded like hundreds of pounding feet. She scrambled under the bed, where she spent another hour hiding behind a dusty suitcase until Tom knocked on her door and told her it was time to get ready. Prior to leaving, he suggested she go into the bathroom and douse herself with aftershave to try hide her scent. She stripped to her knickers and poured almost an entire bottle of Old Spice over her body, prompting a wave of aching desire to see Terry again. Now that they were apart, she could remember the good things about him and their relationship: his honesty, his kindness, his luscious body. She needed something to take her mind off recent events, just for a few minutes, so even though she felt little desire she slid her hand into her knickers and tried to awaken her body. Her middle finger stroked and teased as she imagined herself in bed with Terry, all of their relationship problems forgotten in the urgency of carnal acts. She began to warm to the fantasy, but memories of all the harm she'd done kept forcing their way to the fore. In an attempt to add impetus to her imaginings, she lifted her arm to take a whiff of Old Spice. She breathed too deeply and the searing in her nostrils and lungs kick-started a fit of coughing that killed any chance of escape. She'd pulled on her clothes and trudged downstairs.

"I don't want to sound like a little kid, but are we nearly there yet?" she called out to Tom.

He slowed down to ride beside her and said, "Only another one hundred and forty miles."

"I'm going to take issue with your use of the word 'only' here," Lesley said. "How long will that take us? A lunar cycle?"

"Normally, I'd say nine hours. At this pace, double it."

"You can't expect me to ride that long."

"If time's as tight as you say it is, you have to. Look, it's four in the morning now. We'll be there by around eleven in the evening, provided we have no incidents."

"Whoa there, cowboy. Incidents? You said all the bandits had cleared out."

"That's true, but there are still wild animals about."

"Why didn't you mention this before?"

"I didn't want to worry you."

"Well, consider me extremely fucking worried now."

Tom hiked a thumb toward the loaded crossbow slung across his back. "Nothing will mess with us while I've got this."

"Oh, so this virus has made cows smart enough to recognize a crossbow and keep their distance. That's reassuring."

"Look, you'll be fine. You're not going to set anything off smelling like you took a bath in Old Spice. Which, by the way, was a Christmas present from five years ago. You should have used the Paco Raban."

It was reassuring to hear that Tom, who was after all infected, couldn't detect her unsullied condition. Terry would be proud of her. Yet as she rode she divided her time between dropping her head to grimace at the effort of the steady climb they were now on and shooting anxious glances at the fields opening up around them. It was going to be a long day.

Amazingly, Tom's prediction of an uneventful journey proved correct, although the stillness was eerie, particularly under the lowering stacks of clouds that threatened to dump rain on them at any minute. At first, the ride wasn't too bad. They stuck to the main road, and Lesley's legs ached less as the repetitive motion lulled her into a trance-like state. They left the road twice to avoid checkpoints, which she couldn't see the need for since there was almost no traffic. The only vehicle they passed was an army truck that roared up the other side of the road and ignored them. Once they'd skirted around Perth, though, the road began to wind and the hills took their toll. She began to feel light-headed, and at one point even had an out-of-body experience that made her fall off her bike and skin her hands. Tom gave her fifteen minutes to rest, before pushing on. Past lochs, villages, and glens they slogged, only the thought of the story keeping her going. Lesley had no idea at what time they arrived at the camp; all she knew was that it had been dark for what felt like an eternity. Yet once they'd ridden down the hidden track, she saw that a fire still burned.

"Wait here a minute," Tom said at the end of the road.

He got off his bike and skipped off toward the light source.

Lesley let the bike fall sideways and toppled to the ground herself. Her thighs, bum, back, shoulders, and forearms were having a raucous argument about which hurt the most. She let them get on with it, too exhausted to display even the slightest curiosity about her surroundings. Her eyes drooped and sleep was beginning to take her when Tom returned.

"Follow me," he said.

"You'll have to drag me," Lesley said. "Or give me a ko-carry. I don't care which. Seriously."

And so it was that Lesley, mounted on Tom's back, approached the campfire. As they drew closer she saw two people: a woman with short hair and deep scars illuminated by the shifting light and a boy who had his back to her. The woman rose, tilting her head at a quizzical angle. "Lesley?" she said, her voice rising at the end in a disbelieving tone.

"Do I know you?" Lesley said.

The boy turned. Even though his face had filled out and he wasn't wearing glasses, Lesley recognized him as Geldof. At the same moment, she realized who the scarred woman was. The feeling of déjà vu came on again, so strongly that she let go of Tom's neck and slipped backward. She landed on her shoulders with her legs still held around his waist. The faces of Geldof and Fanny appeared above her, and, in chorus, they said, "What are you doing here?"

The moon had come out from a break in the clouds. It haloed Fanny's head, making her look like an angel. Lesley, her mind and body already pushed to breaking point, dug her fingers into the grass to reassure herself she was neither dreaming nor dead and being welcomed to Heaven by Fanny. "I believe I'm going mental."

An hour later they sat around the fire, up to speed on each other's stories. Lesley clutched a cup of herbal tea, still scarcely able to credit that she'd been thrown back together with the remnants of the Peters family. Those who forget the past are doomed to repeat it, the saying went. She hadn't forgotten the past, far from it, yet here she was anyway. One plus point was that Fanny was alive, although badly scarred, which meant Lesley could remove one death from the tally stacking up against her. Fanny looked remarkably calm regarding the bombshell Lesley had dropped about the real bombshells soon to be dropped. Geldof wasn't maintaining his composure as well.

"I can't believe they'd kill so many people just like that," he said.

"Really?" Fanny said. "Let me give you a few examples. The Holocaust. Hiroshima. Cambodia. Nigeria. Rwanda. Bosnia. Iraq. Syria.

If the human mind is capable of such atrocities, why do you think it can't be done now? You could argue this would be easier. Most of the people in all those countries were truly innocent. In Britain, many have killed. Many will kill again, given half the chance. They can justify it to themselves and others on those grounds. I told you before, people have to choose to be something better. The virus is giving us that pressure. What do they have?"

"Conscience? It's wrong."

"Right and wrong is defined by those with the power to make decisions. We have to assume this is going to happen." Fanny paused to rub her face. "I know you want to stay, and I know I said I would respect your wishes, but this changes everything. When your mercenaries figure out an escape route, and they'll be a lot more motivated when they hear what Lesley has to say, you need to go with them."

"Only if you come with me," he said, hugging himself.

"You know that's not going to happen," Fanny said.

"Then I'm staying. There's no way out anyway, you know that. We can die together."

"While that's a lovely sentiment, let's not get all fatalistic," said a large man in tie-dye, who'd been roused from his bed along with all the other camp residents to hear what Lesley had to say. "If she writes the story about the attack and what we're doing, there's a chance public opinion could stop them."

As Lesley looked at all of the infected calmly gathered around her, for the first time she began to believe it was possible. She'd been one of the most vociferous proponents of sinking the whole damned island into the sea, yet here she sat amongst a group who were most assuredly still people. If they could resist the virus, it stood to reason that everybody else could. If the world knew that and saw humanity still existed on the island, surely they would rise up against the barbarity of genocide. All of those lives saved would compensate for the deaths she'd caused and, with luck, end her jinx.

"You'd better get to work, then," Fanny told her.

Even though she could barely keep her eyes open, Lesley nodded. "Maybe you can come with me, and we can talk while I write. I'll need some good quotes."

Once they were in the hangar and the Internet was ready to go, Lesley opened up Gmail and started typing in her account details.

"What are you doing?" Fanny said.

"I want to get a message to Terry to tell him I'm okay."

"Bad idea. They might be monitoring your and his accounts for activity."

"But they think I'm dead."

"Do you really want to take the chance? We can't give them any warning about this story. You can send him an e-mail after."

Reluctantly, Lesley shut the window. "Can I use your e-mail to send it to my editor?"

"Same thing goes for your editor's account. The only way this story is going out is for it to go viral. We need to send it to every activist, blogger, campaigning group, and newspaper at once, and we need to do it from an e-mail account they won't be expecting. So we use mine."

And so Lesley sat with Fanny until 4:00 a.m., bashing away on the keyboard until she was gritty-eyed and almost seeing double. The story itself was inelegant and awkwardly written thanks to her exhaustion, but it was also a raw and powerful cry for humanity. Fanny had also encouraged her to edit out any details that may give a hint to her location, pointing out that it would be very easy for the U.S. to take them out with a drone. Lesley did, however, make mention of the fact that there was at least one person who was immune. As far as she knew, the young girl Ruan was the only recorded case of somebody who was able to resist the virus. If they started frying everybody, then that person, whose blood may hold the key to a cure, would be lost. They only had one argument about the story, and that came when Lesley tried to withhold her own name. She focused the article on Jack: how he'd come forward with the story, been abducted, and then died. Her role was as an anonymous journalist.

When Fanny read the draft, she poked Lesley in the arm. "Why are you leaving yourself out?"

Lesley didn't have the energy to explain the thoughts that had been swirling around her brain for the last few months. "I just don't think it should be about me."

"That's nonsense. You're a name. You have credibility. You used to

be all for incinerating us. Your name has to be on it and your story central to it. That way people will be more likely to listen."

   Lesley knew she was right and went back to write herself in, feeling sick as she knew her fame would now only grow. When it was done,
they pasted it into the e-mail Fanny had prepared addressing thousands
of people and urging them to pass it on, and hit send. Then they sat
back to wait, which Lesley did face down on the table until a blank
sleep of exhaustion claimed her.

24

The generals sat in the Operation Excision command and control center set up in the bowels of the Pentagon, upturned soda cups filched from McDonald's on the table in front of each of them, beneath a canopy of cigar and cigarette smoke. They'd stayed behind in the otherwise deserted room—not because they had work to do but because it was General Zhang's turn to present his culture through the lens of gambling large sums of money.

They'd kicked off the second leg of the cultural exchange two hours earlier with mah-jongg, which Zhang introduced as a game of skill, strategy, and calculation. To General Carter, as he tried to make sense of the bewildering set of Chinese characters on green and white tiles, it had seemed only like a game guaranteed to fill Zhang's pockets. He didn't make a fuss, though: he won the round of golf and would come out even when the inevitable loss happened. General Kuzkin, who'd finished his round with a score well into three figures and a bank account lighter by four figures, wasn't so relaxed. When Zhang started talking about pungs and chows and big melded kongs—which sounded to Carter like the unhappy aftermath of a fierce electrical fire on the set of a hardcore porn film—Kuzkin had swept his forearm through the tiles and refused to play. Zhang had graciously downgraded to the Chinese variant of Liar's Dice, not that it served either Kuzkin or Carter well. The contents of their wallets gravitated to the Chinese general's corner of the table just as swiftly as they would have done had they stuck to mah-jongg.

"Seven sixes," Zhang said, blowing a stream of wispy vapor up to tickle the smoke detector, which had been disabled with the strategic application of a piece of tape.

The Russian locked gazes with his opponent, seemingly attempting to plumb the depths of his soul to establish whether he was full of shit. Carter had already accepted he would never retrieve his money and was busy cleaning out his fingernails with the edge of his security pass.

When Zhang blinked, Kuzkin slapped the table. "Ha! I knew your inscrutable mask would slip. You are bluffing."

All three men turned over their cups. While Kuzkin and Carter had one six apiece, all five of the dice that had been concealed under Zhang's cup displayed six dots.

Zhang smiled as Kuzkin's face fell. "Sometimes a man blinks when he has smoke in his eyes."

"Or when he is deliberately misleading his opponents," Carter muttered.

The Russian pursed his lips. "What are the odds of all five of your dice coming up the same?"

"One in 1,296. I am very lucky tonight."

"Or you are very cheaty tonight."

"You have already accused me of cheating, and we swapped our dice. Perhaps you think we Chinese have supernatural powers to add to our famous inscrutability."

"I think perhaps you have very fast hands."

"Now you mistake me for Jackie Chan."

"And you mistake me for a gullible fool. I do not know how you did it, but I want my money back."

"Do you really want to know how I won? It is because you are so very scrutable."

"That is not even an English word," Kuzkin said. "If you are going to insult me at least do it in proper English."

"Must I point out that 'cheaty' is not a word either?"

Carter wiped the fingernail gunk from the pass onto the side of his chair and stood up to stretch. "Sometimes the gambling gods smile upon you from up on high. Sometimes they use that height to crap on your head. Just give the general his damn money."

Kuzkin looked as though he was going to continue arguing and barf-

ing up Chinese stereotypes. In the end, he crumpled up his last
hundred-dollar bill and tossed it across the table. "Do not be so quick
to spend it. We still have to play Tiger Has Come."

"Not tonight, gentlemen," Carter said. "My bed is calling me."

Kuzkin resorted to mumbling in Russian as Zhang stuffed the handsome pile of bills into his pocket with some difficulty. Carter was on
his way to the door, already imagining sliding between the sheets, when
a harried-looking aide burst in.

"We have a major problem, sirs," he said after a quick salute. "Intel
has picked up an e-mail revealing every detail of the attack."

Even though Carter was red-eyed from exhaustion and cigarette
smoke, he snapped into professional mode. "Did they block it?"

"Only partially, sir. It's still gone to thousands of newspapers and
bloggers. The first stories are just starting to pop up."

"Any reaction from the zombies yet?"

"No, sir."

"I take it the presidents have been alerted?"

"Yes, sir. A crisis call will commence shortly."

Carter turned to his colleagues. "Thoughts, gentlemen, beyond,
'This is a huge pain in the ass'?"

"Nothing has changed," said Kuzkin, who'd put aside his petulance
and, like Carter, was all business. "They will know, but what can they
do? We go ahead as planned."

"Not true," Zhang said. "We can't use the nerve gas now. They will
not go near any aid shipments."

Kuzkin wrinkled his nose. "That is disappointing. We needed to
use up our stockpile before the expiry date. I suppose we can drop it
on Dagestan when everybody is looking at Britain."

"It goes further than the nerve gas being a goner," Carter said.
"They're going to try to minimize the impact, bunker their leaders,
move strategic assets. The first wave won't be as effective, which will
mean more grunt work later."

"Then we must move the attack forward so they have less time to
prepare," Zhang said.

"I agree," Carter said. "The bombs are pretty much ready to rock,
so it won't be too difficult to shuffle things forward."

"Shouldn't we wait for the presidents to make a decision?" Kuzkin asked.

Carter shook his head. "They won't cancel, not when the fate of humanity's at stake. I guarantee you we'll soon get a call telling us to get our asses into gear. We need to be ready. I figure we can shave three days off the schedule with some rejigging. It might be a bit slap-dash, but it's better than giving the zombies time to hide under every rock they can find."

"There is one other issue," Zhang said. "We have not been able to track their second nuclear submarine yet, and now we have less time to do so."

"We always knew it would be a gamble," Carter said. "Here's hoping the gods are smiling on us and unbuckling their trouser belts over Britain."

"And what if they are not?" Kuzkin said.

"At most they should only be able to get off a few missiles, so our defense shields should take care of the warheads before they reach Washington, Beijing, or Moscow. Given the short distances involved, it's the Europeans who have to worry the most. Just don't plan on taking the kids to Disneyland Paris in the next few days and you should be fine." Carter turned to his aide. "Get our people in here and scare up a pot of industrial strength coffee, more cigarettes for General Zhang, and a big box of Adderall."

"Where would I get Adderall, sir? It's a prescription medicine."

"Break into the pharmacy, and if anybody asks, tell them it's a matter of national security. If we don't wake ourselves up we'll end up bombing the UAE by mistake, and I think we can all agree we need their oil. Now let's get to work."

TWO DAYS TO EXCISION

25

When Tony walked in to the reception of the National Hospital for Neurology and Neurosurgery, Tim was waiting for him with a smug upward tug to his lips. It was just after 7:00 a.m., the only slot Tony could find in another busy day trying to pull Britain back from the brink it seemed determined to topple over. Tony was a bit confused as to why they were in a hospital. He'd expected to be told to come to the zoo, although he supposed it may just have been a question of having the right facilities for delicate brain surgery.

The earliness of the hour might have explained why Tim seemed remarkably compos mentis. He probably hadn't had much time to munch his way through half a box of tranquilizers yet. Tim had called late the previous evening to tell Tony they'd carried out their first operation. Even though he harbored an entire flotilla of doubts about Tim's usefulness, the glowing report card Tim gave himself made Tony wonder if he'd misjudged the scientist. If it really had worked, they could present their data to Piers to show there were options to control the virus. Again, this would hopefully buy them some more time: they had a long way to go from animal testing to proving it could work in humans, but it would at least show there might be a surgical option.

Tim led him through a maze of corridors and swung open a door.

"Ta da!" he said.

Inside the room was a row of white beds, all empty save for one, upon which sat a man with a pinched, hard-life look about him. Old scars on each cheek, which looked like the product of a Stanley knife, gave his face an unpleasant symmetry. A fresher scar punctuated by stitches ringed his shaved scalp.

"Sorry, wrong room," Tony said.

The occupant continued to stare at the floor.

"No, this is the right room," Tim said.

"Where's the monkey?"

Tim looked puzzled. "What monkey?"

"The monkey you did the surgery on."

"Ah," Tim said, and giggled. "I think we may have got our wires crossed. We don't have any monkeys left. They've all been eaten. We went straight to human testing."

"You've got to be fucking kidding me," Tony said, his head starting to throb. "You did this to a person?"

Tim held up his hands. "Don't worry, we didn't just pull somebody off the street. The subject is Ralph Bertram. He's a high-ranking lieutenant in Blood of Christ, probably one of the most violent men in the country. Before the virus, he was serving life for three counts of murder in a gangland killing, which involved a turf war, a hammer, a chainsaw, and a large bath of acid. He, well the whole prison actually, broke out during the unpleasantness, and he joined up with Archangel's lot. He got caught when Blood of Christ burned down a mosque. He was jumping up and down on a burning man's face when our boys arrived. They had to shoot him twice to get him to stop. Even when they brought him here with a bullet in his stomach and one in his shoulder, he still managed to bite off a chunk of a nose, break two arms, and dislocate a testicle."

Although Tony felt like slapping the nervous grin off Tim's face, what was done was done. And he supposed that a successful human test would seem more credible, although significantly more immoral. "Fine, so he's a very bad man."

Tim grinned. "Was."

Tony entered the room and approached Bertram. "Shouldn't you have a bandage on that?" he said, indicating the ugly scar.

"He doesn't care. Watch this."

Tim leaned in until his nose was almost touching Bertram's. "You were a very naughty boy, weren't you?"

Tony flinched as Tim delivered a stinging slap to one scarred cheek. Bertram turned his face to the side. Tim proceeded to drum the top of his scalp, pinch his nose, give him a Chinese burn, and, as a grand finale, punch him in the stomach. Bertram doubled over. When he sat up again, drool was slicking his lips. His eyes were blank and uncomprehending.

"Are you sure you removed just the amygdalae?" Tony said.

"We may have accidentally sliced out a teensy bit of other brain tissue," Tim said, holding up his thumb and forefinger. "But we definitely got the peanuty bit."

The rage woke up fully, stretched a bit, and seized hold of Tony's brain. Tony was gripped by an image of startling clarity, in which Tim's eyes bulged behind his large glasses and his mouth produced a rattling squeeze as Tony's hands encircled his throat. He should have known better than to get his hopes up.

He poked Tim in the chest. "You're a complete and utter fucking idiot."

Astonishingly, Tim looked surprised. "Why? This is a clear success."

"A success? Did you operate with an ice-cream scoop? Look at him: he's a vegetable."

"Aha! Have you ever heard of anyone being killed by a vegetable?"

"If I had a carrot, I'd demonstrate just how vegetables can kill people by stabbing you in the eye with it. Do you honestly expect me to present this drooling mess to the world as our solution to the problem?"

"It's just our first effort. We can refine it."

"No, Tim. We can't. We don't have the time, and it's abundantly clear you don't have the capability. You're fired."

For the first time since Tony had known him, Tim's features tightened into a scowl. "You can't fire me. I'm your chief scientist."

"You're not a scientist. You're a clown without the makeup and red nose. I'd be better off hiring this guy."

Tim took a step back, and Tony thought he was about to slouch away. Instead, he threw out an arm in a half punch, half slap that caught Tony on the upper arm. Spock was nowhere to be found as Tony hauled out his bulky satphone and smacked Tim upside the head with it. The scientist fell backward, landing in the lap of his lobotomized patient. Tony

advanced, the phone held high, his arms thrumming with the desire
to finish the job. The buzz of the device snapped him out of it. He left
Tim sprawled across his intellectual equal and stormed out into the
hallway to answer the call.

"This had better be good news," Tony snapped down the line.

There was a moment's silence, before Glen's voice came through.
"I'm afraid not," he said. "Where are you?"

"With Tim, wasting my fucking time."

"Get back to Number Ten, right now. There's something you have
to see."

"Can't you just tell me?"

"It's better you see it for yourself."

The story was everywhere: in every newspaper, on every blog, across
every social media platform. Tony read as many different versions as
he could, searching for some kind of inauthenticity that would flag it
up as the product of an overactive imagination. It was an act born of
desperation. The story rang true in every way, from the way it tied in
with what he believed was going on behind the scenes to the descrip-
tions of the resistance group, which he knew for sure existed. It also
cleared up the mystery of the helicopter on the East Coast, although
the Glasgow incursion remained unexplained.

It was strange that this journalist, once so keen to make a bonfire
out of Britain, had changed her tune. From the impassioned nature of
the article, she clearly believed her story would make a difference—
and there was no doubting the significance of an uninfected woman
living alongside the infected with no bloodshed. It showed there really was hope. Yet Tony knew it would achieve the square root of fuck
all. Public pressure only went so far. When a government had made
up its mind, it was usually too late. Anyway, a quick browse showed
him the response was muted. The campaigning group Avaaz had put
out a call for petition signatures, as it always did, but elsewhere in edi-
torials and social media there didn't seem to be a groundswell of support for the attack to be halted. People clearly knew it was in their
interests to have the infected killed. They would wait until after the

genocide to condemn it, when it was safe. Secretly they would know they were complicit, but that wouldn't help anybody in Britain.

Only one aspect of the story gave him hope, but it was short lived. This young girl was immune, and he almost convinced himself that would provide a reason for the attack to be called off. Then he thought it through. They would only need a cure if the virus spread, and killing everyone would take care of that threat. Trying to extract the girl would be a risk for them; they didn't even know if she was truly immune or just asymptomatic. Nobody would take any chances. Even if they brought the girl in themselves, he would have to reinstate Tim or find somebody else to analyze her blood and synthesize a cure. That was an exercise in futility.

Glen sat behind him while he read, and Tony could sense he was champing at the bit. During Tony's time in front of the computer, Piers called eight times. Tony ignored each call. He needed to be sure he could talk calmly when the time came. It would take some doing. He was tempted to ponce a tranquilizer, but knew his mind had to be clear. Finally he sat back, rubbing his eyes and trying not to show his fear. The first thing he did was send a driver to take Margot and Vanessa to the bunker at Northwood. Until he knew they were as safe as possible, he wouldn't be able to think straight. The next time Piers called he picked up.

"I know it looks bad," Piers said, "but let me assure you this is utter fiction. This journalist has taken all the ill-informed rumors swithering around and bundled them into a story."

"That's an interesting defense. This is the same woman who got the story out the last time. Seems to me that she has a track record of exposing your little plots."

"I admit she was right once. That doesn't mean she's right again. She was probably missing all the attention of a big scoop and decided to get her name in the headlines again."

"That's weak. Why would she ruin her career making something like this up?"

"Ask her. I can categorically state that this is false. And this Jack Alford character, he was a notoriously flaky nobody. He wasn't privy to that kind of information."

"If he was such a low-level flunky, why'd they abduct him and dump him in Scotland?"

"You know what our American cousins are like. They get a bit keen."

"So you're admitting that part of the story is true?"

Piers, the dumb shit, fell silent when he understood he'd been trapped. "Look, we've been preparing for any eventuality. But we'll take no action unless it's in response to aggression from your side and is authorized by the UN General Assembly."

"Tell that to Saddam," Tony said. "If you can dig him up and get the worms out of his ears."

"That was different. You actually do have WMDs, and we know that any hostilities started by us could prompt you to use them."

Piers's use of "WMDs" instead of "nuclear weapons" caused a brief moment of panic, which subsided quickly. If they knew about the missile development, they would have blown it up by now. Again, he desperately wanted to make his threat, but knew he needed to be smart. He took several deep breaths, assumed his best Spock voice, and spoke slowly down the line. "I believe you."

"What?" Piers said.

"I know you're a cretin, but I believe your bosses are smart enough to know what would happen if you came at us. Let me assure you that we won't do anything rash in response to this story. We'll only act in self-defense."

Piers's sigh of relief was so loud that it distorted the speaker. "That's good to hear."

When Tony hung up, he got Amira on the line and filled her in.

"We need to draft a statement," she said.

"Are you almost at the camp?"

"Be there in a few hours."

"Right. Once you're there, write up a press release saying that while we're disturbed at the media reports of an impending attack, we have been assured by the international community that they have no basis. Bring out the spiel about us being committed to a peaceful solution, blah, blah, blah. And then get that video out pronto, so it looks like we're still trying to prove ourselves. That might buy us the time we need."

"The time we need for what, Tony?" Amira said, her voice flat.

Just as he'd wanted to tell Piers about the missile, Tony now felt the need to tell Amira he wouldn't fire it. She wouldn't have a chance to see Glen again before it was ready, so it would be safe to do so. However, Glen was still standing behind him so he kept quiet. He would call her later when he had some privacy. "They're going to kill us all, Amira."

"You don't know that for sure."

"You'll find the journalist who wrote the story there. Ask her if she made it all up."

"But . . ."

"No buts, Amira. Just do it."

He cut the line to avoid further discussion and turned to Glen, who was tapping his foot furiously. "How long until we're ready?"

"Five days."

"Make it two," he said, feeling like Captain Kirk talking to Scotty. "They were supposed to be attacking in just under a week, but now they know we know, they're probably going to move faster. We need to do the same."

A grin split Glen's face. "Then we'll go ahead?"

"Just get it ready," Tony said. "I'm coming up to oversee this personally."

"Don't you trust me?"

"You're one of the few I do trust. I just need to be there."

Glen looked piqued, but Tony couldn't reveal his real reason for wanting to be present. He had to see the submarine slide under the water with his own eyes before he could start threatening Piers. Most of all he needed to be standing beside Glen in the control room when he told him the missile wouldn't be fired. Glen had been so excited at the prospect of playing with his new toy that, in his childish tantrum at being denied, he might decide to fire it off anyway. Tony wanted to be the one holding the radio at that moment.

As Glen left, Frank pushed past him, his face red, and threw a copy of *The Sun* down on the table. "The fucking tabloids have got ahold of it."

Tony put his elbows on the desk and rested his head on his hands, staring at a drawing of a giant Uncle Sam standing with his foot over Britain, which was portrayed as a beetle lying on its back, legs flailing in the air.

"Bollocks," Tony said. "I'll make a live address. Tell them it's not true."

"Isn't it?" Frank said.

"Of course it is. But we need to avoid panic. Let's get our arses over to the BBC studio pronto."

They ran out of the door together. The last thing they needed was millions of people on the move again. Tony didn't feel bad about lying and telling people to stay put. The bombs they thought would be falling on them would never come. He would make sure of that. Tony began composing his speech in his head, his intention to call Amira back forgotten in the heat of the latest crisis.

26

Ruan was hacking at a tree with her saber in a quiet corner of the commune when Geldof found her. The first she knew of his presence was when she swung the sword back for another swipe, prompting a yelp of fear. She spun round to see a lock of ginger hair float from his fringe to the ground.

"Sorry," she said.

"It's okay," Geldof said, although the look of abject terror on his face suggested otherwise. "I needed a haircut anyway."

She grunted in response and buried the edge of her blade in the tree trunk. She left it quivering there and rolled her shoulder, which was aching from half an hour of brutalizing the vegetation.

"I thought you were a tree hugger, not a tree stabber," he said, looking at the raw wound in the bark.

"It'll live. Maybe."

They'd been thrown together again the previous day when Fanny assigned Geldof to help Ruan with her chores. She suspected an obvious attempt to get them together, but she hadn't really minded. Despite his shaky start, he displayed a level of maturity she hadn't encountered in boys of his age. Even the obvious effort he expended in not looking at her breasts seemed born from a desire to respect her boundaries rather than from the fear of being caught like a startled rabbit in the dazzling glare of her headlamps. Or perhaps she was being too kind. Still, there was something different about Geldof. She couldn't quite figure out what it was at first. After all, he looked very much like a boy: the hair follicles on his face were still in hibernation, his cheeks were as rosy as Rory's, and there wasn't so much as the rumor of a wrinkle on his smooth face. Admittedly, his body wasn't the typically lanky and awkward frame of a boy with years of growing still to go. She knew a swimmer when she saw one; he had that characteristic triangular shape that spoke of long hours pulling his upper body through the water. It was only when he closed his eyes for several seconds that she got it. With his lids down, he looked barely fourteen, never mind sixteen. When he opened them again, the years piled back on. His eyes were those of somebody twice his age.

It struck her again how much her world had changed. All of her experience with boys her age came before the virus, when the worst thing they had to worry about was exam grades or whether the risqué pictures they'd texted to their girlfriends were going to be circulated around the school. Geldof had been through so much more. When she asked him to tell her what had happened after the virus, he just started talking matter-of-factly. The more he talked, not even flinching when he described his father dying, the more she felt a desire to open up herself. It would be good to tell somebody who could understand what she'd been through. But when he finished and looked at her with an unspoken question between them, she hesitated. Sensing her reluctance, he'd moved on the conversation—another sign that he was unusually in tune for a boy of his age.

"I know you're upset," Geldof said. "We all are. But we'll find a way. If Lesley's story doesn't stop them, I'll make sure the mercenaries get you out. You're immune. They're bound to take you in to France or wherever."

"Yeah, so they can stick needles in me and poke about in my brain to find out why I don't get it? No, thanks. I'd rather just be anonymous."

"Then I'll get them to take you somewhere quiet, where nobody knows who you are."

"It isn't about me," she said, dropping to sit on a log.

"Then what is it about?"

"My parents."

"It's hard to lose people you love."

"No. You don't understand."

Geldof sat beside her, keeping a respectful distance. "Do you want to talk about it?"

Looking at the poor tree that had borne the brunt of her frustration, Ruan once again felt the need to share. It was either that or she would end up deforesting half of Scotland. She began to talk, and, once the cork was out of the bottle, she couldn't stop.

Ruan only stopped when she reached the point where her parents had chased her down the stairs, too emotionally exhausted to continue. At some point in her narrative, Geldof had taken her hand. She'd let him, grateful of the contact. Now she realized she'd been gripping it tightly and that he wore an expression of patient discomfort. She let go.

"Sorry," she said.

"No, I'm sorry," he said, shaking out the injured hand. "That's horrible."

"It was my own fault. I shouldn't have gone back, shouldn't have listened to the stupid voice in my head that told me they would be fine."

"You had a fever."

"No, I'm just stubborn."

"Must be why you like my mum so much."

They fell silent for a moment. Even thought it had been painful to recall what happened she felt lighter for having unburdened herself.

"What did you do then?"

"I tried to get the virus."

Geldof's eyes widened. "What?"

"I'd only seen the infected in the camp, so at first I didn't know they only took a proper maddie when there was somebody around to infect. When I realized that I thought that if I got myself infected we could be together again."

"You're immune though."

"I know. But I was lonely and desperate. I figured if I got attacked enough times, maybe it would stick. So I went out of the city, looking for somebody to infect me. I came across this skinny little woman on her own out in a field. I let her bite and scratch me, but she just wouldn't stop."

"Because the virus wouldn't cross over." Ruan nodded. "How did you get away?"

This was something else Ruan didn't want to remember, but she'd come this far and needed to get the poison out. She swallowed hard. "I killed her. I didn't mean to. I just started fighting back, hard. She fell over and hit her head on a rock. It was easy while she was still attacking me: she had that look the infected all have, like she wasn't human. When she died, though, her face relaxed and she was just this fragile farmer again."

"How did it make you feel?"

"Have you ever killed anyone?"

"No."

"Then I hope you never have to. I don't want to talk about it."

"How did you make it through all of that time without going insane?"

"Mental discipline. I'm very good at pretending things aren't happening."

"And you plan to do that for the rest of your life?"

"What else can I do?" Ruan said, her voice small.

Tentatively, Geldof reached out again and took her hand. It felt good to be able to relax and touch another human without still clinging to a faint worry about the possible consequences, as she did any time she was close to Fanny's crew.

"So," Geldof said, "what's upsetting you now?"

"When I came here, it gave me hope. I thought Fanny and her people could teach my parents to control it. Then I began to realize they hadn't even tried to resist the virus. They just tried to kill me."

"And what do you think that means?"

"I think it means they didn't really love me."

"Don't you think you're being a bit harsh? You don't know what it's like to have it."

"Your mum managed to stop herself from attacking you."

"Yes, but my mum hates the mainstream and couldn't possibly have allowed herself to go with the flow. If everybody was controlling it, I guarantee you she'd set up a movement calling for everybody to start killing each other. As willful as she is, you saw how much she had to struggle. Maybe they'll learn to control it. You could see them again."

"No, I won't. I've spent the last few days trying to pretend they were dead. It was easier to deal with than imagining they couldn't even stop themselves from attacking me. The problem is, now they're really going to be dead."

"You don't know that. Maybe Lesley's story will stop the attack."

"Do you really think so?"

She could see the doubt in his eyes, but still he tried to reassure her. "There's a chance. Look, I'm not telling you to forgive them just yet. It was a horrible thing to go through. I just want you to understand this was the virus, not them. How could they not love you?"

This time Ruan squeezed his hand. "Thanks for trying."

His cheeks bloomed red and he looked away. "Come on. It's almost lunchtime. You must be starving after giving that tree such a hard time."

He got to his feet and hauled her up. She reached over to grab the sword, still holding on to his hand, and together they walked out into the camp. No sooner had they emerged from the bushes than Eva came running over. "There you are. Come on, we'd better get you locked away in the hangar."

"Why?"

"The BBC is here."

"More arrivals?"

"We do appear to have been quite popular recently. Anyway, they want to make a video about the resistance."

"I've not been on the telly in ages," Geldof said. "Can we be in it?"

"They're infected."

"In that case, we'd better hide."

They hurried to the hangar, where Lesley and the mercenaries were hovering outside. Just before they went in, Ruan caught sight of Rory. He was staring at their joined hands, his face grim. She let go hurriedly, feeling a pang at the loss of contact, and went inside.

27

They were in the hangar for two hours while the infected members of the commune talked with the journalists. The mercenaries passed the time with a game of charades, in which they took turns to act out not films or books but wars they'd fought in. All of the wars looked the same to Lesley and suspiciously like the games boys had played at school—mimed machine gun fire, valiant tossing of one last grenade despite multiple bullet wounds, lots of flopping to the ground dead— but somehow the mercenaries got them all correct. While the four grown men were throwing themselves around, Geldof and Ruan sat one buttock apiece on the stool in front of the computer, giving a running commentary on the spread of the story. Lesley tried not to listen: she couldn't bear the thought of her name on everybody's lips again.

Now that the article was out, too late to recall, she was filled with doubts as to whether she'd done the right thing. Not to overegg the pudding, the decision she'd taken could alter the course of human history. Sure, Tony Campbell had tried hard to come across as reasonable but she couldn't forget their interview and the sight of the sharp little teeth behind his rigid lips as he lost it and threatened to kill her. Who knew what he would do now? She couldn't even work up the enthusiasm to talk to Geldof and the mercenaries about their mission. It was a great story, but she didn't want to write any more great stories. She just wanted anonymity. More than anything, she just wanted to be back in New York with Terry, lost in the simple pleasure of pressing up against his warm body.

And so, when Geldof and Ruan retired to the corner to whisper to

each other, she commandeered the computer and began typing the
e-mail that Fanny had forbidden her from sending earlier.

*Terry, I'm not dead and I'm sorry. Not sorry I'm not dead, obviously.
I'm sorry for everything I've put you through over the last few weeks.
I'm even sorrier for the months before. I spent so much time trying to
become the Lesley that everybody thought I was that I didn't think
about what you were going through. It's important you know I wasn't
trying to become famous. I just wanted to deserve my success. But the
reasons for being an absentee girlfriend don't matter. I should have
been there for you more. It must have been so hard on your own.
Anyway, by now you'll have seen the story. You know where I am. If I
somehow get out of this mess, I want to come home and try to make
things right between us. I've never told you I love you, because I'm not
sure if I do. I'm not even sure if you love me, or if we can love each
other. But, if you're willing, I want to find out. This time, I promise I
won't kill the goldfish.*

Lesley.

She hit send instantly so she wouldn't have a chance to overthink
and rewrite. It was still early in the morning in New York and Terry
would be asleep, so there was no point in sitting there and obsessively
refreshing in the hope he would get back to her quickly. She opened
the metal hatch to see what was going on with the visitors and stifled a scream as she unexpectedly came nose-to-nose with Fanny's
scarred features.

"She wants to talk to you," Fanny said. "Apparently she has something important to tell you."

"Isn't she infected?"

"She'll stand far away and shout. The wind's blowing the other way
anyway. Plus you're locked in and we'll sort her out if she tries anything."

Lesley nodded her assent and Fanny stepped aside. The chubby
little journalist was standing in the middle of the camp, looking in
her direction.

"I'm here," Lesley shouted. "What do you want to say?"

"For the last few weeks every soldier in the army has been donating blood. At the same time, at Faslane, they've been working on converting the warheads in the nuclear missiles to carry a different load. A bloody load. In a few days' time they'll be ready. Then they're going to fire them at France."

"Sorry, I don't quite understand you," Lesley said. "What kind of bloody load?"

"I meant it literally, not pejoratively. They're filling the new warheads with infected blood. Tony thinks it's the only way to stop the attack. If the virus gets out on continental Europe, there won't be any point in destroying Britain because they'll be too busy dealing with it. Supposedly."

"That's crazy. It'll kill billions."

"Why do you think I'm telling you this?"

"Won't they be able to shoot them down?"

"Apparently not. The missiles are too fast and they're traveling a short distance."

"It doesn't make any sense. As soon as those missiles go up, they'll think they're nuclear. They'll launch everything they've got at the U.K."

"That's what I said. This is a last-ditch measure. Tony was trying to find another way, but when he read your story I think it made him believe he doesn't have anything to lose."

Lesley gripped the edge of the hatch so hard that her fingers ached. The pressure was the only thing holding her up. As a direct result of her actions, the virus was going to get out into the world. From Europe, it would spread everywhere: to New York, where Terry would soon be feeling hope again, and to Kenya, where her mother and father were living out their last years in peace. Her jinx had been globalized and would wipe out half of humanity. All she needed now was a big cloak and a scythe.

"Can't you persuade him not to do it?" she said. "My story might make a difference. People will protest, won't they?"

"This isn't some campaign to stop Israel and Palestine knocking lumps out of each other. People know this country is a real and direct threat to their lives."

"I don't believe that," Lesley said, more to convince herself than because she disagreed with the woman.

"It doesn't matter what you believe. It matters what Tony believes. He's the man with his finger on the button."

"How do you know what he believes?"

"I'm not really a BBC journalist. I'm his spin doctor." Fanny shot her a sharp look, and she held up her hands. "Hey, I think this is as wrong as it's possible to be."

"What do you want me to do with this information?"

"Write a story. Tell the UN. Get them to bomb the submarine before it leaves Faslane. I don't want this on my conscience."

"And I don't want it on mine. You tell the bloody world about the bloody missile. I just want to be left alone."

"You don't have that luxury. You're Lesley McBrien, global expert on the infection."

"I'm not an expert!" Lesley shouted. "I'm a useless, jammy fuck-wit who spouts her gob off on TV about things she doesn't really understand."

"And that," the spin doctor said, "is the very definition of an expert."

Once the woman had gone, they all gathered around the table on the pier for an emergency meeting.

"So, what do we do?" Fanny said.

Lesley had by now calmed down. She knew that as much as she would like to curl up into a ball and quietly decompose, she didn't have that luxury. Too many lives depended on what they did next. "This is my fault. If I hadn't written that story, they wouldn't be about to fire the missile off. We have to do what she says."

"No," Scholzy said. "If anybody outside of Britain gets a whiff of this, the entire island will be burnt to a crisp instantly, us included."

"And if we say nothing, the entire world is fucked," Lesley said. "You have people you care about, I assume?" Scholzy nodded. "All dead. Or turned."

Fanny had a faraway look in her eye and, unbelievably, a slight smile on her lips. "You know," she said, "I've always wanted to stop Trident."

"What are you suggesting?" Lesley said.

"Faslane isn't too far from here."

"And?"

"We attack the base."

"Have you lost your bloody marbles?" Scholzy said. "It'll be crawling with soldiers. You'll all die. Badly."

"They won't be expecting an attack from land. And we have you. Look, do you think all of this is a coincidence, that you came here, and Lesley came here, and this woman came here to tell us, probably the only people who could do anything about it?"

Scholzy snorted. "You think this is fate?"

"Maybe. Maybe not. What I do know is that it's the only real option on the table that won't see mass slaughter here or in the rest of the world."

"No way," Scholzy said. "It's suicide."

"Don't you want to fight for a cause just once?" Geldof said.

"We always fight for a cause. Not necessarily a just one, mind you. And we're used to being paid for it."

"I'll give you another million," Geldof said. "If we succeed, you'll all be rich men. If we do nothing, there won't be a world for you to go back to anyway."

"You're not in a position to be promising more money," Scholzy said.

"I'm in," James said. When Scholzy stared at him, he just shrugged. "He's right. I don't want to live like this for the rest of my life. I want to go home."

"I'm in, too," said Mick, giving Fanny a lingering look. "I've always wanted to see if the Brits are as good in a barney as they claim."

Peter said something unintelligible behind his mask.

Scholzy's fingers drummed on the table as he looked around the set faces. "So you all want to be heroes, heh? Fine. Let's just try to make sure we're not dead heroes."

Lesley looked around the table, scarcely able to believe what she was hearing. This was a risk she wasn't prepared to take: not because she was afraid of dying, but because she knew they would fail. And when they failed, those missiles would shower infected blood over the continent. She couldn't let that happen. She pushed off the table, intending to go straight to the hangar and send an e-mail.

"Where are you going?" Scholzy said.

"To do what's right and tell the UN."

James barred her way. "No, you're not. This is the only shot we've got at surviving. You don't get to make this decision for the rest of us."

"And you don't get to gamble with the lives of all those people out there just so we can survive," Lesley said.

When she tried to push past, James wrapped his arms around her waist and lifted her off her feet. Her legs kicked fruitlessly as he addressed Fanny, "Where can we lock her up?"

"There's no need for that," Fanny said. "Lesley, I promise you that if we fail we'll tell the UN and let them do what they have to. At least give us a chance to keep the bloodshed to a minimum."

"And who's going to tell them if it doesn't work? We'll all be dead."

"We'll hold one person back with the satphone to make the call."

Lesley stopped kicking. "Do you give your word?"

"You have my word."

"Then let's do it quickly."

Fanny nodded and James dropped Lesley. She sat back down at the table.

"Now," Scholzy said, "we get to the difficult bit. Does anybody have any ideas on how we're going to actually get into a heavily defended military base, never mind find a way to destroy these missiles?"

"Isn't that your speciality?" Geldof said.

"Hey, I'm trying to be collaborative here." Nobody piped up with any suggestions. "How about we all go away for a few hours and come back with ideas to brainstorm?"

There was a murmur of assent. As they got up, Fanny looked along the length of the table. "Has anybody seen Rory?"

"Not since this morning," Tom said. "He said he was going for a walk."

"Well, we don't have time to worry about him right now," Fanny said. "I'm sure he'll turn up soon enough. Now let's see if we can come up with a plan."

28

As everybody drifted away in groups of twos and threes, Ruan and Geldof gravitated together. This was the point where it would have been permissible for Geldof to suggest they have wild, life-affirming sex to laugh in the face of Death, who, judging from the plethora of ways to die he was strewing in their path, seemed grimly intent on reaping them. After all, from the exhausted and drawn look on Mick's face and the corresponding look of satisfaction on his mum's this morning, others were clearly thumbing their noses at old Mort. He'd thought he would feel angry if his mum gave in to Mick, but when he saw how relaxed she looked he couldn't hold it against her. His dad had been dead for seven months now, and in such difficult circumstances all that mattered was that she found some fleeting happiness. While the thought to suggest similar activity did cross Geldof's mind, it was in a vague, theoretical way—more as a nod to the books and movies he'd devoured in Croatia that detailed such situations. He did find Ruan attractive, but as he had no chance it was a waste of mental and emotional resources to entertain the notion. He'd been there and bought the T-shirt, cap, and souvenir snow globe on that one with his crush on Mary.

He sensed no particular attraction from Ruan's side, although he could count the number of girls who'd fancied him on a fingerless hand and so had no idea what signals they gave off on such occasions. He'd often thought that life would be much easier if women's nipples swelled in the same proportions as penises when their dander was up. Even he wouldn't be able to miss the signal of long nipple fingers pointing him out as the object of desire. Anyway, when he held Ruan's hand it hadn't been an advance on his part. She'd looked so small and lost as she related her story that it felt like a natural response, the kind of gesture a friend or brother would make. And that, he realized with a start, was how he felt toward her. Before puberty smacked him upside the head with its big hormone stick, he had female friends. After, his scrambled brain only allowed him to speak to girls in mortified mumbles. With Ruan, the initial awkward bumping of heads over her name aside, he'd been relating to her as he would with any boy he liked. A female friend. Of all the crazy events that had swamped his life, this one surprised him most.

"So, you've got a million dollars lying around in pocket change," Ruan said.

"Absolutely. I wipe my bum with tenners."

"Only tenners? That's not very extravagant."

"They're brown, so it seems to fit best."

"Nasty!"

They laughed harder than the joke warranted. Geldof's amusement came from the sense of liberation at being able to say whatever he wanted without feeling he would scupper his chances of a snog. He could be himself. Which was why, halfway through a particularly large chortle, he sat down heavily and addressed the elephant that was rampaging around the room, knocking over furniture, trumpeting, and generally making itself very hard to ignore.

"I'm scared," he said. "I'm pretty certain I'm shortly going to die a horribly painful death."

"Hey, we're going to be heroes," Ruan said. "How many people get the chance to save the world?"

"Don't heroes usually have some kind of fighting skill? You've got your gun and sword, Mum's got her bow, Scott's got his big stick, and the mercenaries have got enough hardware strapped onto those bikes to cause a mass extinction event. Even Andy has his eggs, although I still think that's plain weird. What am I going to do when we go in? Let them eat me and hope they're fatally allergic to gingers? Squirt my contact lens solution at them? Challenge them to a Sudoku death match, loser blows his brains out?"

"You could stay here," Ruan said. "Nobody would think any less of you."

"I can't do that while the people I care about go off to fight."

"Then we'll figure out something for you to do. First, though, we'd better come up with some kind of plan."

"A plan. Let me draw on my extensive knowledge of storming army bases and knock something up."

"Come on, you're a boy. Didn't you play shooting games?"

"I prefer puzzles."

"There you are. You must have developed some strategic thinking."

"I suppose. It would be easier if we had schematics of the base."

"And where are we going to get those?"

"Maybe they have a gift shop. Plastic mushroom cloud replicas, Trident-branded mugs, pens in the shape of nukes, and detailed plans of the base, £4.99 a pop. We could nip down and buy one." Geldof got up and chucked a stone in frustration. It sailed through the sky and pinged off the satellite dish. He stared at it and slapped his forehead. "Of course. How stupid am I?"

"What?"

"We don't have schematics, but we've got the next best thing. Google Earth."

An hour later they'd collected armfuls of aerial views of the base, from a bird's-eye image showing all approach roads to sections at maximum resolution. They didn't have any kind of plan, since they didn't know which building was which or how a submarine base operated. Still, it was something. The mercenaries would surely be able to make sense of the images and figure out how to approach it; they must have chalked up more assaults than a psychopathic skinhead at a gay pride march. Geldof and Ruan went outside with their bounty and headed back toward where a few people had already gathered. As they approached, Geldof looked out across the water.

"What's that?" he said, pointing.

Ruan shielded her eyes and peered. "Looks like boats. Coming this way. It's the Noels."

"Eh?"

"The people from Arrochar. They all look like Noel Edmonds."

"Maybe it's the start of a new infection. The people they bite turn into Noel Edmonds, too. Can you imagine the horror?"

"This isn't something to joke about," Ruan said, chewing at her lower lip. "Last time we met, a mob of them tried to kill me."

"We'd better find my mum."

Fanny was sitting cross-legged with Scott, Eva, and Tom in the living room of one of the houses and passing round some of the sweet-smelling weed as a creative aid when Geldof and Ruan burst in. As the others giggled, Scott was laying out a plan that involved weaving a giant net in the shape of a vagina and lowering it into position over the missile tube from a hot air balloon.

"How much have you had to smoke?" Geldof said.

"He's right, it's ridiculous," Eva said. "The balloon would never carry the weight. We'd need a helicopter."

Fanny put her hand on Geldof's arm as the others laughed. "Just some light relief. We really are trying to come up with a plan."

"We've got something else to worry about," Ruan said. "Boats are coming from Arrochar."

The laughter cut off and everyone ran outside. The two boats were close enough for Geldof to count a total of six bearded men. As far as he could tell across the distance and through all that blond facial hair, they looked decidedly cross.

"They've never bothered us before," Fanny said. "You guys had better make yourselves scarce while I find out what they want."

Before Geldof could move, one of the Noels stood up and pointed a long, shiny object toward them. What felt like a host of tiny insects whizzed past his ear, accompanied by a distant bang and smoke rising from the boat. Scott wailed and Geldof looked to his left to see Eva crumple to the ground. Even though he'd been shot at before, his body still hadn't developed the combat reflexes that would have sent him diving for cover. Standing there like a spare tit, he presented an easy target for the Noel in the other boat who was raising a shotgun in his direction. Fanny hauled him to the ground as shotgun pellets whizzed through the space where he'd been standing.

"Get into the hangar and stay there," she shouted, before getting to her feet and zigzagging away.

Scott was dragging Eva away from the water, while Ruan was sprinting back toward the houses, no doubt to procure her weapons. Geldof didn't intend to cower in the background but had no idea how to make himself useful as anything other than a moving target that would draw fire while the others fought. As he prevaricated, another Noel stood up and let off his shotgun. Pellets dappled the grass in front of Geldof's face. He got to his feet and ran toward the quad bikes. The mercenaries had appeared out of the bushes and were strapping on weapons. Mick was wearing a manic grin as Geldof arrived beside him and crouched down behind a bike.

"Now this is more like it," Mick said, plucking a grenade from his bag.

He pulled the pin, waited a terrifying few seconds, and lobbed it at the Noel Armada. It exploded in the first boat. In the brief and surprisingly small flash of light before smoke wreathed the boat, Geldof caught a glimpse of a body falling backward. The occupants of the other vessel jumped into the water.

"Amateurs," James said. "What're they thinking, attacking in broad daylight in those crappy little boats?"

"Let's teach them a lesson," Mick said.

"You need to still be alive to learn a lesson."

"Fine. Let's just kill them."

The mercenaries opened fire. Splashes kicked up across the water in an arcing line until the bullets found the men wading through the shallows. Geldof turned away. That was when he saw what was charging in from the main entrance. He clutched Mick's arm.

"We've got a bigger problem," he shouted.

A swarm of Noel Edmonds look-a-likes was rampaging in, waving an assortment of weapons that ranged from iron pokers to cricket bats to garden forks. At the vanguard, two men sat atop hulking Highland cows. The wind ruffled their beards around bared teeth. The cows looked even more ferocious, their wide nostrils flaring and shaggy

ginger hair rippling as they thundered toward Geldof and the mercenaries. Mick turned, just in time to be caught by a shotgun blast from
one of the cow riders. He flew back and his head smacked against one
of the metal boxes attached to the quad bike behind him. The other
mercenaries spun and unleashed their weapons on the advancing mob.
The two men riding the animals fell; the beasts kept on coming even as
bullet holes ripped into their muscled flanks.

Geldof felt as though somebody had yanked his brain out through
his ear, dipped it in a vat of potent hallucinogens, and then unceremo-
niously stuffed it back in. His body responded to the chaotic scene just
as vehemently, every quavering muscle demanding that he run like hell.
He ignored his cowardly body and bent over Mick, who lay unconscious
with blood gurgling up from his shredded trouser leg. He picked up
the fallen gun, waved it in the vague direction of the horde and pulled
the trigger. The weapon leapt in his hand; his bullets fizzed over the
heads of the attackers and into the trees. While he was shredding the
foliage, James appeared next to him with a long tube on his shoulder.
A rocket whooshed through the air and hit one of the cows smack on
the forehead. Its head disintegrated into a cloud of red mist that doused
the surrounding attackers, and its huge body came sliding forward on
its knees. The Noels behind hurdled the steaming corpse and kept
coming. As Geldof brought the weapon down, an arrow whistled through
the air and took the other cow in the eye. It let out a long moo and
staggered sideways, crushing another three of the attackers who were
running alongside it. Still the rest came on.

Three individuals peeled off from the mob. At their head ran Rory,
his cheeks purple with rage. The little shit, wracked with jealousy, must
have gone across the water and told his friends there were uninfected
people in the camp. They were heading straight for Ruan, who stood
calmly with her sword drawn. Fanny had gained the vantage point of
a rock by the water's edge and was busy pumping arrows into the main
body of the crowd, while Scott was crouched over Eva at the far end of
the camp. Lesley was now beside the mercenaries, raising a handgun
she must have grabbed from their weapons stash. The rest of the commune was sprinting toward the diminishing mob armed with sticks,

stones, and knives. Nobody was paying any attention to those closing in on Ruan.

Geldof closed his eyes, trying to block out the madness for long enough to bring some clarity to his fuzzy mind.

You can do this, he thought. *You have to do this.*

As calm as he was ever going to be, which in truth was not very calm at all, he brought the gun around. The angle meant that if he opened fire he would most likely hit Ruan, particularly given his wayward aim. He ran closer, hoping to get a better shot. One of the men pulled ahead and reached Ruan, who sidestepped nimbly. Geldof had known her sword must be sharp, as she spent enough time running its edge along the rocks, but he didn't fully appreciate just how deadly it was until it flashed forward and sliced through the front of the attacker's neck. He took another few steps before he toppled. Rory was next in line and Geldof expected to see Ruan deal with him in a similar manner. Instead, she paused before pulling the point up and clobbering the boy on the temple with the solid-looking hilt. He dropped to the ground.

The delay gave the final assailant time to step inside Ruan's guard and punch her full in the face. She fell and landed heavily on her back. The Noel stood over her, his legs tensed to pounce. Before he could leap, a small white object flew through the air and smacked him in the right eye. He took a step backward, wiping at the sticky fluid running down his cheek. From the corner of his eye Geldof saw Andy, who'd appeared from nowhere, snap his arm forward. Another egg cartwheeled toward the Noel and cracked in his other eye.

Geldof took the opportunity to let fly. He kept the barrel low this time, hoping to compensate for the rise, but his aim was off to the right. The bullets missed the Noel and shattered the last bolts holding the old iron guttering to the houses. An entire section creaked forward and swung down like a club. For a moment it looked like the long splinter of iron sticking out of the top would spike the man through the skull, but he stepped back at the last minute, and it impaled his foot to the ground. Geldof pulled the trigger again, yet somehow managed to miss the stationary target. Eyes now egg-free, the Noel started tugging at the guttering. Geldof moved closer to finish the job. Once he was six feet away, a distance from which even he couldn't miss, he jerked the trigger. The gun clicked.

"Oh, come on!" he shouted.

The Noel looked at him with crazed eyes and ripped his foot out of the guttering without a grunt of pain. He picked up Ruan's fallen sword and raised it. Geldof chucked the gun at him. It sailed over his head. As the Noel stepped toward him, Geldof raised his arms in a hopeless attempt to ward off the coming blow, sure that his prediction of dying a horrible death was about to come true. The blow never came. Ruan, who'd regained her feet, stepped up to the Noel and put her pistol to the side of his head. One shot rang out and the Noel went down.

Ruan lowered the gun, her face expressionless, and faced Geldof. "Are you okay?"

"I was supposed to be saving you," he said, his voice hoarse.

Geldof stepped toward her, but she held up a blood-slicked hand. "No. The virus."

He stopped. In the heat of the moment he'd forgotten about the infection risk. Now that his fight—if his actions could be dignified with that term—was over, Geldof became aware the sound of gunfire had died away. He turned to see that the remnants of the Noels, no more than ten, had come toe-to-toe with Fanny's troops. They were taking a pummelling. At the center of the battle Nayapal whirled and twisted, a look of such calm on his face he could have been stroking a kitten. One of the Noels swung a metal pipe at his face. Nayapal dropped, his back arching and hands bending backward to touch the ground. The bar passed over his body and he brought himself up into a handstand, flipped back up to his feet, and drove his heeled hand into the nose of his attacker. Scott had left Eva to join the fray and was whirling his staff around his head, cracking skulls. Tom had brought his hands together into prayer position and, as a Noel charged, stepped forward into a wide-legged stance and drove his index fingers up the nostrils of his opponent with deadly accuracy. It was over within minutes. The members of the commune stood in the middle of the bodies of their vanquished foes, some twitching and moaning, most of them still.

"Now that," Scholzy said, with genuine admiration in his voice, "was fucking awesome."

When the bodies were piled off to one side for burning and the surviving Noels—including Rory—were trussed and locked in the spare
hangar, they gathered around the table, upon which incense sticks had
been placed to mask the stench that would soon follow. Ruan had
cleaned herself up. This time she was the one to take Geldof's hand.

"How do you feel?" she said.

"Hmm. Let me think. Ineffectual. Inept. Hopeless. Feeble. Inad-
equate. I think that about covers it."

"Don't be so hard on yourself. You did save my life."

"How do you figure that?"

"I'm assuming you deliberately shot the gutter down."

He snorted. "Yeah, right. I literally couldn't hit a cow's arse at twenty
paces, but I managed to shoot a bolt at the same distance. But you were
amazing. You didn't hesitate."

"You can't allow yourself to hesitate when somebody's trying to kill
you."

"But how do you do it? I mean . . ."

Geldof trailed off. He'd seen so much violence in his short life; his
muted reaction to a bloody massacre that a year ago would have left
him traumatized told him he was growing far too used to it. Thanks
to his crapness in battle he'd yet to take a life, which somehow provided a layer of insulation that made it easier to bear. And while the
impersonal distance provided by a gun meant he may have been able
to shoot somebody, he knew that driving cold steel through a human
body would always be beyond him.

"How did I kill so easily?"

"Yes."

"Mental discipline again. I visualized them as sheep. Big, woolly
sheep with sharp teeth. I'm pretty good at that kind of thing."

"Why sheep?"

"When I was eight a sheep bit me in a petting zoo. It gave me the
Orf virus and a swollen, seeping thumb. My brother Bryan called me
Thumbelina and the bloody name stuck. After that I couldn't even
watch a cartoon sheep without wanting to kick the screen in."

"And after they're dead? Do you still see them as sheep?"

Ruan blinked several times. "I don't look at them after. Anyway, I did hesitate. I didn't kill Rory."

"Why not?"

"I couldn't see a sheep, just a hurt little boy. It's my fault he went off the rails. I laughed when he came on to me."

Ruan looked so distraught that Geldof wanted to wrap her in his arms. Nobody their age should have to endure so much. Before he could act, a roar of pain and a jumble of swearwords came from the house where James was tending to Mick's wounds. Everybody looked over, grimacing as one. They'd been lucky in terms of casualties. Only Hannah, who'd been guarding the entrance when the Noels rode in, had died. Eva and Mick would both live.

Fanny, who'd been visiting with Eva, came striding over. "Right. If we don't stop that missile, this insanity is going to play out in every town, village, and city across the globe."

Geldof looked at the pile of bodies and tried to extrapolate. There was no way he could come up with an equation to work out what percentage of the world population would die in the event of the missile going out. There were too many variables, but it would easily reach hundreds of millions. That many bodies in one tangled heap of flopping limbs would dwarf Mount Everest. He shivered and slapped the images of the base down on the table. "We've got these for starters."

Scholzy spread the documents across the table. "How recent are these?"

"No idea. Could be a couple of months old."

Scholzy jabbed his finger at one long pier, where a submarine was docked. "The best way to do it would be to swim down the loch and plant magnetic charges on the underside of the sub, presuming it's in one of those berths and not a dry dock. Problem is, we didn't come prepared for an underwater mission and they're bound to have boats patrolling. In the water with no way of submerging we'd have no chance. A full-frontal assault is out, too. That was just a skirmish with a bunch of untrained idiots. That base will be full of well-trained soldiers. We'd have to fight across hundreds of meters to reach the submarine. We don't have the personnel or weaponry."

"So we should just give up?" Lesley said.

"I didn't say that. We need to find another way."

Peter said something then, although it was impossible to make it out through his chunky air filter.

"For God's sake, just take the bloody mask off, heh?" Scholzy snapped. "If Mick can get it on with one of these people and be fine I'm pretty sure you can breathe a bit of unfiltered air."

"Did he tell you?" Fanny said.

"No," Scholzy replied. "He's a gentleman that way. Let's just say you were both rather loud. Impressive stamina, by the way."

Fanny blushed as Scott gave her a sly little nudge. By this point, Peter had unstrapped his mask. It was strange to see him without it. His features looked pink and naked, in much the same way as the freshly shaved face of a lifelong beard wearer. "That interlude gave me an idea. It's a bit wacky, but I think it's our only shot." He paused, as though unsure whether to continue.

"Spit it out," Scholzy said. "It's not like we've got any other bright ideas."

"Do you remember that time in Somalia, when Kenya's military accused the insurgents of planning to use donkey bombs?"

"I remember. I also remember the terrorists quite rightly took the piss out of them for coming up with such an idiotic accusation."

"Maybe they were too quick to dismiss it. It would've carried the element of surprise. Who's going to run away from a donkey?"

"So you want to storm the base with suicide donkeys?"

"No," Peter said. He pointed to the steaming ginger corpses of the cattle. "I've had some bovine inspiration. We use cows."

ONE DAY TO EXCISION

29

This, Ruan thought as she prepared to open the gate that led into the field of cows behind Arrochar, *may well be the stupidest thing I've ever done.*

They'd ridden into Arrochar in the old truck, authorized for use since if this didn't qualify as an emergency nothing would. There must have been women and children left in the village, since the Noel invasion was exclusively male—unless there'd been bearded ladies in there as well—but they didn't show their faces. The truck had undergone some modifications: a hatch just big enough for one person to scoot through had been cut between the storage space and the cabin. The truck now sat idling at the bottom of the path leading to the main road in the village. A ramp led up into the back.

The plan was simple. She was to serve as bait to lure the cows down from the field and into the back of the van. Once in, she would jump through the hatch and Scott and Tom would slam the rear doors shut, capturing the herd for use in their upcoming assault. It was the quickest way to round up the cattle. They couldn't afford to waste a whole day of infected members of the commune chasing them around the field and trying to herd them toward the truck. They had preparations to make. Ruan had been chosen as the bait by virtue of a foot race with Geldof and the mercenaries—a battle she won with five meters to spare over the bulky Scholzy. Even though Geldof trailed in last, he still tried to convince her to hand the responsibility over to him. She knew he was still smarting from his ineffectual role in the battle, which had only confirmed his fears that he would be useless in the final assault. While she felt sorry for him, she'd refused to step down. He wouldn't make it ten paces.

She also knew that Fanny was working up to denying Geldof an active role in storming the base, largely because Ruan herself had suggested his participation would result in him at best being a burden and at worst getting killed—a thought that curdled her stomach. The way she understood it, the old Fanny would have had no problem in delivering this message. The new Fanny was agonizing over how to reconcile her decision to give her son freedom of choice with the fact that this freedom could lead to his death. Still, that was for Fanny and Geldof to worry about. Right now she had her own large and meaty concerns, which were grazing at the far end of the field. Unfortunately, she was upwind from the cows, which meant she would need to get dangerously close to give them a whiff of her scent and set them on the hoof. She started off by jumping up and down and shouting, hoping they would be able to detect her purity by sight alone. The cows merely glanced in her direction and went back to chewing at the grass.

They're just like bloody men, she thought. *The ones you actually want to chase you aren't interested, and the ones you don't won't leave you alone.*

"Try insulting them," Scott called from beside the truck.

"How d'you insult a cow?"

"Tell them they've got saggy udders," Tom replied.

"No, tell them the grass isn't greener on the other side," Scott said. Tom screwed up his face. "That's not an insult."

"No, but it's an unsettling thought. It might make them lose hope."

"I told you not to have that third joint," Tom said. "We need to get them angry, not depressed. They won't chase her if they've lost hope."

"Maybe they'll want to take their frustration out on somebody."

"They don't speak English, so how could I insult them?" Ruan said.

"That's what you think," Scott said. "This cow whisperer bloke I used to know organized a stand-up gig in a field for the cows. Got a comedian to tell them jokes. He swears they all laughed."

"What's a cow laugh sound like, then?" Tom said.

"I wasn't there, so I can't rightly say. A bit evil, I imagine, like: Moo-ha-ha!"

They both laughed until Ruan glared at them. "You do know I'm about to risk my life, don't you? You could at least try to be solemn or tense or something."

"Sorry," the two men said in unison.

Ruan shook her head. These were the people who were supposed to be saving the world tomorrow. She would need to ask Fanny to ration the dope supply. She trudged up the hill, noting points where hillocks, potholes, and piles of dung might trip her up on the way back. She was now worryingly close to the cows and still they hadn't clicked. At this rate she would have to go right up to them and stick her armpit in their noses. Then she had an idea. Fear sweat slicked her armpits, producing dark rings on the gray fabric of her jumper. She pulled it off, along with her T-shirt. Goose flesh rose on her bare skin. She picked up a rock, wrapped the garments around it to give them some weight and chucked them at the animals. The clothes bounced off the flank of the largest cow and came to rest amid their snuffling snouts. They abandoned their chewing with angry snorts and began banging heads as they all tried to get their teeth into the bundle. Two animals got a hold of it and engaged in a tug of war, which ended when it ripped in two. Still they ignored her.

"Sod it," Ruan said under her breath and sprinted the rest of the distance.

She booted the closest cow up the arse and, before it had even swung its head around, bombed back toward the truck. There was no need to look back to know their tiny brains had finally got the message that there was something tastier than grass and cud in the vicinity. The collective moo swelled and dipped as the out-of-sync individual voices came together and broke apart. It sounded like the kind of noise an emergency vehicle would make in a world run by cows. She focused on this thought, transforming the beat of hooves into the chug of an engine, and imagined an ambulance, flashing blue horns protruding from its roof, rushing a cow with an udder blockage to hospital. That turned out to be a bad idea, for the image was so daft she momentarily forgot the mortal danger she was in. Her adrenaline levels dipped and so did her pace. Only when she felt the wet slop of a snout on her back did she snap out of it and accelerate.

She leapt up the ramp and dashed through the truck. She'd spent hours the previous evening practicing diving through the hatch, resulting in bruised forearms and shins and a black eye from the one time she nailed it and sailed through to thump her head on the dashboard. This time she managed to force most of her body through before her feet caught on the opening. The truck shuddered as the cows mounted. Something snagged her trouser leg and started to pull. Scholzy, who was in the driver's seat, grabbed her hand. The rear doors slammed, which meant the cows were now trapped—just as she would be if the cow managed to haul her back in. Scholzy's grip was slipping on her sweaty hand, and she felt herself sliding backward. Just as she was sure she was about to disappear into the back to be trampled to death, cloth ripped and she shot forward.

A massive cow head rammed through the hatch, eyes rolling and tongue lolling. Scholzy punched it square between the eyes. The cow didn't budge, snapping left and right. Fortunately its neck and shoulders were too wide to allow it to push its way through farther. It looked like a necromancer truck driver had mounted a head on the wall of his truck and brought it to life.

"That'll have to do," Scholzy said.

He rolled down the window to talk to Scott, who was peering in. "You guys are going to have to walk. We've got an uninvited guest in the cabin."

Scott nodded and Scholzy put the truck into gear. "Let's get this lot back to the camp and then come out for the second run."

His voice prompted an ear-splitting moo and increased snapping from their trophy head.

"Second run?" Ruan shouted over the din.

"We're going to need more cows than this," he said. "There must be some in the other fields around here."

"Fantastic," Ruan said. "Another chance to have a cow chew on my backside."

They moved off, the truck swaying as the enraged animals blundered around in the back, fighting to reach the source of the enticing smell. Ruan shrank as far as she could against the passenger door and just hoped the truck wouldn't topple.

Geldof moped around the camp, playing hide-and-seek with Fanny. He could tell from the way she kept chewing her lip and shooting him sidelong glances all morning that she wanted to tell him something. He had a good idea what it was. To be honest, after his performance during the attack of the Noels, he couldn't blame her. He hadn't even qualified as bait, which was usually the role set aside for those who couldn't do anything else. Even a blind, wriggling earthworm was useful enough to be jammed on to a hook and plunged into the water to draw in the fish. The same worms would probably be more use than him at Faslane. They could at least dig a tunnel under the fence or something. His mum finally cornered him after Scholzy and Ruan returned with the cows, which were shuttled into the livestock pen by the commune members, growing quieter as soon as the uninfected were out of nostril range.

"I know," he said before she could even open her mouth. "You don't want me to fight. You're right. I'd just get in the way."

Fanny looked relieved. "Some people just aren't fighters, Geldof."

"Some people just aren't anything."

"You're being hard on yourself."

"Am I? What have I done that's any worth since I got here?"

"You came here for me even though you knew it was dangerous. You brought the mercenaries. We wouldn't have any chance without them. And the way Ruan tells it, you saved her life."

"Yeah, right. I flukily shot a pipe and nearly got stabbed in the face. She saved me."

"If you hadn't tried, she'd have been dead. That's what matters: you always try. Most people would've run away. I'm proud of you. Your dad would've been, too."

"I wish I was more like him. He'd totally kick arse down there."

"He wouldn't want you to be like him. He killed a lot of people. It messed him up."

"What about you? You've killed people, too. You were always a pacifist."

"I'm not happy about doing what I did or what I'm going to do. But there are bigger issues at play. We do what we must."

"So, I suppose you want me to stay here and hold the jackets while you fight?"

"Not at all," she said. "We have a job for you."

"Really," Geldof said, perking up a little. "What kind of job?"

"You'll be helping Mick."

"What, am I going to push his wheelchair?"

"Not quite. I'll let him explain. Look, about Mick . . ."

"It's okay, Mum. I don't mind."

"Really?"

"Yeah. Deep down, he's a good man."

"You think so?"

"No. But that's not important. The real question is whether he's a big man."

Fanny looked puzzled for a second before she got Geldof's meaning. She laughed long and hard. Geldof watched her momentarily carefree face and hoped it wouldn't be the last time they shared such a moment.

30

The HMS *Vengeance* looked every bit as deadly as Tony had imagined. The vessel was almost as gray as the water under the floodlights, and the two side fins and conning tower at the top gave it the look of a sleek, mechanical shark—an implacable, imperturbable machine with no imperative other than to kill. He brushed his fingers against the cold metal of the missile as it slid past on the way to be loaded. The accelerated timescale meant Glen's boys only had time to get one ready. One would be all they needed. He closed his eyes and imagined the multiple warheads inside, sloshing with blood. If he ever did have to give the order, this huge metal phallus would spurt its infected load over Paris. He tried to picture how it would be: blood raining onto upturned faces, hands stiffening into claws, shrieks and yells echoing through the streets, people trampling each other as they tried to flee. He could put no faces to these virtual Parisians; he could only see Margot and Vanessa down in the bunker, clinging to each other and waiting for the end.

He could also clearly picture the people who would die in Britain. He'd seen thousands of them streaming along the side of the road as he and Glen drove to the airfield to catch a helicopter up to Faslane that morning. These were the skeptics—those smart enough not to believe a word that came out of a politician's mouth and perceptive enough to see his speech for the gargantuan fib it was. They weren't so smart as to travel light, mind you. Half of them were sweating from the effort of dragging wheeled suitcases or pushing shopping trollies full of all kinds of unnecessary household crap. One individual was even carrying a flat-screen TV on his back. Perhaps he hoped to continue its use as a shield against real life and deflect any bombs that may drop on his head. They were all heading out of London, no doubt hoping to hide out in the countryside when the cleansing began.

He again told himself it wouldn't come to that. Now the missile was on board, all that remained were final checks and provisioning. Soon the sub would be ready to slip under water and head out into the open sea. Then he could call Piers and they would all be safe. He could only hope the bombers weren't already on their way. The next meeting of the UN Security Council, directly after which the attack had been due to take place, was set for four days from now. With luck, they weren't ready yet. They'd only had one day to react to Lesley's story and would have to rethink as well as accelerate their plan.

He left the submariners to their final preparations and returned to his quarters, where he picked up the satphone and called Margot.

"Where are you?" she said.

"I can't tell you. How's Vanessa?"

"Terrified. She overheard some of the security guys talking about that journalist's story. She thinks we're all going to die."

"Put her on."

Vanessa's voice came on the line, small and trembling. He could almost see her, clutching her Peppa Pig doll with one hand and the phone with other.

"Mummy says you're scared."

"The men said they're going to drop big bombs on us."

The abject terror in her voice made him want to cry and beat the living shit out of Piers, the embodiment of the cause of her fear, at the same time. Nonetheless, he faked his best cheery, confident voice. "Those men are silly big fibbers."

"They are?"

"Yes. They work for the government. Everyone who works for the government has to pass a lying test to get the job. If they're caught telling the truth, they get fired into space to go live on the moon."

"Why do they have to be good at lying, Daddy?"

Realizing he'd opened a can of worms and that Vanessa, now at least distracted, would keep asking him questions he didn't want to answer, he changed tack. "Just because. Anyway, are you sure they said 'big bombs'? I think they must have said 'big bums.' Now wouldn't that be funny?"

Vanessa giggled. "Yes." She paused for a minute, and he could almost hear her little brain whirring. "Who would clean up all the poo poo?"

Tony laughed. "I don't know, darling. Just know that Daddy won't let anything bad happen to you. Ever."

"Cross your heart and hope to die?"

"Cross my heart and hope to die. Can you give the phone back to Mummy, please?"

"Okay," she said, back to being a carefree four-year-old just like that. God, how he envied that ability to bounce back.

Margot came back on the phone. "What were you telling our child? She's run off to get a brush and pan to 'clean up the poo poo from the big bums'."

"I may have got a bit carried away. But she's fine now, isn't she?"

"Yes, she is. Thank you. I'm not, though."

"You don't need to worry, love. It isn't going to happen."

"Don't soft-soap me, Tony. It's real, isn't it?"

"Yes. But in a few hours it won't matter how many bombs and guns they assemble. They won't be able to touch us."

"Why? What are you up to?"

"I can't tell you. You just have to believe me when I say all this fear ends tonight. Tomorrow I'll be home, and we'll be able to start building a future. A real future."

Margot's breathing grew thick and heavy. He thought she didn't believe him and expected her to begin sobbing. What she said next came as something of a surprise. "Thank God. Because I'm bloody horny. We haven't had S-E-X in days."

"What's sex, Mummy?" he heard Vanessa shout.

"Bloody precocious child," Margot muttered, before saying, "Go watch television, love. I need to talk to Daddy privately." He heard footsteps, the brief blare of cartoons, and finally the click of a lock. "I'm in the toilet. We're having phone sex."

"Seriously?" Tony said. "You do know I'm trying to save Britain right now, right?"

"Oooh, a hero. That just makes me wetter."

Tony looked out of window. Dozens of men were ferrying boxes and crates onto the submarine under the floodlights. In a few hours he would be able to keep the promise he'd made to his wife and daughter. Until then, all he could do was wait and worry. There was still a chance he could die. If the bombers were coming and got here before the missile was ready, Faslane would be the first to go. With that possibility in mind, he knew he should be saying a poignant farewell just in case, although Margot clearly was not in the right frame of mind. He gave it a go anyway.

"You and Vanessa mean more to me than life itself," he said. "I love you so much that it hurts deep down in my bones when I think of anything happening to you."

"Great. I love you, too," Margot said. "Hear that? That's the sound of my hand running up my stockinged thigh. Guess where it's going? Now come on, unzip that fly. It'll only take a few minutes. Then you can go back to saving us."

Then again, he thought as the whisper of his cock stirring against his boxers answered the whisper of fingers on silk, *nothing says "I love you" like filthy phone sex.*

"I have no idea," he said. "Why don't you tell me? In great detail."

He forgot that he held the lives of millions in his hands, for those hands were soon full of something else. Margot was right. It did only take a few minutes.

DAY OF EXCISION

31

The world was awash in flickering green light as Geldof lay on the damp grass, peering through night-vision binoculars at Scholzy and James snipping the fence at the far north corner of Faslane. Beside him lay Mick, patched up but unable to walk without assistance, which meant Geldof was still knackered from bearing half his weight on the slog up the hill. The Irishman was positioned over a long sniper rifle fitted with a night-vision scope, which he'd already used to dispatch two guards at the north gate. Geldof swept the binoculars across the base, looking for any patrols. At the moment, all was still.

Mick nudged him. He lowered the binoculars. "What?"

"I'm not really a sociopath, so. I just say that to seem harder. I'm actually perfectly well adjusted and a nice bloke. When I'm not killing people."

"Why're you telling me this?"

"Well, you know. Now that me and your mum are an item . . ."

"You and my mum are temporary fuck buddies."

"Ah, come on. I like your mum more than that. There's something special about her."

"Are you looking for my blessing?"

"I suppose I am."

"Now's not really the best time."

"When would be the best time? When we're all dead?"

"Fine," Geldof said. "If it'll shut you up, you've got my blessing. Just try not to let her shag you to death."

"Now that," Mick said in a dreamy voice, "would be a grand way to go."

Geldof shook his head and looked through the binoculars again. The fence now had a large semicircular hole in it, wide enough to accommodate the cows that would shortly be let out the nearby truck. They would then chase a remote-controlled spy car, fitted with a video camera and a microphone. Strapped around the neck of each of the ten cows like a deadly bell was an explosive charge. These bombs would be set off once the car, to which they'd fastened a rag rubbed in the pits of every uninfected member of their party, had led the animals down to the dock to plunge into the water. Individually, the explosives wouldn't cause significant damage to the sub: collectively, they would be powerful enough to send it bubbling to the bottom of the loch. At least, that's what Peter said. If it all went to plan, they would melt away into the night with their lives intact.

Geldof had three jobs: help guide the car, which had a narrow field of vision, to its target; spot for Mick, pointing out the location of any guards he didn't see through the equally narrow focus of his scope; and, if they failed, call the number Lesley had given him, tell the person who picked up what was in those missiles, and get the hell out of there before bombers rumbled overhead.

Scholzy and James retreated to the bushes while Fanny and Scott unlatched the door and lowered the ramp. A few cows poked their heads out but didn't venture down until the little car scooted past. The cows clattered down the ramp, in hot pursuit of the car as it skittered toward the gap in the fence. Even from up on the hill, Geldof could hear their moos and bellows. The soldiers would hear them, too, but that was the insane beauty of the plan. They would think a stray herd had got in somehow rather than make the gigantic mental leap necessary to realize they were facing a cowmakaze squad.

The car had to stop briefly on the other side of the fence as the cows all tried to squeeze through the hole at once. For a moment, Geldof thought they were going to get stuck, but once the first two squirmed free the clog cleared. They stampeded across the empty car park, heading toward the massive white rectangle of a hangar by the water's edge. Beyond the hangar were squat buildings of various shapes and sizes, and still farther Geldof could make out the outline of the moored sub. They had a long way to go across the sprawling base. Just as the cows reached the first hangar, two small figures emerged from a guard post.

"Soldiers," Geldof said.

"Where? Mick said, his eye glued to the scope.

"Left a bit."

"Give me it in time!"

"Twenty-four-hour or normal?"

"Just tell me!"

"Eleven o'clock."

Mick shifted the rifle. "Got them."

He didn't pull the trigger immediately. The soldiers were clearly bemused by what they saw, just staring at the cows stampeding toward them. However, as the toy car zipped past one of them gave it a long, hard look. The cows were close behind, and one of them lost its footing and thumped into the guard post. It paused, just a few feet from the soldiers, before rejoining the tail end of the pursuit like a racer after a pit stop. The soldiers ditched their confused stance. One of them hauled up his weapon and ran out after the herd.

"They must have seen the explosives," Mick said, pulling the trigger before he'd even finished speaking.

The first soldier went down. Before Mick could let loose another round, the other soldier dived back inside the building. Klaxons began to sound.

"Bollocks," Mick said. "This is going to get messy."

The cows disappeared behind the hangar for a few seconds and then reappeared, heading down the narrow road that hugged the water's edge. Tiny figures came running out of a low house a few hundred meters ahead.

"More soldiers ahead," Geldof said into the radio. "Can you see them on the camera?"

"I see them," said Tom, who'd been handed control of the vehicle thanks to his professed proficiency at Scalextric. "Is there another way around?"

Geldof panned the binoculars across the base. The soldiers were blocking the road and there were no turnoffs before them. "No."

"What do you suggest I do, run over their toes with my tiny little tires?"

"Let me try to clear a path," Mick said.

He began to pull the trigger methodically. Three of the soldiers dropped before the rest ran for the cover of another hangar, opening up the road for the car and its wake of cows. The car whizzed past the corner of the hangar. For a moment Geldof thought it was going to make it, particularly since Mick was pinging shots off the side of the building to keep the soldiers hemmed in. Then he saw sparks fly off the concrete around the car as the soldiers fired at it. The car tumbled and came to rest. The cows swiftly caught up and clustered around to rip at the rag.

"There goes plan A," Mick said.

Lesley peered over Tom's shoulder, feeling nauseated in equal parts by the bouncing ground-level view on the video screen and the possibility that they may have to enter the heavily guarded base themselves if the cow plan failed, which she fully expected it to do. She'd seen a lot of crazy shit since the onset of the virus, but exploding cows? That was just ludicrous. Given half a chance, she would have sneaked into the computer room and sent an e-mail to the UN. However, James, who clearly didn't trust her, wouldn't let her near the building. That meant she'd been unable to check for a response from Terry. If she survived, she could pick up the conversation. If she died, at least she'd said what she had to say.

As she watched, the display stopped moving. Hooves appeared. The display veered upward, and she got a close-up of a cow's long tongue. The screen cut to static.

Tom tossed the controller aside. "The car's down."

"What happened?" Scholzy said into the radio.

"Somebody shot the car," Geldof said. "The cows have stopped to munch on the rag."

"One of us poor uninfected sods is going to have to go in and lead them down," Peter said.

"That's not going to fly," Scholzy said. "We'd have to get all the way

to the cows, avoid getting shot by that large group of gun-toting soldiers, and outpace those big fuckers down to the dock. Fat chance."

"Then what?"

"We make the best of it. Are they close to the soldiers?" Scholzy
asked Geldof.

"Maybe ten meters away."

"That'll have to do."

Scholzy nodded at Peter, who was holding the remote detonator.

"Are you ready for a big cow-boom?" Peter said. "You get it, right?
Explosions normally go kaboom but I said . . ."

"I think I preferred you with the mask on," Scholzy said. "Just press
the bloody button."

"Fine," Peter said, and did so.

A massive fireball bloomed in the middle of the base. As the shockwave reached them, everybody save the mercenaries ducked instinc-
tively. A whole cow, still unexploded for some reason, soared into the
air above the expanding flames like a lump of rock spewed up by an
erupting volcano. The flames died out, sucked into a roiling black cloud
of smoke that obscured the cow just as it reached the zenith of its climb.
Lesley, her ears ringing and heart pounding, came out of her crouch.
The sheer force of the blast must have killed a good number of the
soldiers, but the submarine remained undamaged. That meant only one
thing: they were going in, God help them.

The bang blew away the last remnants of sleep clinging to Tony, who
had only just woken in alarm with the blare of the Klaxons. He hauled
on his trousers and ran outside in his bare feet. Glen had emerged from
his neighboring room, and together they looked at the cloud of smoke
rising above the buildings.

"It's started," Tony said, switching his gaze to the sky to see what
was dropping out of it. He saw nothing against the dark sheath of clouds.

Glen had his radio out and was talking urgently into it. "Is it an air
raid?"

Tony didn't catch the reply.

"Car bombs?" Glen said.

"No, cow bombs," the crackly voice on the other side said, more loudly.

Glen and Tony stared at each other incredulously.

"What the fuck is going on?" Tony said.

"I have no idea. But we're clearly under attack."

"We need to get the sub out now."

Glen got on the radio again, giving orders as the screams of wounded men reached Tony's ears. This had to be the first phase of the attack. While he couldn't see the warplanes, he was sure they were tearing overhead somewhere and about to follow-up on the ground assault. And if they were here they would also be over London. All of his carefully laid plans were shattered. It was too late for a deterrent, and Piers would never answer his calls now the attack was underway. He was too cowardly for that. The rage came on, so strong that he didn't even think of Spock. Margot and Vanessa would be safe in the bunker, for the moment at least. He wouldn't survive this first wave, but that no longer mattered. All he knew was that the moment he'd thought so much about was upon him. He didn't rehash all of the moral arguments, didn't think of the lives that would be lost, didn't think of anything except the one action he could take. It wasn't too late to keep the promise he made to Vanessa. Even if they launched their neutron bombs, there would be no reason to continue with the next wave once the virus was out. Margot and Vanessa could emerge from the bunker in a few weeks, into a new world where nobody would try to kill them because they were different.

"Tell them to fire the missiles as soon as they get to open water," he said, his voice low and guttural.

"Gladly," Glen said. "Now let's get to the control room."

32

"How many did we get?" Scholzy said into the radio as Ruan gaped at the black cloud drifting toward them.

"I'm not sure," Geldof said. "There's a lot of smoke. I can see at least a dozen coming toward the explosion."

"Then we'll try to go around them. Geldof, talk us in along a clear path. Make sure that mad Irishman keeps them pinned down."

Scholzy stood up, shifting the strap of the RPG launcher slung across his back. He also had his automatic weapon, and the pockets of his cargo pants were stuffed with spare clips. The other two mercenaries were similarly well-armed and protected by body armor. Ruan had her pistol with fresh clips provided by Scholzy. Lesley toted Mick's automatic weapon. Fanny and Tom clutched bows. Scott had his staff. Andy carried a bag of grenades, foisted on him after he'd initially insisted he would stick to his eggs. Nayapal had only his fists, which Ruan had a sneaking suspicion would be of limited use against a hail of bullets.

"We're going to have to do it the hard way," Scholzy said. "Are you ready?"

Absolutely not, Ruan thought. She'd been in enough combat to understand what it took to face death. This was different. It would be like stepping into a proper war zone: bullets and grenades flying from all angles, a distant enemy trained to kill, noise and fury and pretty much certain death. But she had to do it. She'd bought Lesley's argument that a missile launch from that submarine would prompt an instant nuclear response. That meant they would all be dead anyway. Lesley's story leading to the attack on Britain being called off was a slim hope, but it was the only one they had. She nodded along with all the others. Their fear was apparent in the stark, shadowy lines drawn around their mouths.

"We're going to have to stick the last charges onto the sub manually," Scholzy said. "Me, James, and Peter will lead. Try not to get in our way or get shot. Consider yourself substitutes. If one of us goes down, pick up the gun and follow whoever is left."

Giving them no time to answer, Scholzy and his men sprinted toward the hole in the fence. They moved with easy confidence, like this was something they'd done a hundred times before. Of the others, only Fanny looked like she belonged with them, an arrow nocked in the bow and a half smile on her face as she loped alongside Ruan.

"Can you try not to look like you're enjoying this so much?" Ruan said. "I'm crapping myself."

"Can't help it," Fanny said. "I've wanted to storm this base for over twenty years."

Geldof instructed them to turn left, away from the concentration of troops and the smoke that would obscure their vision. They ran along the fence, Ruan's pulse hissing in her ears as she waited for bullets to come spraying among them. A cluster of trees hid the column of smoke from view as they emerged into a large car park where bright fluorescent lights shone down on dozens of bulky military vehicles. They ducked from one to another, keeping low. The radio crackled into life.

"You'd better get a move on," Geldof said. "There's loads of people around the sub, all climbing down the tower thing on top, and a couple of guys are untethering. It looks like they're getting ready to go." The radio went dead. When Geldof came back on a few seconds later, his voice was urgent. "Soldiers, coming your way from the right."

Scholzy motioned them to a halt and they crouched behind a truck. Ruan lay down and saw boots weaving toward them. Scholzy nudged Andy, who plucked a grenade from his bag and tossed it over the truck. As soon as it exploded, the three mercenaries ducked out and opened fire. Andy lobbed another grenade. This time, the explosion was so close that shrapnel pattered along the ground under the truck.

"For fuck's sake, try and get them a bit farther," Scholzy shouted.

"I told you I couldn't throw grenades," Andy said. "The weight's all wrong."

Lesley, her face chalk white, ducked out from the other side of the truck, intending to fire. She skipped back in when bullets whined off the bonnet, and cowered behind the thick tires where those without guns were already taking shelter.

"Geldof, I need Mick to take these buggers out or keep them pinned down," Scholzy shouted into the radio. No answer came. "Geldof? Mick? Where the fuck are you?"

Geldof watched the group take cover behind the truck, growing cold with vicarious fear as soldiers fanned out and took up positions behind cars. Their weapons spat out ribbons of green fire, sending tracers zipping toward the truck.

"Mick," Geldof said urgently.

The Irishman didn't look up from where he was reloading. "I know," he said. "Give me a minute."

As Geldof fretted, something brushed against his trouser leg. A second later he felt a sharp nip.

"Ow!" he said and twisted his neck around.

Squatting on his calf, a feral look on its tiny face, a skinny rabbit was busy trying to gnaw through the thankfully thick fabric of his trousers. Geldof scrabbled to his feet and shook his leg. The rabbit hung on by its teeth and refused to let go. He hit it hard with the binoculars to force it to release its grip and delivered it a hard boot. It sailed away into the night like a furry football. Mick clicked a new magazine into his rifle just as another dozen rabbits hopped out from the bushes.

"Yegads!" Geldof shouted.

In their eagerness to face the human threat, they'd forgotten about the dangers lurking in the woods. Scholzy's cry for help fizzed through the radio, which lay abandoned on the grass.

"Shoot them, Mick!" Geldof shouted.

The Irishman, now aware of the new danger, shook his head. "Not at this range. Try to stop looking so much like a fecking carrot and deal with it."

Geldof stared at the rabbits closing in. Down below his family and friends were engaged in deadly combat with fierce soldiers. Up on the hill, he was about to do battle with fluffy bunnies. Given his fighting prowess, it seemed pathetically apt. Even though he felt like a prize tool, his frustration at being so crap and his irritation at the Mick's ginger jibe bubbled over. He let out a fierce battle cry and stepped forward to meet the charge. He began by trying to stamp on the rabbits but they were too fast. One by one they avoided his blows and leapt at him, until they'd all fastened themselves to his clothing—save for one that was nipping at Mick's legs, forcing him to stop shooting and club it with the butt of his rifle. Geldof flailed and spun, but the rabbits wouldn't be dislodged. He could feel their little teeth grinding through his combat outfit, pinching his skin. They would never be able to nibble him to death, but it would only take one of them to gnaw through his clothes, and he would have the virus.

He looked down at the biggest rabbit, which was clinging on to his black shirt between his nipples. Its baleful gaze was fixed on his.

You can't even beat a cuddly bunny, its eyes seemed to say.

Geldof, utterly humiliated, stumbled backward and tripped over Mick's outstretched leg. Small bones snapped as he thudded to the ground.

"Roll!" Mick shouted.

Geldof understood Mick's intention and rolled for his life. The rabbits still wouldn't let go, and he grimaced as his body weight mashed them into the ground. The ball of boy and rabbit gathered pace as it went downhill, squeaking like a kid's toy. When the last of the squeaks died away, Geldof dug his hand into the grass to arrest his momentum. He got to his feet shakily, looking at the ruined balls of fur strewn around him.

"Congratulations," Mick said. "You've got your first kills. Now get your arse back up here."

Cheeks flushed with embarrassment, Geldof stumbled back up the hill and grabbed the radio. "If we get out of this alive, you'd better not tell anybody what just happened," he said before pressing the button.

The fire from the soldiers intensified, flashes of light crackling across the concrete like sparklers as slugs ricocheted around the truck. Everybody was now cringing behind the enormous wheels of the thankfully bulky vehicle, which rocked on its suspension under the force of the incoming projectiles. The air hissed out of one of the tires as a bullet found it, sending fragments of hard rubber pattering onto the concrete. As Ruan pulled her body in even tighter to the wheel's metal rim, the windscreen of a nearby car shattered. The zips and whines that filled the air seemed like expressions of frustration from the bullets that had yet to find their intended targets. Ruan knew they wouldn't be frustrated for long.

"We need to do something fast, or we're fucked," Scholzy said. "They'll probably bring out the heavy artillery any minute."

Ruan blinked rapidly, trying to picture herself in a sunny field just to deliver a few seconds' respite and clear her shell-shocked mind. She found herself in a field all right, although she was accompanied by a herd of zombie cows keen to substitute cud for her juicy buttocks. She remembered then how she'd herded the assault cows into the truck.

"I can't believe I'm doing this," she said, and peeled off the fleece and blouse she'd borrowed from Fanny.

"I'm not sure a naked protest will help here," Fanny said.

"They don't know we're uninfected yet. I'm going to let them know, see if we can stir them up a bit."

She took off her boots, wrapped the clothing around them, and moved back just far enough to allow her to toss the packages over the truck in different directions. The gunfire continued unabated for a few seconds, then slackened off on her side off the truck. In its place came angry shouts. The radio crackled again and Geldof's voice came through. "We're back. Mick's going to try to keep them pinned down."

That was as good as it was going to get. Before good sense could return, Ruan scrambled out from behind the tire and sprinted toward the soldiers, praying that her plan would work. From behind the truck, her comrades sprayed bullets toward the soldiers who were still firing. Those soldiers returned fire at their assailants, leaving Ruan free to continue her advance. Near where the fleece had landed other soldiers were running from cover, guns forgotten in their eagerness to reach the source of the enticing scent. She curved close enough for them to get a whiff of her, knowing she had them when the closest soldier bared his teeth and changed direction to follow her. The soldiers on the other side— one or two still in pajamas—quickly got the message and began scrambling over the bonnets of cars. They didn't make it far. Something streaked through the air from the other side of the truck, so fast that she barely registered it, before a jeep, and the soldiers flowing around and over it, disappeared in a searing wall of fire and noise. A blast of hot air buffeted Ruan, and she fell sideways, not even trying to break her fall. When her shoulder smacked into the concrete, she used the momentum to roll under the truck.

Some of the remaining soldiers fell as automatic weapons chattered. The others remembered their training and raised their weapons to return fire. The ensuing firefight could have lasted ten seconds; it could have lasted ten minutes. Ruan just pressed her body to the ground, her nostrils full of the stink of engine oil and cordite, and hoped a stray bullet wouldn't find her. When the guns stopped, there was absolute silence before the moans started. She peeked out and saw that all of the soldiers who'd been following her were on the ground. Two of them were writhing on the spot; another was pulling himself along the concrete on his arms, his wild gaze fixed on her. He only managed to travel a few meters before the light went out of his eyes and his head flopped to the ground. She rolled the rest of the way to the other side of the truck and lay there looking up at the sky, not trusting her legs to bear her weight.

Fanny grabbed her hand and hauled her to a sitting position. She then began patting Ruan's body, looking for wounds. "Are you okay?"

"My shoulder's killing me, but I think that's it. How's everyone else?"

In answer, Fanny looked to her left. Ruan followed her gaze and saw Scholzy on his knees, bent over the still forms of Peter and James. Blood was oozing out from beneath them, coating the sides of a discarded rocket launcher.

"I'm sorry," she said.

Scholzy looked around. His face held a rigid lack of expression, his facial muscles fluttering as he fought to keep them in check. "It's been a long time coming," he said, his voice barely above a whisper. "Funny thing is, I never really expected it to happen. None of us did, or we wouldn't have been doing this."

As he brushed his friends' eyes closed with gentle fingers, the radio came alive.

"The sub's moving," Geldof said.

Scholzy kept his head lowered for another few seconds and then got to his feet. "We've still got a job to do. Tom, Scott, take their weapons. Ruan, you take the charges."

Ruan focused on James's chest, all too aware that his face was a bloody ruin, as she pulled the two explosive devices they'd kept in reserve out of his webbing.

"We're going to have to sprint for it. Everybody follow me and Ruan. Give us cover if there's any more engagement," Scholzy said.

He opened communications with Geldof again. "How do we get to the sub?"

"Straight across the car park, between the two hangars, toward the crane. Turn left at the water and straight down. You can't miss it."

"Any enemy in the way?"

"Not that I can see."

Scholzy and Ruan pulled ahead as the group ran. When they hit the foot of the towering crane, a floodlit section of the dockside came into view. The sub was already away from its berth, churning water in its wake and fading into the blackness. Scholzy snatched the charges from Ruan, dropping the radio over the edge of the dock in the process, and lobbed them after the departing sub. They splashed into the water well short of the target, but Scholzy activated the remote control detonator anyway. A flash of light illuminated the water, followed by a spray of foam and a dull crump. The sub continued, undamaged. Tom, Nayapal, Scott, and Andy caught up with them, and they stood together, watching the dark silhouette meld with the darkness around it until all they could see was the blinking red light from the conning tower.

"We're done here," Scholzy said. "Time to bug out."

"Aren't you going to tell Geldof to make the call?" Ruan asked.

"Unless you want to dive in and get the radio, then no. There's no point anyway. By the time they get the message the sub will be underwater. Only depth charges will do the job, if they could find it. Anyway, they'd never get a warship close enough before the missile went off."

"So everybody's going to be infected," Ruan said.

"Looks that way. If it's any consolation, I doubt we're going to be around to see it. The bombs will be flying soon enough."

Now that the battle was over and her mind was able to look more than a few seconds into the future, Ruan realized she was more scared than she'd ever been. In all of her time scrabbling for survival, even during the overwhelming chaos of the assault on the base, she at least had something in front of her she could fight, some measure of influence over her destiny. What she felt now was the helpless terror that came with lack of control, like that of a nervous flyer relying on the skill of a pilot and a flimsy belt buckle while lightning crackled through the clouds around the bucking plane.

"But I don't want to die," she said, her voice that of a frightened little girl.

"Join the fucking club," Scholzy said.

33

Lesley brought up the rear of the running group, trying to focus on the job she'd been given. The barrel of her gun was up, ready to swing in the direction of any movement from the peripheries, but it was shaking so much she doubted she would be able to hit anything save through blind luck. Again it was her fault they were here at all. Again people were dying all around her while she hadn't suffered so much as a scratch. And despite the sacrifices, they were going to fail. The missile would go up, the virus would come down, and her hand of doom would erase the lives of billions of people. The black cloud drifting over the base was nothing compared to the evil miasma of death that must be billowing invisibly around her.

Still, when something flickered in the corner of her eye she jerked her gun in the direction of the movement. She didn't have time to fire, but she recognized the man who was disappearing into a building. She stopped dead, her hands suddenly steady. Perhaps it wasn't too late after all. She cut away from the group and headed toward the door. A hand fell on her shoulder. She whirled round to see Fanny.

"You're not going to call the UN are you?" Fanny said. "We're not done here yet."

"I just saw Tony Campbell go into that building. You know what they say about cutting off the head of the snake."

"I'm coming with you."

They entered the building, weapons at the ready, and crept up a narrow flight of stairs leading to a doorway. Lesley stuck her head around to look in to an open area filled with computer terminals. At the far

end, Tony and another man were bent over a monitor atop a table clut-
tered with other equipment, including a radio. As she tried to figure
out what they were doing, a boom rattled the windows. Tony ducked
beneath the table. The other man didn't flinch. For a moment Lesley's
spirits soared, taking the weight of all the lives that would be lost with
them. The explosion must have been Scholzy taking out the sub. As
the top half of Tony's head appeared above the table, the other man
walked over to the window and cupped his hands against the pane.

"It's okay," he said. "The sub's still intact."

Lesley ducked back in as he turned, feeling sick to her stomach. A
few seconds later, she heard the man speak again. "How long until
you're in a position to fire?"

"Ten minutes," somebody replied through the radio speakers.

"They missed it," she whispered into Fanny's ear. "We have to kill
them."

"It won't make any difference. They've clearly already given the order to fire. You need to convince Tony to call it off."

"And how am I going to do that? Last time we talked he threatened
to kill me."

"You're the wordsmith. So smith some words and persuade him."

"I can't," Lesley said, close to hyperventilating. "I don't know what
to say."

Fanny grabbed her shoulders and leaned in so their eyes were inches
apart. "I never told you this, but I always admired you. You're a strong
woman, Lesley. You can do it. You have to do it."

"I'm not a strong woman. I'm a walking disaster area."

"That's not true. When it came to the crunch, you shot Brown, didn't
you? You saved my son's life. Now you can save a lot more lives."

In lieu of a brown paper bag, Lesley cupped her hands over her
mouth and took several deep breaths. It didn't do much to calm her,
but it would have to do.

"Tony!" she shouted.

"Who's that?"

"It's Lesley McBrien," she said, sure he would fly round the corner
and attack them.

"What're you doing here?"

"I just want to talk."

"Right. That's why all those bombs were going off."

"What did you expect? What you're going to do is wrong."

"I thought you'd decided killing us wasn't such a good idea after all. Seems I was wrong. You're just like every other journalist. Anything for a good story, right?"

"I don't know what you mean. This isn't about a story. It's about what's right."

"Right for who? You're going to kill everybody I care about. This is the only way to stop that happening. You're making me do this."

"Nobody's making you do anything. If you fire that missile, it'll be your decision, nobody else's."

"And the alternative is what? I just stand back and let the bombs drop? This is war. We didn't start it. But we're going to finish it."

"By infecting the whole world?"

"We'll have peace when everybody has the virus."

"That's your solution? I'm sure it's very peaceful in the grave. Shame the dead are too busy decomposing to enjoy the lovely silence. Don't you get it? This is the virus talking. You're angry, so you're not thinking clearly. Billions of people are going to die if you do this."

"Not my family. That's all that matters. Nothing you can say will change my mind, so you may as well send your soldier friends up to finish the job."

Lesley slumped against the wall and clutched her hair.

"I don't know what to say," she told Fanny.

"Don't give up," Fanny said. "We've still got a few minutes."

Lesley stared at her mutely. She'd spoken to Tony for less than a minute but already knew she didn't have the words to talk him down, mainly because she didn't blame him. She blamed herself. In a few minutes the missile would slide out of its tube and she would have killed half the world. She shook her head and looked at the floor. Fanny nudged her out of the way and edged toward the door.

"Unless your family is more than seven billion people, you can't do it," Fanny shouted. "Don't you get it? The needs of the many outweigh the needs of the few."

"What did you say?" Tony said, his voice hoarse.

"I said the needs of the many outweigh the needs of the few. Do you think you're the only one with a wife and child? Are you really going to kill millions of families just to save your own?"

The only sound from the control room was heavy breathing and the soft tick of a wall clock. As the silence stretched on, Lesley halted her slide down the wall. She grabbed Fanny's forearm.

"I didn't know you were a *Star Trek* fan," she whispered, not wanting to interrupt whatever thoughts were running through Tony's mind.

Fanny shot her a puzzled look. "I'm not."

"Never mind. I think you might have gotten through to him."

Tony stood by the radio, stunned into stillness by the words of Spock coming out of the unknown woman's mouth. Always he'd conjured up the Vulcan, but only in relation to the small things, as a way of quelling his anger. He'd never applied Spock's logic to the big picture. Every decision he made had been driven by the sickening rage conjured up at the thought of those he loved being killed. He hadn't allowed Spock to come because he didn't want to see the truth. Now he breathed deeply and, for the first time, properly asked himself what Spock would do. It wasn't a question that needed any thought, since Fanny had already given him the answer. He saw Spock in the reactor core, his face bearing the scars of radiation poisoning as he slid down the glass pane and said farewell to Kirk after making the ultimate sacrifice. From a purely logical point of view, it was a question of numbers. Billions versus two, or millions if you counted all of the others in Britain. Spock wouldn't do this, he knew. But it went far beyond logic, as Spock's human side would know only too well.

Yes, Tony had been furious when he told Glen to fire the missile and so didn't think further about the consequences. But he'd paved the way for that split-second decision in all of his thoughts over the previous weeks. All along he'd been doing what he vilified the international community for doing: dehumanizing the people he would kill, trying to dismiss them as statistics. This was the kind of decision world leaders took every time they went to war. They gave commands, people died, and geopolitical influence changed as if it were

just a big game of Risk. He'd never seen himself as one of those people. He took up politics as an ideal, not a career. He'd been a leftie, a
backer of an ideology that protected the masses from the excesses of
the few. Many others started out the same way. In order to rise to the
top they gradually compromised and chipped away at their ideals until, like a statue carved by a sculptor too heavy on the hammer, all that
remained was a shrivelled lump of rock. He'd vowed this would never
happen to him. All those years he'd kept quiet as the party moved to
the right, telling himself he was staying in the system so he could
eventually change it. Yet he'd never actually done or said anything,
supposedly waiting for the right moment as he rose and rose. He'd
compromised himself through inaction and silence. And now here he
was, as bad as those leaders who would destroy his country without
thought for the loss of life.

For the first time, he allowed himself to see the gravity of his
actions. There were millions of Vanessas out there, each tucked up in
their own bed, each with a father and mother who would do anything
to protect them. He realized that he hadn't really tried to picture them,
how they would scream and bleed and plead for their mummies and
daddies when the infected came for them. He would never see the bodies, but that didn't mean they wouldn't be there. He let the memory
of the journey back from the hotel engulf him, this time transplanting
the endless vista of broken and battered corpses onto the streets of
Paris, Berlin, Istanbul, Moscow, New York, New Delhi, Buenos Aires,
Johannesburg, and the other cities he'd visited and thus could visual-
ize. That is what he would be unleashing upon the world. Each one of
those deaths would be a tragedy, overwhelming when stacked up in
their millions. When it had occurred to him that firing the missile would
make him the same as Archangel, he talked himself out of his com-
parison by considering motivation. But his motivation wouldn't matter
to the dead. Wrong was wrong. If he did this, he would never be able
to look Margot or Vanessa in the eye again, knowing he'd bought their
lives with the deaths of so many others.

Still, he couldn't do nothing. There had to be some other way. Piers
wouldn't answer the phone, but maybe he could reason with whomever was directing this assault. He'd observed enough conflicts to know

that escalation took two parties, and as he thought back over what he'd done, he understood his posturing had only inflamed the situation. He'd acted like a tin-pot dictator, threatening to nuke the shit out of the world. Even worse, much of his aggressive stance had been driven by his hatred for Piers. He'd never been calm or logical when talking to the man, remembering only that he'd tried to steal Margot. Maybe, just maybe, if he showed he was prepared to step back from the brink they could find a peaceful solution.

"Let me talk to the commander," he said.

"You just talked to her," Lesley said.

"What's your rank?"

"Err, activist?" the other woman said.

"What's your military rank?"

"I don't have one."

Tony looked at Glen in puzzlement. His military commander was staring at him intently, a frown on his face. "What do you mean? You're army, right?"

"Don't be daft. Do you think the army would attack you with a herd of cows? They would just have fired missiles from one of those warships they've got out there."

Tony grabbed at the table for support. Of course it wasn't the bloody military. He'd been so caught up by the explosions and the dash to the control room that he hadn't paid much attention to the farcical method of the initial assault. "So who exactly is attacking us?"

"The resistance."

"What resistance?"

"The people you sent your spin doctor up to talk to."

"The leaflet people?"

"Yes. She told us what you were going to do. We decided to stop it."

Amira. He'd completely forgotten he was going to call her back and tell her he only planned to use the missile as a deterrent. Determined to stop it, she'd told these people he was going to fire it. Which prompted them to storm the base. Which made him believe the UN was beginning its final solution and give the order to fire. He'd almost destroyed the world because of one forgotten phone call. As utterly idiotic as the situation was, it also meant it wasn't too late to stand down. He could cancel the fire order and get on the phone to Piers. This time, however, he would be calm and rational. He would be Spock personified. He plucked the microphone from Glen's hand.

"What are you doing?" Glen said.

"We have to call it off."

"This mission is going ahead," Glen said, his voice soft and full of menace.

Tony looked up and found himself staring down the barrel of a gun. "You can't be serious. They're right, this is insanity."

"No, it's God's judgement on the unbelievers."

Glen took several steps back and, with the aid of his side, pushed up his sleeve. On his forearm was a tattoo of a chalice, red blood spilling over the top. Tony gaped at it. "You're the leak."

"Finally, he gets it," Glen said.

Tony felt like a fool. It had been so obvious all along. Only one person had been pushing for this missile as the answer to their problems and that answer just happened to coincide with the goals of Blood of Christ. He'd assumed Glen was just excited about firing off his missile, and the fact Glen sought his approval before preparing the weapon had blinded him to the truth. And Glen's ethnic background had contributed to throwing off the scent: he just couldn't imagine somebody with Glen's skin tone associating with such a blatantly racist organization.

"How long have you been a member?"

"Long enough to see you were leading this country to oblivion. You're weak, Tony. Archangel isn't. He has a vision. We're going to cleanse this whole planet."

"But you're black."

"So? It isn't about color. It's about godlessness."

"Don't be so stupid. Most of Archangel's guys spent half their time in the eighties stomping around in bovver boots and waving Union Jacks. Do you think they're going to stop once the Muslims and atheists are gone? He's using you."

"No. We're all one under God. He told me that."

Tony shook his head at Glen's blinkered view. There would be no convincing him. Still, he needed to keep him talking while he figured out some way to grab the gun. "Why didn't you just develop the missile quietly and fire it? You're in charge of the military."

"People respect you. I used to respect you, until you proved to be so pathetic. And not everybody in the armed forces backed this. Somebody might've leaked it out if I'd done it under the radar, and that would've caused problems. Better to have it come from the top so nobody could question it. Now, enough chitchat. Put that microphone down, or I'll kill you."

So much for keeping him talking, Tony thought, and prepared to make a mad leap for the weapon.

As the two men talked, Lesley peeked around the corner and saw the gun pointed at Tony's head. She could see the coldness in the gunman's eyes, so similar to that in Brown's. She knew if Tony began to speak into the radio, he would pull the trigger and that would be that. The events that would follow flashed through her mind: people and animals turning on each other in heaving masses, cities and whole countries reduced to ruins as nations yet uninfected fired off whatever weapons they possessed to stop the relentless advance of the virus, society crumbling and the world population dwindling. She would walk through this global valley of death, somehow always surviving. When she saw herself standing alone on the wasteland with the cries of the creature she'd just crushed echoing in her ears, it didn't feel like a dream. It felt like a vision of the future.

No, she thought. *Nobody else is going to die because of me.*

She wasn't a big Trekkie, but the quote Fanny had inadvertently spoken was famous enough for her to know it. Fanny hadn't quite captured the entire sentence or its full meaning. The needs of the many outweigh the needs of the few . . .

"Or the one," she said.

She raised her automatic weapon and charged into the room, feeling Fanny's fingers brush against her shoulder as she tried to hold her back. The gunman's head snapped around. His nostrils flared and his neck tensed into cords as his teeth snapped together. Tony initially reacted in a similar manner, but he then bizarrely raised both of his eyebrows and put his index fingers together. As Tony stepped back, the gunman leapt over the table, narrowly missing kicking the radio with his swinging boot, and charged toward her.

"Get on the radio," she shouted at Tony, unsure if her words would get through to him.

The gunman was only a few feet away when she pulled the trigger. From that range she couldn't miss. A spray of bullets caught him in the stomach, rippling up in a diagonal line to his shoulder as the gun jumped in her hands. The impact of the bullets sent his trunk backward, although his legs kept pumping. As he fell, his gun hand came up and a single shot sounded. He crunched to the ground, dead. Lesley found herself gasping for breath. She felt wetness on her chest and looked down. Dark liquid was gurgling from a hole in the T-shirt above her left breast.

"Ah," she said, and sank to her knees.

The room blurred and canted sideways as she fell to the floor. She was vaguely aware of Tony babbling into the microphone. A hand slid under her neck and lifted her head. Fanny's face swam into focus, her blue eyes filled with warmth and sadness. Below Lesley's neck there was nothing but numbness. As her mind went fuzzy, she tried to picture the wasteland, but saw only a rolling field of bright-green grass buzzing, scurrying and teeming with life. In the distance, the buildings of the city stood tall and intact, reflected sunlight winking at her from thousands of windows behind which lovers kissed and children played without a care in the world.

"Looks like I'm not a jinx after all," she said, and stepped into the bright field with a smile on her face.

Tony watched the scarred woman cradle the journalist's body to her chest. Now that she was dead, the urge to kill faded as quickly as it had arisen. Lesley, a woman he once considered bloodthirsty, had died to save the people he would have killed. She was more Spock than he. Well, he still had time to put it right. He dug out the satphone and dialed.

"What are you doing?" the woman said.

He paused before answering, wondering if what he was about to do was a good idea. He still had the missile and so could return to the initial plan of using it as a deterrent. Now, thinking about it clearly, he knew that wouldn't work. Waving a viral missile at the world would be akin to a lunatic waggling his dick at the doctors: it would only further strengthen the misconception that Britain and its new leaders were as mad as a bag of snakes. They couldn't let such a threat stand. All the stops would be pulled out to find the submarine carrying the missile and destroy it. Eventually they would succeed. After that, it would be bye-bye Britain. This missile had been an awful idea from the start, and in his desperation he'd failed to see it. And now, thanks to Lesley and this woman, he knew for sure the virus could be resisted. When Lesley had burst into the room, her scent ramming up his nostrils and piercing his brain like a hot poker, he wanted nothing more than to sink his teeth into her jugular. He hadn't had the love of his family to hold him back this time, but he and Spock worked together to deny his itching fingers and aching teeth. And this woman, he could tell she was infected. Yet she'd held Lesley in her arms, getting that untainted blood all over her, and remained calm.

"Putting my faith in humanity," he said. "And crossing my fingers really, really tightly."

Piers answered after ten rings, his voice thick with sleep. "Tony. You're starting to make a habit of waking me up."

"We used to be friends, didn't we?"

Piers didn't answer immediately. When he did, his voice was guarded. "Yes, we did."

"Then pretend we're still friends and answer me honestly. Do you still love Margot?"

"God, not that again."

"I'm not attacking you. Please, just answer me."

Piers held his breath. Finally he let it out in a long hiss. "Yes."

"Then for her sake, and for the sake of her daughter, listen to me very carefully. I believe we're better than this virus. I believe we can beat it. And I'm prepared to prove it to the world. I'm going to restore the Internet. I'm going to let everybody see us for what we really are. I'm going to let you judge us. No matter what you do, we won't resist.

We won't fire off any nukes. We won't do anything. Blood of Christ doesn't represent this nation. I promise you I'll find the evil bastards and crush them. All I'm asking is that you do what you can to save Margot. Tell your bosses what I told you. Tell them that what they're doing is wrong. Tell them to give us a chance. They're going to kill people, Piers. You're going to kill people. You can stop this."

Piers said nothing for a while, his breath hissing heavily down the line. When he spoke, his voice was ragged. "I'm just a messenger boy. They don't listen to me. They don't even listen to the prime minister. They take the piss out of him, you know that? Everyone calls him Pie, short for prime minister in exile. Britain's a spent force. The Americans, Chinese, and Russians are the ones calling the shots."

"You can still try. Tell them what I said. Whatever happens, my conscience will be clear. How about yours?"

Tony hung up. When he turned around, he saw the woman had disappeared with Lesley's body. Near where she'd lain, Glen sprawled across the floor, staring sightlessly at the ceiling. Tony didn't know if his new approach would work. Perhaps he'd condemned them all to die. But when he returned to the bunker he could pull Vanessa and Margot close and know that he'd retained his humanity, even if just for a few more days. And wasn't that what he'd been trying to achieve all along?

34

Once the gunfire and explosions had ceased and Geldof saw the group gather on the dockside with no soldiers in view—a sight he was grateful for since the radio had stopped working a few minutes earlier—he helped Mick down the hill. He picked his way past the bodies strewn around the car park, trying not to look too closely, and joined the little band as they sat on the dockside in the growing light. He ran to his mum and gave her a bone-crushing hug. He realized she was covered in blood.

"'Are you okay?"

"I'm fine, Geldof. I'm fine."

"Did you stop it?"

"Lesley did."

"Where is she?" Geldof said. "Off writing a story casting herself as the hero, I suppose. I smell another best seller."

"Actually, she's dead."

Fanny pointed to a body. Light brown hair cascaded out from beneath the jacket covering the face. Geldof sat down heavily. "Who else?"

"Peter and James."

For the first time since Geldof had known him, Mick looked genuinely upset. When he saw Geldof looking at him, the Irishman turned away. There had been so much death that Geldof could barely assimilate it all. That would come later. For the moment, the grief was a blanket that wrapped them all in its dark folds, chilling instead of warming. Without any spoken agreement, they all sat on the edge of the dock and huddled together, seeking comfort in closeness, the warm pulse of blood and hiss of breath that spoke of life.

"This is a really shitty vibe," Scott said.

He reached into the inside pocket of his jacket, tie-dyed in dark colors in a nod to the camouflage that had been required for their mission, and pulled out a five-skinner. He sparked up and passed it around the group. Geldof declined. The last thing he needed in his current state of mind was a burst of unfamiliar sensations brought on by a drug he'd never taken.

"They died saving the world," Ruan said. "That's not a bad way to go out."

"Shame we couldn't save ourselves," Mick said.

"Don't be too sure about that," said Scholzy, who was walking along the dock toward them. "What happened to you two up on the hill?"

Mick looked at Geldof and raised an eyebrow. "We had our own fight. Vicious beasts, they were. Geldof took care of them."

"Well, consider that your last engagement. I've found a boat. A nice little high-speed commando inflatable with muffled engines."

"Do you really think you can make it out? Everybody else who tried got blown to bits," Geldof said.

"Everybody else isn't me. I'm like a ninja ghost. We can cling to the coast and head south. Once it's dark, we'll nip across the English Channel. We'll be having croissants, coffee, and Gauloises for breakfast in no time."

"Presuming you make it past the ships, how are you going to land in France? They've got machine gun posts coming out the wazoo along the coast."

"This is a naval base, isn't it? And what do you think they keep in naval bases?"

"Navels?" Scott said.

Geldof turned on him. "Now's not really the time for jokes, is it? Our friends are dead, and we're probably going to be clobbered by a very large bomb any minute."

Scott sucked on the joint and looked shamefaced.

"I beg to differ," Mick said. There were streaks on his face that looked suspiciously like tear tracks. "Now's exactly the time for jokes, otherwise we'll bloody top ourselves. What did you find, Scholzy?"

"Scuba gear. We'll dump the boat a mile offshore and then swim. Except we won't try for the coast. We'll go right up the Seine at Le Havre and come out of the water a good few miles upstream."

"Sounds like it could work," Mick said.

"If it could work, why didn't the British military do that to get the virus out instead of filling a big missile full of blood?" Geldof said.

"Because they were fucking idiots," Scholzy said. "Anyway, we'd better get going. Geldof, Mick, Ruan, say your good-byes. And Mick, if you want to say cheerio to Fanny in your own special way, you've got five minutes. I'm pretty sure you can get the job done in half the time."

"Do you think I went through all this just to toddle off and leave my mum again?" Geldof said. "I'm not going anywhere."

"I'm afraid you are," Scholzy said.

He grabbed Geldof and hauled him to his feet. When Geldof tried to shake himself free, he found the mercenary was just as strong as he looked. "What are you doing? I'm paying your wages."

"No, you're not," Scholzy said. "Your grandfather is. And he says no money unless I get you out of the country."

"You told him I was here?"

"I did," Fanny said.

Geldof goggled at his mum. "What?"

"I borrowed the satphone and rang him. I told him to tell Scholzy to take you out."

"But you hate him!"

"Yes, I do. Unfortunately, he's the only man who could make you leave."

"You said I could stay."

"That was before we found out they're going to wipe this country clean of every living thing. You have to go."

"But you don't know that they're going to attack for sure. Lesley's story . . ."

"Will change nothing. I should know, Geldof. I campaigned for enough causes to see how little difference the ordinary citizen's voice makes. I know you're going to hate me for this, but I'd rather you were alive and hating me than dead."

Geldof looked at his mum. Whereas before he would have seen a willful woman intent only on getting her way, he now saw the pain of a mother doing what she thought was right for her son. But he was old enough to know what was right for him. Being carted off against his will to run a coffee empire wasn't it. Without further ado, he bit Scholzy's hand as hard as he could. When the mercenary released his grip, he ran for it. In the few seconds it took Scholzy to stop swearing and start pursuing, Geldof had opened up a decent gap. He aimed for the nearest hangar, hoping he could get inside and lock the door. He could tell from the gaining footsteps that he wasn't going to make it. Then he saw a dead soldier, blood pooling around his body. Unbidden, Ruan's words about trying to get the virus so she could be reunited with her parents came back to him. He knew what he needed to do. He veered toward the body and dipped his index finger into the blood. Scholzy was still running toward him, ready to drag him kicking and screaming to the boat. Beyond, he could see the look of horror on his mum's face. He held her gaze and raised his hand to his mouth.

Ruan watched, mouth hanging open, as Geldof shoved a finger in his mouth and sucked. Scholzy stopped. As Fanny ran toward her son, Geldof, his chin bloody, clenched his fists. Then his arms and legs began to twitch and he dropped his head. When he raised it again, his teeth were bared and his eyes were crinkled down to narrow slits.

"I'm going to disembowel you for your treachery, you nefarious oath breaker," he shouted at Scholzy.

He got to his feet, and Ruan was treated to the sight of a muscled killer sprinting away from a slight boy. Geldof was clearly incapable of catching up with his intended target, but Fanny grappled him to the ground anyway.

"What have you done?" she said, her voice dripping with shock.

"Let me go," Geldof screamed, his arms and legs thrashing. "I'm going to bite his pox-ridden nose off."

Scholzy stopped and looked back. "I can't take him now. You know that."

Fanny was too busy restraining her crazed son to reply. As he bucked, she whispered in his ear and stroked his head. Scott came running over to help and held down the boy's legs.

"Right, you two," Scholzy said. "We're shipping out."

Ruan looked at Geldof thrashing on the ground. On the face of it, what he'd done seemed like the act of an immature boy carried out in the heat of the moment, but she knew Geldof well enough to understand he'd been fully aware his actions would condemn him to remaining on this island to face the guns of the invading army. This was an act of sacrifice that spoke of a mind far beyond his years. She knew then that she couldn't leave. Her parents were out there somewhere, still alive. She'd spent all this time running away, trying to pretend this wasn't happening. If she left, she would still be running. Geldof had told her she didn't know what it was like to have the virus. She didn't and never would. Yet she'd seen enough ordinary people turn into raging beasts to know Fanny and her people were the exception, not the rule. She'd been so hurt by her parents turning on her that she assumed it displayed a lack of love on their part, when in fact they were as much victims as everybody else. And she was hardly in a position to criticize: in the camp, she'd made no attempt to save them, choosing instead to preserve her own skin. They might have a few days before the bombs dropped, they might only have a few hours, but no amount of visualizing would prevent her living the rest of her life tortured by guilt if she didn't make some effort to get them out of the city. Maybe they would never learn to deal with the virus, but if they survived long enough then perhaps a cure could be found. She had to give them that chance, no matter what they'd done.

"I'm staying, too," she said.

"And me," Mick said. "I kind of like it here, and they're going to need somebody to protect them when the shit hits the fan. Besides, I'm not swimming anywhere with this leg."

"You're all idiots," Scholzy said, his voice almost fond. "Mick, you mad Irish bastard: try not to get killed or infected."

"Would anybody notice if I did? I'm already horny and violent."

Scholzy turned and walked away. A few minutes later, an outboard motor started up and faded into the distance.

Above his screams and yells and his mum's frantic whispering, Geldof heard Scholzy go. His mum's face was close to his, and he saw her brow knot. He kept fighting as hard as he could, struggling and screaming out every expletive he could think of, medieval or not. Just as a distant engine started up, she put her nose down to his neck and took a deep sniff. Her eyes widened. "You don't have it."

As quickly as he'd gone bonkers, Geldof quietened down and lay still. "You got me." He held up his index finger, still stained with blood, and then put his ring finger in his mouth to illustrate what he'd done. "Oldest trick in the book."

"You devious little shit," Fanny said.

Geldof grinned. "You can talk, going to your dad behind my back. I guess we're even."

Scott let go of Geldof's legs. "Like mother, like son," he said, and began to laugh.

They rode back to the camp in silence, Geldof's gaze fixed to the skies for some sign of the warplanes that would surely be coming. He saw nothing but blue haze and wispy clouds. The bodies of their dead were in the back, wrapped up in sheets taken from the beds of the soldiers for burial. Fanny had wanted to collect the soldiers and burn them out of respect, but Mick persuaded her otherwise. They still had no idea how soon the attack on Britain would begin, and so they needed to flee the obvious target of the base immediately or risk becoming just as charred and dead as the bodies they would have set alight.

When they got home, Scott went running off to the houses to be reunited with Eva while the others got busy digging three graves. They held a brief secular service later that afternoon and marked the graves as best they could with names scratched into lumps of stone rescued from the rubble. It wasn't much of a memorial to three people who died

saving countless lives, but it was the best they could do in the circumstances. Before they sat down to figure out exactly how they were going to survive a full-on invasion of Britain, Geldof went to the hangar
and booted up the computer. He still had Terry's e-mail in his address
book and felt somebody should let him know Lesley was gone. He
stared at the blank screen, unsure how to break the news. He and Lesley had lived through the most intense experiences of his life, yet he
barely knew her. In the end, he just kept it short.

> *Terry, I'm sorry to have to tell you that Lesley is dead. I know it*
> *might not help much, but she died saving the world. Literally. The*
> *virus was going to get out. Thanks to her, it won't. I'll spare you the*
> *details other than to say it was very quick and, according to my mum,*
> *she seemed at peace when it happened. I'm still sort of hoping that her*
> *story is going to save us as well, but that seems unlikely. Still, Lesley*
> *probably already saved billions of lives. I suppose a few million that*
> *slipped through the net won't make much odds in the grand scheme of*
> *things. Maybe you can get them to build a statue or name an award*
> *after her. That's the kind of thing they do for heroes, right?*
>
> *Geldof*

He felt he really should have signed off on a more poignant note
and was about to start reworking the message, but Fanny came looking for him to join in with a group meeting. He hit send.

"Have you forgiven me yet?" he said before they left the hangar.

Fanny glowered at him for a moment and then punched him on the
arm—a tad too hard to be jokey. "Scott was right. You're just as stubborn as me. So I suppose I have to forgive you. Now I just need to figure
out how to keep you alive."

She led him by the hand to the table, where everybody had gathered for what would likely be the last meeting in the commune.

"So, what do we do now?" Fanny said.

"We can't stay here," Mick said. "We're probably out of range of the
neutron bombs, but if it goes down like Lesley said it would we're too
exposed for what comes next. I suggest we run like fuck to the arse-
end of nowhere and hide."

"Even the tallest tree must bend before the storm," Nayapal said. "Which, before anybody asks, means that I agree we should do a runner."

Nods rippled round the table.

"So, any ideas for a good place to hole up?" Fanny said.

"There is a bit of a history of hiding in caves when you're up against it," Tom said. "Robert the Bruce did it. Bonny Prince Charlie did it."

"I know a place," Scott said. "Ten years back I spent two weeks living in a cave up past Ullapool."

"What were you doing there?" Geldof said.

"Taking a lot of acid. Trying to find myself."

"And did you?"

"No. Luckily some spelunkers did, or I'd still be down there in my underpants making cave paintings from steaming turds. It's called Allt nan Uamh Stream Cave. It's in the middle of nowhere, the entrance is hard to find, and we should be able to find game and grow crops. It would take them years to find us, if ever."

"I've always wanted to be a caveman," Mick said.

"You already are," Geldof said.

"Don't talk to your new dad like that."

Fanny slapped Mick on the back of the head. He grinned. "Time enough for rough stuff later."

Fanny ignored him. "Sounds perfect. Let's get ready. Load up the truck and the quad bikes. Scott, you bring as much dope as you can pack up. We move tonight."

"What about the prisoners?" Tom said.

"We let them out when we're leaving. They can take their chances."

"I can't come," Ruan said. "I need to go to Edinburgh and warn my mum and dad."

"No way," Fanny said. "The bombs could drop any minute, and they'd definitely hit a big city like that."

"I don't care. I need to warn them."

"You think they don't know already? Everybody will be shipping out, including them. It'll be chaos. You'll never find them. In fact, you'd never make it anywhere near them. You're still uninfected. You'd be torn to shreds."

Ruan looked stricken as the truth hit home. She sat there in silence as the meeting broke up and everybody ran off to gather what they could. Geldof lingered, reluctant to leave Ruan alone with her pain. "Are you okay?"

"I'll be fine," she said. "I just need ten minutes. Go get ready."

Geldof hurried off after his mum, but halfway to the house something made him stop and look back. Ruan had left the table and was clambering onto one of the quad bikes. He sprinted back as the engine roared into life and got there just as the bike shot forward, forcing Ruan to swerve to avoid him. The vehicle tipped and she came tumbling off. When he reached her, she was lying with her face in the grass, her shoulders heaving.

"You can't help them," he said quietly.

She flinched as he touched her shoulder. When she looked up, her face was contorted. "Don't you dare try to tell me not to go. You came for your mum."

"And fat lot of use I was."

"You're the one who told me to forgive them."

"And you should. But that's different from trying to save them. If you go, you'll die. You're immune, which means everyone will bite and stomp on you until you're a bloody ruin." He paused. "Sorry, I didn't mean that as a joke. I just don't think I could handle your dying."

"I have to go," she said.

As he looked at the set lines of her face, he knew he would probably have to wrestle her to stop her from setting off. That would only end with his lying on the ground with an ego and arse bruised in equal proportion and her zipping off on the quad bike. She was tough, no doubt, but nowhere near as tough as she would have to be. She could only fight off so many infected enraged by her purity until they overwhelmed her. Then it struck him. This immunity that would be her undoing was the key to making her stay.

"Think about it," he said. "Your blood might hold the cure, and if your parents are cured you can be together again. If you go blundering into Edinburgh, that possible cure will die with you. Guaranteed. If we go north to safety first, then we can figure out who to contact about using your blood for a cure. They don't even need to take you out. We could leave a sample for them to pick up somewhere."

Ruan fell silent for a while. "Do you really think it could work?"

Of course it wouldn't work. Once the soldiers were in and busy killing, nobody would take the chance of pulling out one immune girl. They already had all the data they needed on the virus. If they couldn't create a cure from that, they never would. He felt rotten for lying to her, for talking her out of doing what she wanted to do. In her place he would try the same thing. If her parents died, she would never forgive him. But, as his mum had said, she would at least be alive to hate. He really was Fanny in miniature.

"It's the best chance you've got of saving them," he said, putting every ounce of his being into the lie.

"But what if I lose them? They're all I've got."

"That's not true," Geldof said. "You have us. You have me."

He held out his hand, hoping that she wouldn't use it to pull him down, kick him in the nuts, and jump on the bike. Fortunately, she let him pull her to her feet. Her face was streaked with tears, which he thumbed away gently.

"We don't even know how long we'll survive," she said.

Geldof leaned his forehead against hers. "Nobody does. We just need to make the most of the time we have left."

"You're not like other boys," Ruan said.

"Yeah, that's what all the girls say, usually as they edge away nervously."

"No, it's a good thing."

"I'm glad to hear it. Now, are you coming?"

Ruan nodded, and they walked off hand in hand into what little future they had left.

35

General Carter was, to put it mildly, completely hammered when his phone rang. He, Zhang, and Kuzkin had been sitting in a dimly lit meeting room at the Pentagon since midnight, working their way through three bottles of vodka during a game of Tiger Has Come. They deserved the break. They'd spent days working around the clock implementing the reorganization to Operation Excision. Since General Zhang was already snoring in the corner and Carter could barely keep his eyes open, General Kuzkin was clearly going to win back all the money he'd lost from the round of golf and the game of dice, which at least had finally put him in a good mood.

Carter stared stupidly at the ringing mobile, far too drunk to consider picking it up. Eventually, Kuzkin reached across and answered. He grunted, put the device on speakerphone, and sat it in the middle of the table.

"Sir, there's been a development," a voice said.

"I'll say," Carter said. "I can't feel my legs."

After a beat of silence, the voice continued, "We bugged a phone call about an hour ago, from Tony Campbell to Piers Stokington."

"Who are they?"

"The leader of BRIT and his liaison, sir."

"Ah. And?"

"Tony Campbell said, and I quote, 'No matter what you do, we won't resist. We won't fire off any nukes. We won't do anything.' He seems to be backing off from conflict, sir."

Kuzkin raised two eyebrows—well, probably only one, but it was hard for Carter to tell considering the way the room was swimming. He raised his head from the table and slapped his cheeks hard. "Does it seem on the level?"

"Stokington seems to think so, sir. He got on the phone to his superiors. We thought it wise to block the call."

"Good move. So they say they're going to back down. That's very accommodating of them. Sounds like a trap to me."

"Indeed, sir. I should also inform you that Stokington is on the move. We think he might be driving over to tell his superiors in person. He seems quite agitated. From the things he's mumbling to himself, it seems likely he's going to try to persuade his superiors to have the attack called off."

Carter motioned for another vodka and covered the mouthpiece. "The bastard's trying to sabotage our golf plans."

"Your golf plans," Kuzkin said.

Carter knocked back his drink and turned the glass upside down. "Your turn," he said, before speaking into the phone again. "Nobody listens to the Brits. Then again, we shouldn't take the chance. We don't need to bother our politician friends with this. Take him into custody. What time is it?"

"Oh three hundred hours EST, sir."

"Right. Remind me when Operation Excision is due to start."

"Eighteen hundred hours EST, sir. In fifteen hours."

"I might not be able to stand up, but I can still count." He paused. "What time will that be in Britain?"

"Twenty-three hundred hours BST, sir. They're five hours ahead."

"I knew that."

"I also have to tell you that the satellites are still picking up growing population movements. We're not going to get as many of them in the first round as we thought, sir."

"Nothing we can do about that. Proceed as planned. We'll mop up as we go along."

He hung up and looked groggily at Kuzkin, who threw his glass of vodka down his throat. "Fine. You win. Enjoy it while it lasts. I'll take your money back off you at Gleneagles."

His head dropped to the table.

"Hole in one," he muttered, and fell into the deep, dreamless sleep of the young, the innocent, and the very, very drunk.